BLOWN
OFF
COURSE

A John Pearce Novel

BLOWN
OFF
COURSE

DAVID DONACHIE

McBooks
Press

Guilford, Connecticut

McBooks Press

An imprint of Globe Pequot, the trade division of
The Rowman & Littlefield Publishing Group, Inc.
4501 Forbes Blvd., Ste. 200
Lanham, MD 20706
www.rowman.com

Distributed by NATIONAL BOOK NETWORK

British Library Cataloguing in Publication Information available

Library of Congress Cataloging-in-Publication Data

ISBN 978-1-4930-6625-4 (paperback)
ISBN 978-1-4930-6162-4 (ebook)

♾™ The paper used in this publication meets the minimum requirements
of American National Standard for Information Sciences—Permanence of
Paper for Printed Library Materials, ANSI/NISO Z39.48-1992.

To my lovely cousin Joanne,
who has continued to smile
and has remained cheerful,
despite many tribulations.

PROLOGUE

John Pearce knew he was wasting his time almost as soon as he sat down. Besides, in revisiting the Pelican Tavern – a place he had previously avoided – the thoughts both memory and his presence induced were far from pleasant, the whole not aided by the way his day had gone thus far, that compounded by a touch of lonely introspection: he had sent his good friend Michael O'Hagan back to Portsmouth to tell the other two men who formed his circle that matters were in hand that would see them free from worry. Then, as arranged, he had called upon the office of the First Lord of the Treasury in Downing Street, expecting to receive there the results of certain promises that had been made to him the previous evening, letters that would quickly and smoothly ease the lives of his companions in misfortune, as well as a possible commission taking him back to the Mediterranean. Neither had been forthcoming and nor had any explanation been offered for their absence. A request to see William Pitt had been scoffed at, then brushed aside as that turned to a demand. It had been made abundantly plain to him he was not important enough to force the issue and no time had been given to him in which his concerns might be resolved.

Time was pressing; all three of his friends were now in some danger instead of just two, so, determined to force matters and having left an address at which he could be contacted, Pearce made his way to the Admiralty. He had in his possession a letter from Rear Admiral Sir Hyde Parker, which should partially realise what he required, as well as a written submission of his own he had always intended to be used. That the two buildings were not far apart was one blessing: it curtailed his anger at being so badly treated by the King's First Minister as well as his speculations as to what had changed overnight.

He thought he had struck a bargain and, whatever his opinion of Billy Pitt, he had not had him down as a man who failed to keep his word, unlike the other politician who had been present last night. Henry Dundas, Pitt's political fixer, a fellow Scot who commanded many vote in the House of Commons was, to John Pearce, a poisonous snake of a man. Dundas had been responsible for much trouble in his life, as well as that of his late father, the radical orator and pamphleteer, Adam Pearce.

Pitt had been clear in what he wanted – John Pearce had been his messenger before and would be so again. In return he would get, without the trouble of demanding them from the Admiralty, three protections from naval impressment as well as two writs for arrest suspended. Had Dundas been lukewarm, had he changed Pitt's thinking after Pearce departed? He did not know and speculation was useless. That was a matter which would have to wait!

Just to get into the Admiralty building he had been required to excessively tip a sour-faced and deeply inquisitive doorman, a fellow who reacted to his name as though the notion of this visitor holding a lieutenant's rank in the King's Navy was an affront to be taken personally. Finally allowed through to an anteroom, his letters passed on, he had sat waiting to be seen, this while officers of a higher rank and greater heft, arriving later, were waved through to interview, leaving him and the other queuing supplicants to quietly fester at the lack of even-handedness. The morning had gone and so had noon with no sign of him being granted an interview.

Eying those who waited with him did nothing for a mood which grew darker with each passing hour: a captain of advanced years and apparently little in the way of interest waiting to beg for an appointment, lieutenants of various ages seeking employment of any kind – the Impress Service if all else failed. The one thing they all shared, apart from the pique of being constantly passed over, was an air of quiet desperation that underlined their hushed conversations.

Pearce had stayed silent and deliberately morose, his thoughts left him little choice, more than once avoiding a complicit eye that sought to engage him in the kind of talk common in naval circles, of service past and the possibility of shared acquaintance. He had no desire, especially after his reception at the front gate, to even proffer his name, lest in doing so he open himself up to enquiry, for if he wore, like these other men, the coat of a king's officer, he wore it reluctantly.

Quite apart from that, he had his reputation and the means by which he had achieved his rank, which even in an establishment of some two thousand officers would be the subject of common gossip and lurid opinion, neither of which he wished to be exposed: if even a lowly Admiralty porter knew his story, then these others would have knowledge of it too. That he had been right to remain silent was underlined by the raised eyebrows and startled expressions which greeted the use of his name, sonorously announced by a footman.

'Lieutenant John Pearce?' There was a degree of disdain in this fellow's look too, as he responded to an affirmative reply. 'Admiral Affleck will see you next.'

A buzz of animated conversation followed him out, most larded with surprise, or perhaps venom from those who, in recognising the name, would see him as an undeserving upstart. Yet there would be jealousy too, especially from those recently commissioned, who would realise that, if they had been sitting in the same room with a fellow of murky elevation, they had also been within talking distance of a man who had enjoyed the good fortune for which they craved: they had not only failed to nail his identity, but missed an opportunity to press for details, to hear of his exploits from his own lips.

The room he had entered, home to the Board of Admiralty, was spacious and rectangular, lit by three large windows that struggled to illuminate the dark panelling of the walls. Outside could be heard the muted sounds of Whitehall, one of the busiest thoroughfares in London: street hawkers and peddlers, hoarse military commands from the barracks of the Horse Guards, carriages in such quantity and so lacking in discipline that endless disputes resulted on who had the right of way. At one end of the boardroom table sat Admiral Phillip Affleck, the most junior of the naval lords, his indifference to the visitor obvious by the way he flicked a finger and spoke, not to mention the contemptuous tone of his voice.

'Please address yourself to the Secretary of the Board, Lieutenant. I have little interest in you or your business.'

The man in question, Phillip Stephens, sat to one side at a separate desk. He was elderly, arrogant of eye and with disapproving shape to his mouth, features that were set off by the dry, pallid skin of a lifelong indoor man. Having shown no curiosity whatsoever, barely acknowledging his entry, he had examined the letter Pearce had sent in earlier with a jaundiced expression, his greying eyebrows rising towards his like-coloured wig as if the contents were in some way bizarre and the signature at the bottom quite possibly a forgery. He then picked up Pearce's own submission, a request that the persons named, having been released from naval service by the officer in command of the Mediterranean Fleet, be granted exemptions that would protect them from the risk of being once more pressed. Then it was back to the letter, which was waved slightly.

'This in itself does not provide means for your request, sir.'

'I cannot see how it fails to, Mr Stephens. Admiral Hyde Parker penned it on the instructions of Lord Hood. He has freed these men from the navy on the very good grounds that their original impressment was illegal.'

'It does not say that, Mr Pearce.'

'No, but I do!'

That brought forth a snort of disapproval from a supposedly disinterested Admiral Affleck.

'Hardly grounds to give out such documents to . . .' Stephens hesitated and made much of picking up an eyeglass to look at the names, '. . . O'Hagan, Taverner and Dommet, is it? Protections are not things to be handed out lightly at such a time, when the fleet is so short of hands to man her ships. I need hardly remind you we are at war with a most vicious enemy.'

If Pearce was cursing Hyde Parker for being imprecise, he was also silently castigating himself for failing to make sure the intentions of the communication were clear. The release and future safety of the trio had been part of their arrangement, a reward for his services to Lord Hood; that his friends, the men with whom he had been pressed himself, should, in theory, be free to walk the streets of England in safety. At the moment Charlie and Rufus were anchored off Portsmouth, stuck aboard the badly damaged frigate, HMS *Fury*, with Michael on his way to rejoin and reassure them. She had lost all her masts in a ferocious Biscay storm, before rescuing them from off the coast of Brittany from near certain captivity.

The original intention for everyone to travel with John Pearce had been set aside for several reasons, one being – and this was where theory parted with practicality – that two of his companions had writs out for their arrest – it had been these Pitt had agreed to quash, the provision of three protections more gilding than necessity, given he had the means to acquire them anyway. The writs were probably not much of a problem in Hampshire but one that would increase as they approached London.

There was also the cost of four souls travelling at a shilling a mile: Pearce had only a limited amount of money with which to pay, having been required to expend a fair bit of his coin to buy slops and the like from the frigate's purser, for those with whom he had been rescued, this to replace items lost at sea. His own blue coat had suffered so much he had been obliged to buy a second-hand replacement from a Portsmouth tailor on the very good grounds that to appear in Whitehall in a singed and torn garment would not serve.

He had also seen, when seeking to book his passage, how many eager eyes studied the London coach, plus the knowledge he possessed from previous journeys that every post house on the way to the capital was a magnet for those hunting naval deserters. His friends bore the marks of their service: pigtails grown as hobbies could be cut and jaunty clothing discarded but there was no disguising a sailor's gait plus the ruddy complexion occasioned by exposure to the constant wind, while even a cursory examination would spot palms ingrained with tar.

In theory, being with a commissioned officer, someone who could vouch for them, should be protection enough, but the writs out for Charlie Taverner and Rufus Dommet complicated matters. It was no secret that men ran to sea from the law, which always exposed sailors to extra scrutiny from a whole stratum of folk who made their living from the trade in bounties. It was a truism John Pearce knew from his previous travelling life: in a strange setting you never knew who was who and what they were about. As an enterprise travelling together was not only too expensive, it was too risky.

So he had travelled with Michael O'Hagan, the Irishman's safety secured by his coat and, sure that matters were in hand, he had sent him back again with a leave pass which would pass muster on the road and protect him from interference: no one scrutinised a sailor going to a ship, only those who could not prove they were not running from one, and in doing so had inadvertently put him at risk, for now time was of the essence.

HMS *Fury* would not remain at anchor forever; she was slated to be warped into the dockyard for repairs, which would remove the element of safety his friends now enjoyed. That he was angry at this moment, he knew, yet he was also aware that to let that show would not serve with a functionary like the fellow before him: Stephens was accustomed to the tirades of men of much higher rank than he. Pearce hated to beg, it went right against the grain of his being, but he kept in the forefront of his thinking that he was not seeking something for himself. He was pleading for others and that allowed him to suppress his ire and address Stephens in a firm but even tone, speaking more in hope that certainty.

'It is also the wish of the First Lord of the Treasury, Mr Stephens, which I am willing to undertake to confirm. I take it a note from Mr William Pitt, supporting Admiral Parker's letter, will sway matters.'

That got him a crabbed look: the notion that he, a mere lieutenant of limited service time and ambiguous elevation, could call upon the assistance of the king's first minister was surprising. But then Stephens's already hooded eyes had narrowed and flicked towards Admiral Affleck, which told Pearce the secretary had recalled how he came by his rank, gifted to him at the insistence of King George himself. He surely could not call to mind that singular event without also recollecting the circumstances that brought it about, the capture of a French ship of the line, which must cause him to surmise he was not dealing with an ordinary officer. Before him was a fellow for whom the expression 'still waters' could have been coined, for John Pearce ran very deep indeed, perhaps too deep for even a powerful Admiralty secretary or a naval lord to gainsay.

15

'Is it not strange indeed,' Stephens intoned, employing a sepulchral air that went with his desiccated, colourless appearance, 'as well as an indication of the troubled times in which we live, that a man can go from being so recently under the threat of a King's Bench warrant, to being able to call upon the services of the minister who had it issued.'

That had the hitherto silent admiral expelling the air from his lungs through flapping lips, in a way very reminiscent of a bored horse.

'Be assured,' Pearce replied, with a confidence wholly false, 'that I can do so and on this very day.'

It was to salve both his pride and the authority of the Board that Stephens concluded the interview in the way he did: inclined to refuse, he was certain, given the power of Pearce's connections, he must accede, but the least he could do was make the man before him wait for something he could order completed by a mere ring of a bell.

'Call back on the morrow and they will be handed to you.' The eyes went back to the papers that littered his desk, numerous, for Phillip Stephens was the man who really ran the King's Navy, an organisation which in its complexity and reach was the wonder of the world. 'Good day, Lieutenant Pearce.'

'Obliged, sir,' Pearce replied, producing the courtesy, even if he did not feel any had been forthcoming.

As he was about to leave the room, Stephens delivered a parting shot. 'And please remember, Lieutenant, to bring with you the requisite fees for these protections.'

Which left him asking, as he exited the gate of the Admiralty building in a foul temper, recalling, as he did, the way he had been obliged to pay even for the letters granting him his lieutenant's rank, if there was anything the navy did that was not accompanied by a demand for a fee.

CHAPTER ONE

In coming to the Pelican Tavern Pearce had, perforce, to enter the Liberties of the Savoy, that strip by the River Thames where many of the writs that constituted the law of the land did not run. In doing so he had passed many a sharp eye and had been studied with care, looks that belonged to men who made their living from taking up miscreants with writs against their name. Most for debt, many were for minor crimes, like those of Charlie Taverner, who had worked as a sharp in the nearby areas to the north, the Strand and Covent Garden, preying on and duping the innocent or the foolish.

Outrageous schemes promising fabulous returns, forged lottery tickets, fake watch auctions and a bit of dipping had been Charlie's stock-in-trade. Rufus Dommet, an innocent sort of fellow who looked younger even than his tender years, had run from an onerous apprentice bond, a crime in the eyes of an unforgiving law. This was the place where he had first met them and that pair, barring the Sabbath, if Pitt reneged on his commitment, would still be at risk of arrest outside the confines of the Liberties, protections or not.

Once inside and divested of his boat cloak, home to roaring fires and a healthy fug of pipe smoke, he sought out and parked himself in the same seat as the one at which he had first met them, ordering some much-needed food and a tankard of warming metheglin. This gave him, from the very back of the room, as it had on that foul and windy night, a good view of the door through which he had entered.

Pearce had been on the run himself then, from the King's Bench warrant so recently alluded to by Phillip Stephens, as well as the powerful bailiffs employed by the courts to execute such writs and apprehend the putative villain. His crime – in truth, that of his father – had been called sedition, a much more serious transgression than the offences common in the Liberties, one that could end at Tyburn if those who hated radical writings were inclined to press matters to an execution.

From this very perch he had watched Michael O'Hagan lift a hefty pine bench using nothing but his teeth – an indication, if his height and bulk were insufficient, of his massive natural strength. The giant Irishman had been mightily drunk before his feat and even more so afterwards – if he had been sober there was not a press gang in the world could have taken him up without he felled most of those trying. Eyes ranging over the room, Pearce took in the door by the serving hatch through which he had tried to escape, only to run into those set there to catch their fleeing quarry, which brought about his first encounter with Captain Ralph Barclay, the man he now saw as his mortal enemy.

'Such a ferocious stare, sir, I would not want to be the object of your ruminations.'

Pearce looked up at the man who stood before him, into a winning smile in an amiable, handsome face, immediately relaxing his own compressed features. 'I was lost in recollection, sir.'

'Then damned unpleasant they must have been, Lieutenant.'

'I was recalling the night a press gang burst into this very room and carted off all of the able-bodied men, myself included.'

'That was but a year past was it not?' the stranger said, his eye running over the uniform coat with an air of deep curiosity.

'Then you know of it?'

'Sir, it has been the talk of the place ever since, almost the first subject to which I was made aware when I moved my place of business to a set of chambers close by and began to come to the Pelican for refreshment. Allow me to name myself: Arthur Winston, and you, sir, are . . .?

'John Pearce.'

'And you were pressed that night?'

'I was.'

'An act which is illegal in this part of the metropolis?'

That made Pearce smile, so unaccustomed was he to that misconduct being acknowledged. The Liberties of the Savoy came under the legal jurisdiction of the

Duchy of Lancaster, they being the boundaries of the long-gone Savoy Palace, which had been home to John of Gaunt, third son of the King Edward who won at Crécy, progenitor of the bloodline which had produced in his grandson, Henry, the more famous victor of Agincourt. For several centuries, because of its exempt status outside the control of the Royal Courts, it had provided sanctuary for the less salubrious citizens of London and Westminster. One of the statutes of the Liberties, well frequented by Thames watermen, was that it was against the law to seek to press seamen from within its confines.

Seeing agreement in Pearce's expression, Winston added, in a sombre tone, 'But I suspect you are familiar with that to an uncomfortable degree.' He leant forward to see into Pearce's near empty tankard. 'Would you permit me to purchase you a refill, sir?'

A look of suspicion crossed Pearce's face; he could not help it, for life since childhood, traversing the whole of the kingdom in the company of his radical father, had attuned him to distrust unwarranted and too spontaneous generosity, often the precursor to an attempt at chicanery. Yet it disappeared as fast as it surfaced: what possible harm could there be in taking a tankard from this fellow?

'I confess a purpose, sir,' Winston said, his face solemn. 'I am agog to hear of what happened to you and how, in the name of creation, after so short a time, you can be wearing what I assume is a uniform coat of a rank to which you are entitled.'

Avoiding a direct answer, being guarded about the

story of his elevation to a lieutenant's rank, Pearce grinned, invited the fellow to sit down and accepted the invitation to drink, this time a tankard of porter. Perhaps it was the fact that he was nothing to do with the King's Navy, or even that he was an habitué of the Pelican and thus something of a soul mate to his friends, stuck in Portsmouth, awaiting their protections.

As the serving wench, called over with her jug to provide the necessary, came towards them, Pearce, seeing the depth and extent of her visible bosom, as well as the width of her hips, was reminded of Rosie, another fulsome girl first seen on that ill-fated night, one who had enjoyed the favours of Michael O'Hagan while simultaneously fuelling the jealousies of Charlie Taverner. When he mentioned this other wench's likeness to Rosie, his new companion reacted with disbelief, the look on his face one which implied he thought an association between them somewhat unlikely.

'She was an acquaintance of yours, sir?'

'I confess I really did not know her, Rosie being of neither a shape or personality to attract me, but she was at one time the paramour of a friend.'

'And the possessor of the most overwhelming bosom this side of Tartary.'

'The friend in question was Michael O'Hagan and he was pressed at the same time as me.'

'Then sadly, if he still carries a torch for Rosie, he will find his bird flown.'

'A fact he mentioned with some regret.'

'Aye, a farmer came in some months past from Covent Garden market, apparently, with gold in his hand and love in his heart for a wench with such massive udders and he carted her off, no doubt to milk her. I think it was the former, the gold, which swayed your wench, for my information is that he was not overtly handsome.'

Charlie Taverner had also harboured designs of Rosie and he was handsome, but that had availed him little, which made sense of Winston's observation. 'I reckon you are correct, sir: she was also the object of affection to another friend who lacked the means to engage her interest.'

'So, sir,' Winston said, now sat beside Pearce and his eyes full of hope. 'Am I to be favoured with a telling of your tale, or are the memories too painful to recount?'

'There is a great deal to tell.'

Winston waved his tankard, full and foaming. 'I have no pressing engagements.'

John Pearce, as he responded, felt required to mention the fact that he was a stranger to the Pelican himself, having only recently returned from Paris, which had Winston's eyebrows twitching with interest, and that required an excuse be found for why such a thing was so – he had no intention of telling a man unknown to him he had been on the run. So he concocted a tale of seeking out a French acquaintance in trouble, hinting at a woman without actually saying so, which led Winston to allude to the danger of a Briton looking for anything in such a dangerous setting as a city in the grip of the bloody revolution.

Pearce deflected that by admitting to a soft heart, which protected him from exposure and went on quickly to change a subject replete with untruths and in danger

23

of spinning out of control. This he did by recounting the first suspicions he had that something was amiss in the Pelican, aroused by a group of tars, accompanied by a red-coated drummer boy, who had come in after him and had, to his mind, acted strangely.

'They barely drank, Mr Winston, and made no display, which for blue-water sailors is singular indeed, so I began to suspect something might be afoot, but before I could act upon my misgivings the whole press gang burst in, clubs waving. I made for the side door you observed me glaring towards, narrowly avoiding a clout from our Irish friend, only to find a bastard called Ralph Barclay and more tars in possession of the alleyway.'

'You put up a fight, for I am told there was mayhem?'

'I very nearly got clear, sir, but they possessed numbers and there were simply too many with whom to contest, so, once bound, I was done for – and I was not alone, of course: those I had been conversing with previously were taken as well. You may have heard of them too: an old wiseacre called Abel Scrivens, sadly now deceased, and another very likely also gone to meet his Maker, a West Countryman called Ben Walker. He was taken by Barbary pirates and the last I saw of him was as a wharfside slave in Tunis.'

The memory of that made Pearce pinch the top of his nose, his eyes shutting at the same time. Abel Scrivens had died in place of him, less than a week into that first voyage, while circumstances had forced him to leave Ben Walker to his fate and the memory of that, mixed with a tinge of self-pity, never failed to make him slightly lachrymose.

Winston was all apology. 'Sir, I am distressing you, it is clear.'

'It is hard to recall them without sorrow, for if those two men resided here for crimes or misdemeanours, they did not deserve what came their way. But two of the others with whom I became companions are at present safe aboard a ship anchored off Portsmouth, very likely now joined by a third.'

Pearce paused then, wondering whether to mention Pitt and his promises, but he decided that would sound to fantastic to a stranger. Yet it provided a concomitant resolution; if he did not hear from Downing Street he would have to act as if the promises made were not going to happen.

'Tomorrow I go, first to the Admiralty to pick up for them protections, then down to Hampshire to bring them to safety. Not only will they be released from naval service, but also they will have no fear of press gangs or the crimps that line the Portsmouth road.

'And these fellows are?'

'O'Hagan, the aforementioned Charlie Taverner and a young lad called Rufus Dommet.' Pearce raised his tankard, Arthur Winston following suit. 'We called ourselves the Pelicans, a soubriquet that bound us as one. Here's to them and to my joy that I may once again share with them a tankard in their old haunt.'

'You must go ashore,' insisted the master of HMS *Fury*. 'Matters have altered and it has to be so.'

He said these words while looking up into the face of a less-than-enamoured Michael O'Hagan, newly back on board. Behind the master stood the purser, a thin stick of a fellow, as well as a pair of the other warrants permanently attached to the damaged frigate, the gunner and the carpenter. Clearly they saw safety in numbers when it came to dealing with the Pelicans, one of whom was still unhappy at a change of the original plan to travel with John Pearce, while not being made any more confident by the news Michael brought.

'You say he'll be here on the morrow, Michael,' Charlie had said, 'an' maybe he will if'n a pretty face don't take his fancy.'

Charlie Taverner was reminding them the same fellow had left them high and dry once before while he pleasured himself with a high-born lady, which delayed his return from London to fetch them off another vessel, an error that saw all three of them shipped off to the Mediterranean from the very Spithead anchorage in which the were now anchored.

The merchant ship from which they had been rescued, the *Guiscard*, had been taken in by the surveyors to be valued and examined as to the legitimacy of it being a prize, the seamen with whom they had boarded her, being long-serving naval volunteers, had been happy to go with her and, once on shore, to either contact their old captain in the hope of future employment or to sign on in another ship of war.

Charlie and Rufus, debarred from going ashore themselves – they could not just hang about in the dockyard without being attached to a vessel and there had been nowhere else for them to reside. Since the dock at which the frigate would be fitted with new masts was occupied, another plea from Pearce to the captain for them to be allowed to stay aboard, to save money and avoid risk, had seemed the best solution.

'Captain Warren said we was free to stay aboard this barky until Mr Pearce returned.'

Turning to Charlie Taverner, who had mouthed that complaint, the master had his reply ready.

'His commission was over yesterday and he has gone, which you have seen for yourself, but that is not the nub. This ship is to be warped in for inspection at first light tomorrow, which I admit we did not expect, and even if your officer comes he will be too late to save you, and I am bound to enquire if there is a risk he will be delayed?'

'Who knows?' added the gloomy carpenter, not in the least interested in the looks of doubt exchanged by the Pelicans. 'She might be condemned. Her timbers are in a state after years in the Indies and what she suffered in that hurricano we went through damaged more'n just the masts.'

'Please God she goes to the breakers and we get a better berth,' mouthed the gunner. 'I reckon I'm at least due a fourth rate for the years I've put in.'

'That's not the point,' the purser insisted, not in the least interested in the gunner's wish for a bigger ship and a higher rate of pay, or the carpenter's pessimism about the state of the scantlings. 'I have to make up my accounts for the Victualling Board and I can scarce do that with you lot still eating rations as though you belong aboard, without so much as a farthing of payment.'

It was an impasse: Captain Warren, given his place on the captain's list, was due a larger vessel and had been appointed to one, having got his personal followers ashore and away with him. The remainder of the crew, a high number of them Lascars, given the frigate had served on the Calcutta station, had been stripped out within an hour of Warren's departure and sent to another warship unable to weigh for want of manpower. The only reason Charlie and Rufus had been left aboard was their not being listed on the frigate's muster book; nor was Michael.

'There's two ways this can be done,' the master added. 'Either you leave or you will be faced by a file of marines sent to shift you ashore as soon as we tie up, with the dockyard mateys pocketing a reward for turning you in.'

Michael O'Hagan wanted to pick the fellow up by his throat and ask him what he thought they would do if they did go ashore without either a ticket of leave which would stand up to scrutiny or an officer to safeguard them. What stopped him was the man's age as well as his rank: he was not an officer in the strict sense, but he was the most senior of the warrants. To lay hands on him would not be kindly looked upon, but he did pose the question uppermost in his mind, and in a very brusque manner.

'There are ways out of the dockyard, Paddy, and I can show them to you.'

'And then?'

'Get out of Portsmouth and find your officer fellow in London.'

'That sounds as simple as kiss my hand,' crowed Charlie Taverner, his face alight with sarcasm. 'We won't get over the bridge.'

That induced a ruminative silence: the naval base lay near the tip of Portsea Island, connected to the mainland by bridges which, quite naturally, given the propensity of sailors to desert the king's service, were well guarded for those seeking to get onto the mainland. Charlie, quite naturally, made no mention of the writs out for him and Rufus, a serious added danger.

'You will if we give you a boat,' said the carpenter, suddenly, to nods from his mates when he sought their approval. 'If'n you make for the shore beyond Hayling Island you'll have a clear run.'

The carpenter looked quizzically at the master then: he knew about maps and he was not disappointed in the response as the man added, 'Dry land all the way, and I can draw you a route to take that will get you to London.'

'Easy for you to say,' moaned Rufus Dommet, speaking for the first time. 'You get to stay with the ship.'

'Which is our right, lad,' the master insisted, 'but we are of the sea, so you cannot think us friends to those who would press you again, for even if we are not at risk ourselves we still despise the buggers for the low scallies they are. But you don't have a choice: it's take what's on offer or you won't even get out onto the hard. The marines will have all three of you aboard another barky before your feet touch and you can protest till you're blue that you've got protections on the way.

Open your mouth to that, an' they'll make sure you're on a ship about to weigh that very day.'

The implications of that were very unpleasant: once at sea they would be beyond the reach of legal safety and the navy had ways of making sure matters stayed that way. The trio exchanged glances, but in such a situation, with John Pearce absent, O'Hagan was the person to defer to.

'A boat?' Michael asked, eventually.

'You might be best on your own, Michael,' Charlie said, which got him looks of deep curiosity from the warrants.

'No, we're all in the same steep tub now.'

If Rufus looked confused, Charlie understood; Michael was not going to desert them, seeking to use Pearce's ticket of leave that had got him here, which, in any case, might not suffice going the other way, given the scrutiny of such documents was intense.

'The jolly boat,' the gunner suggested. 'Big enough for five and small enough so one of us can come with you to fetch it back.'

'Sure, we need food for the journey,' said Michael.

'An' more besides,' Charlie added. 'Some kind of shore-goin' rig and the like.'

If three of the men before the Pelicans nodded, one did not, though they all knew why Charlie had made that demand. On the way back from the Mediterranean, HMS *Grampus* had caught fire and sank, taking with it most of their possessions. Some had been replaced through the good offices of John Pearce, but not all. It was the fourth fellow who presented the problem.

'What?' the purser demanded. 'Shore-going rig! Have you not dunned me for enough?'

'Mr Pearce paid for what we're wearing,' Charlie protested.

'He's yet to pay for the food you're eating.'

'I ain't got no more'n a few pence left,' O'Hagan growled, with such ferocity that the purser took two steps back and barged into the gunner, standing painfully on and bruising the man's toes. 'And by doin' what you say we could be sacrificing any hope of what pay we're owed.'

'Bugger the pay,' Charlie spat. 'It's a six-month wait to get that at best.'

'You are sure Mr Pearce will return?' the master asked.

'Course he will,' shouted Charlie, with all the confidence he could muster; any doubts he had would not be shared with this lot. 'And he's well found, what with the prizes we've taken.'

More important was the look exchanged between the master and the purser, which implied the latter would have to accede to their request, that was until prizes were mentioned: the word brought a sudden gleam to the purser's eye and, quite suddenly, he was all agreement.

'I shall, of course, charge him a fee in interest, and of necessity it will be a high one, given the quality of what I will provide.'

Seeing Michael's glowering reaction to this promise of daylight robbery, the purser took refuge behind both the master and the gunner, not that the statement abashed him. The other two were looking at Michael O'Hagan, and though he did not say so, the Irishman knew they were on the horns of a real dilemma. To stay was impossible; to run fraught with peril. Never mind what they might face by being sent to sea again, Charlie and Rufus could face prison or transportation once ashore and away from the protection provided by the navy.

As the alternatives ran quickly through his mind, he knew that what had been suggested presented the best course and that included landing Pearce with the purser's bill. That would have to include some coin: what Pearce had given him he had used on the way south and when he said he had only pennies left that was the truth. Without money they would either have to steal or beg and that risked being quickly rumbled and handed over to the local watch, which was worse than being taken by a press gang.

'The other warrants will agree?' he asked.

The bosun, master-at-arms and the cook had gone ashore to carouse in the taverns on Portsmouth Point; the others who had acted as warrants, on a ship so long at sea, had been temporary promotions by the captain, so, not being Navy Board appointments, they had lost their places as soon as she dropped anchor.

'Can't see why they would not,' the master replied.

'Food for a week, and what Charlie said besides, some coin as well as your boat, or on the blood of the Blessed Mary those marines of yours will be carrying us to a new ship and you lot in a foursome of pine boxes to the churchyard.'

A huge Irish fist was slowly raised to make his point.

'Well said, Michael,' added Charlie Taverner.

'It best be done peaceful, like,' murmured the gunner.

'Easy for you,' the purser cried, recovering some of his ire. 'The price is not coming from your pocket.'

'Nor will it be coming from yours, you slimy goat, you'll just be givin' away some of the monies you fiddled from them poor dumb Lascars on the way home from Bengal.'

'Take that back or so help me . . .'

The man stepped right up to the purser, who was by no means the shape of a fighting man, while the gunner was a short and grizzled veteran, nut-coloured from Eastern service, who had served in king's ships man and boy. 'What will you do, turd?'

'Enough,' the master called. 'We are not like to see these poor fellows troubled, so we has no choice but to give them what they need, without grumbling, and rely on Mr Pearce to make good on his promise to pay.'

There was little time for what was required: the cutting of pigtails that had taken months to grow, the preparation of old, lightweight canvas from worn sailcloth, which Michael insisted they must, with needle and thread, turn into clothing that would not only keep foul weather off their head and backs, but stop them being immediately identified as tars. The slop ducks they already wore had to be narrowed: pigtails aside, nothing screamed 'sailor' like wide-bottomed leg wear. Ditty bags were sewn too, with a skill that came easily to Rufus, once an apprentice in the leather trade, much less so to Charlie and Michael, who bled many times from needle pricks.

The ditty bags had to be big enough to carry food, like chunks of portable soup, salt fish, spare shirts, stockings, lye soap, shaving kit and shore-going footwear. The work carried on into the gloom of twilight until it was complete and, in darkness, equipped as best they could, they went over the side, took the oars and, using the lights of the town as a guide, steered away from the dockyard along the Southsea shore to the sound of the tide beating against the shingle.

'And how in God's name,' demanded Rufus Dommet, when darkness fell, 'is John Pearce goin' to find us?'

'We have to find him, Rufus,' Charlie replied. 'And damn quick.'

'So there you have the story, Mr Winston. I, like the others from this benighted place, was trussed and taken downriver, the frigate weighed from Sheerness within a day, and I have to tell you that, if it is damned difficult to get off any ship, it is rendered impossible once they are at sea.'

'This Ralph Barclay sounds like a rum cove I must say,' Winston said. 'Not that the navy is short of his type.'

Pearce shook his head. 'The pity is he is not the worst, sir. There are those who see him as lenient. Besides that, malice is endemic, for I must tell you my companions and I have been pressed not once, but twice.'

Winston's eyebrows shot up. 'That, sir, is singular.

Am I to assume Barclay to be at the seat of that also?'

'Yes, but he had help from a slimy little toad, a midshipman and relation of his called Toby Burns.'

'Who is surely worth another bumper,' Winston replied, signalling for a refill. 'And I am agog to hear more of this Barclay fellow as well as what you observed in Paris. I am a man of business and a first-hand account of the events in that benighted city will be a rare treat indeed.' The break into French was unexpected, but it made Pearce smile. '*Voulez-vous prend un autre boire, avec moi?*'

Pearce replied, amused by the less-than-perfect French, but far too polite to correct it. '*Le même, s'il vous plaît.*'

CHAPTER TWO

It was by a fortuitous accident that John Pearce missed
Ralph Barclay at the Admiralty, for had they met there
would have been blood on the walls. True to his nature,
on entering the same anteroom, Barclay was brusque
with everyone present, they being strangers. Also, given
he had lost his left arm at Toulon, while making it plain
the wound had yet to fully heal – the ligature left in
the wound had yet to come free – his demand that
a lieutenant surrender a comfortable seat on one side
of the fireplace had to be acceded to, that following
on from his loud admonition to the footman who had
shown him in to take care to let Mr Stephens know he
came with the blessing of the Duke of Portland. It was
his way of telling those waiting that he did not lack for
interest in the matter of seeking employment: he was
merely here to find out what ship he would be given.

For all the discourtesy of his entry and manner, such
was the way of the navy, where grovelling to senior

officers was very necessary, every lieutenant present was eager to engage him in conversation, especially since, with such a potent aristocratic connection, he would soon have a command: he was, after all, a post captain with the twin epaulettes of three years in the rank and he had seen action.

When they enquired on such matters they found themselves addressing a man eager to recount his adventures, as well as to air his prejudices: for the former, that led to boasts of prizes taken, a single ship action which, though ending in a defeat, he managed to make sound like a triumph, that followed by his unflattering opinion of the man who held the Mediterranean Command, Vice Admiral Samuel Lord Hood.

'His Lordship made a singular mess at Toulon,' he insisted. 'He should have listened to the wiser counsel of Sir William Hotham. Now, there was a man who had the right of it.'

That had the other post captain present, an elderly fellow who had seemed to be asleep, opening his eyes and sitting slightly forward: a man of Barclay's rank did not lightly traduce an admiral of the status and reputation of Sam Hood without good cause. It was not necessary to say to these fellows that Ralph Barclay was a client officer of Hotham, Lord Hood's second in command, or that he was unlikely to be well regarded by the C-in-C himself; they understood without explanation the nuances of what was being said and so they should, for it was their world. If Hotham were being praised he would be this fellow's patron; anyone who did not have regard for Barclay would be damned.

'And I told the noble duke of Hood's error of judgement in no uncertain terms.' That was accompanied by a hard look to ensure they identified which particular peer he was talking about. 'I daresay Mr Pitt has had his ears burnt already on that matter, given the government depends on support from the Portland faction to properly prosecute the war.'

Explanation, of necessity, had to follow; Barclay had set the scene, while underlining the depth of his own interest. Hood, he insisted, had made a bad bargain with the French in Toulon, not insisting that the Royalist-leaning officers surrender the huge naval base and their ships, instead granting them the status of allies and allowing them to keep control of their powerful fleet.

'We should have seized the port, gentlemen, which was in such turmoil it could not have been defended, but did we? We should have towed out what ships we fancied and immediately burnt the rest, blocking the harbour with wrecks, but did we? We had no need to land and seek to hold the place when destruction would have served our purpose just as well.'

His listeners knew these enquiries to be rhetorical so none bothered to answer. Everyone present would have read the *Naval Gazette* and the London newspapers; in short, they would be au fait with the details of the failure to hold on to Toulon, despite help from Naples, Piedmont and Spain, with Hood landing every man he could spare from his fleet. The siege had lasted for five months, the forces of the French Revolution bloodily determined to take back the main French naval port in the Mediterranean.

In the end, Hood had been forced to abandon the place, taking off as many refugees as he could – nowhere near the number seeking to flee the guillotine and Jacobin revenge. Thousands had died in retribution for their lack of revolutionary zeal and, to cap it all, the destruction of those warships that could not be manned and sailed out had only been partial; in short, given sailors to crew them, the French still had a powerful fleet.

'It is said, sir,' advanced a very junior lieutenant, 'that the Spaniards let us down in the matter of destruction. They did not set alight those ships allotted to them.'

Barclay snorted. 'Only because an old fool who should have been beached long ago gave them opportunity to do so.'

Being by nature a touch insensitive, even Ralph Barclay could see what these fellows tried to disguise: to call into question the ability of one the nation's best admirals was within the bounds of normal discourse – no two sailors ever entirely agreed on a command appointment or a chosen course of action. To call the same man an old fool and past it was coming it very high indeed. He had gone too far; time, Ralph Barclay knew, to recover some ground.

'I have nothing but admiration for Lord Hood and I say he stands high enough in my estimation to not be shamed by comparison to the greatest naval officer it has been my privilege to serve.' The pause was just long enough to tickle their curiosity. 'I refer, of course, to Admiral Lord Rodney.'

That met the stony-faced acceptance politeness

demands, for once more this captain was nailing his partisan colour to the mast. Clearly he had previously been a client officer of the late George Brydges Rodney, an admiral about whom opinion was much divided: a great fighting sailor yes, but a man with a reputation for being a touch free with the notion of lining his pockets as well as playing ducks and drakes with the rules of the service: had he not tried to make his son a post captain aged just twelve years, had he not raided and emptied the rich warehouses of Tortuga merely to get his hands on the value therein? It was also well known that Rodney and Sam Hood, when serving together in the Caribbean, had quarrelled a great deal; Hood insisting personal greed had proved a greater motivation to Rodney than service to his king and country.

'But age, sirs,' Barclay added with great emphasis, 'has come to addle Lord Hood's thinking, as it must come to any fellow in his eighth decade. Sir William Hotham, by contrast, is still in his prime and as clear-sighted as a man of his rank needs to be.'

King George's Navy was like a club, one in which gossip was the stuff of life; indeed, John Pearce had been wont to say that no fishwife need fear comparison with a group of naval officers gathered to discuss their peers. It being their profession, they lived in its rumour-driven web, talked when they were gathered and wrote to each other when not, while in doing so, never failing to air their partialities. In the face of this piece of blatant embroidery, the gathered lieutenants murmured as if in agreement. It was the old fellow on the opposite side of the fireplace who spoke now. Being himself of equal rank he felt no need to defer to opinions with which he did not agree.

'I had a letter from my good friend, Captain Elphinstone, sir, whom I am sure you must have encountered at Toulon.'

'I had that good fortune, yes,' Barclay replied guardedly: Elphinstone was a creature of Hood's and not a man he considered a friend.

'I am bound to say he was full of praise for Lord Hood and his attempt to hold Toulon. He was also of the opinion the government had let Hood down by not sending forth the soldiers he required and which he asked for, and that, had they obliged, it might have been possible to inflict such a defeat of the Jacobins as to render the whole of France vulnerable; in short, to bring to an end the war. I am bound to say I respect Captain Elphinstone's opinions, sir, and most markedly did so when he was my premier.'

'Sir,' Barclay replied, for the first time speaking guardedly, 'we are not, I think, acquainted.'

'Rawlinson.'

This set Ralph Barclay thinking hard: he knew the captain's list as others know their psalms and he searched his memory for the name. Of some four hundred and fifty in total, Ralph Barclay's greatest interest was in the top of that list, to which one day he hoped he would rise, and the name, added to the man's great age, supplied the clue that fixed his position. Barclay was in the top quarter, this captain was at the very apex and it was clear, given the determined look in his eye, the old fellow was willing to carry his disagreement all the way to argument, which might prove unpleasant. Barclay temporised.

'Captain Rawlinson, I am surprised you have not yet been given your flag.'

'I am close to that honour, sir, though it scarce credits a man to want it too much . . .'

Balderdash, Ralph Barclay thought. *I want an admiral's flag more than anything in creation.*

'. . . given,' Captain Rawlinson continued, 'that it requires men of my own age or above to expire before I can be so elevated. You see, Captain Barclay, I was somewhat advanced in years when I was made post myself, but to wish for the death of others would not aid me when my own time comes. I would aspire to meet my Maker with as pure a heart as I can muster, so if I go to my grave lacking the elevation to an admiral's rank, so be it.'

'Your flag, sir,' said that very junior lieutenant, a gleam in his eye. 'What a fine thing it must be. I cannot believe it is not something to be craved.'

Rawlinson produced a sad smile. 'It is a mere title in my case, young man, since, unless I can this day persuade the Board I can be of use, it will likely be a yellow pennant.'

'But the pay, sir,' the youngster blurted out, before blushing, given it was a crude allusion.

That was not the only thing to cause the kind of embarrassment that led to an avoidance of the old fellow's eye. Topping the captain's list at the next round of promotions, he would get a rear admiral's rank and the rise in pay that went with it – a stipend he would hold till the day he died. But 'yellow' admirals were granted no command: the navy took great care to ensure the competence of those granted control of its fleets and it required influence to be granted any of the other numerous appointments in the Admiralty gift.

The conclusion was plain: as an officer Captain Rawlinson had probably pursued an undistinguished career. In that time he had failed to make important connections in the service or politics and, while no doubt competent, did not impress those who ran the navy with his powers of command. If it was not an uncommon state of affairs – there were many more yellow admirals than active ones, just as there were more captains than vessels for them to command – it was rare to have it openly stated.

'Yet I have hope,' Rawlinson added, with a wan smile, 'that I might be gainfully employed in some capacity, hence my presence here among we supplicants.'

Ralph Barclay was about to protest he was better than a mere supplicant when the footman intoned his name from the doorway, adding. 'Admiral Gardner will see you now.'

Barclay nodded happily as he rose to exit: he was about to see the most senior of the present naval lords, Hood, the other, being absent. Added to that, Alan Gardner, in charge of appointments to ships, had been a client of Rodney, so he was assured of a warm reception. The same words made old Rawlinson sigh and recline once more in his chair, eyes closing, as they had been when Barclay first entered the room. He had been passed over yet again, underlining just how low were his chances of success.

Midshipman Toby Burns had decided some time past that Admiral Sir William Hotham was trying to get him killed by continually putting him in danger. The reason was clear even to dim Toby, who was not well blessed in the article of discernment, and it all had to do with his uncle by marriage, Captain Ralph Barclay. In a piece of chicanery to which Hotham had been an active accomplice, a charge of illegal impressment brought by the pestilential John Pearce had been seen off by a farce of a court martial, held in Toulon, undertaken when the main litigants and their damning evidence were safely out of the way, en route to the Bay of Biscay.

Serving aboard his uncle's frigate and in utter terror of the man, Toby Burns had become the chief witness, primed to lie through his teeth that he had been present at the taking of John Pearce and his stupidly named Pelicans, when in fact he had been nowhere near the Liberties of the Savoy on the night in question. Hotham had seen to it that none of the contrary written depositions were introduced and had staffed the court with officers he could trust, both in the presentation of the evidence and in the concluding judgement; Ralph Barclay had thus suffered nothing more than a mild rebuke.

Such an outcome had not brought the youngster security – quite the opposite. Now serving in Hotham's flagship, HMS *Britannia*, and apparently much cosseted by the admiral – his fellow midshipmen, though never in his hearing, called him the admiral's bum boy – he had been sent more than once, on the excuse of providing him with opportunity to distinguish himself, into deadly situations, the irony being that those with whom he now shared his shipboard accommodation were ravaged with jealousy at what they saw as his good fortune.

In Toulon he had faced death or mutilation in the action in which his uncle had lost his arm. At San Fiorenzo, the most northern anchorage in Corsica, Hotham had selected him to help lead ashore the boats carrying the marines to the beach and there he had seen his superior, a lieutenant, end up with a smashed leg. Now he was on a land expedition and had spent the last three days trudging up and through the Teghime Pass, still in the grip of winter, cold and snowbound at this altitude, as part of the so-called liaison with the troops of General Dundas seeking to take the French town of Bastia, helping to haul the naval cannon provided to aid the assault.

From San Fiorenzo to Bastia was no great distance as the crow flies, but the pavé road ran through high mountains and the upward leg had been hellish. At least now they were on the downward slopes, heading for the coast on which the city lay. It was fully expected this was the day they would meet the enemy and, unable to sleep, the youngster was awaiting the dawn with trepidation.

Sat by a blazing fire, his cloak wrapped tightly around him and staring into the flames, he had taken to listing those people whom he saw as inimical to his well-being, one that seemed to grow longer the more he considered the matter. Hotham, Ralph Barclay and John Pearce only headed the growing roll, which extended in his present mood to include his own family, who had failed to see on his last visit home that he did not want to be in the navy at all, never mind stuck halfway up a mountain pass with a party of seamen who showed him scant respect.

In order to hold that view it was, of course, very necessary for him to forget his one-time enthusiasm for sea service, the way he had persuaded his parents to badger a newly acquired uncle – Ralph Barclay had married his Aunt Emily – to give him a place in his midshipman's berth. What a shock that had been! There was no romance below decks on a man-o'-war, no glory; there was filth, thievery, bullying of a kind he had hoped to have left behind when he departed his school, added to a severe risk of being maimed or killed in action, the first of which had seen him wrecked on the shores of France. He had returned to Somerset after only a few months of service as a supposed hero, finding it impossible, under such a burden, to let those so proud of him know of either his unpleasant experiences or of his very real fears.

'Not asleep, Mr Burns? Surely you of all people have no dread of action today?' The voice of Lieutenant Driffield had him shoot to his feet: the fellow might only be a marine officer but he was in all respects his superior. What followed was an emollient apology for so startling him. 'Please, young fellow, there's no need to jump to attention. We are, after all, in the field.'

'You caught me deep in thought, sir.'

'I daresay you were plotting ways to confound the enemy.'

'Of course, sir,' Burns replied, automatically, as Driffield stood rubbing and warming his hands.

'Well, never fear, you will soon have action to get your blood flowing. I have asked permission of the bullocks that my marines and I be allowed to partake of any assaults on the enemy bastions blocking the road to Bastia. No point in coming all this way and not seeing action, what? Be assured, should you wish to accompany me, I would be honoured to include you and I know my men would be inspired by your presence.'

Having turned away from the fire, the cold air helped to fix the features on Toby Burns's face, which enabled him to avoid reacting to this terrifying hyperbole. The last thing he wanted was to 'partake', he did not want to even be where he was now! His heart's desire, which he feared to articulate, was to be back in rural Somerset and even at school, perhaps applying himself in a way he had not done previously to his books, so as to qualify for an occupation that would keep him safely ashore, perhaps as a curate or an articled clerk of law.

'Sit down, Mr Burns,' Driffield insisted, doing so himself. There was a short pause before the marine lieutenant spoke again, and it was with a sideways glance at the midshipman. 'I know, young sir, for I have been told, that you are reticent in the matter of your exploits, modest to a fault, in fact. But here we are, with dawn not yet upon us and with time to kill. If it would not put you out, at all, it would pass some of that if you were to entertain me with the tale of your heroics. I refer, of course, to the events in Brittany.'

Staring into the flames again, Toby Burns was thinking if Jesus Christ had his Calvary, he was not alone: Brittany and what happened there was his. The whole 'exploit', just like his supposed heroism, was founded on a lie and one he feared would eventually be exposed, but he was not going to be the source of that. Obliged many times to repeat the untruths and seeming trapped into doing so now, the words came with an ease born of much repetition, larded, of course, with very necessary modesty regarding his own role. No matter how many times he told the story, it provided for him no crumbs of personal comfort.

'It will not surprise you, sir, that naval officers are sometimes lacking in the very basic needs of their profession.' Driffield nodded at that, perhaps a trifle too enthusiastically, marine officers being much condescended to by their naval counterparts. 'In Lieutenant Hale of HMS *Brilliant* we had one who was not only deficient in that, but deaf to boot, and it was because of his affliction, his inability to hear the heavy crashing of waves on jagged rocks, we found ourselves cast ashore on the French coast, lucky not to be drowned in the maelstrom.'

The tale rolled out, of Hale drowning, he being the only blue coat to survive and because of his midshipman's status, in charge of a party of boneheaded seamen, he was forced, despite being a mere thirteen years of age, to take command, to concoct a plan to get back aboard his Uncle Ralph's frigate. As he spoke, to a silent and admiring marine, the sky took on a grey tinge, slate rather than any hint of blue, and soon, all around them under the heavy clouds, bugles blew and soldiers stirred from their tents to begin to heat their breakfast, both men by the fire brought theirs by Driffield's servant.

By the time Toby Burns, in his story, had got back to England, to be hailed as the first hero of the new war, the trumpets were starting to blow for the troops to assemble, so he was spared the need to recount the way his family had reacted to his supposed success, had failed to discern what he couldn't bring himself to tell them – his desire to forgo sea service.

'A fine tale, Mr Burns, and one you should be more than proud to relate. It says something for a boy of your years, as well as for the service of which we are both a part, that you should be able to command men so much older. I am surprised you did not have a mutiny on your hands when you ordered them to risk their lives.'

'John Pearce would have started one.'

'Pearce?' asked Driffield.

Toby realised he was weary, from worry as well as lack of sleep, that being a name he was not inclined to utter in another's hearing, of a man who had become the bane of his entire life since the events he had just been describing. It was John Pearce who had taken command, not he, Pearce who had shown the leadership and skills he so conspicuously lacked, details of which his Uncle Ralph had suppressed. But he was obliged to respond, given the look on the marine lieutenant's face.

'A sailor who was one of the party I commanded, sir, and a true sea lawyer type.'

'I met a fellow of that name at Toulon, a naval lieutenant.'

'Different fellow, I'm sure,' Toby Burns replied quickly, standing up to cover the blush of his lie: he had spent his entire time in Toulon seeking to avoid that very person on the very good grounds that, not only had he stolen the man's glory, he had, on the way back to England, watched him pressed a second time when he could easily have intervened to prevent it.

'Must be another person,' Driffield agreed, rising also. 'But if they share a name, young sir, they share other traits. The Pearce I met was a very wrong-headed fellow. He wanted me to abandon my guns to the enemy, damn him!'

'Shocking,' Toby Burns exclaimed, seeing it, in the expression of his companion, as the required response.

Driffield puffed himself up to his full height then, pushing out the buttons on his red coat. 'I confounded him, of course, and the enemy. Waited till he had scuttled off and did my proper duty.'

'You must be very proud, sir.'

Driffield's reply was quite sharp considering how friendly he had been hitherto. 'As I said, Mr Burns, I did my duty, no more, no less.'

In a long line the column descended from the Pass of Teghime, the ground underfoot on the switchback road turning from frozen slush to the more slippery, brown-flecked kind, and finally to nothing but mud. But at least, going downhill, the oxen were not straining, the only hold-up caused by wheels dropping into the ruts of a poorly maintained surface. They could see, at times to their right, at others to their left, the Mediterranean – not blue but as grey as the sky it reflected – and between them and it the lower hills that hogged the coast where their enemies awaited them.

That sight was soon lost once they descended further: above and below the sides of the roadway thick forests of pine, oak, chestnut and beech hemmed them in, and where there was a clear patch the earth was terraced, red and rock-filled, with straggling vineyards or olive groves, only very occasionally showing a peasant dwelling, one which was immediately raided by the soldiers. They emerged with whatever of value they could steal: not much from inhabitants who had fled, as country folk do at the approach of any force, hostile or friendly, taking their livestock, sheep and goats with them. On the lower slopes there were fewer trees, but instead they had to contend with the thick, near-impenetrable scrub that was a special feature of the island.

Up ahead there was the occasional rattle of musketry as French skirmishers, using the dense undergrowth, sought to delay the column's progress – pinpricks Driffield called them – though in time they passed one of the fatal results, a red-coated body by the roadside, which did nothing for the state of Toby Burns's mind. Boots covered in mud, white breeches likewise spattered, the bottom of his cloak soaked, he lumbered along, occasionally issuing unnecessary commands to men who knew better than he what to do, receiving in return barely disguised looks of dislike covered by touched forelocks.

Here was another reason to detest the King's Navy: tars were generally indulgent of young midshipmen, he had seen it often enough. Sometimes, it was true, they joshed them into making fools of themselves, sending them to get things like sky hooks and long weights, but it was done, if not with pure kindness, with little malice. No sailor he had served with ever played upon him, benevolently or otherwise; they either ignored him or sought to thwart him in some way. So gloomy had he become, he even contemplated the thought that death would be preferable to his present cold condition – not a painful one, of course, but a demise of the kind where one goes to sleep and merely does not awake. That was until he considered divine retribution.

Yet surely his lies would not count against him in the eyes of the Lord? Forces with which he could not contend had pressed them upon him, so the sin was surely theirs. His Uncle Ralph had known very well it was John Pearce who had led the party that recaptured the ship taken from his convoy, he who had sent him back to England with the despatch extolling his heroism. He had also inveigled him into telling lies at the court martial that had dished Pearce's hopes of retribution, aided, of course, by that sly old bastard Hotham.

No, he was an innocent in all this: should he expire in his sleep, surely he would not be denied celestial comfort, a place in heaven, for what were the transgressions of others. That he had not confessed them either in church or in life was not allowed to interfere with the outcome the youngster mentally desired. It was unfortunate then, that in contemplation, one of the faces to fill his mind was that of his Aunt Emily, estranged wife of his uncle and the one person who, in knowing the truth of what had happened, and being of a pure nature, might one day ditch him.

She had gone back to England with her wounded husband; was she at this moment relating to his family the terrible lies he had told? The thought, which he tried to get out of his mind, would not go, making his misery even more acute. Silently, he imagined a prayer to send over the ocean to her, begging forgiveness, but more than that, her silence.

CHAPTER THREE

Ensconced in a decent set of rooms just off Holborn, near the Inns of Court, her chest unpacked and her possessions put away, Emily Barclay had achieved that which she sought, the freedom to live as she wished without her marital vows impinging on her life. The note from her husband demanding she return to the family home she ignored, merely replying in the negative but suggesting he meet her on neutral ground to work out how they were to find a way of living as a married couple while never sharing the same roof, with the concomitant need to avoid a scandal that would harm Ralph Barclay's career – necessary to support them both financially – and destroy her reputation.

That it would require care by both parties was a given: the world in which they lived did not take kindly to separation or anything that fractured the marriage vows, so it was incumbent on Emily to somehow protect her estranged husband, to find a fiction that society would see as acceptable – not that anyone with half a brain would be fooled. But appearances were all: if he had a ship and was at sea pursuing his career, matters would be eased. Should he fail to find employment, a strong possibility given his missing arm, then things would be much more complex.

She reflected less now on how she could have been so blind to Ralph Barclay's manifest faults. Of course, she was junior to him by twenty years, he was a naval captain and, even lacking a ship, was thus seen as a catch. There had also been a degree of parental pressure due to the fact that the home into which she had been born and raised was entailed to the Barclay family and, due to death and inheritance, had he so chosen, Captain Barclay could have turfed them out and not been required to give a reason for doing so. With an ineffectual father and a single-minded mother the drift from intention, to engagement, then to nuptials had turned out, when she examined it in retrospect, to be seamless.

How supine she had been! It was not hard for her to pin down the exact moment when that had been punctured and her spirit hardened. There had been that first day at Sheerness aboard HMS *Brilliant*, when following on from her own arrival had come those poor unfortunates her husband called volunteers, when she more than suspected, by their bruised and dispirited appearance, they were pressed men. Then he had hit the one called John Pearce for the mere act of looking at her. She had not known his name then, of course, but how much that man had impacted on her life since that first day. Her husband's determination to subsequently flog him for a minor misdemeanour had led to their first disagreement and it had seemed the relationship went downhill from that moment, culminating in his lies about not meeting Pearce while she and Captain Barclay were prisoners in Toulon.

The tap at the door took her mind off both and she opened it to find her widowed landlady, Mrs Fletcher, waiting to speak. 'A gentleman to see you, Mrs Barclay.'

'In uniform?' Emily asked, suspecting it might be her husband, even if she had demanded he do not call.

'No,' she simpered, 'an engaging young fellow, and very handsome he is too, waiting for you in the parlour.'

Her heart had lifted at the thought it might be Heinrich Lutyens, to whom she had sent a note regarding her new address, but there was no way the one-time surgeon of HMS *Brilliant*, who had become her sounding board and many times acted as her conscience over this past year, could be described as handsome.

'No name?'

'He did not give one, but he says he carries an important message.'

'Handsome you say?'

The way Mrs Fletcher responded positively to that, almost coquettish, gave Emily a clue to who it might be, and if she was correct in her assumption, she knew she would have to steel herself for what was coming, given it was bound to be unpleasant.

'I will come down presently.'

When Mrs Fletcher left, Emily went to a chest of drawers and opened it, the scent of the perfumed liners rising to her nose. The papers she wanted were not hidden in any way and, taking them out, she unfolded and looked through the bundle, a copy she had made on the way to London, even though she knew very well what each page said. Selecting the one she thought the most damning, the bundle was returned to the drawer, yet she shuddered as she closed it. Much as you anticipate a confrontation and even when you know you hold all the cards, there is always a moment of anxiety: for all the certainties, matters might not go as you wish.

He was standing, back to the door, looking out onto the street when Emily entered the room, but she knew, by the corn-coloured nature of his hair, even before he turned to face her, it was, as she had suspected, her husband's clerk, Cornelius Gherson. The smile was the same one she recalled from previous encounters, a look that implied an amorous connection, and an intimacy, which certainly did not exist. If there was one man in the world she loathed without a measure of charity, it was this slimy toad.

'Mrs Barclay, I come from your husband.'

'He still employs you?'

'He will have need of me when he gets his next command.'

There was an attempt to keep anticipation out of her voice. 'There is some hope of that, then?'

Gherson's smirk told her she had failed: it was as if

he could see the workings of her mind. 'He has made some very important connections of late; enough, I suspect, to get him a ship of the line. He had a very favourable interview this very day at the Admiralty.'

'And the message is?'

'Simply, that he declines to support you in your desire for independence.'

The fact that Emily smiled threw Gherson only very slightly. 'He does not consider I can support myself?'

The look she got then, for there was one obvious way she could do that, was interesting. 'He requires you to return to the marital home, his home, where he will join you at his convenience. He also bids me to point out to you that there are consequences attendant upon a refusal that encompass more than your own person. I refer, of course, to the remainder of your family.'

'How typical of Captain Barclay to use the innocent to seek to punish those he sees as guilty.'

'Then you admit guilt?'

'If I am guilty of anything it is in being slow to see what a slug I married.'

'Is that a word you would wish me to convey to him?'

'I asked Captain Barclay to meet me on neutral ground. Am I to assume he declines that also?' Gherson nodded. 'Then, much as it displeases me to deal with you . . .'

Gherson's look was a picture; he was so vain, with his absurdly handsome face and near-girlish features, he could not accept even now, and after all the times he had faced her angry rejections, that Emily was not in the least bit attracted to him. No doubt he had contemplated, after her previous words, that he might keep her himself as a mistress.

'Take that smirk off your face, you snake!'

He was not thrown. 'You call me a snake, madam? Physician, heal thyself, I say, for like Eve, it is you who are the betrayer. It is a fault of your sex, as I know only too well from having dealt with many women myself.'

Fists clenched, Emily fought the desire to dispute with him: it would not serve. Instead she held out the paper she had brought from upstairs. 'I will not give this into your hand, since my trust in you is so low I have no knowledge of how you would use it – probably to blackmail my husband, not to aid him. But you may come closer and look.'

He declined to move. 'What can a piece of paper tell me?'

'This is a fair copy of part of a transcript of my husband's court martial, which both you and I know to have been a tissue of concocted lies and perjured testimony before a court hand-picked by Sir William Hotham. It is taken from the original sent to Lord Hood for his confirmation of sentence and it is part of the testimony given by my nephew Toby.'

He had moved closer as she spoke, to stare at the paper she was holding out. Her handwriting was neat and copperplate, so easy to read.

'You will wonder how I came by such a thing and you may do so till hell freezes over, for I will keep my counsel, but I have the court record in its entirety in my possession, and safe. Should my husband fail to support me, these papers will be placed in hands that will see Captain Barclay, and for all I know you with him, had up for blatant perjury. I shall also write to Admiral Hotham to let him know what I am about to do, and he is not a man to suffer disgrace. I daresay any threat to his reputation will see him throw you all to the wolves.'

Gherson was not smiling now; he had on his face a pout that would not have shamed a child denied a sweetmeat.

'Tell my husband to accede to my request for a meeting. Mrs Fletcher will show you out.'

'I don't believe you, madam. You were present at the court martial, these must be notes you made, which renders them useless, since you cannot testify against your husband or proffer evidence against him.'

'Gherson, I do not care if you believe me or not, you are of no account. Good day.'

'Your nephew will suffer most, madam, which in turn will bring shame on your whole family.'

That was a telling barb, but she knew Toby Burns to be a liar and a coward; knew he had stolen, with her husband's contrivance, Pearce's achievements in Brittany. Any disgrace would break the hearts of her aunt and uncle and she had considered the matter before.

'Toby has made his own bed, and so must lie on it,' she replied, well aware that it was far from being that simple.

'A bed that might well be Botany Bay.'

'You may face the same fate.'

'No, Mrs Barclay,' Gherson replied, with such

annoying and resurgent confidence. 'I committed no words to the court that could in any way be questioned by another, Pearce notwithstanding, which leaves it as his word against mine.'

'I am sure you have other crimes that will one day see you transported. Now, get out!'

The slow, elegant bow was infuriating.

Emily was shaking by the time she got back to her rooms, thankful that she had not succumbed to that in Gherson's presence, well aware the snake had spotted the flaw in her proposition. She could not ditch her husband without also ditching her nephew, who had been the chief court martial witness. Could she pay that price? Should she write to him and give him a chance to repent and if she did and he agreed, how would that affect her future life?

Midday found Toby Burns on the steep coastal hills of East Corsica which ran right down to the sea, creating valleys of varying depth, with the leaders of the army, General Dundas and Colonel Stuart, eying the first of the enemy positions through their spyglasses, a redoubt with half a dozen cannon covering the sloping, intervening ground. Beyond that in the distance, hugging the shore, lay Bastia, with the sticks of ships' masts, if not the hulls, visible in the harbour.

The old fishing town was between them and the citadel, which protected that anchorage, the white walls of which, even without the magnification of a telescope, looked pretty formidable. That was underlined by the layered defences, which had been set up in between. The

French had known they were coming and had made their preparations accordingly. They intended to exact a high price from their enemy before they could even think of closing the harbour and investing the city. From fifty yards' distance, Toby Burns observed the negative shakes of the head and a degree of heated discussion: these army officers were seemingly not enamoured of their prospects, which suited him admirably. Uncomfortable as it would be, he would happily re-cross the mountains without another shot being fired. Driffield was closer, within earshot of the discussions, and it was not long before he came striding towards the midshipman, his face angry.

'Damn these bullocks, they are a shy lot.'

'How so, sir?'

'They say that what lies before us is too formidable to assault with the forces we have, and even if we could subdue the outworks they lack the means to lay siege to the city.'

'So we pull back?' Toby asked, careful to sound disappointed.

'After a demonstration, I think, yes.'

'Demonstration?'

'We cannot just retire with our tail between our legs, Mr Burns, without showing Johnny Crapaud our mettle. I daresay Dundas and Stuart will be satisfied to subdue that redoubt before us. It hardly serves to my mind.'

'What would satisfy you, Mr Driffield?'

'Why, Mr Burns, that you and I show them what our service is made of by beating our weapons on their city walls. Rest assured, if they do decide to attack those guns, you and I will be well to the fore. The navy will take a cannon this day or we will expire in the effort, so get yourself two primed pistols and a sharp blade, while I get my marines ready.'

'And the sailors, sir?'

'No tars, this is a task for Lobsters.' Driffield grinned then. 'And, of course, midshipmen of the right stripe.'

Much time was taken up getting the British artillery into position and firing, seeking to subdue the enemy by destroying their outworks, with the obvious concomitant that they were within range of counter battery fire. It was a damned dangerous place to be but Toby Burns had no choice and it was just as well, given his ignorance, he had no need to issue orders regarding range and powder – the gunner's mate sent along saw to that – for, quite apart from his lack of knowledge, he would not have trusted his voice to emerge as anything other than a squeak. Driffield, on the other naval cannon, could not shut up, issuing a constant stream of bellowed encouragement to, 'Give them hell, lads,' and, 'Let us see the true colour of their damned claret.'

Meanwhile the assault parties were forming up, half the available force, officers dressing lines so that their men would not disgrace them by risking their lives in an untidy fashion. Then came the moment Toby dreaded most, when Driffield called to him, gleefully ordering his own men, who had been working their cannon in shirtsleeves, to don their red coats, gather their muskets, fix bayonets and take a heavy tot of the soldier's rum to still their gut. On the marine officer's heels, Toby, the taste of that rum still burning in his throat, was close enough to the major leading the assault to hear the idiot marine thanking him for the chance to face a glorious death.

As the drum started beating, the youngster had to work hard to keep his bowels from issuing an involuntary evacuation, but the terror of exposure had him marching forward as the command was given. They passed the mouth of the naval cannon to a last salvo, followed by loud cheers, with the grinning faces of the tars full of encouragement. For the first time in his naval career, the midshipman issued a command that was stern enough to be immediately obeyed.

'Belay that damned noise.'

'Do not castigate them for encouragement, Mr Burns,' Driffield called, 'for it is only engendered by jealousy. They, I am sure, would wish to be alongside us.'

The first French ball scythed into the centre of the long, thin line of redcoats and took with it two bullocks, the ranks closing up automatically to fill the space, the eyes of the men Toby Burns could see, staring straight ahead, fixed upon their object, with he wondering how they could act so and ignore the bloody corpses of their fallen mates.

'Grape soon,' Driffield said, out of the side of his mouth, as if he was about to be in receipt of a surprise and welcome gift. 'We will charge after the first salvo, I'll wager.'

That grapeshot came as if ordered, the tiny steel balls cracking as they passed Toby's ears. His first thought was to fall to the ground as if wounded, but having already employed that bit of subterfuge in a similar attack on the heights of Toulon he had severe doubts as to it serving a second time. In one hand he had a loaded pistol, in the other a raised sword heavy enough to make his young arm ache, and all his thoughts were on how to employ those weapons on himself, not the enemy. Yet, if he was afraid of the pain of a wound inflicted by others, he was even more fearful of one made by his own hand.

He had, he knew, begun to cry, the tears streaming down his face, his mind in a turmoil of thoughts and emotions, saved from discovery by the sudden command to charge, which allowed him to be dilatory and let those alongside him get slightly ahead. By sidestepping he got himself behind two bulky fellows – soldiers or marines it made no odds, they were taller than he and that sufficed: if a ball came his way they would take it first. Thankfully Driffield had lost all interest in his hero midshipman, his own lust for glory consuming his being. He was yelling and waving his sword like a banshee, and right before him lay the damaged earthworks of the enemy redoubt, still firing grape, as well as supporting musket fire.

Which one of those weapons took him in the chest mattered little: he stopped as if struck by a plank of wood, his body going rigid and seeming to rise from the ground, his weapons in the air as if he was aiming them at the heavens, his black tricorn hat flying backwards and off his head. Then he crumpled, collapsing not falling, first to his knees and then sideways to the ground. Toby

Burns was beside him, kneeling, glad of the chance to stop going forward, looking into the still-open eyes.

'Do not attend to me, Mr Burns,' he gasped. 'Lead my Lobsters to victory.'

It was a relief to Toby Burns that Driffield's eyes closed then, that a stream of bright red froth burst between his lips, accompanied by a deep groan. With the man down, Toby did not have to go any further forward and from his kneeling position he could see that the redcoats were atop the earthwork, taking aim with muskets at what must be a fleeing enemy. He had survived!

The counterstroke was not long in coming. No sooner had the defenders abandoned the redoubt than those who had taken it were in receipt of musketry from their inland flank, a party of French infantry firing from the deep scrub and woods above them, those crowing their victory on the crown of the embankment taking the most punishment, with Colonel Stuart, who had led the attack, calling to them urgently to get down. From being a defensive position that had protected the French it now became one behind which the redcoats cowered, with Stuart, foolishly exposed, spyglass to his eye, seeking to assess what threat they faced, which given the swing of that tiny telescope, seemed to be coming from more than one direction. Toby, having run for that same shelter, was right by his legs as he spoke.

'Humbugged, by damn.' Then the movement at his feet caught his eye, and he barked, 'Stand up, sir, do not let the men you lead see you cower.'

'Mr Driffield is dead, sir,' Toby protested, as a knot of other officers joined their colonel.

'All the more reason for you to appear unconcerned, lad.'

He had no choice but to comply, not least because what officers remained had come to join their colonel. Faint over the ground behind him, Toby could hear shouted commands. A glance backwards showed the remainder of the British force forming up, their lines being dressed once more for tidiness. He could also see the guns being levered round to take a new aim.

'They are coming to our rescue, sir,' he cried.

'Damn me, I hope not,' Charles Stuart said, with a wry grin, as several musket balls cracked over Toby's head and by the ears of the gathered officers. 'But they will cover us as we seek to retire. Mr Burns, I know you to be a brave lad, Mr Driffield told me, so get your Lobsters formed up and ensure they have their muskets loaded. I am in no doubt you are aware of what is required, but I will tell you anyway. They must follow my orders as to when to deliver a volley and then retire at a walk so they can reload on the move. I anticipate the French will pursue, so I will require them to stop on my command and fire again, then repeat the manoeuvre.'

'Sir.'

'See to it, lad, we are short on time. Gentlemen, to your places.'

Approaching the marine party Toby was aware that it was not only Driffield's body lying out in the open: from a detachment of twenty, they were down to fourteen. It was an absurd thought to have at such a time, as he counted their number, to see there was one for every year of his age. With a tremulous note in his voice he issued his orders to a corporal, who looked as if he understood, though there was a definite scowl attached to his acknowledgement for having to take instruction from such a nipper.

'Follow Colonel Stuart in all things. I will issue no more commands.'

'Praise be,' came a growling voice from behind the corporal, who issued a weary, insincere reprimand.

The British cannon opened up and that was the signal for which Stuart had been waiting. In a parade-ground voice he ordered his men to form up, his next command as they complied to give the French a volley. Then they spun and began to walk with their backs exposed to enemy musketry, each man holding his weapon as he first cleaned it, tore open a charge, poured powder down the barrel, followed by a rammed-in ball, the last act being the priming of the pan, then the response: stopping, turning, aiming and firing as ordered, then continuing the orderly retreat. It would have been admirable to see it if Toby Burns had looked, a demonstration of the tight discipline and training of the British redcoat; he was not watching, he had his eyes firmly on the ground before his feet, his shoulders hunched for what he knew was coming.

The searing feeling in his arm was not pain, more like that which you feel when inadvertently touching a very hot griddle, but a look to the side showed his blue coat ripped and the first sign of blood beginning

68

to emerge through his equally damaged shirt. He fell to his knees, part in shock, part in the thought that he would be less of a target, with the notion of being taken prisoner suddenly attracting him.

'On your feet, Mr Burns,' Stuart called over the sound of both cannon and musket fire, 'lest you favour the notion of a French bayonet in your vitals, for they will not take captives, I'll wager.'

Toby Burns was up and running in a flash, getting ahead of the line until another shout slowed him.

The whole body of British forces, once reunited, effected an untidy disengagement, guns being hauled away ahead of the infantry, until they were on the route back up to the Pass of Teghime, one so narrow the French declined to enter in pursuit. A hastily bandaged midshipman was with them, head held high now, feeling for once like a true hero, issuing, much to the annoyance of his toiling tars and very likely the struggling oxen as well, brusque orders which did nothing to aid the task of getting those heavy cannon up the steep hill.

CHAPTER FOUR

Pearce had entertained Winston regarding his sojourn in Paris, before going on to describe serving under Ralph Barclay, and that had naturally led on to the story of his adventures in Brittany, which then required him to recount the events of the second impressment at sea of him and his friends thanks to the supine nature of Toby Burns, this over a tankard of ale it was his turn to provide. Winston was a good listener, rarely interrupting unless he required clarification, but he did enquire what it was like to be flogged.

'Not, sir, that I am a stranger to punishment, given I was a pupil at Eton, where the masters were hearty with the birch. One, I admit before my time, flogged forty boys in one day, which given the strain on the swinging arm, is prodigious.'

'It is said to make a good man bad and a bad man worse, so what it does to mere boys I cannot imagine.'

'But would it not also be true to say that in certain settings, even a school, discipline is very necessary.'

'Command is very necessary, sir, but I have had charge of a ship, albeit not a large vessel and for a very short period. A basilisk eye and a threat to stop grog will serve just as well as the lash, excepting, of course, the endemic hard bargain who might require to be stapled to the deck. But you must understand that flogging at sea is ritualistic in its execution, as much a demonstration of the power to punish as the actual act of punishment itself, so it is often not about chastisement but the glorification of the office of ship's captain.'

Thinking back to what had happened to him, almost a piece of theatre in its undertones, John Pearce felt it necessary to add to his explanation. 'Having said that, it is also the case that the crew of king's ships tend to an appreciation of what constitutes fair play and have thus devised their own methods, as long as they are not dealing with an outright martinet, of mitigating the actual pain inflicted.'

'Mr Pearce, you have been most forthcoming and damned entertaining, and no man could question you have had an interesting life, but you mention you held a command, so you must tell me how you came by, in such a short service at sea, that blue coat.'

Two tankards of porter added to the metheglin had tended to soften John Pearce's natural modesty, so there was just a trace of swank in the way he replied. 'Have you heard of a French capture called the *Valmy*?'

'Who has not, it had the church bells peeling,'

Winston said, before keenly looking at Pearce. 'Was you the fellow who took her?'

'I played a small part in her capture, yes, and it was much exaggerated in the telling.'

'Yet profitable, I imagine.'

'No. I was dunned out of my true share of the proceeds, getting pennies not pounds, but my actions impressed Farmer George: the old booby insisted I be given promotion from midshipman to lieutenant.' Pearce took a deep swallow. 'Wasted, I might add, since I have no intention of any further service to him or his damned navy.'

'I don't follow.'

'I would not accept another commission, sir, though I am forced to admit there is no great queue waiting to grant me one.'

'The navy presents great opportunities in war, sir.'

'That may be true, Mr Winston, but not for me.'

'Then I am forced to enquire, sir, what occupation will you follow?'

'That is yet to be decided. My main concern at present, protections secured, is to find a means to bring the aforementioned Captain Barclay before a court.'

'If it is for illegal impressment, sir, you will struggle, for the tars are good at minding their own. A seaman was killed not six months past in the Thames Estuary by a boarding party intent on pressing seamen. Yet, with the Admiralty fielding its full power in the court, the lieutenant in charge was acquitted even of manslaughter, when he was clearly guilty of murder, he having given the order to fire the muskets, admittedly in reply to one being set off from the ship.'

'I have a possibility of getting him met with a charge of perjury.'

'Perjury, by damn! Do I detect the beginning of another tale, sir?'

Pearce smiled. 'I think, sir, I have assailed your patience enough.'

Winston signalled to the serving girl. 'Another will do no harm and it is my turn to provide it.'

And neither did it harm him as Pearce recounted the details of the travesty of Barclay's court martial, of how he and the true witnesses had been sidelined. He went on to explain the need for evidence – declining to say the pure, unvarnished proof was lost because of a fire at sea.

Winston was quick to allude to the expense. 'There is not a lawyer in creation, sir, who will not rub his hands at such a brief, for deep pockets will be needed and they are masters at the stripping out of wealth from their clients.'

'True,' Pearce replied, draining his ale. 'But if I can get a certain midshipman back from service in the Mediterranean – the aforementioned Burns, who was most avowedly not, as he claimed, there on the night I was pressed – I will have Ralph Barclay regardless. Now, I must finish my drink and be on my way, sir.'

'Before you depart, Lieutenant Pearce—'

'I think Mr Pearce might suffice from the morrow, for once I have collected from the Admiralty the protections for my friends I may discard this blue coat for ever.'

'Yet you have experience of being at sea.'

Pearce laughed, an act made more hearty by the consumption of porter. 'Not a great deal, sir.'

'From your own lips you have admitted to commanding a vessel. What I mean to say, sir, is my line of business occasionally includes the need to ship goods by sea, mostly in the coastal trade, and I must tell you the war with France makes more difficult what was never easy. In short, finding reliable people who will do what I need done and properly.'

'It is very kind of you, Mr Winston, but I shall be wholly occupied for some time in getting Captain Barclay into a court of law.'

'Nevertheless, you must, I suspect, find some form of employment in the future.' Winston reached inside his coat and produced a small rectangular card. 'Upon this, sir, are my details, where I can be found, though I would add I am generally there only in the mornings. Should your needs, not least the lawyer's fees, require you to seek out a way to make your way, then let your feet direct you to my door, where you will be most welcome.'

'That is most obliging of you, Mr Winston, but I am not without means. I am off to see the fellow who represents me in the article of prizes, where I will discover how I am found in the nature of funds. That is one measure of how soon I can proceed with the matter Barclay.'

'You took prizes?' Winston asked, with a slight air of disappointment.

'I was most fortunate in that regard, yes. One in the Mediterranean and another on the way home.'

'Valuable, I suspect, this time?'

'If all is well I should be able to easily sustain my own needs and perhaps have enough to bring my case.'

Winston nodded slowly, then seemed to recover both himself and his winning smile. 'Then it only remains for me to wish you well, sir.'

'Perhaps we will meet again.'

'Perhaps, Mr Pearce.'

The offices of Alexander Davidson were in Harpur Street, on the opposite side of Holborn to the lawyers' chambers of Gray's Inn. He was a man who lived above the shop, his home being on the upper floors of what was a narrow but handsome town house, thus the lateness of the hour – it was dark by the time John Pearce called – had no bearing. He had met Davidson before and that had been an unhappy occasion, one in which he had found the prize agent, representing his one-time commanding officer, to be a fount of unwelcome news. But his exploits in the Mediterranean had brought him a prize ship, a French sloop by the name of *Mariette*, subsequently bought into the service by Lord Hood and renamed. In need of someone to contract his business, he had sent written instructions to the only man whose name he knew to see to the distribution for both himself and the crew he had led.

'Mr Pearce, it is a pleasure to finally meet you,' said Davidson, as Pearce entered his office, the greeting followed by a quizzical look. 'But I have the feeling, a strong one, we have met before, sir.'

There was silence then, as Davidson tried to place him. Pearce had come here just after his elevation to get his share of the capture of the French seventy-four, the story of which he had just been relating to Winston: he had departed with a lot less than he hoped.

'We have Mr Davidson. I came to see you about monies from the *Valmy*.'

'Sir, I place you now,' the man responded, clearly surprised. 'I cannot feel that our previous encounter endeared me to you.'

'You act as a prize agent do you not?'

'For several naval officers, yes.'

'And I take it your actions were not motivated by personal animus in denying me my rightful share of the capture.'

'No.'

'Then might I ask how matters proceed in that case, since my entire claim is not settled?'

Davidson sighed. 'The *Valmy* is locked in the courts, sir, with the legal wolves of Gray's Inn, not more than a stone's throw from where we sit, feeding heartily at the trough of both parties, for, bought into the service at twelve pounds a ton, with both gun and head money, she was a valuable prize. Neither of the litigants will give way and reconcile, and I fear if they do not have a care there will be little of value left to settle on.'

'Then I can only wish them both damnation, sir, but today I have come to see how I stand regarding the vessel I took in Corsica.'

'You did not receive my letter regarding that?'

Davidson was a good-looking man, in his early thirties, sandy-haired and with lively, open features. Now the countenance had about it an air of foreboding, and since Pearce did not respond, his face merely closing up, he was forced to continue. 'I fear you will find yourself in the same boat, with the widow of Captain Benton.'

'Go on,' Pearce responded, his heart sinking.

'She has laid a claim to the captain's share, given her husband was in command when the action commenced. Let me say, Mr Pearce, that she has no choice but to proceed, being in straightened circumstances.'

Pearce was about to allude to the year's pay, which would come her way by right as a serving officer's widow, added to what had been realised by the sale of Benton's possessions – admittedly not much after the purser's twenty per cent emolument – but he checked himself. Benton might have been master and commander but his pay was that of a lieutenant, ninety-one pounds in a calendar year, and that was not great, added to which he had no idea of dependants.

'Which means?' he asked.

'That she will pursue the case to the bitter end, sir, for she has nothing to lose.'

'So what would you suggest I do?'

'A settlement, which is what I proposed in my letter to you: share the windfall with the lady on an equal basis and I think she will be content.' Davidson paused then, slightly embarrassed. 'You do, of course, have the right to seek advice elsewhere. I am aware that I seem to be disappointing you for a second time.'

Pearce looked away from Davidson then, his eyes scanning the portrait-covered walls and his mind ranging over the matter. Others were involved, the crew of HMS *Weazel* who took part in the action, but they would not be affected by any decision he made, and while he was thinking on that Davidson was still talking.

'Naturally we are talking only of the captain's two-eighths, which would not affect your eighth as the sole lieutenant on the vessel, so you would emerge as the superior beneficiary, giving you, if my memory is correct, some five hundred and eighty-one pounds less my fees of twelve per cent and a modicum of expenses. Then, of course, there are the prize court costs.'

'You can quote such figures from memory?' asked Pearce, far from amused.

'God has granted me a head for figures,' Davidson replied.

Pearce looked over his head to where a charcoal sketch sat on the wall, a full-length study of a young officer, in a lieutenant's uniform, and the face was familiar.

'Is that Captain Nelson?'

Davidson brightened, as if relieved at the subject moving to one less contentious, and turned to look at the same sketch. 'Being some seventeen years old at the time he was no captain, Mr Pearce, as his garb will tell you. It was a preliminary drawing made prior to a portrait executed by the artist Rigaud, who was good enough to sell it to me. The actual painting went to his old mentor, Captain William Locker, at present the Governor of Greenwich Hospital.'

'And you have it on your wall?'

'I am happy to say that Horatio is not only a client, but also a close friend of long standing, one I have represented for many a year. If anything, I pursue the profession of prize agent due to him, given I was in the general Canada trade prior to this.' Davidson gave a look of realisation, before adding, 'But, of course, you would have encountered Captain Nelson in your recent service.'

'On more than one occasion.'

'He is an honest fellow, Horatio, and a damned fine sailor.'

Pearce had to stop himself from saying that his acquaintance was slight and also that Horatio Nelson was an absolute booby at times, excessively light-headed in the article of drink and damned silly when it came to the opposite sex, a fellow who caused much anxiety in the breasts of his junior officers, which Pearce had witnessed at a ball in Leghorn. It said much for the man that those same junior officers cared enough to shield him from his own folly, whatever his qualities of command and seamanship.

'I found him so,' was what Pearce actually replied, which was nothing but the truth, for there was an endearing openness about the man to modify his faults. He was thinking that, if this Davidson was trusted by the likes of Nelson, he too was probably honest, if anyone could be said to be that in the modern world, which was important, given he was about to mention another commission.

'What would another prize agent tell me, Mr Davidson, in such circumstances, that you would not?'

'Lieutenant Pearce, there are upright fellows in this game, but there are as many rogues in the profession as there are in others. It is not unknown for one of my stripe to make more in *douceurs* from interested lawyers than they would ever make from a client.'

'Meaning?'

'They would advise you to fight a case you may well not win from what they would gain by the back door – an agreed percentage of the lawyer's fees. I am happy to recommend another prize agent, but if he is honest he will give you the same advice as I have proffered. I might also add, Mrs Benton has a particularly avaricious counsel and even what I have proposed may not go smoothly.'

That was telling: you did not have to serve in the navy very long to hear the stories of prize case disputes dragging on for a decade and more, pride as often the driving force of the argument as mere coin. He needed money and he needed it soon to pursue Ralph Barclay: it would appear best to settle.

'Mr Davidson, I will take your advice on the *Mariette* and also advise you that on my return to Portsmouth I brought in another prize, a merchant vessel, the *Guiscard*.' Pearce reached into a pocket and pulled out a paper showing the details of the tonnage as well as the names of the men he had had with him when he came across her, who would be entitled to a share. 'The details are listed on this. She is at present in Portsmouth being valued, but it is only the hull, there was no cargo, no crew for head money and not even a signal cannon.'

'An unusual capture, sir, I must say. Legitimate prize?'

'Undoubtedly so.'

'Any other king's ship in sight?' Pearce shook his head, acknowledging there could be no other claimants. 'You seem to be a lucky officer, sir.'

'If you knew the means by which we came upon her and what we found aboard you would not say so.'

'Would an enquiry be unwelcome?'

Having spent too much time talking to Winston and relating his adventures, Pearce had no desire to recommence now. 'Another time, Mr Davidson, perhaps, given I have another call to make. I take it all is in order for you to proceed?'

Looking at the paper before him Davidson nodded. 'I will send to Portsmouth immediately advising them of my interest.'

'Can I ask if you satisfied matters at Nerot's Hotel?'

Pearce, on his last sojourn in London, had been obliged to depart that particular establishment in some haste, being bereft of the funds needed to satisfy a bill that included not only his room and food but the uniforms he had ordered made as well. Part of his instructions on appointing the man before him had been to deal with the outstanding bill.

'I did.'

'Good. Could I ask you to send a message to them to say I wish to occupy a room tonight?'

'Of course, sir, and will you require an advance on your funds?'

'Fifty guineas?' Pearce enquired tentatively, knowing the protections would eat off a slice of that, adding, 'I anticipate some immediate expenses.'

'Most certainly, Lieutenant Pearce,' Davidson replied with a confident air, standing and producing from his waistcoat a chain on which was a hefty key. 'Once the matter is settled I will remit the balance to your bank.'

'Mr Davidson, I do not have a bank.'

'Never mind,' the man replied gaily. 'I am happy to recommend Baring Brothers as a sound repository of your monies.'

Pearce and Ralph Barclay were not shadowing each other, but the post captain was likewise with his prize agents, sitting in the opulent offices of Ommanny & Druce overlooking the Strand, nursing a fine crystal glass which contained within it a very superior Burgundy wine, this while the two partners of the well-established practice quite openly flattered him. Barclay could not but contrast their behaviour with his last call at these premises, when, at the outbreak of the present war, he had been newly appointed to his frigate after five years on the beach. Half-pay and the mere expenses of living – not least in the caring for his clutch of sisters and the acquisition of a new bride – had left him seriously short of the monies he needed to fulfil his duties.

The reluctance of this pair to advance him any on his prospects had forced him to pay the high rates of a City moneylender, but what had hurt more than their parsimony had been their disdain – they had treated him like a beggar – which was the precise opposite of their present behaviour, for Ralph Barclay was now a man of substantial means, having taken a fully laden merchant vessel in the Levant trade from under the nose of a Barbary pirate, his two-eighths of that capture alone exceeding ten thousand pounds.

There was another, even more valuable Indiaman locked in a dispute between whether it was a prize or salvage, which if it came in as the former, would more than double his gains: he had been sailing under Admiralty orders and was thus entitled to three-eighths. Added to that, his interview with Gardner had gone well – the admiral was well disposed, in any case. The name of the Duke of Portland was of inestimable value too, an ounce of interest, as the old saying went, being worth a ton of ability, and this pair had heard that his prospects were excellent. If there was a fly in the ointment of his pleasure it was that Samuel Hood, as his commanding admiral for the Levant vessel, would get an eighth of the value of that; also, that the Gibraltar Prize Court, into which his claim had been submitted, was home to the most rapacious adjudicator on the planet.

'Admiral Gardner did not name a vessel, Captain

Barclay?' asked Ommanny, looking as prosperous and self-satisfied as Barclay remembered him. He was a man with a belly and rubicund face that spoke of long indulgence in the good things in life.

The reply followed a draining of his wine. 'No, but he assured me that my claim for a command was high on his list, and would be met as soon as I was fit enough to go back to sea. I have high hopes of a seventy-four, HMS *Semele*, at present refitting at Chatham.'

That was followed by a keen look to observe what these men knew and the nods told Ralph Barclay that his connection to the Duke of Portland, if it could be called that to one of the most supercilious, condescending bastards he had ever met in his life, was well known within these walls. They would also know that HMS *Semele* was near-ready for sea. Before him was a pair who sniffed gossip as a hunting hound sniffs spoor, picking up rumours as much as hard fact as an aid to their business activities, which went well beyond merely acting as prize agents to some of the most successful sailors in the fleet.

Several admirals, always the men to profit most by the exploits of their captains, taking a full eighth of any prizes brought in, were their clients. Indeed, Ralph Barclay had been introduced to them by none other than the late Lord Rodney, his one-time patron, and on their walls sat an imposing painting of that sailor's most famous Caribbean victory, the Battle of the Saintes, in which he had bested the fleet of the Comte de Grasse. He and Alan Gardner had already shared claret and memories of the admiral's part in the action.

'Then we wish you joy of your prospects, sir,' added Druce, the smaller of the pair, raising his glass, only to realise a toast was impossible. 'But, sir, your glass is empty.' A flick of a finger brought forward the liveried servant, the crystal decanter and a silver tray to top Barclay up, as Druce moved on to business. 'I think, Captain Barclay, we must look at some investments for your profits.'

'Which, of course, we would be happy to advise you on,' Ommanny added. 'The major portion should be placed in the Consolidated Fund, naturally, but there are certain speculative ventures from which you might benefit handsomely. We act as agents for several canal and turnpike trusts, which promise good returns, some as much as ten per cent per annum.'

'There is something of a building boom in progress in my native Frome.'

There was mischief in the statement, his way of guying this pair, a touch of revenge for their previous attitude. What he was saying clearly did not please them, much as they feigned interest. They wanted his money to play with and profit by, which would not be the case if he favoured his own notions.

'Added to that, I have always thought land around my birthplace a good area to invest.'

'Fluctuation, sir,' sighed Ommanny, in a theatrical manner, 'has too often been the death of wise placement. Land rises and falls in value, especially if we have peace. Buildings, and I take it you mean domestic dwellings, require close supervision, or those carrying out the construction will find a home for your materials that is to their profit, not yours.'

'If you are at sea, Captain Barclay . . .' Druce added, merely opening his hands, not seeing the need to add any more.

In truth, the man drinking their wine wanted nothing more than to see income without effort on his part, a dream he had carried since first he went as a lad to sea, the hope of every naval officer, the capital of prize money earning by its mere existence. But trust was not a virtue to which Ralph Barclay was given and he certainly did not repose it in this pair, who, if he lost on their proposed investments, would ensure that they did not suffer likewise. It was the way of all projectors, men who never took a risk with their own funds, unless they could make a killing by some chicanery, like inside knowledge of guaranteed outcomes. These were investments into which their clients were never allowed.

'I employ a man who deals with my affairs,' he said, his eye acute enough to see the slight change in their expressions. 'Not that he will be ashore when I have a ship; he is, after all, my clerk, but I will task him to work with you, to look over what you propose, for he has a sharp mind, unlike me. I am, after all, more of a sailor than a man of business.'

'As you wish,' Ommanny replied.

Both partners were well aware of what Barclay was saying: your investments will be studied and your fees scrutinised for any signs of excess payments by someone who knows the byways of financial transactions. You will not treat me as you normally treat naval officers, safe off at sea and usually too unquestioning for their own welfare.

'I shall send him to you and you may show him a list of your speculative proposals. His name is Cornelius Gherson.'

Had Ralph Barclay not drunk deep then, and had he not been quite so self-satisfied, he might have noticed that the name registered with Mr Druce, and whatever connection he made was not a happy one.

CHAPTER FIVE

The grinding of the jolly boat on the soft, sandy beach, on a cold, grey and misty dawn, still left several feet of shallow water to be crossed, so the trio of Pelicans, having thrown ahead of them their sack of provisions, came ashore with wet feet, albeit their newly sewn trews were rolled up and their shore-going footwear, stockings as well, were safe in their ditty bags. Michael O'Hagan crossed himself as the boat, relieved of their weight, floated off immediately, with the carpenter, who now had the oars they had used to get to this point, quick to drop them into the water and spin round to haul off. There was no farewell, no cheering cry of good fortune to set them on their way, which reflected the silence with which he had accompanied them on the journey: it had not been a trip laced with anything in the way of conversation or advice.

The sight that greeted them, a huge area of flat, damp sand turning to a bank of that mixed with shingle quite some way off, in a featureless landscape, did not cheer either, while one isolated lean-to hut, far away along the highest point of the scrub-covered dune, in truth not much in height, showed no sign of occupancy. Along the seemingly endless shoreline, in the distance, a few forlorn-looking boats were up out of the water, sitting on the baulks of round, tar-soaked timber used to protect the hull from damage as it was hauled above the high-water mark – that a wavy line of seaweed stretching away on either side – while in the direction from which they had come, the faint outline of what they had been told was Hayling Island, a thick line of trees, was just visible through the mist.

The sounds were few, the hiss of the waves running up the sand behind them, the odd cry of a gull, always sounding dejected, all under a lowering grey sky that merged with both land and sea. Rufus rolled down his trews and looked set to put on his stockings and the new shoes provided by the purser.

'Belay that,' Michael barked. 'Wait till your feet are dry and free of sand, boy, or they will be bleeding before you have gone a mile.'

'A mile to where?' Rufus responded, with a bit of a pout at being admonished.

'First we must get off the beach and see if we can find something to get our bearings.'

'We should eat,' Charlie Taverner added, as they made to a dune, partially covered in a line of dark green scrub and high tufts of marsh grass.

'Shortly,' Michael said.

Topping the dune through a tiny gap, no doubt

made by locals, looking into the land behind, flat fields of grazing sheep, dotted with stunted trees too sparsely gathered close to the shore to provide any shelter, Michael scanned the landscape, grey where sky and mist combined. He pulled from his pocket the drawing the master had made for them showing, roughly, a route they should follow, which would take them away from the many inlets that dotted the shore, with crosses to denote towns, places to be avoided. He had also written the names, but Michael only knew them from the memory of them having been spoken, for he could not read more than a few words. All he knew for certain was that they were to make sure to avoid the Portsmouth to London road, bound to be crawling with crimps.

'We has to get to the east of a place called Chichester and aim for a town further on called Midhurst.'

'What bearings might we be looking for?'

'Church spires, Rufus,' Michael said, 'though, sure enough, they will be hard to spot in this mizz. You makes your way in England from parish to parish, for sure there is always a path from one to t'other. I swear on the blood of Holy Mary you won't go far in this land before you spot a house of worship, never mind it being one tied to a heathen faith.'

'The Irish are the godless ones,' said Charlie, without rancour.

He spat after he said that; Michael being a papist was not commonly a bone of contention, but Charlie, who would likely never have entered the portal of a church except to steal its plate or raid the candle box, was not about to have his nation's Anglican religion insulted by a Catholic Irishman.

Rufus looked at the grey sky, then at the paper in Michael's hand. 'How will we know we's going in the right direction?'

'Sure, there are ways, and many of those same churches have a pointer to the north on the spire. If in real doubt we will have to ask, will we not?'

'A risk, Michael.'

'One we might have to hazard if the sun don't show. According to the ship's master, London is to the north and east of where we are.'

'To the north and east of where we think we are,' Charlie objected, talking to a man who had turned round to look back out to sea.

'Get down,' Michael cried, immediately dropping behind the deep scrub and scrabbling for better cover. 'A guard boat.'

'Where away?' demanded Charlie, who had followed him down automatically, with only Rufus still visible, that was until Michael took his legs from under him. The youngster collapsed in a heap of arms, legs and swearing that ceased as his landing winded him.

'In the distance to the east, following the shoreline, a cutter by the shape and size, and low in the water from the number of men it's carrying. It's no fisherman.'

A short crawl still gave him cover but also a view over the sea and that showed no sign of their carpenter. He had rowed out of sight in haste and the thought could not be avoided that the men who had suggested this route of escape must have known it would be patrolled for deserters, a notion he shared with his companions and one that brought forth from Charlie a long list of expletives for not being given any warning.

Ignoring him, Michael edged his head out enough to look along the beach. The guard boat, which he had first seen as an indistinct shape in the mist, was now in plain sight and it had not altered course, still hugging the shoreline at a steady pace, but it took no great genius to work out that someone aboard would be looking into the soft sand below the high-water line for footprints.

'We must get away from this shore and quickly.'

Michael was moving as he was explaining. The marks of their landing would stick out like a pus-filled boil and as soon as they were spotted the boat would beach and those aboard would come inland to hunt for them. The only hope he could think of was to outrun them first and find somewhere to hide up next.

'Stop!' Charlie Taverner's voice was so commanding that the Irishman obeyed. 'Now get shod and do as I say.'

Still sat down, Charlie was already scrabbling in his ditty bag to get out and slip on his shoes, talking as he did so. 'We will not lose the men in that boat and for all we know they are armed with muskets, so all they need is a sight of our backs to bring us to.'

'So?'

'Look at the sand we have to walk through to get onto grassland,' Charlie insisted. 'It is damp from the morning dew so we cannot avoid leaving a trail.'

'Shoes won't help,' Michael insisted.

'Then watch what I do,' Charlie commanded.

Standing, he made heavy steps through the sand, sure enough leaving obvious footprints and, as soon as he reached the point where the ground underfoot turned from mixed to pure grass he stopped, then very carefully walked back into his own footmarks. He had just got back to the point where he started when a cry floated through the morning air: the men in the boat had spotted what they were set to look for, a line of prints pointing to where the Pelicans had stopped to get their bearings.

'Do the same, Michael, you too Rufus, then we must look for cover in this scrub, just enough to keep us hidden.' Charlie, frustrated at their lack of speed, positively hissed. 'Will you move your arses or we'll be had up, an' don't you go making it all too neat. Try to make it look as if we was in file.'

As his companions complied, with an air of doubt as to whether what they were about was wise very obvious in their attitude, Charlie had his clasp knife out and was sawing at the branch of a bush, talking all the while. As soon as it separated he spat on his finger, picked up some sand, rubbed that and his spittle together and used it to cover the fresh cut wood, making dark what had been a clear white cut.

'The tide was making when we landed so them coves will not know how long we's been ashore, could be minutes, could be near to a glass of sand. When you'se done, get your shoes off again and back in your ditty bags.'

The air was now full of faint voices, some just shouts,

spliced with the odd clear command, and each of the trio of Pelicans had in their mind a vision of what would be happening shore side of the dune. The cutter being beached, men leaping out with cutlasses certainly, and maybe a musket or two, hard-eyed bastards, maybe marines, more likely press-gang tars, who would be keen to take them up for the bounty or maybe just for the sheer joy of capture.

'They must have known, them sods,' wailed Rufus, sat again and removing his shoes. 'And they said not a word.'

'Course they knew,' Charlie hissed, 'they just wanted rid of us. But no more talking. Get in among them bushes, you too Michael, while I spoil our trail. We don't need to go far to lie down and be hidden and for the sake of the Lord breathe easy when you is settled.'

Crawling through the bushes to the sound of hearty shouting from the beach, ditty bags and the sack of provisions before them, they did not see Charlie back into the greenery, brushing the sand behind them to remove any trace of their passage. He had not gone far when he heard the first sound of shod feet on the sea side of the dune, scrabbling on the shingle, which had him pushing himself down so hard it was as if he wished the earth to swallow him up. Godless he might be, but the prayers he was mouthing now were as fervent as those of Michael O'Hagan had ever been.

'Here, Lieutenant,' called a voice. 'They sat here a while by the state of the sand.'

'How long, man?' came the gruff cry, obviously the voice of an officer by his impatience.

'Hard to say precise, Your Honour, but not too much time has passed. They shoed up here and I can see their marks as they made their way inland.'

'Right, set off a musket, let the inshore picket know we are on the hunt.'

The crack of the fired weapon rent the air, which had all three hidden Pelicans digging their fingers into the sand, as though the weapon had been aimed at them; noisy birdcalls were aired too and for the same reason. For Charlie it was worst of all: closer than the others to the gap, he could see the striped woollen stockings and boots of the man leading the hunt. They soon disappeared and another dozen legs went by, one with white stockings, which had to be the officer, the whole party a mass of eager, mumbled voices, the one of the man in charge the only clear sound, his voice gruff.

'We must hurry, lads, and keep a sharp eye out, we don't want those scallies at Bracklesham Church to get the bounty for three men run, do we now? There an extra pot of ale for the one to spy them first.'

The sound of movement and voices died away, the last discernible order from the officer for his men to spread out a bit and cover more ground, with Rufus whispering, 'Christ, that were close.'

'Be quiet,' Charlie hissed. 'There will be fellows still with that boat.'

Michael crawled close to Charlie's ear. 'Sure, you were sharp there, Charlie boy, but what do we do now?'

'We must get along the shoreline, the way from whence they came, and lay low until dark.'

'And then what?'

'Pray to your papist god for a moon, Michael, for without one we will be stuck.'

The progress was slow, great care taken to ensure that no one could see them, with Charlie's cut branch employed continually to hide their trail, this as the cloud cover began to lift and the first signs came of a watery sun. Hundreds of yards away from the point at which they had come ashore they found a clump of low trees and bushes in which they could at least sit up and occasionally stand to study the land around.

'Best rest up here,' Michael said. 'The more we move the more we risk till the hunt is called off.'

'Those sods, curse them,' Charlie moaned, with neither of his companions needing to enquire of whom he was speaking. 'And what makes you think those after us will give up?'

'It's a hope, brother.'

'We ain't got a prayer,' groaned Rufus.

'We always has a prayer,' Michael replied, 'and, sure, if you say enough of them an' mean it, the good Lord above will hear them.' Those words, and the way they were delivered, got the Irishman a look from Charlie that would not have shamed Old Nick himself, so full was it of doubt. 'The question is, how far will they go afore they see they has missed us, and give up. They might set pickets out overnight.'

'If there's a bounty, Michael,' Charlie snorted, 'an' there surely will be, then it is not just their pickets we need to worry on. Every bumpkin in creation will be on the watch for miles inland.'

'For three tars, Charlie, remember our guise of weather tarpaulin.'

'That won't suffice if we are had up close to shore.'

'No, but it is a start, Charlie, and we must find a barn or outhouse and look to steal some tools.'

'What kind of tools?' asked Rufus.

'Farm stuff, or maybe the kind of shovels that will let us pass for men working to repair the roads.' Seeing the doubt in their faces, Michael had to tell them that in his travels along the byways of the land he had seen, many a time, small parties of men, paid by the parish to keep the roads in decent repair. 'Not that they stay free of holes, so it is permanent work that folk are obliged to do.'

'Poor souls' labour,' opined Rufus.

'Our ditty bags we must keep hidden,' Michael added. 'We must not be seen as travelling men.'

They sat there until the light began to fade, the inside of the hiding place made darker by the overhead cover, eating the biscuit they had been given, grateful it was shore-made and no more than a few days old, for, lacking water or any other liquid, real hard tack would have been inedible, though it was hard to swallow, even with cheese.

'That was a clever ruse, Charlie,' said Michael. 'Where did that notion of the bush come from?'

A bit of praise lifted Charlie's spirits. 'I got it from an ancient fellow who was done for thieving when a nipper and transported to the Virginia Colony, that was until the Jonathans decided they did not like King George any more'n we did in London town.'

97

'Sure, he is not much loved in Ireland, brother.'

'This old cove worked his time and took to farming, then fought the redskins when they was siding with the French, an' he told us some of their wiles, for, as he said, you could never see the buggers in the forests. But there were locals who knew what to look for, and brushing away their trail was one of the signs, as were fresh broken twigs.' Charlie suddenly waxed lyrical. 'Often thought, when things weren't too good, that I'd have liked to go to the Americas.'

'Too late now,' Michael said.

'What about walking backwards?' Rufus asked.

'That were my own notion,' Charlie replied. 'Which is a handy one to use when you is seeking to break and enter over soft ground, like a vicar's flower bed.'

'Sharp, Charlie.'

'Were it, Rufus? I don't think it were that sharp. If'n I'd had my wits about me, I would have had us walking backwards as soon as we landed. Then those bastards in the guard boat would have rowed right on instead of stopping, thinkin' we was just fisher folk going out on our common business.'

'Now that, Charlie, is a sound notion.' Charlie had to peer at Michael in the gloom to make out his smile. 'Holy Mary, I have walked too many miles in my days to take pleasure in it, an' being a tar for all this time has not endeared me. What better way to get to where we need to go than by boat?'

'You have noticed, Michael, that we ain't got one?'

'There was boats along the shore, we saw them, and the master, who did that drawing, penned the shoreline as well, all the way to the waters that lead up to London.'

'With neither oars or the means to raise a sail in the buggers, if the folk that own them have a brain.'

'Can we not steal those?' asked Rufus. 'Instead of shovels.'

Charlie laughed, the first sign of real humour the whole day. 'You'se spent too much time in my company Rufus, you'se come to think like a felon. If we get back to the Liberties, I'll send you out a-dipping along the Strand.'

'There'll be no fear,' Rufus replied, with more force than he usually employed. 'Was a time I would have worried, but not no more, mate.'

Michael was not finished. 'The only thing we must have is some water. Sure, with that, we could sit here till things die down.'

'I don't know much about that drawing you're on about Michael, but I do know it has to be a hell of a row all the way to the Thames, and that takes no account of weather.'

'If we have to land, Charlie, and walk after all, at least it will be well away from these men now hunting our hides and the hue and cry they will set up.'

'What about staying hidden?' Rufus suggested.

'And what if they sense we ain't left the area and start a search of every hiding place, which I humbly put forward they will know like the back of their hands.'

'You can be a miserable soul, Charlie Taverner.'

'No, Rufus, I am a man who was raised to think how to avoid either the rope or the transport ship, which is two risks I have faced all my life, an' if I was that officer I would have men out hunting first light. We ain't safe here, and even if it is pitch dark we has to move. We'll try for your boat first, Michael, that being a good notion, but as sure as God made little apples we must be away from this place whatever way we can, and I am going to suggest that the best time to move is afore the light is gone complete, so that we can at least work out that we's going in the right direction.'

'Could we find some water to drink?' asked Rufus.

'First thing,' Charlie replied, beginning to gather up his possessions. 'Christ, I am dry as a witch's tit.'

CHAPTER SIX

The last call John Pearce had made the previous evening had been to the home of Heinrich Lutyens, near St Bartholomew's Hospital, to reacquaint himself with the one-time surgeon of HMS *Brilliant*, and see if any word had come from Downing Street, this being the address he had given. Faced with a negative response he could at least openly fulminate about the duplicity of politicians. An offer of accommodation he declined, but the invitation to stay to supper and share a beefsteak from nearby Smithfield Market was welcome. He was now nursing an after-dinner brandy and the subject had moved on, very naturally, to the potential to indict Ralph Barclay.

'I think I might be damned by the loss of those papers, Heinrich.' The look that engendered, a pursing of the lips and a piqued expression of the surgeon's fish-like face, as well as a dilation of his pointed nose, had Pearce apologising immediately. 'I bear you no ill will for that. You only managed to rescue your sea chest and it was my idea to leave them in your care.'

'And mine to hide them in my instrument chest.'

There was a moment then, when Pearce considered adding that it had been a wise precaution. On the night he and his fellow Pelicans went ashore in Gibraltar, someone, he was sure, had rifled the chest in his wardroom cabin and he doubted it could have been one-armed Ralph Barclay, more likely Gherson; it was that which had decided Pearce to leave the copy of the transcript of Ralph Barclay's court martial with Lutyens, when he had only intended to have the surgeon care for them when he was off the ship for one night. But that was none of the host's concern and something best kept to himself.

'Did you ever find out how the fire started? It had to be carelessness on someone's part.'

There was no denying that as a fact; if there was one overriding fear sailors had, it was of a fire at sea, something that could rapidly destroy a wooden ship, leaving those aboard no time to get off. Great care was taken with lanterns and stoves to ensure nothing could set the timbers alight and buckets of sand were liberally distributed around the vessel to douse anything accidental. The crew of HMS *Grampus* had been as assiduous in that as every other vessel, yet catch fire it did, and quickly, spreading until it consumed the whole vessel and forced the captain, in a very short time, to order it abandoned.

'The culprit is still breathing,' Lutyens added, 'for every man aboard was brought safe back to England.'

Seeing speculation on that as a dead end – no one would admit to the guilt and, if it had not been discovered by now, it never would be, Pearce went back to his primary concern. 'My first task is to find an attorney to handle my case.'

'Does not this Davidson fellow have someone?'

'That places too many eggs in one basket, friend, and the only people I know personally are my father's old acquaintances in the London Corresponding Society.'

The reply was sharp. 'They, I must tell you, are best avoided.'

'That is unlike you, Heinrich.'

'There are moves afoot to curb their activities, John.'

Lutyens made a great play of rising then to poke the fire, which allowed him to avoid the keen look he was getting from his guest. As the son of the pastor of the Lutheran Church in London he was connected to the court, Queen Charlotte being a regular visitor at that establishment, sometimes accompanied by the king, and if they could be dragooned into worship, the royal children as well. It was no secret that Farmer George hated the radicals who made up the various corresponding societies that had sprung up after the overthrow of King Louis, the London branch being the most numerous and vociferous, and in his antipathy he was fully supported by William Pitt.

To John Pearce it was typical of monarchy and those who served them: they saw every gathering of citizens at which free discussion was the aim as inimical to their security. His own father, Adam, had been more *outré* than most society participants, more outspoken in his calls for universal suffrage and an end to the system of rotten boroughs, demanding votes for both sexes and all citizens in equal measures, as well as a curb on the constitutional power of the monarchy, if not its actual abolition, all underpinned by a more equable distribution of the nation's wealth.

These ideas, penned in pamphlets, spoken of on innumerable platforms, were notions Adam Pearce, known as the Edinburgh Ranter, had actually been propounding for his whole life. But the Revolution in France had changed everything, including his father's stature, first being welcomed by a nation that saw itself better governed than its continental neighbour, then causing fear as the excesses of the Parisian mob, egged on by fiery orators, had turned the bright new dawn into blood-soaked mayhem. That change in attitude had resulted in a short stay in prison for both son John and old Adam. They had been locked up and, after their release, given Adam had gone straight back to further writings and speech making, had been forced to flee to Paris to avoid that writ for sedition.

Lutyens took a particularly hearty poke at a log, sending up a shower of bright sparks. 'The king is sure there are mobs who would wish to see the guillotine set up in the Horse Guards parade grounds, with him as the primary victim.'

'Then he has no understanding of revolution and what causes it.'

Lutyens looked at Pearce then, and smiled. 'And naturally, you do.'

Not sure if it was a question, Pearce declined to reply,

but had he done so he would have pointed out that, at its very simplest, it was not mobs of the poor that made revolt a success, but the break between those who sought to wield untrammelled power, and the desire for a say in matters of those with the means to finance their dreams of glory. King Charles had faced the axe over money, or a lack of it; so, in truth, had King Louis: both had lost their heads for hanging on to an outmoded concept of kingship in which they expected their every desire to be treated and provided for as if handed down from the Gospel.

Underlying those thoughts was the very potent truth that, in growing to manhood in Paris, John Pearce had begun to see that his father's propositions, hitherto Holy Writ to a young lad, had within them serious flaws. They took no account of the base nature of the people Adam wished to enfranchise, this despite the observations both had made while incarcerated in the common cells of the Fleet. It was all very well for Adam Pearce to say that better education would produce a better polity: given the venal nature of those with education, like those firebrands in France, there was no evidence to suppose such an assertion to be true.

'If Farmer George was wont to ask my advice I would tell him to surrender with grace that which he cannot keep, for not to do so risks having it taken away by forces, which, once unleashed, as events in France have shown, become uncontrollable.'

'Not words he would receive kindly, John.'

'Axe and guillotine blades are more cruel by far than a few home truths.'

Pearce was unsure where Lutyens stood on such matters. His own ultimate view had been formed in Paris when the bright promise of the overthrow of the monarchy had turned to bloody and uncontainable violence, a bloodbath that had, in the end, consumed his own father: Adam Pearce had discovered very quickly, having fled from the risk of arrest at home, that revolutionaries were no more inclined to tolerate dissent than monarchs or their minions, and had ended up in the prison of the Conciergerie because of it.

'We must change a subject which is, of necessity, an unpleasant one for you.'

His friend had misunderstood Pearce's allusion to instruments of beheading, but he was right. He had been a witness to his father's death, having had to move heaven and earth to recover and properly bury his body, only succeeding with the aid of a sympathetic Revolutionary politician, Regis de Cambacérès. It was a very painful subject, and one which had him fingering the tin of Parisian earth he carried with him, taken from the churchyard of St Sulpice where old Adam was interred – how his father would have hated that as a resting place – he hated all churches, and that one was Catholic. One day, Pearce had vowed, he would be rescued from that cold grave and have his bones taken back to his native Edinburgh and more suitable ground.

'A lawyer?' Pearce asked.

Unbeknown to his guest, that put Lutyens on the horns of a dilemma: the only man he could truly recommend, he had also recommended to Emily Barclay. Would their paths cross?

'Come along, Heinrich, you must know someone.'

Caught on the hop, Lutyens was forced to reply. 'There is a fellow called Studdert.'

'I'll take his address, then,' Pearce said, with soft interruption. 'And then, for I am beat, I must be off to my hotel.'

'Which is?'

'Nerot's in King Street.'

'That, John Pearce,' Lutyens joked, his face lighting up at his coming sally, 'is the last address at which you should reside.'

It was not just a want of oars that made the finding of a suitable boat difficult on a strand of beach that stretched for miles: no owner was content to leave their possession beached without chaining to it a dog, so every approach over the noisy shingle – the craft were pulled up and away from the sand and the high-tide line – was met by first a growl, that followed by barking and, if further approach was attempted, by gnashing canine teeth, the din alone being enough to make the Pelicans sheer off and seek shelter back in the trees, eyes peeled to observe if anyone had reacted, not least if those out hunting them were within earshot.

The morning, since grey dawn, had been spent creeping along the shore with great care: scurrying from hideout to hideout, trying never to expose themselves to sight unless it was unavoidable and of necessity, they were making slow progress. They had at least found a dribble of a watercourse, which had allowed them to drink, thus relieving a raging thirst, but bringing on its own annoyance in the very obvious fact that they had no means of taking any water with them, lacking, as they did, the means to carry it, which had them eying the grey skies wondering if it might rain.

'It's not just oars, Michael,' Charlie said. 'We must find a flagon or suchlike. 'There's no joy in being on salt water without we has summat fresh to drink.'

'Maybe we'll find some beer.'

'Only if there is a God that loves us.'

'He loves the likes of me, Charlie.'

'Then only he knows why, Michael,' Charlie sallied, only partly in jest, given they had a history of dispute, 'for you are a cussed sod.'

The boat owners, those who had possession of both oars and water containers, lived inland in the cottages sparsely dotted about the coastal marshes, far enough away to justify the dogs and to give them some protection from the winds, which on this coast were ferocious, as well as an occasional heavy-tide surge that must overwhelm the shingle barrier. They must make their main living from the fish in the sea and on a day like this most would be out with their nets and lines. It took no great thought to work out the reasons why those who were not had such craft: there were pots by the boats and there would be more off the shore, buoyed on the surface, sitting on the seabed to catch crabs and lobsters, traps not worth visiting on a daily basis.

It was neglect that provided what they were seeking, a boat owner so uncaring of his guard animal that what greeted them when they crept towards it was not the usual sounds but a faint whimpering. The beast lying within the thwarts, a collar and chain round its neck, turned out to be a sad-looking creature and not just in the weak, brown eyes. His coat was unkempt and showing sores, while the very visible ribs underneath spoke of a severe lack of nourishment, so much so that when Rufus proffered a bit of cheese it produced the first response that could be described as animated: the dog grabbed it and consumed it greedily.

'Poor bugger is starving,' Rufus said.

'So will we be if'n you go giving it our grub,' Charlie complained.

Michael was less troubled. 'Sure, give the poor mite another bit, while I go look to see who might be the possessor of this creel.'

'Whoever he is has little fear of Davy Jones,' Charlie said, rubbing the strakes of peeling timber. 'I reckon the only thing holding this in one piece is the varnish.'

'She's a sorry-looking bugger, sure enough, but it will hold three and float.'

'Which we are preparing to row out on if we can find the sticks, Michael?'

'I thought we agreed,' the Irishman replied. 'Water is safer than land.'

Charlie kicked the boat, but not too hard. 'I'm not sure with this under my arse.'

'Has to be in use, Charlie, there's not a drop of water in the thing.'

Rufus, who had been patting the acquiescent dog, reached a bit further to touch the bottom board. 'She's damp, but that could be rain.'

'An' if she weren't used, she'd be turned turtle.'

'Unchain the dog, see where he leads.'

'What if he barks?' Rufus asked.

Charlie pulled a face. 'He ain't got the puff.'

There was truth in that: the animal had to be lifted out of the boat and even then there was no scamper in his gait, more the stiff-legged walk of a beast on its last legs. Once over the dunes and in a clump of trees they could see a tumbledown hovel, too broken to be called a cottage, which, even at a distance seemed to be held together by tarred canvas, not nails, with Michael of the opinion that a creature who let an abode fall into such disrepair was promising.

'Best you two wait here,' he said. 'No sense in we three exposing ourselves. Anyone out hunting us and spotting one person, even with such a mangy dog, will reckon he belongs.'

If the Irishman had expected dispute he was not granted any: Charlie and Rufus were only too willing to stay as safe as they could and it did make sense. If there was a human in that hovel, then a bit of intimidation might be in order and when it came to that, O'Hagan, with his height and build, plus a face which, for all he was a smiling fellow normally, could look very ferocious, was just the man.

As he followed the dog across the ground, soft underfoot for it was marsh, Michael could see, now that the air was a bit more clear, that this flat landscape extended well inland to a very obvious line of dark-green, forested hills, and that reinforced his thought that a boat would be safest. There was a serious lack of cover on such a windswept shore – it was the kind of place where anyone on a high spot, even a man-made structure like a church tower, could see for miles around.

The door, when he approached it, seemed to be hanging off what passed for its hinges, rotten wooden dowels poorly fixed on the main frame, with rusted iron hoops sat over them just adding to the run-down nature of the whole. The dog had disappeared inside, through a gap in the board wall, moving faster than it had previously, no doubt in anticipation of some food, yet there was no hint of anyone being around: take away the sound of the birds overhead and the place was silent. Standing outside, Michael had to consider what to do: if anyone was awake in this hut they could not have failed to see him approach, yet surely the natural thing to do would be to exit and seek to identify a stranger. The other alternative would be to wait inside, in the dark interior, with the means to crown anyone who came over as a threat.

A swift look around failed to locate that which Michael was looking for, oars leant against the exterior walls – he would have to search inside, which had the Irishman crossing himself by habit. The creak of that hanging door as he pulled it open was, to his ears, like a siren call, which had him tensing his jaw, and peer as he might, he could not see anything clearly inside. He stepped forward very gingerly indeed, his voice low as he spoke.

'God bless all here.'

The greeting got no response, which emboldened him to move a little further forward, but he stopped, letting his eyes become accustomed to the gloom before taking another step. The shape was slow to be identifiable and it was as much the dog whining at its feet that had him looking to make sense of it. A man slumped over a table, one hand stretched out and by it a tipped-over dark-brown bottle, the hair dirty, grey and matted but with no other features visible.

A pair of oars sat just inside the doorway, not more than a hand's reach away and that he did. There was a touch of conscience then, for Michael O'Hagan was not of the robbing type and he knew he was about to do that to this poor fellow. Oars were to hand and that bottle might not be the sole thing to hold and carry water, so putting aside his scruples he stepped forward, then stopped. The cold of the metal against his head was enough for that, though the deep voice was another good reason.

'Got him, Jed.'

The head was slowly lifted off the table and Michael found himself looking into a pair of gleaming eyes and the barrel of a pistol – aimed right at his heart.

'Never fails, that old mutt, do it Francis? Jack tars being such soft-hearted sods. They see a starving dog and they just has to come an' investigate. You'll be looking for the means to row that boat, will you not? And what have you found, just two of the sharpest bounty boys in creation, that's what. You got the press running all over the county looking for you, but Francis and I, we know you could not have got away unspotted, so we set our little trap, one that has served us well in times past.'

The other pistol, for it could only be that, pressed a little harder on Michael's temple. 'He's a big bugger this one.'

'Pity being,' the man called Jed replied, in a joshing tone, 'that they don't pay bounties by the pound weight. I can only see his outline, but we could retire on this sod if they did.'

'The other two?' demanded the fellow called Francis.

'What other two?'

'Don't bother with lying, Paddy,' snarled Jed, who had immediately picked up Michael's accent. 'There were three sets of feet came off that beach to the west, and my bet is you has stuck together. All you have to do is halloo from that there door and call them forward.'

'They're too sharp to fall for that,' Michael said quietly.

'Tell them you've found some beer, or maybe even rum. Never met a man of the sea yet who could resist a tot of rum.'

Michael O'Hagan was a fighter as well as a fellow who had done enough bare knuckle in his time to know that the key to the art was balance. As they had exchanged these words his mind had been working, as had his feet, moving slightly apart to give him purchase. He knew, for he had seen them fired, that pistols were not accurate at much more than ten paces, which was about the distance between him and the table. Set against that, the fellow called Jed had a steadying elbow on the tabletop which might help his aim, and that would be further aided by the fact that

Michael was standing silhouetted in the doorway.

'We ain't got all day, Paddy.'

It was only to gain a moment's delay that Michael replied, 'How do you know I'm Irish?'

Jed laughed, though it was more of a wheeze. 'I thinking he's trying to josh me, Francis, to play for time.' The head of the pistol flicked back and forth and the voice lost its tone of banter, turning harsh. 'Do as you'se told to or my friend here will blast out what passes for brains in an Irishman's skull.'

The waving of the pistol, meant to emphasise the threat, did just the opposite: it gave Michael, a man they no doubt thought, given his bulk, would be slow to move, the split second he needed to act. First his left hand shot up to deflect the gun at his head, this as he dived sideways towards the stacked pair of oars, his right hand reaching for the rounded base. The sound of Jed's pistol, fired in such a confined space, was deafening, and if the ball hit Michael he had no way of knowing, for not only was his heart pumping blood to his veins, he had the oar in his hand and was swinging it in a wide arc aimed at the other fellow, this while his foot kicked out to seek to take away his balance.

Time seemed to slow to a standstill: there was Jed screaming abuse, standing now and beginning to move as he turned his discharged pistol into a club. Francis was slow to bring his deflected gun back round and take aim, the barrel wavering slightly, he wanting to make sure he did not miss, so the oar that Michael swung from a position on his knees took his head just at the point where he pulled the trigger, this while the target was trying to get out of the way of the coming ball. What Michael felt along the side of his head was a searing feeling, not pain; what he saw was that oar head take Francis on his temple, with a crack that seemed no less noisy than the pistol shot which accompanied it.

There was no time to wait to see how that affected Francis: Michael had to dive at the knees of the man coming at him with his butt raised to strike and he was in mid-air as his fist shot forward to hit his assailant in the groin, that taking most of the force out of the blow. Yet, coming, as it did, from a man of Michael's build, it did enough, forcing Jed to bend forward so sharply his intended blow hit Michael's shoulders, not his head. Next, Jed was lifted bodily and screaming by the knees as Michael half-stood, off balance but able to use his feet, his weight taking both men back to the table into which Jed was smashed.

Jed knew he was doomed when Michael got one of his huge hands on the pistol-holding wrist and, with a twist, broke it. Now Jed's screams were not imprecations but pleas for mercy mixed with pain, wasted on the Irishman, who had only one aim, which was to see this creature in hell; his blood was up and pumping and his vision was blurred with hate. Michael was above him now, as he lay in the splintered remains of that table, with the giant, using the heel of his hand to protect his own finger bones, pounding at his head until the screams faded to silence. Even then Michael did not stop, reducing the face before him to bloody pulp.

A groan from behind him stopped the assault, and Michael took up one of the legs of the smashed table and went towards the second crimp. One swinging blow was enough, a crack on the head that told of broken bone, and it was raised again, with Michael, chest heaving, just about to deliver a swing that would, if he had not done so already, have killed the man. He stopped, for the first time aware of the blood running down his face, as well as the stinging sensation in his temple.

That warranted no more than a wipe and a curse. Throwing his table leg aside, he gathered up both pistols, a search of Francis producing the means to reload, while the coat Jed had not been wearing had in it a purse containing a little money and, beside it, a sack containing food and bottles. Michael knew he had to work quickly, those two pistol shots, even fired indoors, would have reverberated across this featureless land, which would alert anyone who heard it, and that might include the press gang. He had to get those oars to the boat and get onto water and away. Grabbing them, sack over one shoulder, pistols stuck in his waistband, he ran out of the door, his girth so wide and his aim so unconcerned, it knocked the flimsy thing right off the outside wall.

Would his mates have run, for they must have heard the shots and it was the wise thing to do? Much as he reasoned that, he hoped they had waited. He needed someone to look at his wound, for he had no notion of the seriousness of the damage, and he needed him to tend it as well. It was with a feeling of joy he saw them step out of the trees to greet him, with him gabbling about what had happened as he got close.

Rufus was examining his head, using a spare shirt to stem the blood flow, when Charlie asked him why, in the name of creation, he had fetched along the dog as well? That was before he aimed a boot at the creature, which had it scurrying away.

CHAPTER SEVEN

Pearce woke in Nerot's Hotel to the sound of loud knocking on the door and a grousing voice keen to inform him he had brought his breakfast. It was a voice he recognised from his previous stay and if it was bad-tempered he had a good notion of why that should be.

'Which I wish you would shift to open the door, Your Honour, this tray I'm carryin' being a weight.'

The clerk at the reception table, a haughty sod, had been polite the previous night, if not entirely friendly, an attitude somewhat mollified when Pearce offered to pay for his night's accommodation in advance, as well as asking to leave half his guineas in the care of the hotel safe. Nerot's owners had probably hauled the fellow over the coals for allowing him to get away previously with his bill unsettled, even if it had subsequently been taken care of.

The man bringing his breakfast, if indeed it was

the same fellow, had been all over him like a mother hen previously, in the expectation of a sizeable tip for his care; all he had got from an impecunious John Pearce was one sixpence and a bit of copper and the consequences of that disappointment were in the man's tone. Ordered for eight, Pearce knew he had ample time to consume the meal: the Admiralty might run the King's Navy but it did not in any sense conform to naval time, four bells in the forenoon watch being the best that could be expected prior to anyone being at their labours, leaving him two hours grace.

Opening the door, Pearce stood aside to let the servant put his tray on the table, his nose twitching in anticipation as he registered the odour of kedgeree and pork, probably a chop, the whole underscored by the smell of fresh coffee. That the tray was put down with scant care amused him, which, when the man turned to face him and saw his expression, turned what was a crabbed look into one as furious as a servant dared employ in front of a hotel guest.

'You saw to my needs on my last stay, did you not?'

That made the fellow look as if he had just bitten into an unripe lemon and his voice was a growl, with the added title closer to a snarl. 'I did, Your Honour.'

'Your name is?'

'Didcot.'

'Surely you have a forename too, man?'

'Ezekiel.'

'Well, Ezekiel, I made the singular error, being called away suddenly, of forgetting to see to you on my previous departure, did I not?'

It was an instruction in naked greed to watch the face change from screwed-up aversion to expectation, as well as an indication that if this fellow occupied a lowly position in life, he was far from stupid: Ezekiel Didcot could smell a *douceur* coming from a mile distant.

'Now, Your Honour,' he said, in a voice as changed as his countenance, this before he turned to lift the cover off the breakfast tray. 'We has here for your delectation a fine spread of kedgeree made up from fish fetched in fresh from the Billingsgate Market this very morning, as well as a chop of pork thick enough to satisfy a bulldog.'

He was already pouring the coffee as he added, 'Now, Your Honour, I recalls from your last stay you are not too much of a drinking man, so I did not fetch up for you a flagon of wine, but it would be my pleasure to dash and get some, should you wish it.'

'Coffee will be fine,' Pearce replied, able to grin with his back to the fellow, as he took a half-crown from his purse, a coin that once he got back to the table, was expertly palmed.

'Water is on the way, sir, and I will be here in a trice with strop and razor to shave you, but you has a bell, Your Honour, for meantime needs, and you ring it at your pleasure. Ezekiel Didcot will be here in a flash, upon my soul, I promise.'

'I require writing materials. Also on my last stay, I had certain items made for me, uniforms as well as a chest of the seagoing type, to hold my possessions. I wish to avail myself of the same services on this visit, though for civilian garb and a less nautical trunk.'

'Why, Your Honour, you leaves that to me.' Didcot touched the side of his nose, his face full of cunning. 'And, might I make so bold as to add, that with me placing the business, you will find the articles a lot less costly than afore.'

Pearce had to struggle not to laugh at the response to his own reply: the man's eyes were close to popping out of his head. 'Why, Didcot, cost is not very much of a concern to a man who has taken a number of prizes, as have I. Please be so kind as to order for me a hack to take me to the Admiralty at half past nine of the clock.'

Having eaten, and before being shaved, Pearce sat down to write a letter to be sent to William Pitt, demanding to be told what in the Devil's name was going on, adding that the superscription at the top was where he could now be contacted.

Emily Barclay, content with the early hour, was not happy about Brown's Hotel as a meeting place – the note asking her to meet her husband having come from that establishment – her one condition being that they meet in a public room, one which he must secure, not his own private accommodation. On arrival she was also careful not to compromise him.

'Can I say who is calling, madam?'

'Captain Barclay is expecting me,' Emily replied, turning away to kill off any further enquiries.

It was Gherson who came to fetch her, his smirk much in evidence, and she was shown into a private dining room off the main lobby in which the table had been laid with coffee and refreshments. Seeing Gherson closing the door behind him, her first comment was a sharp one: she would not discuss anything with him in attendance. Her husband, looking set to argue, was probably persuaded by the determined look in her eye.

'Leave us, Gherson,' he said.

'And keep your ear away from the door as well,' Emily added.

'You are too hard on the fellow,' Ralph Barclay said, as the door closed.

'And you are too trusting, husband, which I have to admit I would never have thought I would hear myself say to you.'

'Emily,' he said, moving forward, a soft, pleading look in his eye, which to his young wife, was wholly insincere.

He was met by a held-up palm, which stopped him dead. 'Please, Captain Barclay, no attempt at intimacy. You know what I am here to discuss and it would be best if we get straight to the matter without any false displays of affection.'

The tender look disappeared to be replaced by one Emily knew better, a more habitual scowl. 'I was not aware, madam, that the entire terms were to be set by you. You act as if I have no say in any arrangements, not that, in truth, there should be any at all. Might I remind you that you are my wife?'

'That is not something of which I require to be reminded,' Emily snapped.

'Look,' Barclay protested, 'we must not dispute like

this. Pray take a seat and I shall too, and let us act upon the matter as adults, even if you are scarce more than a child, lacking in experience.'

'I am woman enough, sir, to know my mind.'

'I am over twice your years, my dear,' Barclay said, emollient again. 'Grant that I know more of affairs than you.'

'You know of the sea, sir, and the unbridled use of arbitrary power, which is not a force you can bring to bear in the circumstances in which we find ourselves.'

'A spat, Emily, common in marriage.'

'Is it common, sir, to punish a man for a mere glance? Is it common, sir, to tell lie after lie to your bride? Is it common, sir, to use brute force to gain what the law says are your marital prerogatives?'

'I admit to errors.'

Emily had a flushed face now and she was quietly berating herself, having promised on the way here that the one thing she would not do was lose her temper.

'And, my dear,' Barclay added, 'I am minded to change my ways.'

With a wife still struggling to calm herself, as well as slow the rate of her heartbeat, that was a gambit greeted by silence, which encouraged Ralph Barclay to continue.

'You must understand, Mrs Barclay, that I have had a harsh apprenticeship in the world, sent to sea as a tender lad and raised in brutal company, so if I have rough edges they come from what I was brought up to. I do not doubt such experiences have shaped my way of behaving but I am not without a mind of my own or a desire to be brought to a better way of acting. Might I offer you some coffee?'

If anything, the silky tone, which had crept into her husband's voice as he proffered his *mea culpa*, irritated Emily even more, for it implied that she was some kind of booby, to have her thinking changed by a few words of apology and explanation. Breathing deep to control her voice she replied.

'Captain Barclay, I fear you misunderstand the nature of this encounter. You act as if it were a prelude to a reconciliation and it is nothing of the sort—'

He lost his composure then, his voice a hiss. 'Damn you, I will not have you dictate to me, madam.'

'I do hope that worm you employ as a clerk has told you of the choices you face.'

'By what chicanery, or by what exercise of your feminine wiles, did you come by what you claim to possess?'

'It is not an unfounded claim, sir, I have the documents in their entirety: every word and every lie, and in the right hands it will see you in court and drummed out of your precious navy at the very least.'

Ralph Barclay touched his stump then, alluding to his missing left arm, in what was an obvious plea for sympathy, his voice hoarse. 'Is it not odd, the pain I feel is as physical as—'

'Please, husband, do not seek to say to me that you feel any pain in your heart, always supposing you could locate the organ. You are a sailor, a ship's captain and you wish to remain one. Good, I say. You want a vessel to command and service at sea, even better. I want nothing more than a separation from you, which if it is provided by salt water will be perfect, since my living apart from you will not be remarked upon but be seen as normal. I think that is clear enough, don't you?'

'And if I don't agree?'

'Why bother to ask a question to which you know the answer?'

'You wouldn't dare expose me.'

'Would I not, sir? Let me tell you here and now I will not ever spend another night under the same roof as you, whatever the consequences, and, if I am to be disgraced for it, so will you be, first by a public denunciation of your actions both as a naval officer and husband, and secondly by those court martial papers being put into the hands of those who would bring you down.'

The voice was close to a shout now. 'John Pearce, you mean?'

'If that man is the avenue by which I will achieve my purpose, then yes, I will pass them to him and I do not doubt he will be relentless in pursuit of you.'

'You, madam, are not the only one who can go public! Do not think I have not observed or heard of your association with that rake.'

'There is no association, sir. There is not even mutual regard. I despise the fellow for the very actions of which you accuse him.'

'Is that why you made moon eyes at the fellow?'

'So, Captain Barclay,' Emily replied with forced amusement, 'you add stupidity and jealousy to your other reprehensible traits.'

'Damn you, woman,' he shouted, getting to his feet, 'stop insulting me!'

'And,' Emily added calmly, 'your language is, as it has been many times in the past, both loose and wicked.'

'I am minded to horsewhip you in public.'

'Do your worst, sir. It will be nothing as compared to your head in the stocks, where the mob and I will take great joy in pelting you with the filth of the streets.'

'This meeting is over.'

'It is not,' Emily snapped. 'I require from you the means to live in reasonable comfort, and I also require from you a guarantee to be left in peace when I so desire. In return, I will observe certain conventions in the article of appearances, thus preserving both your reputation and mine – attendance at certain social functions to do with your rank and station, at which I promise to be the soul of discretion. While you are at sea, I will, in all respects, behave as a woman temporarily widowed by your very necessary service to your king and country. In company I will praise you and be admiring of your character. That no one will be convinced matters not, the world in which we live will be satisfied with a dumbshow of a marriage rather than the reality.'

Emily reached into her purse and produced a sheet of paper. 'Here, Captain Barclay, is a list of my expenses, which will naturally be greater the more you require of me socially – dresses, jewellery and the like. There are also the details of my account at Coutts Bank, to which you may remit the necessary funds, I suggest by the calendar quarter. You have my address, and to there you may send word of what I am required to do to still wagging tongues.'

It was a last desperate throw that had Ralph Barclay saying, 'I will not be the only one ruined and you know who stands to lose the most.'

'Sir, Toby Burns lied!' she snapped. 'That is a fact of which he is well aware because it was you who put the words into his mouth. He is also a weak creature who, placed before any kind of examination, will crumble and is thus more of a threat to you than I. Perhaps you mean my parents and the rest of my family, the house to which you have title and in which they live?'

Emily had to work on her voice and manner then, for she cared deeply they should not be hurt. 'They were content to trade my virtue for their comfort. If that virtue is ruined by their enthusiasm to see me wed to you, then they must face the consequences of their actions, as must I for being such a fool to agree to the marriage. I openly admit that I was a fool, openly admit I did not look beyond your prospects and your rank to see what lay behind. Had you not taken me to sea with you, a ploy to save the expense of an establishment at home, I may never have discovered, sir, what a scrub you are.'

Ralph Barclay looked a beaten man as she said that to him. Head bowed, he waved his good arm in dismissal. 'Go!'

'I shall,' Emily said, rising from her chair and taking a second paper from her purse. 'I will give you time to consider, Captain Barclay, and to aid you, here is the paper I refused to give to Gherson to assist you in making up your mind. Shall we say a week?'

Emily went to the door and stopped, as if waiting for her husband to open it for her, which he irascibly declined to do, instead picking up that which she had left him to look at. Exiting, into the lobby of the hotel, she threw Gherson a glare, then noticed that the exchange had been noisy enough to cause the staff that manned the area to avoid her eye.

Gherson entered the room to find Ralph Barclay still reading. 'I hope you have some suggestion of a way to deal with this?'

'Is that the same paper as your wife showed me, sir?'

Head still down, Barclay passed it to Gherson, who gave it a cursory glance, before confirming it to be the case and that led to an enquiry regarding the handwriting.

'My wife's.'

'Might I suggest, sir, first, that this is insufficient for you to be convinced the whole exists and secondly, if the entirety is in her handwriting, as is this, it will very likely be ruled inadmissible in court.'

'Go on.'

'Your wife, sir, when you sent me to her, named this as a copy, which implies an original.'

'Which might be in another hand?' Barclay asked, a question requiring no response.

'She was not witness to the entire proceedings, so that is a strong possibility. If you were to ask for more proof, say another few pages of remarks made when we know she was not present, and originals, I think perhaps your wife could be persuaded to provide them, perhaps by you showing willing and sending her some funds.'

'How do you know she asked for funds?'

The look Gherson gave his employer was such that there was no need to reply: if he had not been listening at the door, then the man had found some other means of eavesdropping, unless, of course, he had just arrived at a conclusion which was obvious.

'I suggest a watch be kept on her if she agrees. Should the papers she alludes to be in her present residence, then that will be made obvious. If not, in order to comply, she has to lead us to where they are.'

'Which might not help.'

Gherson's response was terse. 'It is better than where we are now, sir, in ignorance.'

'Damn you, Gherson,' Ralph Barclay snapped, his old fire reanimated by hope. 'I have had occasion to remind you before to take care how you address me, and after being berated by a near child of a wife I am in no mood to let such a thing pass now.'

'Of course, sir,' Gherson replied, not much put out to be checked. 'But might I suggest if it is to be done, the notion is best executed immediately?'

'Why?'

'I cannot but help feel, sir, that your wife, much as she may have rehearsed for this encounter, is emotionally troubled by it.'

Looking at Barclay, who clearly could not discern the nub of what he was saying, he was, not for the first time, wondering how this man had ever managed to get married at all, never mind to a beauty like his young wife: he might be able to command a ship but he knew nothing whatsoever about the opposite sex.

'You think so, Gherson?'

It would have been too crass to say, 'I know so, sir,' so all he did was nod towards the quill and ink provided by Brown's Hotel.

'Send for Devenow. He can take your note to her, and after that he can keep a watch out to see where she goes.'

Emily Barclay was sitting in the back of a hack on the way back to her lodgings, still suffering from the effects of her interview and wondering what would happen next. She had few illusions that her husband would just roll over and acquiesce, it was not in his nature, but as to what he would do she had no idea. It was a thought which was still troubling her when she got back to her room, which occasioned a great deal of pacing up and down until, after an hour, she resolved to act and prepared to set out once more, this time on foot, for her destination was close by, to be met on the stairs by her landlady bearing the note which had just come through the door.

Quickly perused, she saw it as evidence of the need for what she had in mind, so, stuffing it into her coat pocket she went out the front door and headed off towards Holborn, unaware that she was being followed.

John Pearce, looking around the book-lined ground floor room, thought it had a level of dust which seemed appropriate for the fusty pursuance of the law as a profession, with a decent amount dancing in the shaft of light coming in through the window. The man opposite had a dry quality too, pale skin in a long face over what looked like a spare body, evidence to Pearce's mind of a life spent indoors.

'Thank you for seeing me at such short notice, sir.'

'Mr Lutyens was most pressing that I should accommodate you, Mr Pearce.'

'As you will observe, Mr Studdert, I have done no more than outline the details of my case so that you can look them over. I have a place on the two o'clock coach to Portsmouth where the men named in the document are waiting for me. I collected their protections from the Admiralty before coming on here.'

That revived an unpleasant recollection: having had no intention of being kept waiting once more, Pearce left the collection of the protections as late as possible, yet he still had to tip the blasted doorman just to get into the building, making him reprise in his mind a thought he had harboured before: that if he died and came back again he wanted that as an occupation. It was without doubt the best paid for the least effort. By the time he had paid the fees and got out again, he was lighter by ten guineas in his purse, and not a happy man.

'But if you need to contact me,' he added, 'word can be left at Nerot's Hotel, where I have taken a room.'

'I would appreciate a short verbal explanation, sir,' the attorney said, holding up the papers that Pearce had laid on his desk and which he had quickly skimmed through.

'It is a case of illegal impressments, Mr Studdert.' Seeing the man's facial reaction Pearce was quick to add, 'Which I know to be a difficult area of law to pursue. But when you read through what I have given you, it will become clear that in some senses that is only the trigger for my action, which is, in truth, an attempt to get a case of perjury brought against the man named on the first page. He was the scoundrel that took my companions and I out of the Pelican Tavern on the night we were pressed.'

'Pelican?' Studdert said that in such a strangled way that John Pearce was tempted to ask if he knew the place.

'And the man you wish arraigned . . .'

'Captain Ralph Barclay.'

That was said softly, and followed by an arrangement of the attorney's features, which told the man opposite him that he was about to deliver bad news. 'Mr Pearce, much as I would like to oblige Mr Lutyens, I cannot act for you.'

'Why ever not?'

Pearce's papers were pushed across for him to take. 'That I cannot tell you.'

'Sir, I am no student of the law, but when an attorney says to me that he cannot act, I suspect it is because he fears a conflict of interest.'

Studdert stood up abruptly. 'And I am a student of the law, Mr Pearce, which tells me that I am at liberty to choose or decline whom I represent and to do so without being required to provide an explanation.'

'I cannot believe you are acting for Barclay.'

'What, sir, you believe or do not believe are none of my concern. Now, if you will forgive me, I have other matters to attend to.'

John Pearce wanted to argue, but there was no point in disputing with this fellow. With as unfriendly a glare as he could muster, he picked up his bundle and put it back inside his coat, then turned and left, exiting into a hallway and passing the stairway that led to other business premises above. Behind him a perplexed lawyer was wondering at two things: the name Pearce had used, which he knew, and the word 'Pelican', which was the one-word code that he had agreed upon with Emily Barclay should she wish to send someone to him to fetch from his strongroom the bundle of papers, thicker by far than those Pearce had presented, she had left in his care.

Emily Barclay, walking towards the attorney's office to comply with the request from her husband, was too preoccupied to see that, as she took the first step up to his doorway, she was just about to bump into John Pearce – that is, till he spoke.

'Mrs Barclay!'

He was as surprised as she, though he hid it better. She put her hand to her mouth as if she had seen a ghost and it was all she could do not to scream.

'This is a coincidence,' Pearce said. Then he turned, looked at Studdert's doorway and smiled, a look that was still on his face as he turned back. 'Or perhaps it is not so much of one.'

'Lieutenant Pearce,' she replied, fighting to control herself.

'Yes, the ogre.'

'You may be many things, sir, but you are no ogre.'

'Forgive me if I do not ask you to list what those other things are.'

'Do I find you well?' she asked. It was such an inane thing to say in the circumstances that Pearce threw back his head and laughed, which made her cross. 'What, sir, is so amusing?'

'Your good manners, madam.'

'It does not surprise me, sir that you find such attributes . . .'

'Strange,' he said, finishing a sentence she was struggling to complete. 'In your mouth, no, given you are the living epitome of the polite manner.'

'The way you say that, Lieutenant Pearce, makes it sound like an insult.'

'Then I apologise for it. I would not want to ever insult you.'

That made her blush, which to Pearce made her look prettier than ever, and that broadened the look on his face to a near-grin as he took in the trace of auburn hair under her bonnet and the fresh features of her beautiful face. The voice that responded, as well as the flashing green eyes, made it plain his compliment was not welcome.

'We are in the public street, sir, which is scarce the

place to dispute with you, but I am bound to say, and it makes me cross to add it is not for the first time, your mode of speech is inappropriate. Now, if you will excuse me.'

Pearce stood aside, still smiling, with a very slight bow. 'Of course, it would never do to keep Mr Studdert waiting.'

'How do you know—?'

Emily Barclay stopped herself, dropped her head and brushed past, followed by the appreciative eyes of John Pearce. He, once she had gone through the doorway, spun round to hail a passing hack, too preoccupied to notice the man ducking out of sight, which was not easy for one of his height. A long-time follower of Ralph Barclay, now rated as his servant, Devenow had been sent for to follow the man's wife and he had just witnessed something of more weight than finding out where she went on her errand.

'Now, that is goin' to set the capt'n ablaze, an' no error,' Devenow whispered to himself.

Sitting opposite Mr Studdert, Emily Barclay was unsure of how to proceed. She had come here because she felt the need to discuss with him the preparation of some kind of contract that would bind her husband, the discussion of which could not be anything but embarrassing. The request from her husband for further documents she felt worth compliance, but at this precise moment her mind was reeling from having just met John Pearce on the doorstep and, as a question, that took precedence.

'Mr Studdert, the gentleman you have just had

135

in your chambers, whom I bumped into on the way out.'

'Lieutenant Pearce.'

'Might I ask what his business was with you?'

'None. He wanted me to act on his behalf in a matter and I declined to do so.'

'Why?'

Studdert's hands met before his lips, the long fingers tapping together like a church steeple as he considered his reply. Despite the look of impatience which crossed Emily Barclay's face, he was not about to be rushed, being a man who was wont to say it would never do to ask a lawyer the time, given the reply would be so delayed by caution as to render it useless. He was free to speak if he wished: the woman before him was a client and Pearce was not, but the lieutenant had likewise come from Heinrich Lutyens, and that altered the case somewhat; best be sure of other factors before being too open.

'I do believe I must respect the confidentiality of his request.'

'Was it about my husband, Captain Barclay?' Emily demanded.

Forced to accede, Studdert nodded. 'I declined to represent him on the grounds that I have a strong suspicion I could not do so for both you and he, simultaneously.'

The connotation in that statement, as well as the way it was said, and not least because it was delivered with an unblinking gaze, made Emily blush. She being a very attractive young woman and Pearce being

136

a handsome fellow of near the same age would lead anyone to certain salacious conclusions. For the second time in as many hours she found herself defending her reputation.

'Be assured, sir, that my relationship with Lieutenant Pearce is a social one, and "strained" would be the best way to describe it. In fact, I cannot abide the man!'

'These matters are none of my concern, Mrs Barclay, and I suspect it is not the subject on which you wished to consult me.'

'No, it is not.' Studdert nodded, inviting her to continue, but Emily had another question, which threw her previous statement into doubt: it really was foolish of her to ask the lawyer, before she proceeded to other matters, if he had an address for John Pearce.

CHAPTER EIGHT

For all it was one of the best-travelled roads in the country and was maintained by the government as an important artery, there was nothing restful about coaching to Portsmouth, either in the ten hours it took or the solace afforded to the passengers, so it was an irascible John Pearce who, after an overnight journey, arrived in the naval port – a mood not improved when he discovered that HMS *Fury* no longer lay out in the Spithead anchorage, but was alongside the dockyard mast house with her old poles already removed, her crew broken up and every officer aboard her from captain to the most junior lieutenant reassigned.

He could not enquire for his Pelicans until he knew if they had managed to stay aboard and, if they had not, to where they had either gone or been taken. Once on the ship, watched with some curiosity by the dockyard workers, he called out along the gun deck for his friends, but there was no reply in a vessel small enough for him to be heard even on the orlop, and that brought on a terrible sinking feeling – had he once more delayed too long and let them down? That the fault did not lie with him was scant comfort.

He went in search of those who might know, unaware that the gunner had seen him coming along the wharf and warned the carpenter, they being the only warrants still aboard: both had taken great care to make themselves scarce, their attitude being that the only man who had to deal with him, the purser, was not on board, leaving Pearce to enquire of those whom he could talk to. He had no real experience of dealing with dockyard workers, though he had heard from every naval lip that they were the most pernicious bunch of scoundrels in creation, thieving bastards who would steal your eyes and come back for the holes. He had always assumed a degree of exaggeration in these tales, but his contact with the breed working on the wharf, as he passed them, made him wonder if that were indeed true.

Going further below in search of information brought him across knots of mateys sitting around smoking pipes – a wonder, until he discovered, and it was a fact given with little grace, that the hull was being surveyed. His question as to why that had not been undertaken before the vessel was warped into the dock was met with incomprehension, even when it was posed to the surveyor himself.

'And what damned business, sir, is that of yours?'

'Mere curiosity, which I am told is a human condition.'

'I suppose that is an indulgence in levity!' the man snapped.

He was not a big fellow, this surveyor, he was small and flabby, his most prominent feature being a belly that, slack as it was and hanging over his belt, spoke of idleness, his purple face implying he was wont to wash down what he ate with generous quantities of wine, not that added height or muscle would have altered Pearce's response. He had that air of the functionary about him, which John Pearce had encountered too many times in his life, an expression that implied that nothing at all was any of his business.

He had been dunned by an avaricious Admiralty doorman, paid out to a supercilious clerk nine golden guineas for protections, been refused representation by an attorney and had not slept properly but uncomfortably in a post house, this backed up by dozing in a crowded coach and it was quite possible the men he had come to rescue had been shipped off as they had been the last time. His mood was therefore not forgiving.

'Can you swim, sir?' he asked, in a cold tone.

'I fail to see that is relevant.'

'It is that, for if you address me in that way again I will toss you bodily into the harbour.' The man opened his mouth to protest but Pearce was not finished. 'I am about to ask you a question and any answer less than civil will, I assure you, test the nature of my threat.'

'I will have the magistrate upon you, sir.'

Aware that those dockyard workers close by were grinning and nudging each other – clearly this popinjay was not loved – Pearce felt secure: if he took this fellow by the scruff of the neck they would not intervene.

'He will take an age to arrive, by which time you will either be drowned or a laughing stock. Where, in the name of creation, are the warrants?'

'I have no idea.'

'But they are aboard?'

'The carpenter is, as for the rest I have no idea.'

'Do you know where the carpenter is?'

The surveyor was in the process of recovering some of his conceit, it was in his face, but that melted under the stony glare he was getting from this naval lieutenant. His reply was accompanied by a slap on one of the hanging knees.

'He should be here, sir. We are, after all, discussing the parts of the ship for which he is responsible and a damned poor state they are in. The scantlings are bad but these knees are soft enough to take my finger . . .' The man stopped, given the impatient growl from Pearce was very audible. 'He said he needed to go about his occasions, so I suspect he is in the roundhouse.'

'Thank you,' Pearce replied, striding off.

Behind he heard the man hiss. 'Damn cheek of the fellow, why if I were ten years younger he would pay for addressing me in so cavalier a manner.'

'Ain't gone far, Your Honour,' a sarcastic voice replied, obviously one of the lounge-about mateys. 'You'se still has a chance to put the upstart in his place.'

'I have work to do,' the surveyor replied, his voice louder and still carrying enough to reach the companionway, 'and I suspect that you too have labours which require your attention.'

141

'Watching you be toil enough, mate.'

Striding along the gun deck, Pearce was increasingly both worried and angry, so when he opened the forepeak doorway to the heads, to find two men standing there talking softly, who, by their shocked expressions, had to be people seeking to avoid him, he was ready to do murder – a mood not enhanced when the gabbled explanation was provided as to how his Pelicans had got off the ship.

'We had to get them away, sir, or they would have been taken up for certain and a boat was the best option.'

'Who took them?'

'I did,' the carpenter replied. 'Dropped them off past Hayling Island.'

'I need you to be more precise.'

'I grounded at Bracklesham Bay, just past the sandbar known as East Head.'

'And what are their chances of getting clear from there?'

The gunner wouldn't look him in the eye. 'Master drew them a map of sorts, though none of your lads can read, but they knew the names to avoid and the route to follow.'

'That's not what I asked.'

'We did our best for 'em, Your Honour,' the carpenter protested.

'I need to follow in their footsteps. Which is the best way to get to where they landed?'

'Boat, Your Honour, same as I did, and any local man will know East Head.' About to hurry away, Pearce was brought up with a round turn when the man added, 'Mind, there is a bill from the purser you has to settle, for he saw to the needs of your men, though if I was you, Your Honour, I would argue about the total, 'cause he be as tight as a duck's arse.'

'He will have to wait.'

'You have no idea, sir, how that cheers me.'

Hiring a wherry in Portsmouth was easy enough – they were ten a penny in such a busy anchorage and those who manned them were secure from the press – though he got a curious look when he named the destination. It was not long, in the nature of things, before he was conversing with the man steadily rowing him, a cove with a weather-beaten face and a pleasant manner, with Pearce intimating he was on a social errand. What he discovered, when, in a very roundabout way, he alluded to press gangs and the like, was not information to make him feel happy.

'A happy hunting ground for 'em round Wittering and Bracklesham. It ain't a part of the world I go to without I had my protection, an' even then I will not hang about once I land you.'

'Why so?'

'Stands to reason, sir, for it takes no genius to see that getting off Portsea Island, or Hayling for that matter, is hard, seeing as it means you'se obliged to cross a guarded bridge. Bracklesham Bay is the first bit o' land that gives a clear run without crossing water, so it be a place much made for by those on the run from the Spithead fleet.'

'A fact no doubt known to those who would take them up?'

'Both kinds, and though the press might respect my paper, there be lobcouses who work that area who would take me up and damn my protection.'

'How long have you been a waterman?' asked Pearce, changing what was a worrying subject.

Pearce had no way of knowing if he had arrived in exactly the same place as his Pelicans and it was a very forlorn hope indeed that they might catch sight of him and come rushing to make contact. His boatman was as good as his word, rowing quickly away from the shore once his passenger had landed, leaving behind a man thankful for the service and also the way the fellow had advised him to go just before the boat grounded.

'Just keep the water in sight on your left hand, Your Honour, and afore long you will see plain the tower of Wittering Church. Make for that and you can get directions to where you is heading from there.'

He crossed the shingle strand and stood atop the dune, looking over the same featureless landscape which had greeted his friends, but there was scant point in stopping – his task was simple: to find out if his friends had got away from this shore or had been captured by the men who patrolled it. In another time it would have been a pleasant enough walk over land that, edging the sea, had at many times been inundated, making it perfect pasture for sheep and, where there was rise enough to keep the ocean at bay, fine farmland. The numerous watercourses that cut into the shore were well bridged, and edged with tamarisk hedge. The trees, where they stood in clumps, rose to a decent height, where they were individual they showed by their bent nature the power of the winds that could lash this exposed coast.

Walking in such a setting took him back to better times. More than once John Pearce had traversed this kind of landscape in the company of his father, just as he had experienced every other type in the extensive travels they had undertaken together: hill and dale, flat farmland, endless towns, the odd city – he had seen as a growing lad more of his country than most. Sometimes, when they had been static enough to allow him some formal schooling, those with whom he mixed had alluded to the peripatetic life he normally led as strange, when what was alien to him was to be in one place for any length of time; a bed was as likely to be under the stars as under a roof and that seemed natural, for he had known precious little of any other.

Education for him had been an 'all day, every day' affair, not just in the rudiments of Latin, Greek and numbers, books which he carried in his satchel, but it also encompassed what lay around him in the countryside through which he and Adam travelled. Thus he knew, without much in the way of registering the fact, the cries of the different birds – terns, lapwings and curlews – knew the markings of the different types of ducks that filled the watercourses and crabbing pools, could register sea lavender or a yellow-horned poppy as he passed by them.

Beneath his feet it was as often sand as salt marsh grass and as he plodded along, his mind moved from worries about his at-risk friends to mix with memories of his father, and that led to recollection of many of the places Adam had stopped to speak as well as the many variations in the way they had been greeted. Sometimes they had been obliged to depart in such haste that they barely managed to stay ahead of the stones aimed at their backs. At the other end of the scale – and there had been every variety in between – they had received such a warm welcome that to leave after several days was like a wrench, while on more than one occasion a local worthy, men of open mind and keen to dispute, had set them up as guests in their own homes and let them stay for months.

Such thoughts led on to a re-examination of subsequent events and the eventual need to flee. In truth, what his father had expounded in both his written and spoken words should have been tolerated in a secure society, but John Pearce knew that the lands ruled by King George were far from that, even if those with enough possessions to secure comfort and full bellies crowed about the freedoms of John Bull's Island. The three polities of Scotland, Wales and England were a seething mass of inequality and discontent, for most in this land of plenty went without a morsel of meat in their diet – so much for the roast beef of old England. All Adam Pearce had sought to do was to point out the absurdity of so many people near to starving, especially in times of harvest failure, while those who owned the greater tracts of land existed in such conspicuous and arrogant luxury.

'Never underestimate the indifference of the rich to the plight of the poor.'

He had inadvertently spoken those words out loud, a quotation much espoused by his father and it was true, though there were exceptions to the mass who genuinely sought to alleviate suffering, good people who knew all was not well. But most men and women of means made pious noises before reassuring themselves that poverty was brought about by the sloth of the poor, not circumstances. Yet could he excuse himself? Pearce knew he might not be so very different: had he not taken the full measure of what had been available to him when they had fled to Paris, where his father was famous, while being aware of beggars in the streets? Was he, indeed, as much of a hypocrite as the mass of his fellow countrymen?

Not a man to berate himself for any great length of time, thinking of Paris led to more pleasing memories. There he had come to manhood in what was a sparkling milieu of glittering salons and excited speculation, had mixed with great thinkers and engaged famous wits, met the most important men of the Revolution and, more pleasurably, their womenfolk. Some were esteemed for their conversation, but being his age, healthy, good-looking, tall and of fair unblemished skin, other matters took precedence and he had not been left disappointed, garnering to himself a beautiful mistress. It was her image that filled his mind when the church bells broke the pleasing train of thought.

The village he entered was small, self-contained, with a jetty and a muddy main street that included some shops, a covered market and, at either end, that ubiquitous feature of the English town, the tavern. He

147

made for the first of those, given he was sharp-set and his stomach was rumbling for a hunk of cheese, some bread and perhaps an apple. The interior was, as ever, smoke-filled and warm, with each of the small rooms having a healthy fire in the grate. Being a stranger, he was examined; being in a naval boat cloak over his uniform, such examination was not excessive, that is until, in one snug arbour, he espied a group of pipe-smoking men, a half-dozen in number, one in the same garb as he, albeit the coat was very well worn indeed, the remainder in short blue jackets, far-from-white ducks and wearing striped stockings.

'Good day, gentlemen,' he said, taking a chair not too far away. 'I trust I find you in good cheer.'

The looks he got were not actually unfriendly, they were just emanating from faces of overall ugliness that would find amiability impossible and he knew, without having to be told, that he was in the presence of a press gang, which, if it was fortuitous given his purpose, produced in his belly a slight tinge of utterly unnecessary apprehension: he was a naval officer and in no danger at all.

'An' good day to you, sir,' came back a gruff reply from the lieutenant, a man with black eyes and several scars on a heavily pock-marked face. 'Are you from these parts?'

'Passing through,' Pearce replied, 'but it is good to see a blue coat.'

'Not many pleased to see these coats,' said another of the group, a remark that produced amused and general agreement.

'Gentlemen, I suspect I know your purpose.'

'Ain't hard to guess,' came the reply from the very furthest away; they seemed to be talking to him by turns. 'Seeing there ain't no ship o' the line in the offing.'

'I am told it a good station for the task you perform,' Pearce advanced, adding, 'the very *necessary* task.'

'We takes up more'n a few,' the lieutenant agreed.

The fellow had a voice no more refined than his inferiors, not that Pearce was surprised: the Impress Service was no place for gentility and that extended to those who officered the bands. It also seemed to be something of a republic, the whole party drinking together and no sign of any deference to hierarchy in their manner or response, and they spoke as they chose. Momentarily distracted by a serving girl and his order for food and a tankard of ale, he resumed his conversation when she left.

'Had much recent success?'

It was as if he had thrown a bucket of cold water on what had been an already low level of bonhomie, for to a man their faces closed up. 'Forgive me if I seem overly curious, but I have not met many men who undertake your kind of work.'

'Never pressed?' demanded one of the group, clearly incredulous.

Pearce never had, yet he knew it would be foolish to say so, given every naval lieutenant would have, at some time in his service, even as a midshipman, been sent out with a party from whichever ship he was serving on to find men, willing or not, to man her in time of war, an almost common state of the nation for these last hundred years. Even those who thoroughly disagreed with the practice were obliged to undertake it.

'I meant a real professional. It seems to me that I might learn something from your experiences, given we all know how hard it is to find volunteers.'

'That's not a breed we come across often,' their officer responded. 'Our task in these parts is to take up the boobies that think a boat to yonder bay will put them beyond our reach.'

'Ah yes,' Pearce acceded, 'we sit in a favoured spot for deserters from Spithead.'

That got sage nods, and since silence followed as the men drank from their tankards, Pearce was left at a stand, one easily solved by offering them all a refill.

'You taken a prize ship, then, has you, sir?' asked one, the first to acknowledge his rank, so great was the power of liberality.

'I confess to having the good fortune to have done so.'

If Pearce had expected congratulations he was sadly disappointed: these fellows looked very put out and one actually said, 'All right for some.' But he was grateful really, for they showed a singular lack of the common curiosity when given such a statement: in any other gathering of naval folk he would have been immediately pressed for details. Silence ensued until the drinks arrived, then Pearce raised his own tankard to toast them.

'To you, gentlemen, enjoying the same measure of success as I have, albeit your aims are different.'

150

The toast was acknowledged and reciprocated, with the lieutenant, at least, showing a glint of good humour. 'Happen most folk don't know how dangerous our task be. I daresay, in your success, you faced a degree of shot?'

'I did,' Pearce replied, thinking immediately of the number of occasions when he had done just that.

'Well, we ain't safe just 'cause we're on dry land, my friend. The men we seek to take up are prone to deep violence to avoid being collared.'

'Armed an' all, now,' said one of his men, his pipe stem aimed at John Pearce's face. 'You would not guess on that, now would you?'

'You surprise me in that, I must say,' Pearce replied.

'Right now we is on the trail of a fellow that near killed two men.' Pearce could not breathe and it did not get easier. 'Part of a trio that arrived on the beach not two mornin's past. We lost them ourselves but they were threatened by a pair of crimps seeking to steal our bounty.'

'They bastards got what they deserved, I say,' came another voice, soon matched by a third.

'One of the parties out hunting heard the pistol shots and went to see what was what.' A coarse rumble of a laugh, which spread to the others, followed those words. 'Found a right to-do, with blood everywhere.'

'That's right,' the lieutenant said. 'It be a grievous assault.'

'Should have heard them bleat when they could talk.'

It was hard for Pearce to make out who was speaking, not that it much mattered.

'Had their guns pinched and their grub and beer, so there is stealing from a person to face up to and housebreaking.'

'The place was falling apart, didn't take much breaking.'

The lieutenant finished the litany. 'All they now need is to employ those pistols in highway robbery.'

'Serious crimes,' Pearce was obliged to respond.

'Never fear, it will not be brought to civil justice,' the lieutenant maintained. 'The culprits were run sailors and we will have them back, though we might be obliged to hand over the one who did the damage. A Paddy, we were told, a giant of a sod by all accounts, so right now we are waiting for a list from Portsmouth of sailors run recent. Soon we'll have his name, and the others. With names and a right good description we will have them by the heels in no time.'

One of his companions had an opinion. 'Might be best to hand 'em in for a better bounty from the magistrates, and who knows, the whole three of them might be strung up, which will be a fine sight to see.'

Slowly Pearce lifted his tankard to cover his face, mouthing into it, in words that sounded as hollow as he felt in the pit of his stomach, 'Then I wish you joy of it.' He could not, of course leave it there, and once he had composed his face he put forward the obvious question.

'You are sure you will catch them, Lieutenant?'

'Once we has the names. They're in a boat, but I

have been told it is a leaky bugger, so they won't outrun us in our eight-oared cutter.'

'They might take to the land.'

'They might at that, but with their names and descriptions put out, I don't give much for their chances. Better we catch them than the law!'

CHAPTER NINE

Forced to eat his food, even though his appetite had gone, and also keep up a genial conversation with men he considered beneath contempt, it was near to half an hour before he felt he could decently get up to leave. Once out of the tavern he made his way to look out at the flat, muddy tideway and stood in contemplation: what to do? Should he go in pursuit of his friends, or head back to Portsmouth? For the former, he would need a boat and several oars willing to row for however long it took, days perhaps, and he had no guarantee of catching up with them, just as he had no idea if they were still afloat. If he went back to Portsmouth and HMS *Fury*, that at least promised the possibility of an effective outcome.

He made for a knot of what he assumed to be local fishermen to bespeak a boat for Portsmouth, only to find, despite their garb, their physical build and the smoking pipes, they were women, leaving Pearce to surmise their menfolk had either made themselves scarce because of the presence of those he had just been drinking with, or had been taken up by the navy already, leaving their spouses to keep fishing to feed their families.

Even the women seemed unwilling to chance what they saw as dangerous waters; the best they would agree to was to drop him on the Southsea shingle and at no small cost, so he found himself in the thwarts facing two creatures who, despite his high regard for the opposite sex, he could not in any way regard as attractive. Short on teeth, square-faced and ruddy, they swore, spat and pipe-smoked in such a way that no man need fear comparison for his manners, just as in the article of cleanliness the odour of fish they gave off was quite offensive. He was heartily glad to hear the keel grind onto the beach, even if they had been informative on the dangers of the part of the world in which they lived.

That left a long walk into the city, along a barren foreshore above a strand of exposed and blustery shingle, so it was very late in the day when he got into the dockyard, which meant he was heading for the mast house at a time when the lamps were being lit. The frigate was where he had left her, with just enough westerly light left to show that, if her decks were free of labour, her lower masts were in and seated. He ran aboard, making his way straight for the wardroom, where a light showed through the casements.

As luck would have it the master was there as well as the other warrants, cook included, but not the purser, all sitting round a bottle and the remains of their dinner, the smell of which hit a man made hungry again by that walk along the strand. Time had allowed Pearce to rehearse what he was about to say and to discard any other avenue than anger: persuasion, an appeal to better nature, was unlikely to produce the result he sought and his voice was already loud as soon as he had cleared the doorway. He was received in shocked silence when he began to berate them for sending his friends into an area where they were almost certain to be caught.

'I have just come from that very place, which is cursed with a press gang that damn near resides there. I have a good mind to turn you in.'

'The purser were in on it an' all,' the carpenter protested, an exclamation that got him a glare from the master, who was, by his high expression, not a man to be easily browbeaten, while the gunner would not catch his eye. The bosun, master at arms and the one-legged cook, who had had nothing to do with the whole affair, just looked affronted.

'I cannot see, sir, what it is you can turn us in for.' the master protested.

'Is it not an offence to aid and abet a man wishing to desert from the navy?'

'Which I did not do,' the bosun insisted, to nods from his two drinking companions.

'We acted for all,' was the response from the senior warrant, seeking to make them equally responsible. 'It may be that such an act is an offence, yet you have no proof unless your men have been caught, which I take leave to doubt, for you would have told us so if they had.'

'Are you saying you will deny granting them that aid?'

The master held up a hand to shut up those complaining who, unbeknown to Pearce, had been no part of the arrangements. 'We most certainly will, sir, though I fail to see how we could be posed with the question, given your trio had no business to be on this ship anyway. We looked at the problem with care and did the best we could for them, even to the article of my drawing for them a map and allowing the use of our jolly boat, so that's an end to it.'

'Not supposed to be on the ship?' Pearce asked, trying not to look confused.

'Not mustered, was they?' the gunner said, finally emboldened enough to speak. 'They ain't on the ship's books, so how can they run from a barky in which they had no business bein' aboard in the first place?'

Pearce had come here to threaten them with exposure, on the very good grounds that to do so was to ensure their silence as to the identity of his friends and it was only on hearing what had just been said he realised that the tactic was not necessary. That press gang lieutenant could ask till he was blue for the names of recent deserters, but the Pelicans would not come up. That did not get them off the hook, there was still a description out for Michael, but without a name to put to it, half its use would be lost. You could not apprehend a man merely for his size and birthplace.

'What do you mean you did your best for them?' he asked, really to gain a little time to think.

The response was gabbled as they tried to get their part of the story in, with three particularly claiming ownership of the notion of the boat, which sent the carpenter puce with rage and turned the whole thing into an argument, but out of their disputes came the alternatives to what they had done and they were all worse. Well aware of what an admission of error by him would achieve, Pearce adopted a humble tone.

'Gentlemen, I owe you an apology.'

'You have the right of that, sir,' the master insisted, only partly mollified and still glaring at his companions for their temerity and failure to see how his superior intelligence had so readily found the solution to an intractable problem.

'Yet I am bound to seek to find out what will you say if you are asked about my men?'

'Sir, we will deny any knowledge of your friends, even if, in order to lessen their own punishments, they say we helped them. Why, I would not even admit they were aboard the ship and neither, sir, would any one of us. As far as HMS *Fury* is concerned they do not exist.'

'The purser would say the same?'

'He might be a robbin' little bastard, sir, but he is no fool, and by the bye, he is looking out for you.'

That got a shrug: the man could wait. These fellows had given Pearce what he had hoped for, even if it had come about in a different manner. His threat to turn them in had been posed to gain their silence; they would cling to that anyway. A warrant and description might come as far as Portsmouth, and if it did would any of these men see it and make the connection? If they did, would they tell the authorities or keep their mouths shut for fear of involvement? If the answer could not be definite, the conclusion was likely to be that, given human nature, for not to do so was to risk punishment themselves of an unspecified nature.

'Any road,' the gunner, said, 'you was gettin' them protections.'

'Which I have in my pocket.'

'Then,' the master spoke again, obviously confused, 'where is the difficulty?'

'The difficulty, sir, is this. I now have no idea where they are, so I would be obliged if you would draw for me the same map you penned for them.'

Not, Pearce thought, that such a thing would be of the slightest use!

Over his own dinner and a bottle of wine it soon became obvious he only had a single course of action and that was to keep an eye out at the one place he could be sure they would seek to get to, the Pelican Tavern. To go charging about the country asking for them would be to put them in jeopardy, not rescue them from arrest. He just had to trust to them to find their own way to London and into the Liberties, while he kept an eye on the sources of news in case they were apprehended. With that in mind he would return to Nerot's Hotel and wait, making daily visits to the Pelican to see if they turned up. Then he recalled his letter to Pitt and there was some pleasure in thinking if the sod had replied and wanted his services, Pearce would have the pleasure of telling him he would damned well have to wait.

There was one useful task to perform before looking

159

for HMS *Fury*'s purser and departure, one he undertook the following morning, which was to see how the prize he had taken was being valued. That took him to the offices of the port admiral, who acted as vice admiral of the coast for this district and oversaw the work of the Portsmouth Prize Court. There, on enquiring how things were proceeding in the matter of the merchant vessel *Guiscard*, he was asked if it was any of his concern.

'I am the officer who took her as prize.'

The clerk before him opened and thumbed through a ledger, making a great play, once he had found the page he was seeking, of taking his time to read what it contained, though the entry was clearly so recent he must have known what it said.

'Says here she is claimed as the property of a religious order, a French and papist one by the look of the name.'

'What?'

That led to another slow perusal of what was written. 'They claim to be émigrés run from the mayhem over yonder water and that they set sail in this boat you're claiming as a prize. Can't be that if they own it and have come to England to escape.'

'They don't own it. The man who owned it was killed trying to flee the mouth of the Loire. The priests and nuns we found aboard were his passengers.'

That got him a direct look from the clerk. 'So they was, indeed, running from the Revolution, sir?'

'Yes, but they would have been victims of the Jacobins if myself and the men I led had not got aboard.'

'There is a comment to say they rescued some British sailors who were adrift and a request to be granted any reward for the service.'

'You may find this hard to accept from religious folk, but that is a lie.'

'I would not put it past a papist to produce an untruth,' the clerk said, gravely, 'Nor an Anglican divine for that matter.'

'I was adrift with men from HMS *Grampus*, it is true, but it is we who rescued them, not the other way round.'

'You will be Mr Pearce, then,' the clerk said, his name information once more extracted from the ledger. 'And your representative is a Mr Davidson, right?'

'It is.'

'Well, you best take it up with him, for word has been sent of the counterclaim by the Order of St Eufemia that the boat be their own and if it is to be sold then any monies raised should go to support them.'

'How do I prove it's a prize?'

'The only way is to go to the prize court, sir, which is overseen by a judge and let him decide. Or you might come to an amicable settlement. Mr Davidson, your prize agent will advise on the route to follow. I take it you has witnesses to back up your claim?'

About to answer in the affirmative, Pearce realised that at least three of the witnesses could not be called and when it came to the others, members of the crew of HMS *Grampus*, they could, by now, be anywhere.

'Tell me, is there such a thing as a prize taken which is not disputed?'

'Rare, sir, very rare.'

Outside the port admiral's office, Pearce made straight for the London coach, having decided that, given the state of his purse, and the news he had just received, the purser of HMS *Fury* would have to wait.

The look on Ralph Barclay's face when Devenow told him of his wife meeting and talking to John Pearce had been a picture of pure spleen, which had him volubly cursing the fact that he had ever come across the man. He was not in the presence of people who were about to point out to him he was the author of his own misfortune and neither was Barclay the type to admit such a truth to himself. He glared at Devenow as though he were the cause, but the man was accustomed to that and took no notice – to him his captain could do no wrong and that included the number of times he had been fetched up at the grating for his endemic drunkenness and flogged. Ralph Barclay was, to Devenow, a hard man, but a fair one.

'Unpleasant as it is to hear, sir,' Gherson had said, 'it does not alter the real purpose of Devenow's task, in which, I have to say he has succeeded admirably.'

That compliment had got Gherson a sour look: Devenow had no time for him because he was a slippery cove, secondly because he was too close to the man he admired, and lastly because, when it came to serving Captain Ralph Barclay, he was fresh to the duty. Devenow had served in Ralph Barclay's ships during his previous commissions and had missed the man when his captain had been beached before the present war, which he thought madness on the part of those who ran the service. As soon as he heard on the grapevine that his old commanding officer had been given HMS *Brilliant* he had volunteered and got aboard her fast, unaware that, on seeing him, his hero was not entirely pleased.

The reason was straightforward enough: Devenow was a drunk and bully, inclined to browbeat those weaker than he into passing to him their ration of grog, an article he would hoard until he could drink himself near to insensible, at which point, whoever in authority was unfortunate enough to come across him, found they had a right handful to deal with, given Devenow was a real hard bargain and almost always the toughest member of the crew. For all his reservations, Ralph Barclay had found Devenow to be as useful as he was pestilential, and in action at Toulon the man could have been said to have come close to saving his life, an act for which he had been rated as a servant, though he was singularly ill-equipped for that role.

'We have,' Gherson had continued, 'the name of the attorney to whom she went, and if that produces the evidence we asked for, then it indicates clearly she has lodged the original papers there.'

Devenow, who could not read, had badgered people in the street to tell him what the brass plaque on Studdert's door said, and being a large brute with an ugly face and a threatening manner he had not waited long to be told. A little snooping had established that the man's place of business occupied no more than the ground floor and that there was a barred window at the rear to his main office.

'That does nothing to tell us how she came by them.'

For Gherson the temptation to sigh needed to be suppressed: the captain was being stupid, for matters had moved on. It made little or no odds who had supplied those papers, even if it was Sam Hood himself, and that was very unlikely: if he had been inclined to act he would have done so off Toulon where his authority was near absolute. What mattered was that they existed and were in the possession of someone who could harm Barclay's career. If he was to prosper he needed to keep the captain out of trouble; in short, Cornelius Gherson had to ensure that nothing blighted his chance of another command.

'We must wait and see what happens,' Gherson had insisted. 'Only then can we formulate a plan to deal with the situation.'

'It must be resolved before I go to sea. I do not want to be in the position of turning down a plum because of this.'

'Even, sir, to the point of illegality?' Gherson had asked.

Ralph Barclay had been about to reply in the affirmative, but he checked himself, looked at Devenow and, despite the fact that he reckoned the man would never betray him, requested him to leave the room, only realising when he did so, that he should have troubled to come up with some excuse, even if it was only to assuage the fellow's pride. Devenow, in what was a rare event, had given him a look that reeked of disrespect, not that it lasted long, being transferred to Gherson in quick order.

'Devenow, trust me, man,' Barclay had said. 'It is for your own good I desire this.'

That had been received with a growl of, 'Aye, aye, Capt'n,' and, shoulders dropping, he had departed.

'When you say *illegality*, Gherson, what do you mean?'

'I cannot see how we can come by those papers by honest endeavour, sir, and I would remind you, that as of this moment, our supposition that they are stored in the offices of this Studdert fellow are mere speculation.'

'Let us then, for a moment, see that as being the case.'

'The only way to secure them is by theft.'

'Do you see yourself up to such a task?'

'God no!' Gherson protested.

'Then,' Ralph Barclay had demanded, far from pleased at the response, 'how in the name of damnation are we to go about it?'

'Sir, the requirement is to break into a building without alerting suspicion and once inside to open, if this fellow is anything like his peers, at the very least a well-padlocked strongbox, for if your wife has left those papers with him she will not have done so without saying that they are of value.'

'I'm waiting,' Ralph Barclay had growled.

'There are people who can undertake this, so it is a case of finding them.'

'A task, I suspect, for which you *are* admirably suited.'

Gherson demurred. 'Let us say, sir, that I know

whereabouts to look, but, and I say this straightaway, it will take time and, given there is no cash reward for any forced entry, the payment for the services of the kind of fellows we require will need to be a substantial one.'

The two men had locked eyes, Ralph Barclay sure that if Gherson took funds for a payment to some felons, then not all of them would reach the men he needed. Gherson was well aware the captain knew and was not in the least fazed by the direct stare. He was tempted to say their association was one of mutual benefit but that would be too open: as long as it was understood, it did not have to be stated.

'And who will these fellows be, Gherson?' Ralph Barclay had asked eventually.

That had got the captain a wry smile. 'Just as you were wise enough to send Devenow away, so that there would only be me to witness this conversation—'

'Which I will deny ever took place.'

'Precisely, sir, and for the same reason, should I be able to find the right person, you will have no contact with those I will employ to carry out the aforementioned task and they, I am sure, will not be able to incriminate a man whose name they do not know.'

A soft knock at the door had Gherson going forward to open it at Barclay's nod. The small package that passed through was soon opened and Barclay read part of the testimony from his court martial.

'Is that what we think it is?' Barclay nodded. 'And not in your wife's writing?'

'No,' Barclay replied, his face growing furious, for in

his mind he was back in the captain's quarters of HMS *Brilliant* when she had barely weighed from Sheerness, in his hand then a letter given to him by a reliable member of the crew, a strange letter, not least in its contents but in the singular style of the writing. 'But, by damn, I recognise the hand, for I have seen it before. This was written by John Pearce.'

If the journey to Portsmouth had been full of discomfort it had, at least, been made in a spirit of hope; the return, no better, was made in a very low state of mind indeed, given he now had three cases in dispute for prize adjudication. Yet, that was not his main concern: in his mind's eye he could not avoid the recurring picture of his friends being taken by either a press gang or as the result of a hue and cry. In the wild imaginings which plagued him, the very least they suffered was a sound beating; at worst they were shot by musketry or dangling from ropes hastily thrown over a tree branch. There was also the nagging fact that he was not as well off as he had supposed himself to be, one that came back with full force when he finally entered the lobby of Nerot's Hotel; would he be forced to once more run from a bill?

'Lieutenant Pearce, sir, there are several letters for you.'

Anticipating William Pitt, he was disappointed: two were from Davidson, one regarding the lack of a settlement yet with Captain Benton's widow, the second referring to the *Guiscard*. But the one that intrigued him most was a note from Emily Barclay, requesting a meeting, at his convenience, but as a matter of some urgency.

What, in the name of creation, he asked himself, can she want to talk to me about? A silly question really, since it could only relate to her husband. Then the thought occurred that, if she named it as urgent, then he was master of how it should proceed, and it was not just curiosity which had him pen, in his reply, that if they were to meet and talk, it should, at the very least, be over dinner, which would not be taken at the ungodly hour employed by the navy but at a later time, when with candles lit and time to converse, perhaps John Pearce could go some way to mitigating the impression Emily Barclay had of him and damn the expense.

There was another thought, but that had to be suppressed as too fanciful.

CHAPTER TEN

Sometimes the right thing to do was to let Charlie Taverner take the lead in things and this was one, he being a fellow who had spent his life seeking to outwit the law. If he was troubled by what Michael admitted he had done in that tumbledown hut, he hid it well, merely acknowledging that if it had needed violence to get clear, so be it, though he knew and said plainly that it increased the danger they faced, which gave extra impetus to the rowing that went on throughout the rest of the day. They remained offshore even when the light began to fade, though they closed to within sight of the breaking waves.

What followed was a cold and dispiriting night afloat, each taking turns to snooze, with only the light from a weak moon to show them the white line of the shore, wondering if the calm sea on which they were bobbing up and down would stay that way; they knew the English Channel for what it was. Daylight came and breakfast of a shared bottle of beer, bread and cheese, did little to lift their spirits. Having been in a brown study since then, taking his turn both rowing and bailing the boat, for it was indeed a leaky one, Charlie announced, very emphatically, they must abandon it and get back on dry land.

'Why?' Michael asked.

'It be about odds, mate, and I don't reckon this weather to hold all the way to the Thames. We might find we're bein' driven on to a beach where we don't want to be. Best to pick our spot to go ashore. Apart, think where we are and the direction in which we is going.'

If Rufus looked confused, Michael was not. 'Soundings.'

There was a death knell quality to the words, though in peacetime it meant a happy return: in war it was the hunting ground of both naval vessels and floating press gangs, the place where most sailors were taken, because the law stated that, once a cast lead found the seabed, then they were within the limits that they could be legally coerced into naval service. For all the brouhaha about innocent landsmen being pressed ashore and with violence – true, as the Pelicans knew to their cost – most hands, real seamen of the kind needed to properly work the ships of war, were recruited out of merchant vessels returning to these shores from foreign parts, and their destination was the same as their own: the narrows between France and Dover, the anchorage at Deal and finally the River Thames and London.

'And what happened to us the last time we was in

such waters?' There was no reply necessary to that: they had been pressed for a second time.

'What do you suggest, Charlie?'

'We keep going till the tide is low, Michael, then we should look for some rocks by which we can land without leaving a trace and sink this bugger so it stays on the bottom when the tide comes in.'

'Why not just leave it?' Rufus asked.

That got a sharp response. 'You might as well hang a flag. What do you think anyone looking out for us will say when they see an empty boat bobbing about?'

Michael responded more gently. 'Sure, we need them to be confused, boy.'

'Agreed?' Charlie, demanded, looking at the Irishman, satisfied when he got a nod. 'Those pistols you got loaded?'

'No, Charlie, 'cause I don't reckon to use them.'

'Why ever not? From what you told me about the way you dealt with them two buggers in that hut, there's precious little to lose.'

'Sure, doin' murder won't help us.'

'Might scare some fool off.'

'No, Charlie.'

'Suit yerself, Michael. That you're here at all is good, 'cause I ain't sure you needed to be.'

'Why Charlie Taverner, you're goin' soft.'

'In the name of Christ, row,' Charlie growled.

They had to bypass the first set of rocks – black, low and slime-covered: there were womenfolk with children crabbing in deep pools, and further on the shore opened out into the strong outflow of a river and that required some hard rowing to get clear. Then the sea state got up, creating a heavy swell, and with the tide starting to make enough to cover the low strand of sand, Charlie settled for shingle, backed by flat ground. He insisted that the boat be sunk as far out as they could manage, so it was a soak to the waist they got, in freezing sea, on a far from warm day.

Even then it took many blows with the butt ends of the oars to make holes big enough to let water flow in at speed, added to downward pressure from all three to take her from wallowing to sinking, this while waves came in to hit them chest high, with the wind chilling them even more. The oars were just as much of a problem: they would float whatever they did, so they had to be taken ashore and hidden.

'We need a fire,' Rufus moaned as he sat on the shingle, dripping water.

'What we need and what we get are two different things,' Charlie insisted, though he was shivering as much as the others. 'Now, let's get shod and away from this shore; happen when we find some shelter we can light a fire.'

'Has anyone got flints?' Rufus asked.

Michael laughed as he crunched his way up the bank of stones. 'Holy Mary, flints! Do you not know how to get a fire going with two sticks?'

'I was born in a house, not a cave.'

'Rufus,' Michael joked, 'we are in need of someone born in a manger.'

'You'll do if you can make a fire.'

As they walked inland, Michael gathered the wind-dry tops of the marsh grass for kindling and had his friends pick up old and dry twigs. They found, not far from the shore, a deep series of connected copses bordering fields both fallow and tilled, then a clearing where the light could penetrate the tree cover and still hide them from view. Michael used his knife to make a point in a finger-thick piece of straight wood, and with patient spinning into a second bit of dry timber, accompanied by the careful laying of cracking leaves and dry grass, got first smoke and eventually a glow from the dried grass, gently adding the tiniest spills as he blew on air.

A hint of flame allowed him to add the spills, then twigs and finally bits of wood, albeit thin. It took an age to get anything like a real fire going, and a lot of hunting about by the others to find the means to keep it fed, but in time the trio were sat round a blaze, feeling truly warm for the first time in two days.

John Pearce was happily warm, standing legs spread and back to a glowing coal fire, looking around the private dining room he had booked, though there was a wonder at what it might cost when he got the bill. The table was set with an excellent display of fine crockery, silver cutlery and crystal glasses, set off by the deep-mahogany colour of a round table large enough to accommodate eight people. To one side there was a narrow board of the same wood, with water-filled hotplates in the middle, a decanter of wine at one end. He was dressed in a dark-green coat, which had taken a great deal of effort to acquire in time – and a handsome tip to Didcot – for he had no notion to appear before Emily Barclay in naval uniform.

He had checked both the setting and the menu – careful, in the way the seating was arranged, to avoid any hint of intimacy: they were set as far apart as the table would allow, though there were two deep and comfortable chairs on either side of the fireplace for a more relaxed conversation, and a long settle against the far wall which, Pearce was sure, had witnessed much activity of a carnal nature in the past. He doubted there would be any of that tonight.

'Your guest, sir,' Ezekiel Didcot intoned from the doorway, as he showed the lady in. As she passed him, and as Pearce moved away from the fire, the servant threw the kind of look one man affords another when he is in the presence of a rare beauty.

'Good evening, madam,' Pearce said evenly. He did not wish to use her name, or allude to her married status and he waited until Didcot had taken her cloak, hat and muff, then exited, closing the door behind him, before apologising for the formality of his greeting.

Her reply was pointed. 'I hope, sir, it will set the tone of the evening, for this is far from a social occasion.'

'Mrs Barclay, I had hoped that by taking dinner together we could perhaps show each other the degree of courtesy we once enjoyed.'

'I agreed to dinner, Lieutenant Pearce, because you insisted you would not see me otherwise.'

Pearce could not avoid a slight smile. 'So you doubt my motives?'

'After your disgraceful behaviour in Leghorn, sir, how could I do otherwise?'

'I am curious to know by what means you arrive at the conclusion that my actions are any of your concern.'

Emily reddened a little, and it had nothing to do with the heat from the fire, which highlighted her eyes. That same fire, and the candles all around the room, were picking up the colour of her hair too, which, given her slightly arch mood, made her look stunning.

'Sir,' she responded, 'if a man is found in the streets of an Italian city in nothing but his smalls, having been obliged to flee from a lady's bedchamber, I cannot see how it is not the concern of any right-thinking person. You shamed your nation, sir, and your colleagues serving in the British Fleet.'

Pearce threw back his head and laughed. 'Would that include your husband, madam, whose actions are so exemplary?'

'I have not come here to defend him.'

'Nor, I hope, the officers and midshipmen you accuse me of dishonouring, most of whom, while I was dallying with a lady of some beauty and high rank, not to mention delightful conversation, were enjoying their time in the whorehouses of that same city of Leghorn. I think, by comparison, given I confined myself to company of some refinement, I come out of the time we spent at anchor there very well.'

'I find this conversation untoward, sir,' Emily protested.

'No doubt, because polite society does not allude to the very common fact that most of my sex find their pleasures in fleshpots, not connubial bedchambers.'

'I erred in coming here.'

'You are not my prisoner, Emily.'

That got a full blush. 'I do not allow you permission to use my given name.'

The gentle knock at the door, to which Pearce responded, brought a halt to their dispute. Didcot entered carrying a tray on which sat an ice bucket, from which protruded the neck of a bottle, wrapped in a linen cloth.

'Your champagne, Your Honour,' Didcot said, 'as you ordered. Would you care to have me serve it now?'

'Please,' Pearce replied, quite taken, and in truth, part-amused by the way Emily Barclay was suppressing her fury at his temerity in producing such a celebratory offering.

Part of her wanted to storm out, for the advent of that most inappropriate wine was like a deliberate insult, almost as if he were saying 'you cannot resist my charm'. Running through her mind she reprised every conversation she had ever had with this man, in not one of which, as far as she could recollect, had she been in control: it had always seemed to be him, and his assurance was infuriating, never more so than at this very moment.

Underlying her anger was the knowledge, regardless of how deep she sought to bury it, of the reason for that. She found John Pearce attractive, had done the first day she clapped eyes on him; not in his behaviour, which was reprehensible, but in his manner, which was the very antithesis of her husband: Pearce was compassionate where he was cruel, humorous where Ralph Barclay was a grouser, a man dedicated to the pursuit of women, with a very clear idea of how to trigger a compliment and bring on a blush, as against one who had no notion of the workings of the female mind at all.

Emily was not so naive that she would miss an attempt at seduction and she knew Pearce had attempted that more than once, quite ignoring her married estate, in a way so much more assured than that of any man who had ever paid court to her. He had about him a natural urbanity so at odds with the provincial mores with which she had grown up. There was no bumbling shyness with this man – his aims were direct and obvious: she had spotted that in their first exchanged glance, the day her husband had clouted him for that very kind of look.

'Fill the glasses and leave till I ring for supper.'

Now he was staring at her, not with any trace of wickedness; in fact, his eyes were soft, brown and warm and, if he was not actually smiling, there was nothing strained in his features, underscoring that, if she was nervous, and she was, he appeared not to be. Try as she might, Emily could not avoid thinking he looked both elegant and handsome in that well-cut green coat, the concomitant thought, which she failed to stop herself from conjuring up, being that he had looked good in his naval uniform as well. Salvation for the direction in which her mind was going came from avoiding his steady gaze to look around the well-appointed room.

'It was unnecessary to go to such trouble, Mr Pearce.'

'That will be all, Didcot.'

The servant was taking an unconscionable time to pour two glasses of champagne; nosy, as all servitors are, no doubt hoping for a snippet of gossip to take down and share with his confrères in the basement: if he had no absolute knowledge of what was going on, the atmosphere was crackling enough to provide a damn good guess – that settle, which had seen much service, he knew, might see more this very night.

'Your Honour,' Didcot replied, gravely. 'I shall await the bell.'

As soon as the door closed Pearce picked up both glasses and presented one to Emily, who hesitated to accept it.

'I thought, since we have both survived our recent travails, that a toast to our shared good fortune might be in order. Surely, madam, you would not decline a celebration of being alive after being cast adrift in an open boat?'

Taking the stem, aware that what she had just heard was an excuse, Emily looked into the golden bubbles rising to the surface. 'Is it not bordering on treachery to drink such an obviously French wine?'

'This,' Pearce replied, grinning, 'is a monarchical pressing. The grapes were no doubt picked when King Louis was still on his throne. So a toast, to you, to all of the crew of the *Grampus* and to a happy return, excepting, of course, the fool who set the ship alight.'

'The last time I drank champagne was in Toulon.'

'Sadly, I doubt the Toulonnais are drinking it now, but I will happily add to my toast a wish for the safety of those poor unfortunates we had to leave behind.' With a quick nod, Emily acceded to that and drank, feeling those bubbles tickling her upper palate. 'Now, might I suggest, we sit down and you can tell what it is you must so urgently see me about?'

She did not move. 'I would have thought, sir, that was obvious.'

'If it is obvious to you, it is not to me.'

'You would force me to say it.'

'You must, in truth, do so at some point in the evening.'

'I believe you intend to ruin my husband.'

'If I can, I will.'

'Might I be permitted to ask how you intend to proceed?'

'Only if you both sit down and having done so assure me that you have come to plead for yourself and not for him.'

'Would that make such a difference?'

'At this point I have no idea, but I must say I would be disinclined to do anything that would simply aid your husband's cause.'

'You hate him so much?'

'More, madam, than any man alive.' That was not strictly true: there was one man he hated more, even if he had never met him, a Jacobin zealot called Fouché, whom he held responsible for the death of his father. 'And I must tell you that hating my fellow man is not a normal state of affairs for me. I was raised to think otherwise.'

'I know nothing of your background.'

Emily was lying; quite apart from what she had picked up in conversation, especially with Heinrich Lutyens, she had been obliged to translate a letter for her husband shortly after HMS *Brilliant* weighed from Sheerness, one Pearce had written seeking intercession to get him released from the navy, and once his true name became known, for he had been entered in the frigate's muster book as 'Truculence', his parentage was rapidly established. If she had never heard of the Edinburgh Ranter before, her husband had told her much about Adam Pearce. It was, and she knew John Pearce would smoke it, nothing less than an attempt to delay the real object of her visit, to soften him up so that a blunt refusal of her plea would be harder to make.

'Would you like to know?' Pearce asked, his motives for allowing the subject to be aired very different from her own. Before she could say yes, which by her expression she was about to do, he added, 'That is, of course, a two-way affair. You must, in all fairness, share the story of your upbringing as well.'

'I fear, sir,' Emily replied, for the first time allowing a smile to cross her face, 'you will be mightily bored.'

'No,' Pearce said emphatically. 'There is no way in creation that you could bore me.'

'Perhaps,' Emily gasped, taking refuge in her glass to hide a blush deeper than any which had preceded it, 'it would be best to call for dinner to be served.'

Having spared no expense – he was after all engaged in an attempt at seduction, even if he doubted progress would be achieved on this occasion – John Pearce set out to show that he was a man who knew his way around both board and cellar. The food had been carefully chosen as had the wines, and while he obliged Emily by telling her of his peripatetic upbringing, that was interspersed not only with enquiries as to her background but with comments on what they ate and drank, not in a swanking way, but showing he was a man of the world.

The oysters were fresh from Whitstable, which allowed him to discuss the relative merits of those and their Normandy cousins; the fish, a deep-water bass, had been cooked in thickly packed salt to keep its flavour, the crust having no effect on the taste once filleted, accompanied by a wine from the Upper Loire; while the cut of beef, set off by a robust Hermitage, was a cross-grain one called an *onglet*, uncommon in England and served in a mustard sauce with small roasted potatoes.

'Such detail, sir, the careful observation of what you consume, is not an English habit.'

'But, madam, it is very much a French one, which is why I think their cuisine is so much more varied than ours.'

'I was raised on plain fare to your tastes, I fear – roast meats and game.'

181

Pearce lifted his glass of red wine. 'Then I shall recommend it to your entire sex, given the result it has produced is one of great beauty.'

She dropped her eyes. 'Sir, you must not address me so.'

'I would have you tell me why I must not speak the truth as I see it.'

'It is unbecoming.'

'Because you are a married woman?'

'Yes.'

There was a lightness of humour in Pearce's tone as he responded to that, for he had no notion to spoil what had become a pleasant mood by mentioning to whom she was wed. 'Then I can only conclude that it is an estate the French treat with the same attitude as they do food. To a Frenchman experience is all, in whichever room it is attained.'

'Sir!'

'You blush at a compliment, which I do assure you I mean.'

'That is the whole point. You should not say what you mean.'

'I cannot stop myself.'

'You must,' Emily insisted, feeling in her extremities a tingling sensation that went with the beating of her heart. 'You are too forward.'

'Then, if I am less so, do I have any hope of penetrating your reserve?'

There was only one avenue that would deflect the way this conversation was going. 'I came here to request you to desist in the action you propose to take against my husband.'

'I know.'

'On the grounds that others will suffer should you succeed in ruining him.'

'I am aware of that too, but I hope you have not come here to plead for your nephew as well as your husband.'

'My pleas would be for myself. If you bring him down, you will also damage me.' Looking into Pearce's eyes, which were not soft now but hard and uncompromising, Emily knew she must be totally honest: nothing else would serve. 'I must tell you that I have taken a decision to live apart from Captain Barclay. You may have suspected he sent me here to intercede with you . . .'

'It would not come as a shock to me that he would do that, but I do think you would decline, even if he had a grip on your affections.'

'It is enough that you understand it is not so. In fact, my being here would only increase his fury.'

'Perhaps,' Pearce smiled, 'I understand more than you are saying. I must also add that nothing would give me greater pleasure than that your husband should have good grounds for his feelings.'

There was no flippancy in the words – much of the evening had been spent in a kind of banter – neither in John Pearce's mind, nor in the way they were delivered, and in his eyes was a directness hitherto lacking: there was no way to miss the seriousness of what he was saying and Emily Barclay did not, which caused her to stand up.

'I made an error in coming here and I must go. Please call for my coat and hat.'

'Depart, with nothing resolved?'

'It seems to me, sir, that you have made plain the price you would extract for compliance and it is not one I am prepared to pay.'

'Emily Barclay,' Pearce sighed. 'You are beautiful beyond measure and you are also honest and very brave, which I know, for I have seen you tend to wounds on men that would make a matron twice your age blanch. It is because of that I have gone too far, pressed too assiduously, but I do assure you it is not a thing I embark on lightly.'

'I do not follow your drift.'

Pearce was aware of a subtle change in his feelings: in setting up this meal he had approached Emily Barclay in the same manner, and with the same purpose, as he would have done with any other attractive female. Yet right now he was acutely aware that he wanted her to think well of him, in a way that had nothing to do with his initial aims. It was not a shock, it did not come as a bolt-from-the-blue revelation, but John Pearce knew he was actually smitten in a way he had never been in the past. He wanted her to like him as a person and he badly wanted her company in every imaginable respect.

'You see me as a rake, hence your objection to my behaviour in Italy and, being honest, I cannot deny that the opportunity to engage with you in a conversation that might prove amenable was too good to resist, yet—'

Emily gave him no chance to finish, for she lost her composure then, as much angry with herself as with

John Pearce. 'It was more than that! You have set out to charm me, sir! You have set out to seduce me with your wines and food and your interesting life story, which does not want for a degree of sympathy, and this taking place in a private room away from prying eyes. I was a fool to accept your invitation and I should have departed as soon as I saw it was not to occur in a public place.'

Pearce had stood up with her, as a gentleman should. Now he came closer and was impressed by the way she stood her ground, which was typical of her nature. Emily Barclay would not back down and it was very endearing.

'You will, I think, not thank me for saying so, but having spent the last hour or more in your company, my interest has moved on to a degree I could hardly have thought possible.'

'What are you saying, sir?'

He took her hand and lifted it to plant a kiss on the back. 'You know exactly what I am saying, Emily.'

'My things,' she croaked.

'Only if you insist.'

'Which I do.'

'Of course,' Pearce replied, moving to ring the bell for Didcot. 'But with nothing decided, I think you and I must meet again.'

They stood in silence till Didcot responded, each with their own thoughts, each assuming they knew what the other was thinking, which, in the way of such things, were entirely at odds with the truth. Pearce was castigating himself for being too open, while Emily saw in his sad smile an attempt to engage her sympathy and get her to change her mind and stay. He saw in the firm set of her jaw a determination to resist him come what may: to her it was set in anger at the way her thoughts were so unclear. Part of her wanted to remain in the room and she hated herself for the weakness of such a position.

Naturally, Didcot, ordered to fetch her outdoor garments, did not help either of the principals with his mixture of obsequious acceptance of his instructions, mixed with his barely disguised smirks over what he assumed had happened. To his mind, the man he was set to serve had tried it on and got an elbow for his pains. Once in her cloak, Emily merely nodded to Pearce, thanked Didcot as her manners demanded and left.

It was odd, the consequences of her departure: for John Pearce, as he surveyed the disturbed table, there was the realisation of a degree of disappointment that had nothing to do with thwarted carnality. For Emily Barclay, sat in a hack, there was a feeling of emptiness in the pit of her stomach that, having eaten and drunk well, she found inexplicable.

'I'm damned if I will see him again,' she swore, in the way that one does to seek fortitude.

Ralph Barclay sat stripped to the waist, feeling an apprehension of forthcoming pain of the kind he had experienced too often of late, which caused him to ask the doctor attending him for a tincture of laudanum. The man's frown was annoying, as was his Scottish burr as he advised a dependence on the opiate to be injudicious, unwelcome advice to a fellow who had come to see it as something to ease not just physical discomfort but those of the worried mind as well. He was also wondering why it was all medical men now seemed to be Scots, a damnable race even to a man whose antecedents, and indeed his very name, were Caledonian, though so far distant in the past that such an association could be discounted.

'Are you ready, Captain?' the man asked, once he had sunk the black and bitter liquid.

'Aye,' Barclay replied, though he would have preferred to wait till the laudanum took full effect, not a welcome notion given he was paying this fellow by the hour.

The doctor approached his stump and leant to sniff, seeking corruption, grunting that all seemed well. 'There is no anger on the surface either, sir, so I propose to give it a wee tug if you are game.'

Game! Ralph Barclay thought, this is no damned game, but he nodded for the fellow to proceed.

The string of the ligature hung from the end of his stump, the skin around it puckered and pale, the arm above now wasted where it had once been muscled, for it was never used now. Gently the doctor took hold of the end and his patient closed his eyes in anticipation, keeping them so and wondering what this quack was doing. He only opened his eyes when the doctor spoke.

'Come away clean, sir. Your arm is fully healed.'

Looking down at the stump, Ralph Barclay saw the

ligature was no longer there and only then did he see it swinging in the hand of the smiling doctor. His heart lifted and not just from the lack of hurt, for testing it previously had always been painful. With the wound healed he could return to duty. HMS *Semele* would be his.

CHAPTER ELEVEN

Having never met a special pleader before, John Pearce was unsure, having spent an hour of the morning with one, whether he was glad to have broken that run. Not that Theodore Lucknor was an unpleasant fellow, far from it: he had a lively countenance on a head somewhat too large for his body, a mass of thick, curly and unruly black hair, eyes that positively sparkled with the various emotions he took no care to conceal, added to a booming voice – exaggerated by the confines of his cramped office – and a mischievous grin when the occasion warranted it. That he saw the justice of the case this man before him wanted to pursue, he left in no doubt, it was how to carry it forward that puzzled him and that was his occupation in life, to prepare court papers in pursuance of the wishes of his client.

'Perjury, sir, is a crime that must be pursued in a criminal court, it is not a matter that can be brought before a judge as a civil matter. The question, and it is a trying one, is how to get that unwieldy article, the law of the land, to act.'

That last statement was accompanied by a loud smack of his fist on the desk, which both sent up a cloud of dust and dislodged several spills of paper: Lucknor was not a tidy man, nor did he take much care in his dress, while his fingers, stained black with ink, showed how much time he spent with a quill in his hand.

'If I had those court martial papers . . .'

'I am bound to say, Mr Pearce, that the case would not be advanced one jot by their survival. True, given other factors, they would have proved deadly in court, but it is the very things, those other factors, which you must have.'

'There is no doubt, Mr Lucknor, that an illegal act was committed in the Pelican, and there are folk who still frequent the place who know that well.'

'But you must have evidence of the identity of the perpetrator, sir, and that can only be provided in an unquestionable manner – given you say that Barclay did not enter the tavern – by those with whom he did the deed. I refer to the members of your press gang, and they, I hazard, will not come forward and volunteer to incriminate themselves in an act being touted as illegal.'

'So my testimony, and that of my friends, would carry no weight?'

'I think you do not know a court of law very well, Mr Pearce, so you do not understand what a good defending counsel can achieve. You openly admit that two of your companions in misfortune are under threat for their past misdeeds, which leaves you with your

Irishman, who may be, as you said earlier, one of the most upstanding fellows you have ever met in your life, but it will be easily established that he is partisan in your case, while you will be asking a jury to take his word against that of a senior naval officer that . . .' Lucknor paused then to glance at the notes John Pearce had given him, '. . . the act was deliberate, not, as he stated at his court martial, an error brought on by an inexperienced midshipman mistaking the nature of where they had landed.'

'Which is a blatant lie,' Pearce barked. 'Something you do not seem to wish to accept.'

Lucknor held up a hand and smiled, not in the least put out by his client's tone. 'Mr Pearce, I am on your side, but it is necessary that, in the execution of my duty to you, I am obliged to point out the problems as well as anything we can use to advantage. We are, after all, talking of seeking a conviction which can only be brought about if the commission of the alleged offence is beyond reasonable doubt, reached by a jury who will have more in common with your Captain Barclay than a lower-deck witness, and that is a high standard to meet, one which brings with it a very serious sanction. A conviction for perjury can send a man to the gallows.'

'I wondered if you believed me.'

'That is not an unusual reaction.' A hand swept through his mass of curls, making what was already unkempt even more so. 'I do not doubt for a second your assertion that the court martial of which you speak was a travesty and I do not doubt that lies were told, but to get your Ralph Barclay before a judge will not

191

be easy, for as soon as your motion to do so becomes public the Admiralty will move heaven and earth to have it dismissed. You are challenging not only one of their officers, but as they will see it the whole area of press gang conduct, as well as the verdict of, to their eyes, a properly constituted court martial. You allege deliberate corruption on the part of one of their senior admirals, and, if not collusion, then a blind eye turned by Lord Hood to a tainted result. In short, you are proposing to put, in a time of war, the whole structure of national defence on trial. I fear you have not understood the magnitude of the task you have undertaken.'

'Are you saying it is your opinion that my case is doomed?'

'Most assuredly not, but what is required is an unimpeachable witness and . . .' Lucknor looked at Pearce's submission again, 'perhaps, one more who, you suggest, will wilt under any sort of examination.'

'Toby Burns has the backbone of a worm.'

'You can only be sure he will do so if you have another witness, in this case I suggest the midshipman who was actually with Captain Barclay on the night in question.'

'Richard Farmiloe.'

'You say here he is a decent and upright young fellow, this underlined by the fact that he was sent away with you to the Bay of Biscay; in short, Captain Barclay would not have been able to persuade him to lie.'

'And Lieutenant Digby, what of him?'

'He was aboard HMS *Brilliant* when she was berthed at Sheerness, was he not? It was he who

192

commanded the ship in which you were diverted to La Rochelle, but he was not present at the actual illegal impressments.'

'Is he of any use?'

'If he would swear that Toby Burns *was* aboard HMS *Brilliant* on the night in question, he will be of vital interest to a court, for he can establish without peradventure the boy is lying, and that is the only question to put to him, of necessity in writing.'

'Everyone you have mentioned is at present serving in the Mediterranean.'

There was a thought then that he might be going there himself soon, that was until he reminded himself he had heard nothing from Downing Street for days: it was not to be relied upon.

'And' Lucknor added, 'you do not have the power to command they come home to make the case, only a judge can order that.'

'So?'

'We write some letters, Mr Pearce, carefully worded ones to both get from Farmiloe and Digby the truth of various assertions. With the former, we just need him to confirm that he was with Captain Barclay while Burns was not. If Digby supports that by saying the lad was on board the frigate, then we have a strong argument to confound any attempt by the Admiralty to apply for the case to be thrown out as specious. We can then demand that the people in question be returned to England for a proper trial and that Captain Barclay be held pending that.'

'And Burns?'

'He must be asked for the truth, and if he is tempted to lie once more, he may, and I shall make this plain in a roundabout fashion, be digging a grave for himself deeper than the one he is already in. Perjury is as much a capital offence for him as it is for his uncle. If he tells the truth, your case is made without the need for any other witness. Damn me, sir, he could bring down this Hotham fellow, to boot. Would that not be a coup!'

Lucknor paused then and looked directly at John Pearce. 'Now, sir, there is the matter of my fees for the work described, and I must enquire of you how you are going to fund what will happen if we succeed in getting your case to court.'

'Perhaps if you could give me some indication of costs?' Pearce asked.

It was a chastened client who left the lawyer's office, a man wondering if he wanted either Farmiloe or Toby Burns to be brought back to England, for if they did return he would need a king's ransom to make use of their presence.

When it came to travelling overland Michael O'Hagan was much better equipped to cope: he had not only done it previously, but he was country bred, having been raised on an Irish farm, albeit one wracked by debt and too many children. Having walked from there, crossing both his own island and much of England in search of work, while needing many times to sleep under the stars, he knew what to keep an eye out for in terms of where north lay as a constant: the russet colour of tree bark, the leafing on trees, which tended to the south and the sun, even on a path, where the cold side would be muddier. There was also the matter of shelter and getting fed, which depended on the skill to snare and cook small creatures like birds and rabbits, but also to spot where there might be a chance of some labour in exchange for a meal.

He also knew they must find some kind of watercourse to follow: to have something to drink was essential, and common wells were used by too many people, while around such streams wildlife and vegetation were abundant, cover was easy to find, for there were always bushes and trees, which in turn meant wood for a fire as well as a modicum of shelter should rain threaten. What he found first was hardly more than a brook, with little in the way of flow, but it served to provide the means to assuage their thirst and allow them to shave, each man taking it in turn to employ their guard razors to scrape off the beginnings of another's beard, eased with the lye soap they had dunned out of *Fury's* purser, though in the case of Rufus that tended towards fluff – something he had been much ribbed about aboard ship, where a clean chin and upper lip was an absolute requirement of the service.

'It never does to appear like a beggar when you're looking for a bit of work or wishing to avoid the eye of a watchman.'

'Careful with that blade,' Rufus replied, as Michael worked on his neck.

'Be better plucking that than wasting a well-stropped edge,' joked Charlie.

'Where do we go from here, Michael?' Rufus asked, his chin still in the air.

'As long as the sun comes up to our right hand we are on the true path. Brooks lead to bigger streams and rivers, rivers is where towns are . . .'

'And the law,' Charlie insisted.

'So we skirt round them.'

'How far did that master say we had to travel?'

'Some sixty-plus miles to London, land miles, but we will need to work a longer route to stay away from trouble and most of all, if we can, bridges. Do you not recall our shipmates saying to stay away from them?'

How to avoid being taken up when on the run was a constant topic below decks and there were those who boasted they could travel from one end of the country to the other without risk, but they always insisted bridges were the most dangerous places, for too many were locations that could not be crossed without paying a toll, which meant queues to get through and folk watching out for miscreants, as well as just plain nosy bastards.

'As I said before, we go by church spires as much as we can, for there will be a walking right of way twixt two, used by all. Spot one on the horizon and that is a hamlet, two or more is a town, one that seeks to touch the sky is a city and those we avoid like the Black Death. Lacking those, we use the signs of which I have told you. We will seek to stay off roads and keep to fields and not travel too far from the rise of the sun till it starts to dip, for as soon as it does we must look for shelter, wood and set snares in the hope of adding to our food.'

'We're bound to come across folk,' Rufus opined, rubbing his new-shaved cheek.

'Sure, we give them a cheerful top of the mornin', for to be sullen or to avoid their eye will make them wonder.'

'Some will wonder, whatever,' said Charlie. 'There are folks whose nose is never still.'

'You can spot trouble, Michael, can you?'

'As much as he can cause it, Rufus.'

Michael looked at Charlie as he said that, wondering if he was referring to what had happened with those crimps, but the man was smiling, so perhaps it was the memory of what Michael had been like when full of drink in the Pelican. Better still, it could be just a jest, for if they had rubbed up against each other in the past, Michael's sticking with them had tempered the way Charlie seemed to behave towards him.

'You're a town boy, Rufus, and Charlie, well he's London, where there are any number of folk looking to make their way by dobbing their fellows as a way to feed themselves. Country folk are less inclined to think ill of a man just for being on the same path and, as often as not, the farm owners will trade a meal for labour at a time of sowing and planting, though harvest is best, so we might find we has a chance to work to eat, as I have done many times in my life.'

'And those folk will say, "Where have you come from?",' said Charlie, 'so we need a story to tell.'

'Can you talk like an Irishman, Charlie?'

'Why would I want to do that?'

Michael hooted his reply. 'Christ in heaven, Charlie, no one ever asks a Paddy what he is doing in this country of yours, they just think we have come to make our way.'

'To steal our work, more like.'

'Which,' Michael grinned, 'would never have caused you any harm, given you've never done an honest day's toil in your life.'

Charlie cupped his hands in the brook and pulled out some water, replying with very evident pride as he sucked at it. 'I will drink to that, Michael.'

'So where now?'

'Through these trees, Rufus, to the meadow beyond, which being left fallow, will not be tended till the time comes to cut for hay. We will keep to this water and hope we come across a blind farmer with three lovely, lustful daughters and flagons of cider in his cellar.'

Rufus looked excited by that, until even in his slow mind the unlikelihood of such luck was obvious.

'Cost apart, Heinrich, it will take for ever, if my man Lucknor has the right of it, even if I were to carry them myself. A month or more to get a letter to the Med and as much to get one back again, that is if they trouble to reply.'

'If you do get sent out you can take a deposition.'

'But are they going to tell me what I want to hear?'

'You think they might not?' the surgeon asked.

'Farmiloe and Digby might look to their careers before they look to my needs, and I doubt that little shit Burns will respond to a letter at all.'

'As would you, if things were reversed.'

'True, but that little bugger will run a mile just at the sight of me.'

'How did you find this Lucknor fellow?'

'Davidson put me on to him.'

'I seem to recall you mentioning something about eggs and baskets?' Lutyens said.

'I had little choice when your man refused to represent me.'

'He had good grounds and he did send me round a note of explanation.'

'I encountered Emily Barclay on his doorstep, so I don't need one! Mr Studdert clearly feels he cannot act for both her and I, even if what you tell me is true and our cases are in no way related.'

'It does not put me in a happy position either, John.'

'For which I cannot be blamed, brother.'

'Emily confides in me.'

'She is "Emily" to you?'

Lutyens responded with a grim smile. 'When you have worked together to cut the limbs of a screaming man it brings you close.'

'I had dinner with her last night.' That surprised Lutyens, a fact very evident in his wide-eyed expression. 'The meeting was at her request, but it did not go as well as I had hoped.'

The reply was a touch sour and very sarcastic. 'I

cannot begin to guess what you hoped for, John.'

'Don't be so pious, brother, I am a man and she is a fine-looking woman. But I'm sure you can take a stab at what she was after. She came to ask me to drop any action against her husband. Can you guess why?'

'Easily, since she had told me she intends that he should support her. Ruin him, destroy his career and she will be damaged too, by being left without support.'

'I have thought on this, Heinrich, and it does not add together. Can you see Ralph Barclay volunteering to support a wife who will not share his bed?' When Lutyens did not reply, Pearce added, 'I wonder, if she confides in you and she seems to think it a possibility, whether she has intimated what lever she can use to persuade him to do so?'

Lutyens threw up his hands. 'I have no idea, John.'

'You could ask her, brother.'

'I will do no such thing. Please remember I am friend to both of you.'

'Then, as a friend to both her and I, would you ask if we could meet again?' The way John Pearce said those words got him a very sharp look from his friend. 'I am serious, Heinrich, and you can say to her that the meeting place can be one of her choosing.'

'What reason would I give her?'

'Tell her I very much want to apologise.'

Looking at the tall brick house he knew so well, Cornelius Gherson wondered what had become of the lady who had resided there: was she still in place, or had her husband,

Alderman Denby Carruthers, got rid of her in the same manner he had tried to rid himself of the man who had seduced her? Certainly the old booby was capable, and that brought on a shiver as Gherson recalled the night the toughs employed by the alderman had tipped him half-naked over the parapet of London Bridge into the fast-flowing Thames. If he had not landed right by the boat from HMS *Brilliant*, he would be dead for sure, just another battered and unidentifiable cadaver found on some downriver sandbank.

To come here might be seen as foolish, but given Carruthers would think him long dead, and he was here at a time when he suspected the man to be occupied about his business affairs – he was wont to visit Lloyd's Coffee House each day at this time – Gherson saw the risk as minimal. He had spent the morning at the offices of Ommanny & Druce, where he had happily pored over the accounts for the portfolio of Captain Barclay, before listening to various ventures proposed by the Druce partner of the firm.

The fellow had quizzed him about how he had come to serve the captain, as much as the clerk had made pointed enquiries about their proposed investments. Such curiosity had not bothered Gherson: he saw it only as an attempt to discover the nature of the man they were dealing with, and he had been sharp enough to pick up the very subtle hints that his welfare might be better served by taking the advice of the firm rather than rejecting it – in short, the man was seeking to find out if he was open to act more for them than for Ralph Barclay.

It had been a pleasant game and one Gherson enjoyed – nothing openly stated, many possibilities delicately hinted at, suggestions advanced only to be partially withdrawn, expressions of hope that a less calculating mind would have easily missed. The replies Gherson had made were suitably evasive without being totally negative. He had also not sought to avoid any enquiries of a more personal nature, seeing them as natural breaks in an interrogation that, too intense, would be obvious. Besides, the story he had told was one well filleted and vague: there was no mention of his previous life in London or of the employers for whom he had worked.

What was on offer would add to those ambitions he already entertained, and the possibilities for personal gain that might accrue from an acceptance of what Druce had been hinting at could be substantial. That had to be set against both what he had now and that which he hoped to gain in the future. There was no regard for Ralph Barclay in his thinking, the man was merely a means to an end, and if he knew his place on the captain's list, so did Gherson.

Barclay's prospects for employment, with his arm now healed, were excellent – right at this moment he was on his way to Chatham to look over the ship he hoped to command – and there was money to be made as a clerk aboard a third-rate ship of the line. In time, if he survived, Barclay would get a first-rate and one day he might get an active appointment as a flag officer – that was where the real wealth lay when there was a war on!

Whatever, Barclay was helping him establish his credentials in a service where fortunes lay in wait, and if he prospered, Gherson would remain in his employ. If Barclay faltered or got himself killed, then he had some hope of being so recognised that another post would quickly become available. Ultimately, he wanted to be the senior administrative aide to an active admiral on a profitable station, for he had heard quick enough that such functionaries, whom no admiral could do without, were the ones who really coined it; if a clever mind could purloin a profit from a single ship, what could one extract from a fleet? Perhaps, one day, when he had the means to do so, he would confront Alderman Denby Carruthers and see how he reacted to the notion that, in trying to dispose of him, he had not only failed but paved the way to him making his fortune.

Cornelius Gherson would have been less sanguine about where he stood and the thoughts he was reliving had he read the mind of Benjamin Druce, who knew that a man he thought long departed this world, was alive, well and parading around the streets of Westminster. If Gherson had seen in the prize agent's enquiries a desire to establish his character, Druce had been more concerned to fix his true identity, not that he had been in much doubt. His wife's brother had come to him previously in some distress and unsure what to do about his young wife's infidelity when he discovered what was going on.

A man of the world, Druce was no stranger himself to the more refined form of brothel. He had counselled against any act which might bring about disgrace to the family, such as exposing Catherine Carruthers – the ripples of such revelations could spread to unforeseen places. The cause of the problem lay with the young swine who had seduced her – remove that pestilence and the boil would be lanced, and given he dealt with the navy, and collected bounties on behalf of Impress Service officers, the finding of the men to do the deed required presented a minor problem.

He had considered telling his brother-in-law of Gherson's re-emergence, but what had previously been a cost-free bit of aid would not fall into the same category now: if no commitments had been made in their conversations, there had been a very clear understanding of where advantage lay for both parties, and in the information Druce held, he had a very useful lever on Barclay's clerk, one that might produce great future benefits. The man would be going to sea soon, so matters were better left fallow.

Sat once more in the Pelican Tavern, on his now-daily visit, John Pearce ruminated on his prospects, which did not look brilliant given the lack of a word from Pitt. Mind, he was accustomed to that – his fortunes seemed to be, and had been for a very long time, in a state of flux. He was aware that not being in the true sense a naval officer hampered him greatly – had he taken the normal route from midshipman to his present rank, he would very likely have served with dozens of people and met hundreds more, for the navy was a very social organisation: no two ships could be anchored in sight of each other without invitations flying across the intervening water.

With such contacts it might have been possible to discreetly seek news of Michael, Charlie and Rufus, without in any way alerting those he did not want to, certainly in Portsmouth, which must act as the natural headquarters of the Impress Service. Not being a member of some kind of London club, places to which provincial news-sheets might be sent, left him in ignorance of any hue and cry, plus descriptions, which the local chronicles would publish.

Then there was money, that perennial bugbear, which he was going through at a rate and doing so without any certain knowledge that more would be forthcoming: he had heard enough tales not to enjoy any certainty that matters would proceed smoothly. Thankfully, his captures were legitimate, a warship and an empty merchantman. Taking cargo vessels, especially neutrals, was fraught with peril, indeed, many a naval officer had found their supposed captures declared illegal, then faced the need to make the kind of reparations to the owners that induced bankruptcy.

From his coat pocket he extracted and looked at Arthur Winston's card – he had looked out for him in person but to no avail. The fellow did his business in the city, which was only to be expected, his place of work being not far off, hard by Blackfriars Bridge. Tempted as he was to call, he had to put it aside, given nothing could be done until he knew the whereabouts of his companions. Lucknor had sent the proposed letters off to the Mediterranean, carefully worded missives, which asked questions and invited replies that would in no way incriminate the correspondent.

That, of course, did not apply to Toby Burns: he had been informed of what he faced if he continued to lie.

———

CHAPTER TWELVE

The further inland the Pelicans progressed, the safer they felt and, if they looked odd on a rainless day to be wearing loose-fitting, foul-weather tarpaulins, then it seemed not to trouble any soul they came across – mostly farm labour types who, if they looked at them with some misgivings, displayed only the natural reaction of any bumpkin to a strange face or a soul that might steal their labour and thus the bread from their mouths. They walked the said footpaths through fields and over stiles that had been in place for centuries, kept between one house of worship and another. Many of the churches, being part of multiple benefices served by a single vicar, were closed – those with open doors they avoided – though the graveyards provided a place to rest weary limbs.

Charlie Taverner, if you left out being pressed into the navy, had never been out of London, so much had to be explained to him: every village was a parish, every parish had a church and, given there would have been at least a curate in olden times, hard by that would be a decent dwelling, and often the whole would be contained in the grounds of a substantial manor house, owned by some local worthy, who both lorded it over the neighbourhood and held the right to choose the divine who said Mass in what they saw as their private chapel, into which they would allow their tenants and workers for Sunday service.

Very occasionally they would skirt round one of the truly great residences, huge mansions of red brick and grey stone, with stable blocks and coach houses attached, deer in the park and guards on the dovecotes. The homes of magnates, these places often sat in their own shallow valley, served by a tower set on a nearby high point, the sure indication of its presence long before the house itself came into view, with a circulating donkey on the ground floor, plodding wearily, drawing up from the well to a cistern so high every room in these near palaces could be supplied with running water. When encountered, they crossed any part they were obliged to with a weather eye kept out for stewards and gamekeepers, for the owners of such stately piles were jealous of their possessions, which extended beyond the sheep and cattle in their fields to the game in their woodlands as well as the fertiliser in those dovecotes.

If they got close enough there would be farm buildings as well, some soundly built houses for the higher estate workers. There were cottages too, these for the people who tilled the soil and tended the livestock, and it was telling that Charlie, who rarely gave an impression of caring for another living soul, was incensed by the tumbledown and damp nature of the contrast when he spotted the many that were so badly maintained as to be near-uninhabitable.

'You would be a leveller, Charlie?'

Michael asked this as they passed a row of low stone buildings, with unpainted, broken-down doors, gaps where there might be windows, great holes in the roof thatch, that had got Charlie going: they were also being examined by a dozen near-naked children, covered in farmyard filth, who looked, with their stick-like legs and pot bellies, in great need of nourishment, while behind them lay a field full of fat sheep and beyond that another showing the first signs of growing wheat.

'I'm beginning to see the sense of what Pearce's old pa was about, mate,' Charlie opined, 'there bein' those who has plenty and them that has nowt, though I confess I have seen worse in my own backyard than those poor mites we just passed.'

'Then, Holy Mother of God, don't cross to Ireland, Charlie, for there are sights there that will make you weep.'

'Is it time to stop yet, Michael?' Rufus asked. 'Being at sea does not do much for your walking legs.'

'We're on an estate, Rufus. We will be chased off, maybe with a fowling piece, if we seek shelter here. We have to keep going until we are well away from any buildings and further yet if the woods we seek border a village.'

That had already been explained: villagers poached,

which meant that the lords of the manor, or the farmers who tenanted them, employed men to guard their game down to the last grey rabbit or fat pigeon, and, given poachers could be vicious – they were likely to be doing the deed for need rather than pleasure – those fellows were often armed.

'I still say you should load those pistols, Michael.'

There was an undertone in that: Charlie had suggested not only loading them but also sharing and Michael had refused both. 'No, Charlie, for without a ball and powder they can't be a threat; while loaded, given we are novices in the use of them, they could see us hung.'

Walking on they came to a long, straight roadway wide enough to take a coach and, given the numerous ruts, it looked well used. With the sun on the dip and the road going in the direction they sought, with no one in sight and ample woodland cover on either side, it made sense to use it to make some easy mileage, though they stayed close to the forest edge. Twice they had to take deeper shelter, alerted by distant sounds, once for a carriage, the second time for a lone horseman with big saddlebags on what looked like a shire horse, so large was the animal in the flank, but given the fact that it was a good roadway there was surprisingly little traffic, which meant they were covering a lot of ground with minimal effort. It was Rufus who first alerted them to the bridge; he had spotted the slight hump in the road before the others and it looked as if the road continued straight beyond it and, more importantly, there was no sign of any dwellings nearby.

'Maybe we should stop now,' the youngster said, not without a certain note of pleading in his voice: if the road was easier than field, hedgerow and furrow, he was still wilting.

Michael looked up at the sky to make a judgement, though there was little to see given the woods hemmed them in. The forest either side was not of the thick kind, the trees were various, with numerous bushes jostling for growth and the ground carpeted with leaf mould, fallen branches and the occasional rotting trunk, seemingly extensive and perfect for their needs, as had already been proved when they got out of sight quickly and easily.

'Looks the same t'other side, Rufus, and the time it will take to get over the bridge is of no consequence. We'll find a place to rest then.'

Walking on, they saw the stone trough on their side, a place for horses to drink and maybe a spot where someone was employed to keep it topped up, which induced caution, though there was no indication of a soul about and the birds seemed lively in their singing. Above the trough, when they came close enough to see it, a fresh-looking poster had been tacked onto a tree and it was only natural to look at it.

'Holy Christ!' Michael swore.

The drawing was not him absolutely, and he struggled with all the words excepting Irishman, which he knew only too well, while the written numbers the trio could, between them, decipher, but it did not take much in the way of sense to ask how many men of Ireland, of well over six foot in height and with girth to match, set over a square head bearing a mass of black curls, wearing ill-fitting clothing that was close enough to canvas, could be found walking the roads in these parts.

'Theft and assault,' said Charlie, those being words he knew only too well.

Rufus was silly enough to add what he could read, albeit he traced it with his finger. 'Is that a twenty shillings reward?'

'Enough to keep a yokel for a year,' Charlie answered.

Michael was not listening: he was already heading for the bridge and the woods on the other side. There would be no easy progress now!

HMS *Semele* was a mess, but that was only to be expected: a good half of her rotten timbers had been ripped out and replaced with fresh wood, as had her entire deck planking. Floating on the inner reaches of the River Medway now, just out of dry dock, she sat very high in the water, showing a great deal of her copper and Ralph Barclay was just in time to see her innards right down to the keel before they began to add ballast, and was thus happy to know that the hull looked very sound. Even with all his years at sea, he had never been in a ship that did not stink of bilge and rot, so it was a pleasant and unusual feeling to tour one which smelt only of freshly hewn wood and the caulking tar.

'English oak in the main, sir,' said the assistant shipwright, who had been deputed by the dockyard supervisor to show him around, trailed by a rather silent carpenter. 'But with so much construction under way there is some Holstein timber and the knees are from the Adriatic.'

The visitor nodded with understanding: every dockyard in the country was working flat-out to build new warships and there was only so much suitable oak growing in English forests, never, indeed enough, while he was also aware of how many tens of years a tree must be given before it could be of any use for shipbuilding. Added to that, when it came to shaped pieces of wood like the riders, as well as hanging and transom knees, single pieces of wood that had to be whole and the correct shape – so-called compass timber – Italy seemed the most fecund source. 'Nothing much grows straight south of the Alps' was an old naval joke.

His greatest pleasure was to enter the area of the great cabin and admire the space – free of any bulkheads it seemed enormous, but already he was imagining the furniture and carpets with which he would make it habitable, this while Devenow, who had come with him, inspected the pantry. There was a pang then for Ralph Barclay and it was not just the idea of Devenow cooking and serving his food: the furnishing of his cabin should be a discussion between him and his wife, not that he wanted his quarters to look anything but manly, but women had a way with decoration, an eye for the little things which he knew he lacked.

'When will she be ready for sea?'

'Once the ballast is in, sir, she will be ready to take in

her stores, much of which are those that were stripped out and warehoused when she went into dock.'

'The rest?'

The reply had a certain sour note. 'Sir Charles Middleton's innovations mean they are already allocated, sir. There will be no delay once an officer is commissioned to command her.'

'I sense a degree of disapproval.'

'And you are not mistaken, Captain Barclay. We have enough trouble with pilfering in the dockyard without having warehouses full of everything a ship requires sitting and waiting to be lifted by the thieving mitts of the population of Chatham. The walls of the dockyard require to be patrolled hourly and the gates watched in case they succumb to bribery. The people on the Navy Board do not understand the difficulties.'

Middleton's 'innovations', as the fellow called them, had been to create a way to ensure that every ship laid up in ordinary – most of the fleet in peacetime – could be quickly got to sea in the event of war. In past alarms months had gone by while stores were purchased and delivered, the ships sitting idle for want of such obvious things as the means to feed the crew. As comptroller of the Navy Board, Sir Charles had bought everything the fleet required in advance of need and had them tagged, warehoused and ready: spars, sails, barrels of pork, beef and peas, cables, rope for rigging, turpentine, nails, vinegar for cleaning, barrels of powder – just a few of the thousands of items needed to get a ship to sea in condition to take on the enemy.

The discussions that followed for Ralph Barclay, with the rest of the warrants, were entirely satisfactory; he had under his feet as fine a seventy-four-gun ship as the navy possessed, albeit her guns were not yet loaded. All he needed now was a decent set of officers and a crew. For the former, his table back at Brown's Hotel was full of requests for a place: word got round quickly in the service of his possible success and he seemed to have had submissions from every unemployed lieutenant in creation. For the latter, he would need to get busy: he would be provided with the basis of a crew, but HMS *Semele* required over six hundred souls to sail and fight. It was to be hoped the Impress Service was up to the task of finding them, for anyone who had a mind to volunteer had long since taken the bounty.

Once back in London, he sent a letter to the Admiralty, which underlined his good health, as well as his desire to be commissioned into HMS *Semele*, and another, more obsequious, to the Duke of Portland requesting that he use his influence to secure the appointment. Then, in strong anticipation that he would soon have his ship, he began to riffle through the pile of applications. Word had also gone out regarding midshipmen, so he had letters from Somerset to attend to – the usual number from clergymen keen to find a place for their sons – as well as communications from old shipmates, many no longer serving, asking that their offspring be considered; if he did not know most of the lieutenants, he could check for some notion of their competence.

With the youngsters needed to fill his midshipmen's berth, a captain was never sure what he was going to get. Had he not been landed with Toby Burns on his last commission!

That Michael was thrown by that poster could not be in doubt, and in discussing it with his shipmates, after a fitful night's sleep, it soon became obvious that the greater distance they could put between them and the deed the better. Hitherto, if it had not been dilatory, their progress had not been rushed, but that needed to change, which in turn increased the risk of arousing suspicion. Charlie and Rufus killed off at once the idea that they might split up: such a notion did little to lessen the risk to them while very much increasing it for Michael, though the Irishman wondered if their opinion was as much generated by fear as sympathy – if it came to a fight to get clear of trouble, then he was their best hope.

Light and darkness told them they had been four days on the road, but that gave them no idea of how far they had travelled and how much further they still had to go. The weather, which had held good for that time and made at least their morning point of travel an easy decision, suddenly changed and the rain began to fall steadily and continually from a sky full of heavy clouds, which made direction-finding that bit more uncertain.

The further they went, the more inhabited and fertile the land seemed: now the country through which they were walking was high rolling downland

– valleys and hills of verdant grass, tilled fields, the smoking chimneys of numerous dwellings, which meant people to be avoided. There were trees aplenty, but they were woods or small copses, not forest, and rarely of a size; added to that, the route they followed was dissected by many rutted tracks, while if there were milepost signs, they were to this trio unreadable unless they said London, which none did.

Two days of bad weather wore them down. Footsore now, with chafed and aching legs, dripping water off their outer clothing they looked and felt a sorry sight and Michael suggested an early stop as soon as they could find a suitable place. They ended up being halted by a fast-running, clear stream with no real idea of which direction in which to proceed, upriver or down, and while there was shallow water close to the bank it might be too deep to wade in the middle. There the trio spent a miserable night: after so much rain the lighting of a fire was out of the question, for even under the tree cover the leaf mould and any wood they could gather was soaking wet.

The morning brought a break in the weather, a hint of sunshine but little joy, given the trees were still dripping, while the middle of the river was covered in a fine mist. The provisions provided for them had nearly run out; what bread was left was green with mould, the little amount of portable soup could not be heated and also, they looked like what they were, fugitives: unshaven, their clothing stained, and given the course of the stream and the place where the sun rose, a bridge to cross whichever way they travelled.

'We should rest here for the day and seek to stock up on some fish.'

'Are we like to eat anything we catch raw?' Rufus moaned.

'It won't kill you,' the Irishman insisted. 'Many is the time on my travels I had found the need to eat uncooked fish.'

Charlie had his objections too. 'Can't see how you going to catch any without a line.'

'Then for a thief, sure, you're a poor specimen, Charlie,' Michael replied, beginning to remove his shoes. 'These are skills no city fellow will know, so watch as I teach you to tickle them out of the water.'

The stockings followed, to be put away in his shoes. Next he rolled up his trews and his sleeves, waded gently from the edge, over the stones, until the water was near his knees and then stood looking for what seemed an age, the pair on the bank watching him. After a while Michael leant over and gently lowered his hands, wide apart at first, then slowly coming together under the water, a position he held for what seemed an eternity. Finally he stood up, in his hands a fine-looking trout, its shiny body flecked with brown, which did not flap as a caught fish might, but seemed content with the finger being rubbed back and forth across its belly.

'As fine an example of tickling as I have witnessed and enough to see you before the beak at the next Assizes.'

Michael was frozen in place, Charlie had turned his head slowly; only Rufus reacted with jerky fear to the voice, but it was not long before they were all staring at the muzzle of a double-barrelled fowling piece, this in the hands of a leather-clad fellow of ruddy complexion and square build, standing with his high-booted legs set apart. Obviously out hunting, he had come upon them silently, able to get close because of the damp leaves that carpeted the floor of the woods to their rear. Across his breast he wore a powder horn, and on one shoulder he had a satchel with which to carry his kills, while at his side were two dogs of the bird-fetching kind, with dappled brown and white coats, big brown eyes, lolling tongues and soft mouths.

Charlie began to move his hand towards Michael's ditty bag, which contained the pistols, which, even without powder or balls, might pose a counter-threat. 'Stay still, you!' There was no doubting who the hunter meant and Charlie withdrew his hand as the muzzle moved towards Michael. 'Drop the fish.'

That was a command not obeyed. Michael lowered the trout slowly back into the stream and watched it as it swam lazily away. 'You would see a man had up for a creature he has not eaten?'

'Poaching is poaching, man, as you know well, and this stretch of water is on my land, as is this wood. Come ashore.'

'One fish?'

'You will be telling me you would have stopped at one, which I would choose not to believe. Now move, but with care.'

Michael came out of the water with the same ginger steps he had used to get in, his mind trying to work out if he could, once on firmer ground, get to that muzzle before the fellow could fire it off. A gun of the sort he was carrying, and he being out with his dogs, would be loaded with pellets meant to down a bird, not of the kind to easily kill a man. Maybe it was his look that made it seem as if the landowner read his mind. The muzzle jerked again.

'Don't think I will not use this and you, big fellow, will be the first to feel it. Your throat would be the best place to aim, for there is enough weight in each barrel to make a mortal wound on such soft flesh.'

The message was plain, just as the voice was steady and lacking in tremor. Michael knew he was too far off to get to him before the trigger could be pulled. Indeed, looking into the fellow's steady eyes he suspected he would not panic, for there was no indication he was the sort to get flustered. No, he would hold off until Michael got really close, and then do as he promised at point-blank range, take out his throat.

'We are going downstream and you will walk ahead of me, so you two sitting, get up slowly.'

'My shoes?' Michael asked.

'Can stay where they are, which will take away from you the temptation to run. I detect, by your voice, you are Irish, so know this: you will be first in a line of three. Who brings up the rear I care not, but whoever it is will have my weapon close to their very head, which I will take the top off if any tricks are tried, like seeking to escape. The same holds true if any of you seek to reach into a pocket, where I think you might have a weapon.'

'We ain't,' Charlie lied.

'Allow that I don't believe you.'

'Our dunnage?' Charlie said, reaching down.

The word produced a frown on that ruddy face, as if it were unfamiliar, but all three could see understanding dawn, that being a sailor's expression. 'Leave it be. You will have no need of it where you are going.'

'Happen we should take our footwear off too?' asked Rufus.

That brought forth a humourless laugh. 'So you can chuck one at my head, boy? I might be a farmer but I am not a fool. Stay shod and move.'

There was little choice but to comply, there being one barrel each for Michael and probably Charlie, while this hunter had the build to take on and deal with Rufus. These were odds he had probably calculated before he spoke and he clearly had no doubts that help from another source was not required. The muzzle waved again and Michael started off downstream, on a path that was full of the tangle of undergrowth. He could feel the prick of nettles on his bare legs and more than once a bramble caught and scratched his flesh. Before long the wood ended to show an open, rolling meadow, which, as soon as it was reached had the dogs barking and running off.

'Down the hill after them,' their captor commanded. 'You will see the smoke from my chimney; head for that.'

Rufus was at the rear praying the other two did nothing stupid and Charlie got as close to Michael as he could, whispering at the Irishman's broad back, 'We must get out of this, Michael, you most of all.'

The reply was just as soft. 'I will see to him if I can get close, but I doubt he is fool enough to let me.'

'Should have loaded those pistols and had them ready to use.'

'Too late now, Charlie.'

'Is that you plotting up ahead?' the fellow called. 'Well know this, I have been a soldier and I fought for my king in the Americas, so I have seen the wiles of better men than you, and note this especially, that my aim is true.'

The house they were heading for had several chimneys, not just the one, even more windows, was well built and painted a buff colour, all of which told the three captured Pelicans that the man was not of poor stock. From the elevation provided by the hill they could see barns too, more than one of wood and another stone-built, while all around were grazing cattle and ploughed fields. They came to a stile and he saw them over it before commanding them to kneel with their hands between their knees while he crossed himself, breaking the barrels so that he could do so without the risk of setting off his gun, underlining what he had just said to them about wiles. The weapon snapped shut again as soon as he was over and on both feet.

Once past a pen of grunting and snuffling pigs and a duck pond, they came to the house and the cackling geese that guarded it at night. There was a well in the middle of a gravelled area, while around and on the walls were pots and sconces of flowers, and the dogs, having run to their home, were lolling in the doorway; the whole looked idyllic and the smell of wood smoke finished off the impression of a place of rural bliss. They were on the gravel, close to the wall of the well, when their captor spoke again, this time a shout.

'Mrs Pointer, I require you to come to my aid and fetch some rope from the barn, for I have caught three villains trying to poach our fish.' Before they heard the feet of the man's wife on that same gravel they were ordered to kneel, wincing as the stones dug into their flesh.

'Mr Pointer,' the female voice rasped, 'are you mad to apprehend three men on your own?'

'Three boobies more like and I am telling you they are better sport than pigeons.'

Michael had been looking at the stones under his knees, seeking to shift, for with his trews still rolled up it was more painful to him than his companions, but he looked up to place the voice and when he did his jaw dropped, for before him was a woman as broad in the hip as her spouse, with a face he knew well.

'Rosie!'

Her head came forward as she peered into his unshaven face. 'Michael, is it you?'

'God be praised, it is indeed.'

'You know this man?' Mr Pointer demanded.

'She knows me too,' said Charlie.

'Mrs Pointer, my question?' her husband asked, his

ruddy face now bright red and his eyes near popping out of his head: he was clearly not pleased. 'Do you know these villains?'

He was irate, but ample Rosie had never been a shrinking violet and she had a pair of arms to match her other attributes, while in her previous existence she had never struggled to chastise anyone who she thought took a liberty with her. If her husband's eyes blazed, so did her own and her voice, when she replied, held not the slightest trace of apology.

'I do, sir.'

'I demand to know how.'

'Demand, Mr Pointer?' Rosie bellowed, loud enough to have the dogs scurrying away, tails between their legs. 'You can withdraw your demand, sir, for you do not have the right to make it.'

'I am your husband, madam.'

'Michael, Charlie,' she cried, 'get off your knees, you too, boy, for I do not know your name.'

'Rufus Dommet,' was the soft reply, though it was questionable if it was heard over the farmer's shout.

'Stay kneeling, damn you, or I'll shoot you down.'

'You will do no such thing, sir!' Rosie moved then, to stand between the Pelicans and her husband, cutting him off from their view, which only underlined her ample dimensions. 'Put away that weapon, Mr Pointer, for you do not require it.'

'They were stealing my trout.'

'*Our* trout, husband, and I for one would not see them troubled for it.'

'I demand you explain.'

'Which I shall when you deal with your temper.'

'My temper is justified, for I suspect these three to be sailors run from the navy.'

'It is not as simple, as you will discover. These are pressed men and I was present when the foul deed was done.'

'That is not a licence to poach in my river.'

They could not hear what Rosie said then, she moved close to her husband and dropped her voice, but it was not too difficult to work out what it would be, with Michael having the sudden thought that if Rosie was too open the danger might not decrease, he having lain with her many times. Whatever words she used it did the trick, for they heard the sound of the barrels breaking once more on the fowling piece, which had them standing up, for it was not a move they were inclined to make while it was ready to fire. Rosie turned round to find all three rubbing their pained knees.

'What, in the name of the Lord Almighty, brings you to my door?'

'Sure, Rosie,' Michael said, with that big grin she knew so well. 'It has to be that very same deity, bless his grace, the one my two companions so mistrust. But by all that's holy you're a long way from the Pelican.'

She grinned then. 'Further than you think, Michael O'Hagan.'

They could see her husband again now, and if her explanation had seen him take away the threat of his weapon, it had done nothing to erase the fury on his face, which creased even more when Rosie indicated they should enter his house.

'No daughters,' whispered Rufus to Michael, 'but I'll take a wager there is cider.'

Rufus was right, but if there was refreshing drink and proper food, taken at a fine board in a comfortable kitchen, there was also an atmosphere that could be cut with a blunt knife – Mr Pointer was not a happy man and it was obvious, as he listened to Rosie talk with the Pelicans, he was also cocking an ear for the slightest hint of anything that went beyond friendship. Neither Michael nor Charlie could ask if he knew about his wife's previous life – that was a jar of worms best left well corked – and at the same time they had to ensure that Rufus, in his innocence, did not let slip anything untoward.

'It's good to see you so happy, Rosie.'

Michael wanted to say he had sought her out not a week past but dare not. He looked around the well-appointed room, with a huge hearth big enough to roast an ox and from which they had earlier been treated to some thick vegetable soup. The bread they were eating was fresh that day, the remains of the stew they were eating was gently bubbling in a suspended pot above the glowing logs. Copper pans hung on hooks from the thick, low oak beams, blackened but good-quality implements for cooking surrounded the fireplace, while through an open door he could see a parlour with fine furniture and an invisible clock that chimed the quarter hour.

'She was happy afore, she tells me,' Pointer responded, as if he had heard a slur on his own person.

Rosie stood from her chair and went to stand by her husband, placing a hand on his shoulder. 'It cannot be told to you what the love of a good man will do, Michael.'

Thankfully, Rufus's nose was in his plate, so he did not see Rosie wink, and for Charlie and Michael, forced to keep on their faces a pair of fixed grins, it was questionable what she was implying. There was no doubt that Pointer was comfortably off, and recollection would remind both that Rosie had always had an eye for a coin, which was the root of the jealous competition between the two.

Michael, when he came to the Pelican of a night, had the wages from his daily labouring, ditch-digging for the endless house building taking place around the capital, which, since there was more to be had on the morrow, he was happy to spend. Charlie, grubbing for work on the bank of the Thames, rarely had more than the cost of a pot of ale, and too often not even that.

'I will not complain of what went afore,' Rosie continued, 'but I cannot say it compares with my contentment now, for Mr Pointer is not only a good man, but a fair one too.' That sat ill with the expression on his face: he looked like a hangman might study his coming victim, one who took pleasure in his work. 'Now, tell us how you came to be in our woods, and what has happened to you this twelve months.'

That took a long time and all three taking turns to relate their tale, though it was, of necessity, filleted. There was only a passing mention of John Pearce, but an account of his getting them protections was paramount to putting them in a good light. For what had happened since they last saw Rosie came sadness for Abel Scrivens, whom she remembered, and a bit of a prayer for Ben Walker, whom she did not. Nor was it a wise notion to say why Charlie and Rufus had been resident in the Liberties, while care had to be taken about the nature of Michael; any mention of what had happened to create that poster they kept to themselves.

'So,' Charlie concluded. 'We need to get back to the Pelican, 'cause that is where the mentioned Lieutenant Pearce will be awaiting us.'

Michael had spent much time watching Rosie's husband, who had shown no sympathy for the fact that they were wrongly pressed, nor any reaction to the harshness they had lived under as unwilling tars, his only vocal reaction being a snort at the notion of protections. He could be placed by all three Pelicans if they cared to: he was an English yeoman, John Bull to the top of his high boots, a forty-shilling freeholder with a vote and few feelings for those who lacked his means. They had all met his type before, a man convinced of the glory of his country and the way it was ruled, who would tell his friends over a pot of ale that the poor were idle, the Irish untrustworthy, the Scots worse – for they added wily cleverness to their guile – and the Welsh mad. The one thing he could not do was tell his wife what was right and wrong.

What arguments ensued they were not witness to, having been sent by Rosie to fetch their possessions, but on their return they were promised a good night's sleep in a warm bed, a tub to wash in with hot water and a mirror with which to shave, some old shirts of Mr Pointer's to wear, as well as a promise to get them safely to London. Michael O'Hagan's gesture of a pair of fresh-caught and tickled trout for the table was only seen as unwise when he presented the fish to the man who owned them.

CHAPTER THIRTEEN

For Heinrich Lutyens, broaching the mere name of John Pearce to Emily Barclay was bad enough, but he suspected he was being asked to play Cupid and that with a woman for whom he had a very soft spot indeed. Not that he harboured any thoughts that he himself might play the suitor – he was not one of those fellows able to entertain delusions about his own prospects, given he prided himself on having a mind attuned to the vagaries of human nature. Had he not left his profitable practice and gone to sea as a lowly surgeon in order to study his fellow humans in situations of stress: battle, storms, the sheer difficulty of sharing such a confined space with so many others? The volumes of his notes sat on his shelf awaiting the day when he would be able to sit down and compose a paper on his conclusions.

Looking at Emily as she sipped her tea, he wondered if the story were complete, for his ambitions had been met in so many unforeseen ways. Not only had he been able to observe and note the actions of the common seamen and the men who led them, but he had been gifted a group of men so varied in their backgrounds as to appear as a Pandora's Box of attitudes. Pearce had, of course, been the most interesting because of his background, but his fellow pressed men and those who saw him as an enemy had been just as rewarding: the bully Devenow, the slippery Gherson, the experienced hands on HMS *Brilliant*, proper blue-water sailors who had split into two camps: those who sided with the captain as against those who saw that Ralph Barclay had a down on one man and for questionable reasons.

And last of all was the gift sitting before him now, looking as radiant as ever, a sweet, country-bred girl of decent education and upbringing, thrown into the maelstrom of a newly commissioned naval warship. It was not just her relationship with her husband that had brought on fascination, there was the approach she had used to deal with a world so very unfamiliar, the 'tween decks of a man-o'-war, stinking of bilge, unwashed humanity and the flatulent effect of a diet that produced compacted bowels; the way she had aided him with men wounded in battle, squeamish at first, certainly, but overcoming that to become a competent helpmeet with gaping wounds and screaming amputations, as well as showing a natural aptitude for the compassion required for the aftercare.

'Why are you smiling in such a way, Heinrich?' Emily asked.

'Am I smiling, my dear?'

'And staring, too, at me, in the oddest way.'

'Admiration?' That brought on the most endearing blush: if Emily knew she was a beauty she had none of the conceit that usually accompanied such a gift. Knowing he had made her uncomfortable, Lutyens quickly added, 'I was thinking, my dear, of how you have changed between now and the first day we met.'

'It would be true to say,' she replied, dropping her head slightly and smiling sweetly, 'that a lot of water has flowed under the keel since then.'

'A most apposite pun on the old cliché, Emily, yet I have known people face much and change not one whit.'

'We are all changed, I think.'

'None more than John Pearce.' The cup and saucer clinked, a sure sign that the name had an effect. 'You had dinner with him, did you not?'

Those alluring green eyes narrowed slightly. 'Only he could have told you that.'

'I think,' Lutyens replied, temporising, for he was far from comfortable, 'that there is no role so awkward as mediating between two people of whom you are fond.'

'Are you mediating?'

'I have been asked to, Emily, and there is no need to add by whom, is there?' The slight shake of the head allowed him to continue. 'John told me of your meeting, told me what you wanted of him, and also how it ended.'

'And?'

'He asks me to convey to you an apology and a request that you meet with him again, this time at a place of your choosing.'

232

She did not reply immediately, but sat in silent contemplation for what was no more than half a minute, yet seemed like an eternity. 'Thank you for not interrupting my thoughts, Heinrich.'

'Which are?'

'That I should refuse immediately, without any hesitation.'

'Yet you do not.'

'No, and it has nothing to do with his action against my husband.' She looked straight at him then. 'You do not seem surprised.'

'That would be, my dear, because I am not.'

The animation was sudden. 'Why is it I cannot dislike him? Why is it that I cannot wipe from my mind a man who behaves as he does? What is wrong with me?'

'Which question, Emily, would you care for me to respond to?' She shrugged and looked at the cup in her lap. 'Let us take the first, and the answer to that is he is not an easy man to dislike, given there is no hypocrisy in him and much humour, added to a sound sense of his and others' place in the world.'

'Is he not a ferocious radical?'

'No, but he is a gentle one. His father was the ferocious one, but I suspect, though I have no actual evidence, that Adam Pearce would not have hurt a fly. He was a man who sought justice for all, not retribution for a few.'

'Unlike his son.'

'One of the difficulties you have in making up your mind about John is you have not spoken with him often enough.'

That got a sharp rejoinder. 'I have exchanged words with him many times, and on each occasion Lieutenant Pearce has shown the nature of his intentions.'

Given a sudden memory of eavesdropping aboard HMS *Grampus* on the conversation Pearce had had with Lutyens on the subject of those court martial papers, Emily was made uncomfortable, even more so by the fact that she could not admit she had taken them from his instrument chest before abandoning ship. If she had a best friend in London it was he, and she felt by her lack of honesty to be deceiving him. Fortunately, too busy with the train of his own conversation, he did not sense her disquiet.

'I think John Pearce admires you greatly.'

'Then it is unbecoming.'

'I admire you too, my dear.' Seeing a hint of alarm, the additional words were quickly delivered. 'As a dear friend.'

'I do not know if that is flattering or not, given the other friend you mention is a rake, and a self-confessed one to boot. His own pleasure, his own needs seem to be the only thing that moves his mind and the devil take the hindmost. Look at his behaviour in Leghorn, which I challenged him with. Did he blush, did he admit fault? No, he was more inclined to recall the incident with pleasure, and that in my presence! The man has no shame, nor does he have the slightest knowledge of what constitutes proper behaviour. You do not dally with the wife of another man, even one you dislike intensely. You saw my husband strike him that first day at Sheerness, what you did not see, and he did, was the look Pearce gave me and that was not the only occasion. He was flogged for the same act . . .' She paused then and glared at the surgeon. 'Why are you smiling?'

'Methinks the lady doth protest too much.' Heinrich Lutyens held up his hand to stop her snapping at him. 'Do not forget, that I am an observer, and I have seen the way you sometimes look at him.'

'I have done nothing untoward.'

'You most certainly have not, but I have a nose for such things . . .'

And a very strange nose it is was a thought Emily could not express.

'Firstly, do not judge John by what he has done – nothing wrong in his own eyes, I assure you – judge him by what he would do.'

'Which is?'

'That is a question which does not require an answer. Meet him, accept his apology, perhaps ask him again to abandon the pursuit of your husband, though to that I do not think he will agree.'

'Then what purpose is there in another encounter?'

The look they exchanged then spoke volumes on both sides, but neither party was inclined to spell it out. She was attracted to John Pearce and repelled by him in equal measure and Lutyens could imagine how his friend would cope with that, not by abject and insincere contrition to win her favour, but by a defence of his right to do as he wished.

'Are you happy, Emily, in your present circumstances, and how do you see your future?'

She was aware of what he was hinting at, but she was not going to give him the satisfaction of a negative response, an attitude he discerned from the way she arranged her features. Emily did not set out to make herself look heart-stoppingly lovely, that was a mere by-product of her need to appear positive, but it induced in Heinrich Lutyens a pang of jealousy for whoever it was who would steal her heart in the future. That someone would he had no doubt: Emily Barclay was never going to be an old and crabby creature tied for life to a rank hypocrite of a husband. Yet her options in that regard were limited: when it came to hypocrisy the world in which they lived was full of it.

King George, a one time rakehell, now preached domestic bliss while his sons openly lived with their mistresses and the offspring of such liaisons; indeed it was suspected the Prince of Wales had secretly married his and she was a Catholic. Adultery was rife in the upper echelons of society, yet those same people would cut anyone who failed to observe the conventions to which they did not themselves adhere, all this overseen by an Anglican Church more noted for its venality than any true piety. Divorce was impossible, while too open an association, outside marriage, was the route to social death for someone of the stratum to which Emily belonged. She knew all this, but if it troubled her it was not obvious.

'Happy no, content yes, and if I can persuade Captain Barclay to my way of thinking I will remain in that state.'

'You may meet John here if you wish.'

'With you present?'

'If that is what you desire.'

'I will leave it to you to arrange, Heinrich, but I do not wish to be alone with that man.'

That would be, Lutyens thought, *because you do not trust yourself.*

Ralph Barclay was not a man much given to mirth but he was laughing now at a pair of Gillray cartoons he had purchased, one showing William Pitt pissing into the Portland Vase, and a second of the said duke, the owner of that famous piece of antique glassware, pouring those same contents over the first minister's head: in both, a drunken Henry Dundas, Pitt's claret-soaked political fixer, was shown in an equally unflattering light, in the first soiling himself and in the second grovelling at Portland's feet with a written plea for votes.

'I wonder if this Gillray fellow takes commissions, Gherson.'

His clerk looked up from the list of stores at present being loaded off Chatham, two and a half thousand tons in all, which presented to his mind a degree of tempting opportunity. 'I doubt he needs to, sir, given the money he makes from his prints.'

'Should be in the Tower, of course, for if these are not libels I do not know what is. At any rate, they will have pride of place in my great cabin. But I would dearly love something unflattering on Lord Hood to gift as a present to Sir William.' That took the amused look off Barclay's face. 'He's a hard man to know, Hotham, difficult to guess how you stand with a fellow who keeps his own counsel so much.'

He had HMS *Semele* and the possibility of a return to the Mediterranean, so that was a matter of much import: Hood was still in command, so he would need Admiral Hotham to protect him from what he saw as the older man's malice. Putting aside the drawings, he picked up the list of officers and midshipmen he had compiled: how different this was from the way he had been treated with HMS *Brilliant*. With the frigate he had been denied his own choices, and Hood, then *in situ* as the senior naval lord, had foisted onto him men he did not know.

Now he had his own people, all of them known from previous commissions, either in ships in which he had served or those of men he trusted. These fellows would owe their future advancement to his good offices, so they would do whatever he required to run his ship properly and be grateful to him for even a kind word. That was the way it should be: a captain must be lord of his own domain, safe in the knowledge that his list of instructions, in addition to the Articles of War, the overriding laws by which the navy was run, were as a bible to his officers.

'I looked over your suggestions from your investment talks with Druce.' That brought Gherson's head up sharply, the tone not being one of outright approval and there was a goodly amount of personal gain resting on acceptance. 'All I have to say, Gherson, is do not steal too much.'

'Steal, sir?' was the reply as Barclay turned to stare at him.

'I have had occasion to say this to you before, man. I am not of a trusting nature, and while I expect you to look to your own needs up to a point, I also expect that my requirements will be paramount. Now, going over your suggestions again, which one is the high risk?'

The pair locked eyes, but it was an unequal contest; it always was with Ralph Barclay, who was as much a pilferer as his clerk. They had, between them, got a very profitable enterprise going in Toulon, by trading stores from the French arsenals and warehouses for a promise to evacuate a certain number of the officials and their families should the siege collapse – not necessarily a promise they intended to fulfil. HMS *Brilliant's* holds had been full to bursting with powder, cables, sailcloth and many other easy-to-sell artefacts. The loss of Barclay's arm had ruined that, given he could no longer command the ship and oversee the disbursement; the whole lot had ended up in the harbour, thanks to the loss of nerve by the frigate's premier, a fellow called Glaister.

'So?' Barclay demanded.

'The proposed canal to Buxton, sir.'

'Because?'

'Buxton is on a high elevation, so it requires a great number of locks, they are expensive and hard to calculate in terms of construction time and costs. There is a question of whether the projected revenues will meet the interest on the acquired debt, since the traffic projections are speculative.'

'And if they are sufficient?'

'You stand to make a fortune.' The look those words got forced Gherson to add, 'With the concomitant that you could lose everything if the usage is poor.'

Ralph Barclay nodded as he pulled out his Hunter and looked at the time. 'We will put that venture in Devenow's name, then. If it goes wrong he will not mind a debtor's jail and I will get a power of attorney to look after his profits, if they materialise. Now, Gherson, I must be away or I will miss the bargains.'

Ralph Barclay was en route to the auction sale rooms to find the furniture and carpets he needed to furnish his great cabin, the goods of one-time wealthy folk fallen on hard times, of which there were always a number. To have them made, with waiting times of up to a year or more, would take too long.

Rosie's husband hated the idea of waiting till Sunday to travel, though that was tempered somewhat by the free labour he was given over the two days the Pelicans were resident on his property, their presence a curiosity to his normal workers, one he was brusquely disinclined to satisfy. Come the day, he also drew the line at using his coach to transport them to London: for a man like him, such a conveyance was his pride and joy, a measure of his standing and he would not have it sullied by men he still saw as thieves.

From Rosie, more in hints and winks than words, it seemed the farmer had not told his friends and neighbours of the nature of her previous life, while he would hope none of the upright souls who would wonder why he was not at church on this day had even been in the Liberties of the Savoy; if they had, their silence was assured for the sake of their own reputation.

Whatever legend he had concocted to explain her arrival Rosie would stick to, but it did provide for her a very strong lever over Mr Pointer's behaviour.

Thus he found himself driving one of his carts through Dorking and taking, as well as paying to use, the turnpike road that led to London, with Michael O'Hagan laying in the back, not actually hiding completely but keeping his large frame out of view, while Charlie sat up front with Pointer, more by habit than inclination seeking fruitlessly to engage him in conversation, his comments met with grunts, not replies.

'You've got yourself a stalwart there, Mr Pointer. Old Rosie is a right brick.'

That got more than a grunt. 'You would oblige me by not speaking of my wife in that fashion.'

'Suit yourself.'

The words Charlie had used must have played on his mind, for Pointer, when they were well past the turnpike toll, eventually asked in a gruff tone how long Charlie had known Rosie, a question which got Charlie a warning knock on the back from Michael.

'Why, I have known her for an age, sir, and never have I met a gentler soul to a man in need.' That got a look that Charlie understood very well. 'When I says that, Mr Pointer, I means a man in need of a shoulder, for the likes of me, well, I've had a hard life. Never knew my birth mother and I ain't alone in having no idea of who was my sire, my only good fortune bein' that when I was put into the ballot at the Foundling Hospital I was admitted.'

Rufus dug Michael in the ribs and grinned, for

Charlie was spinning a right tale. He had hated both his parents, which he was wont to say often, them being drunks and wastrels, and had known and been raised by them, if being left to fend for himself and needing to steal to eat could be called an upbringing.

'Now I don't know if you is aware of it, sir, but when a little 'un is left for a foundling the hospital takes a token from the poor mother, something by which to identify her child if she should come back one day to claim him.'

The snort that got told all three that Pointer thought any foundling, and their mother for that matter, did not deserve consideration.

'Now, I found out, and you will not mind me refusing to say how, that my token was of value, not just a piece of flotsam, which is the usual. That led me to suspect that I might be the child of a well-born lady.' Charlie's voice dropped a notch, to become conspiratorial. 'Further nosing about, 'cause I is skilled at that, Your Honour, led me to believe that I stood in the way to inherit a goodly estate.' The tone changed again – he became guarded. 'You must not ask how I came by this knowledge, sir, no, that would never do, for other, innocent folk, would be put in jeopardy by disclosure, but I am sure that I am heir to a proper fortune, only I lack the means to make my case.' Now the voice took on a note of well-practised ire. 'I hope you never had to deal with a lawyer, Your Honour, for never was there a more rapacious set of folk than they.'

Michael and Rufus were enjoying listening to this nonsense, thinking Pointer should have known by Charlie's tone that he was being joshed, yet he responded as if what he was hearing was the literal truth, and gruffly. 'I have dealt with attorneys and I agree.'

'Great shame, not having the small amount I need to get my case heard. No more'n ten guineas would do to start a hunt.' Charlie sighed, as deep and heartfelt as it was false, for this was a tale he had told many times, to fools who had been sucked into belief and a share of this mythical money. 'But it is not to be, for the Almighty has never fixed me up with the means. I got close, many a time, but never there, always short by a head.'

Rufus was the first to laugh; both he and Michael had been shaking with silent mirth and he could not contain himself and, of course, that made the Irishman follow suit. Then Charlie could not hold himself back and his tone was larded with humour as he insisted on the need to keep his hand in.

''Cause,' he insisted. 'I won't get nowhere depending on you two for fodder.'

'Spare me this,' Pointer barked. 'I asked about my wife.'

It was Michael who answered. 'Sure, you must take her for what she is and I will wager from the look in her eye and my memory of her, Rosie will never give you cause to doubt her.'

'I am curious as to how you know her so well.'

'And, sir,' the Irishman said emphatically, as it was Charlie Taverner's turn to grunt, he never having reconciled himself to losing out to Michael, 'curious you will stay.'

Rufus got a dig in the ribs: he was still laughing.

* * *

The rest of their journey was undertaken in silence, the only words spoken Pointer's insistence that he would not pay the high toll to cross the London bridges; they would have to walk or boat across the river. Being Sunday they were safe from arrest: the tipstaffs who looked out for felons were obliged to observe the Sabbath Day, and having walked too much since leaving HMS *Fury* they elected for a boat, using some of the coin taken from those crimps to pay for their passage, which given the tide was incoming, was swift.

Landing on the northern bank induced strange feelings: for Charlie and Rufus, it was a kind of homecoming, even if it was to a cold hearth. For Michael it was no longer to be a place from which he could come and go, he too would be stuck here now and that was not a thought to cheer his soul. Just as strange was the sensation of once more entering the Pelican on the only day it was quiet, for those forced to reside in the Liberties took full advantage of the day of worship. There were one or two nods as they made their way to the very seats two of them had occupied the night they were pressed, using more of the money they had to buy some food and porter.

That was where John Pearce found them, sitting in a row and it was Charlie who spoke first.

'I do believe that it's your turn to stand us a drink.'

Pearce grinned. 'It was ever so, was it not, brother?'

'There's no future in staying here in the Liberties, John-boy,' Michael O'Hagan insisted, 'and that goes double for you.'

244

Both tales had been told, of the trio's adventures, Rosie's good fortune included, and what John Pearce had been about in their absence – excepting what had happened with Pitt and Dundas – raising the hopes of Rufus and Charlie for a pardon was unwise given there was still no response to his letter and a journey to the Mediterranean for Pearce, should it ever come about, would lead to questions of how it affected his friends.

The problem with the prizes caused dismay, while the Irishman was only partly reassured by the knowledge that his name was unknown and likely to remain so on the south coast. The discussion had moved on to what course to follow next. Pearce knew from previous conversations of how hard life had been for the men from the Liberties before their impressment – eking out a living was hard and sometimes near to impossible, and he also knew that placed a burden on him of support, an added charge on prospects already strained.

'But there is the problem of keeping you all safe.'

If he had expected some suggestions from the likes of Charlie Taverner, Pearce was disappointed, a lack of any from Rufus being more usual. If they could not stay in the Liberties, and barring Sundays they could not move out of them, then some form of escape must be found. Wild flights of fancy, like a journey to the Americas, he kept to himself, but that did bring on the thought that they would be safer on a boat than on land, with the caveat that the notion would not include the King's Navy: each now had his protection. Pearce still had Arthur Winston's card and that might promise two things: a method to get his friends away

245

from the clutches of the law, while also providing him with income.

'There's a fellow I met that I will go and see on the morrow.' Then he looked at Charlie, he being the most likely. 'You might know him since he uses the Pelican, a man called Arthur Winston?' That got a negative shake from all three. 'Well, he knows you, Michael.'

'Big bugger like him is hard to miss,' Charlie responded, smiling.

Michael's answer was equally good-humoured. 'Need to look behind the wainscoting to find you, Charlie, you bein' a mouse.'

The exchange pleased John Pearce: these two had always had a slightly abrasive relationship; shared danger seemed to have eased that. 'Can you find a place to rest your heads?'

'We can if we can pay,' said Charlie, 'and we ain't got much coin left.'

'I will see to that,' Pearce replied, reaching for his purse, the immediate thought on feeling it that it was not the bulging appendage it had so recently been: it was too damned light now and he had serious doubts if, under the circumstances, Davidson would advance him more.

'Who is this fellow?' Rufus asked.

'A man of business that I encountered in this very place, who might be able to put something our way.'

Pearce did not want to elaborate on what any gainful employment might entail, his reason being he had no desire to hear objections until he had something concrete to propose. If it meant going back to sea, albeit on a merchant not a naval vessel, he might find they were reluctant, not that they could truly baulk, given the alternatives.

Having passed over some money, more than enough for bed and board, Pearce stood up. 'I will be back tomorrow, once I have seen this fellow.'

'Where are you off to now?'

'I'm off to see the queer fish, Rufus.'

'Then give him a hail from us, the creature,' cried Michael, for if Lutyens had the soubriquet of 'queer fish', and was known for his strange ways, he was nevertheless well liked.

What Pearce did not say was who else was going to be present.

CHAPTER FOURTEEN

Having sat drinking tea for nearly an hour and indulging in polite conversation, Heinrich Lutyens had had enough. With John Pearce in a chair on his left and Emily Barclay sat on a settle to his right he felt like some sort of games net with the inconsequential sallies lobbing over him, back and forth, to no conclusion. He had watched this pair for a long time and knew well what they would not openly act upon: that there was a high degree of mutual attraction between them which had foundered on the twin rocks of Pearce's endemic levity and the upright stance of the well-brought-up and slightly prudish Emily.

John had apologised for his previous behaviour, which got a nodded acceptance. Talking, since then, the avoidance of anything contentious could have been amusing if it had not been so fraught with a fear of a gaffe by either party: thus any mention of acts or places in which they had both been involved, like being on board HMS *Brilliant*, the events off Brittany or the siege of Toulon, or people that might spark a disagreement, brought on sharp changes of subject.

The problem was compounded by a lack of directness from John Pearce, to Lutyens his most endearing trait. He was behaving like the worst kind of supplicant bumpkin, fearful when he spoke lest anything he said should give rise to dispute or engender a low opinion. If anything, the atmosphere and mode of conversation suited Emily more than he: this was a game she had played many times in her life as a growing girl of some beauty, attractive to a reasonable list of local suitors who had come to take tea in her parlour and pay her court, with the surgeon deputing for the parents who had many times overseen such visits and ensured proprieties were observed.

The only thing which had kept him amused, and that was an imagining rapidly running out of steam, was the vision of Ralph Barclay in such a setting. He could imagine the room in which he would have made his opening moves to gain Emily's hand, a well-furnished and comfortable Somerset parlour, with the sunlight shining in though the large sash windows on a group that in its formality was like a quadrille. Emily's mother would be an older version of her daughter, a woman who had herself been wooed in like fashion and knew the game in its entirety. Her husband was probably a bluff country fellow, who would huff and puff while wondering when the suitor would get to the only point on which he had concerns: was he in search of a dowry?

Also present, perhaps jealous, would be the main player's female siblings, younger than she but sure they were the better person, seeking to engage the eye of this gruff naval captain while slipping in barbed comments to diminish their sister, asides which would be sat on by a mother who had already made her mind up as to the suitability of the match: Ralph Barclay, on tenterhooks lest he let slip some gaffe which would scupper his chances, would have already been weighed up and assessed as to whether he was an acceptable husband, and that before he even came through the front door. What a farce it was this marriage game!

'What do you think, Heinrich?'

The question caught him off guard, for lost in his visualisation of Ralph Barclay seeking to woo Emily's parents he had not been listening. 'About what, my dear?'

'Why, the suspension of habeas corpus.'

'Is it to be suspended?'

'No,' Pearce responded, 'but it is much talked about and I would not put it past Pitt to recommend it to the king.'

'You, I take it, John, would not approve.'

'Of course not, it's the basis of the citizen's individual liberty. Without it we are at the mercy of tyranny.'

'John,' Lutyens observed, 'we are subjects in this country, not citizens.'

'Which I, for one,' Emily stated, 'am perfectly happy with.'

Lutyens looked at Pearce in anticipation of the

objection, one which should have been automatic; he looked in vain, though his observant eye informed him that his radical friend was having some difficulty in keeping his views to himself. If anyone else had mouthed such an opinion they would have been treated to a discourse on the difference between a polity subject to the whims of a monarch and the serious advantages of a republic.

'Everyone is, of course, entitled to their own view.'

'Dammit, John, say what you believe and stop this pussyfooting around!'

Because of the unbecoming language, that demand got Lutyens a look of shock from Emily and one of surprise from Pearce, who knew the surgeon to be a man who rarely swore, even in exclusively male company.

'Forgive me, both of you,' he continued, 'but I cannot bear this sparring.'

Emily's nose went up and she looked away. 'I cannot think what you mean.'

'You know precisely what I mean, both of you.'

'And,' Emily spluttered, 'I am surprised at your use of language.'

John Pearce was trying to look as shocked as she, but he could not hold it and his shoulders began to shake with suppressed mirth, which rendered the words he spoke a touch breathless.

'For a man who never blasphemes, to do so in such a setting argues he is serious.'

'I am serious, John,' Lutyens replied, his face assuming the same level of dudgeon as Emily Barclay. 'I cannot conceive of what you hope to gain by a total denial of everything you believe in. Tell Emily what you really think.'

That stopped his mirth. 'I fear if I do so I will end up talking to myself.'

'Sir, you make it sound as if I cannot accept a contrary opinion.'

'Emily, will you stop being so arch.'

That got Lutyens a withering look from her half-closed green eyes. 'I look to you for support, not complaint.'

'Support in what, my dear?' was the soft reply. 'Do you wish me to remain silent while you behave foolishly?'

'I was not aware—'

She got no chance to finish, for Lutyens cut right across her, not in a louder tone of voice, but one which was very direct. 'My dear, you are very aware. The only problem you have is in acknowledging what you know to be true.'

'Which is?'

'That you are as attracted to John here as he is to you.'

'There am I,' Pearce said, 'having a care to say nothing contentious, and along comes a fellow known for his circumspection—'

That, too, was interrupted, and more sharply. 'To bring matters to a head! You said, Emily, that I did not see the look John gave you the day he first clapped eyes on you, but I have seen such looks since.' About to speak his upheld hand silenced her. 'And I have seen you, too, look at him in a certain way.'

'Never.'

'Many times.'

'Are you seeking to play Cupid, Heinrich?' Pearce asked.

'Lord,' Lutyens replied, with deep feeling, 'what a tedious time that child of the Gods must have had, if he had to deal with the likes of you two.' He stood up abruptly. 'I am going to leave you alone, and please do me the favour of talking to each other like real people instead of two characters in a badly written play about manners.'

'Were we so?'

'Yes, John, you were.'

Then he was gone, leaving them both silent for a while, until Pearce asked, 'Does he have the right of it?'

'The right of what?' came the soft reply, delivered into her own lap.

'I think it behoves me to make a declaration.'

She looked up then, her face a picture of misery. 'I am not sure that I want to hear it.'

Pearce responded with a wry smile. 'You must, I fear, for Heinrich will settle for nothing less. I am about to speak and I would like to do so without interruption, is that acceptable?' The response was a short nod. 'I will not seek to deceive you; when I invited you to Nerot's Hotel there was, in my mind, albeit without any real hope of success, an attempt at seduction.'

'That, sir, was very obvious.'

'I do not apologise, nor will I do so, for the kind of man I have been, for that would be hypocrisy, to which

I am not given, I hope. I do not think you can doubt that I am attracted to you—'

'Just as I do not feel singular in that regard.' She looked at him then and bit her lip before adding, 'Apologies, you said without interruption.'

'There's no need and you are, of course, correct in your observation, for I can hardly deny being a man. What I hope is that you can – though I admit I did not fully do so myself at that time – see the depth of that interest, something which only came to me on that night. Experience tells me . . .' That got a flash of irritation: it was his experience that damned him in her eyes and he was forced to repeat himself. 'Experience tells me that the upset I caused you was not because I had insulted you by my actions, but that you feared what might occur if you stayed. That, I think, is what our friend is driving at.'

'I have no notion of how to deal with this.'

'It might please you to know, Emily, neither have I.' Since she did not object to the familiarity, Pearce stood up and moved over to the settle. 'May I sit beside you?' She agreed, but moved so they would not be touching. 'I confess that I am smitten.'

'And I confess that I have no idea how to respond. The way you speak, and what you speak of, is anathema to everything I have ever been brought up to believe. Heinrich asked me on my last visit here if I was happy and I lied, for I am not, locked as I am in a relationship with a man I have come to actively dislike.'

Pearce reached out and gently took her hand, feeling, as he had previously, that buzz of electricity up his arm. 'Tell me how it came about.'

Which she did, in a soft voice devoid of animation, and it was a story that was familiar in the society in which she had been raised, a match driven by that very English disease called 'property', rather than affection or love. In telling her tale she had to, perforce, admit of the reasons her parents had been so keen on the match, his only response to take a tighter grip on her hand. A few gentle enquiries led Emily on to a more open explanation of her previous life, as well as the attributes she had seen in her husband, which she now knew to be drawbacks, with an admission that the caused of her lack of discernment came from being too provincial.

'For you, John Pearce, have seen much of the world, and I have seen so little.'

'Not true, Emily. You have seen more than most and I am obliged to tell you that you have seen it with rare clarity. Your bravery, for instance, astounds me.'

'I do not think of myself as brave.'

'People with courage never do, but you have had the pluck to challenge your brute of a husband, which I know was not easy. I cannot think, having listened to you, how your upbringing could have prepared you to act that way, given repression of feeling seems its abiding rule.'

She looked at him for the first time in an age. 'It was not you that brought on my dispute with him, it was the sheer injustice of his actions.'

'For which I will happily settle.'

'Did you think it was for you?'

Pearce laughed gently. 'I have, as you know, a degree

of conceit, but not even I thought you were acting solely on my behalf. Yet I did hope you might have done so, and the real question is, Emily, if that act were repeated, would it be for me now?'

'I am in a state of utter confusion, so I cannot tell you.'

'Which is only to be expected.'

'No! I should know my mind, I should know what it is I want and what I am prepared to do to get it.'

'That flies in the face of the human condition. As creatures we are all confused, with so many varied pressures pulling on our emotions. It does not do for you to berate yourself.'

John Pearce was in a quandary: he had on the tip of his tongue words that would explain the solution to Emily's dilemma, yet he was also unsure if it would be wise to employ them. He wanted to tell her about Amélie Labordiére, high-born, beautiful and married, with whom he had enjoyed a wonderful *affaire* in Paris, tell her of how a French woman would have approached her problem, really with indifference. In France, the fact that she despised her husband would have raised not a single eyebrow, nor would his indifference to their liaison, given that he had his own mistress. Given 'mutual attraction', as Heinrich had termed it, there would have been no doubt as to which way matters would have proceeded.

It was, he knew, not so very different in London, if you took account of the behaviour of the upper social orders: had he not enjoyed a brief fling with Lady Annabel Fitzgerald just after receiving his commission?

It was the attitude of her middling class which prevented Emily from moving naturally on to the next stage of their relationship and Pearce feared to be too open in broaching that such a conclusion, such intimacy, was inevitable if they were to remain in each other's company for any length of time, and in thinking on that, he wondered how that, with all the other problems he faced, was going to be achieved.

Lost in his own thoughts, Pearce had failed to see the tears that began to well in her eyes and she had gone quite rigid in an attempt to prevent them. It was only when a very suppressed sob escaped her lips that he became aware and that, sad as it was, it allowed him to pull her gently towards him and put his arms around her shoulder, feeling, as her body came into contact with his, the jerking of her dismay. Pearce could smell her: not her scent but the actual musk of her body, and that produced in him an unbearable depth of desire, one which, with any other woman, he would have turned into action. Yet he could not and it was fear that stopped him: fear of acting too swiftly, fear of giving offence, as an emotion one which was entirely novel to him.

'It is such a sin,' she sobbed.

'What is?'

'To contemplate loving a man other than my husband.'

'I am happy that you can contemplate such a thing, Emily, but it is far from a sin and also it is far from uncommon.' Those words, too, had required restraint. 'How can anyone term tender feelings for another as "sin"?'

257

'It is in the eyes of God.'

'Dry your tears and imagine that God cannot see you.'

'He sees everything.'

Pearce sighed, for in saying those words Emily had informed him of the height of the hurdles he had to overcome. She had been brought up in awe of a doctrine in which he did not believe and for a short period he was back with his father, listening to him as he ticked off his objections to the teachings of the Church, the calm way they were expressed rendering them absurd: God made the world in six days and rested on the seventh, he also made man and woman. His own son was the product of a virgin birth created by a visiting angel to a woman who was married – what about poor Joseph, had he been debarred by divine instruction from consummating his marriage? Death and resurrection and a Holy Trinity of three beings in one were what the worshipers were supposed to believe, never seeing or suffering from the outrageous venality of those who were supposed to carry out his ministry!

'What if he does not?' Pearce asked in a soft voice.

She raised her head off his shoulder and looked at him with reddened eyes. 'To even contemplate such a thing is blasphemy.'

'I wish, Emily, you had met my father, surely the most Christian man I have ever known, yet one who did not believe in God.' Seeing the look of shock he continued quickly, 'Yet he believed in his fellow man, often when the evidence before him flew in the face of that belief.' Pearce smiled again. 'It will not surprise you to know we disputed long and often on that.'

'You, I think, were born to dispute.'

'I am forced to ask you, Emily, having got as far as we have this night, what you see happening next?'

'I do not know.'

That was, of course, obfuscation: Emily Barclay might have been raised in circumstances of rigid propriety, but like everyone else on the planet she knew what the alternative was, given even rural Somerset could not be entirely bereft of scandal. But the step at which John Pearce hinted was, for her, a leap into a sort of hell.

'You do know, the sole question is whether you accept that what should happen will.'

'You are too direct, sir.'

'I think by now I might be "John", not "sir", and someone has to be, as our good friend so recently observed.'

'I need time.'

'If there were three words I feared, it was those.'

'You cannot expect me to . . .' That was a sentence she could not finish: to even acknowledge what Pearce was driving at was beyond the limit of what she was prepared to say.

'No, of course not.'

His reply was full of an understanding he was not sure he felt, yet to push now would be to create a barrier, not remove one, and she did need time, for whereas a man embarking on a serious liaison with a married woman would suffer the minimum of opprobrium, the lady would not: she would be damned by a society steeped in double standards.

'We must meet again,' Pearce said, with a smile intended to soften her fears.

'Yes?' The positive response was a whisper.

'Shall I see you to your lodgings?'

'Perhaps not.'

Pearce laughed, which occasioned a frown.

'What is so amusing?'

'You are, just as you are sweet, good-natured, kind, beautiful . . . and I have run out of superlatives, which is just as well since I have driven you to the blush.' Her face was indeed suffused. 'But, and I will not brook any objection, I am going to kiss you.'

He could see a flash of fear in her eyes as he moved towards her, but then, and this lifted his already heightened emotions, a sudden sign of that determination he so admired, that resolve not to allow fear to rule. A hand round her narrow waist hauled her in, and they did kiss, in a way which was deeply satisfying for Pearce, but more so for Emily, who had never been properly kissed in her life.

The parting, once Heinrich Lutyens had been brought into the happy conclusion of their talk, occasioned one of those periods when neither party really wants to let go, which much amused the surgeon, though he took care to keep that hidden. When Pearce finally left, with a promise to meet upon the morrow, he and Emily were left alone.

'Am I doing the right thing?' she asked.

'All I can say, my dear, is that you must do that which will make you happy.'

'Is happiness possible?'

The reply was typical of the man. 'Not without a concomitant degree of misery, my dear, the two go hand in hand.'

'Even if it were possible, my husband would never release me.'

'In that I think you are correct.'

That induced tears again, for Emily Barclay lived in a world where divorce was near to impossible for a man, and doubly so for a woman.

CHAPTER FIFTEEN

Pearce was up bright and early to visit Arthur Winston, pleased to find the fellow was not as dilatory as those who staffed the offices of the Crown. Indeed, the bustle of the city was reassuring: not for the inhabitants of this place a ten-of-the-clock attendance on their tasks. On being admitted to Winston's chambers – a busy apiary of small offices staffed by men all engaged in various commodity trades – claiming to have been at work for several hours he immediately proposed to whisk his visitor off to a large and satisfying breakfast, refusing to allow Pearce to demur, only popping his head into an adjacent room to ask that another visitor he was expecting be requested to call back.

'Tell him I will send word of a convenient time. Now come, let us eat, for I am hollow.'

His description of the breakfast, of John Dory fillets followed by a pair of mutton chops, the whole washed down with a robust claret, was not mistaken and the first question, once they were settled at their board in a tavern crowded with like souls, was an obvious one.

'My friends are safe, if you can call being confined in the Liberties such a thing.'

'Protections?'

'Valid and in their possession.'

'That is good to hear, so let us toast their health properly this time.' Goblets raised they both drank deeply. 'And how proceeds your case against Captain Barclay, Lieutenant – or should I say, given your coat is no longer blue, Mr Pearce?'

'I fear you had the right of it when you alluded to the difficulties, and as for the costs, well, I have no idea where they are to come from, that is, if the man I have engaged to prepare the plea has provided an accurate figure of what they might amount to.'

That statement led to an enquiry as to the state of his prizes, the answer to which had Winston frowning. 'The law is well termed an ass, sir, be it in an Admiralty Court or the King's Bench.'

That name and the confident way it was used made Pearce stiffen: the latter court was the highest in the land when it came to common law and the one which had, at the bidding of William Pitt, or more precisely his friend Henry Dundas, issued the summons against him and his father, a threat so serious there was no option but to flee abroad. Too often the King's Bench was an instrument of state power rather than justice. Winston noticed his reaction – he could hardly fail to – and his face showed concern as well as a degree of embarrassment, which led to an apologetic explanation.

263

'Your name, Mr Pearce, rang a bell, but not, I admit, until I was well on my way home and I saw it perhaps as a coincidence that you were in the Pelican on that very night, when you were quite open about not being a regular visitor. I hope it does not offend you that I made a few enquiries only to find out you had misled me, not I hasten to add, that you did not have the right.'

Pearce was not entirely mollified. 'Even when I had declined your offer of employment?'

'I confess to having too much curiosity for my own well-being, but I would in my defence add that, as a man of business, intelligence is all when it comes to ensuring profit. I seek out information often without any idea as to its use, yet I cannot tell you how many times such idle digging has inadvertently aided me in my affairs. I would also hazard that I am about to be rewarded. You have not sought me out for the sheer love of my company, so what I gleaned from my burrowing may well have a bearing, is that not so?'

This produced a delicate moment: Pearce had come here to seek some way of making money or at least halting the decline in his expenditure. It was also the case that, with his friends dependent on his charity, if they could be included in some form of paid work they would be less of a burden. Winston had mentioned the need for a man to command a trading ship: what better place than a merchant vessel for a trio with protections from impressment to be safe from the other threat to their liberty, the common law?

The problem was one of openness: to tell all was to

diminish his ability to negotiate both a decent return for his services and his chance to gain work which would include them. The question of his own competence worried him less – he had briefly commanded a ship of war and that was a much harder task than some lumbering trading vessel ploughing the waters of the North Sea with the coast in view and just enough of a crew to handle the sails.

'Let us leave that aside for a moment,' Winston said, which indicated to John Pearce he had hesitated too long in replying to the previous question. 'We will return to your perjury case. You mentioned the costs, so I assume they are not insignificant.'

'Cost and time, sir,' Pearce replied, going on, while he chewed on his mutton chop, to detail the need for letters to fly back and forth to the Mediterranean, without, of course, mentioning any hopes, very diminished in truth, for any proposition from William Pitt that might take him there.

'And time on its own is an expense, for you must pay lawyers even when nothing is happening.'

'You have smoked the problem, Mr Winston.'

A warm and expansive gesture was followed by Winston's proffered hand. 'Please, sir, my given name is Arthur, and once I have taken breakfast with a man it ill behoves me to maintain any reserve. If you will allow it, I will call you John from henceforth.'

Pearce took the hand and shook it. 'Please do.'

'Now John, let me sum up what you are not saying.' Given Winston was grinning as well as chewing it was impossible to be in any way slighted. 'You need some form of paid occupation for, even if all your chickens come home to roost, you feel you will struggle to meet the cost of bringing your man to justice. Am I correct?'

'You are.'

'And, I hazard, that with your friends recently returned to the Liberties they will not eat and drink as a man should unless you are there to support them.' Given a nod, Winston continued. 'Added to that, there they are with a most valuable document in their possession, but one which is of no use to them in their present location.'

'A near-perfect summation.'

It surprised Pearce that there was no triumphant reaction from Winston, indeed he went very quiet and pensive, eating slowly, not looking at his fellow diner but at his plate. Eventually he did speak, but only to say he was thinking on a particular problem, which left John Pearce to concentrate on his own food, while catching snatches of the conversation going on around him: discussions on the price of sugar and other tradable commodities and the rising insurance rates, with more than one damnation of the King's Navy for the way French privateers seemed able to operate with impunity.

'Forgive me, John, I have been gnawing on a conundrum as well as my chop.' The look he gave Pearce was very direct, as if he wanted to ensure that what he was about to say was seen as really important. 'I have need of a man who can command a ship, that I have told you, but what would you say if I also told you I have need of a man who has been a fighter as well as a sailor?'

'Go on.'

'I would add, before I do, that having alongside him men who would also be useful in such a situation would make that man very valuable to me.' Pearce, being intrigued, made to speak, but Winston was not finished and his insistent look induced silence. 'It would also be a task that, successfully concluded, could pay so handsomely that certain burdens of yours would be eased, if not removed. There is a question of trust involved and what I was ruminating on just now was just that. Can I trust you, John?'

'If I said "yes", I might be lying, and I would add it is not a question to which any man would answer "no".'

'Just so, which makes it a question of my judgement and so I am going to lay out the very barest bones to you. I have a need which requires a slight evasion of the law, one which may, though the chances are small, turn violent, yet it is one that will return me such a profit, as well as a high level of satisfaction, as to allow for a rare degree of generosity in the matter of payment for services rendered.'

'How generous?'

Winston threw back his head and laughed, but it was short in duration and the look that followed the humour was serious. 'The nub, for you, I suspect.'

'I am also curious about how a man "slightly" evades the law. From my experience you are either on one side or the other.'

'Is that true, John? Can you not be placed outside

the law merely by the malice of certain government ministers?'

'Going back to your question regarding trust, I am not in a position to answer yea or nay.'

'Which makes me aware I must say more.'

John Pearce pushed his plate to the centre of the table and leant close to Winston. 'Arthur, you must say everything.'

That induced another period of silence. 'Very well! I have a vessel in a certain harbour loaded with a valuable cargo. Those goods, bought and ready to be shipped over the Channel in peacetime, are now worth more, much more, because we are at war. They are, in short, the kind of commodities which have become scarce because of the conflict.'

'No genius is required to deduce these goods must be French in origin.'

'Correct! And it is also the case that, quite apart from duties, which in peace I would have been subjected to, now we are at war with the Revolution such trade is banned even for neutral vessels.'

'An ordinance much flouted, I suspect.'

'True, John, the Dutch make hay while the honest British trader suffers, as long as they are not caught and investigated, which is such a small risk with naval captains cautious and so few Revenue cutters on hand to intercept their cargoes, while a well-placed bribe at the dockside will answer to prevent too deep a search. So you see my problem. It is not only securing my cargo and getting it to England, it is also the act of landing it on home shores.'

'Now it is pure contraband?' Winston nodded. 'So you require a captain to sail it, some men to crew it and of the type not to be fastidious about where it is landed, given bringing it into a port would be very hazardous.'

It wasn't shock on Winston's face, more a sense of wonder. 'I see, John, I do not have to explain to you as much as I thought I would be required to. You have a sharp brain, friend, one that would, I suspect, make you a great deal of money in the city.'

'The only way to make money in this city is to have a great deal to begin with.'

'That I would challenge, but this is not the time, for you have, with your shrewd appreciation, not to say quite remarkable deduction, leapt very far ahead of where I thought I would be.'

'Yet you are still not far enough, Arthur, for me to commit to what it is you require.'

'True, so I must tell you more: I must tell you that in this piece of business I had an associate, a Flemish trader, who was in a position to gather the goods for which I paid and get them loaded aboard a vessel which I own, all for a very respectable remuneration. This he was in the process of doing when war was declared, which, though it made the trade illegal, raised the intrinsic value of my cargo to a point where a mere doubling was conservative. Can you, for that, work out what has gone wrong?'

Pearce thought for only a short moment. 'Your agent has assessed that his fees, given we are at war with France, are insufficient and he is demanding a higher payment to release to you your cargo.'

'Damn me, sir, you are amazing. I cannot think of another soul who would have reached such an accurate conclusion from so little information.'

'Why don't you pay him?'

That brought on a very clouded expression and Arthur Winston's voice rose to a high and much louder pitch. 'I'm damned if I will! This is a fellow who owes any prosperity he has enjoyed for a decade to my faith in him as well as the trade I have put through his hands. Also, I have been fair, more than that throughout our association, downright generous, in fact, and what do I get in response? Naked greed! I have paid him for his services already, I will not give him another brass farthing.'

Realising, by the silence around him, that he had made himself an object of attention, Winston dropped his voice again so that only Pearce could hear. 'Besides, paying him more does not get my goods into England and sold, so it would be money down the drain. This fiasco has gone on too long, ever since war was declared, and I have been out of pocket because of it.'

'So, the task you wish carried out is for your vessel to be wrenched from this fellow's grasp, an act which he is bound to object to?'

'Yes.'

'The value?'

'Of the cargo?' Pearce nodded. 'In peace it was, in terms of market value, just in excess of twelve and a half thousand pounds sterling, prior to what was owing in customs dues.'

'And now?'

'Take out the duties, then ask yourself what French brandy will fetch, likewise Lyon silk or Calais lace.'

John Pearce might have been out of England for a while, but no one could fail to notice how such commodities had risen in price – threefold was a reasonable guess at the buying end. Always open to being smuggled, such an occupation, almost an industry on certain parts of the south and east coasts, had become more dangerous with so many Royal Navy ships now in the narrow seas seeking prizes. Where neutrals could sail in safety – navy captains would baulk at the financial risk of impounding an innocent vessel – an indigenous smuggler was at high risk and that meant the cost of supply had increased and, quite naturally, it had also raised to fever pitch the desire for those who could afford such outlay to have and display something so hard to come by.

'Let us say, John, it has risen so much in value, and the getting of it being not without risk, I am prepared to split a third of what I can sell it for with the man who helps me get it ashore in England. With a higher margin on my goods and my ship returned, I would be well content.'

It was natural that a period of silence followed that statement: Arthur Winston was doing no less than offering Pearce a fortune, not a wage. That it was not without risk, and he suspected Winston of playing that part of the matter down, only served to make it more tempting. If he had enjoyed anything this last year it had been the excitement that comes from action, the knowledge that in a situation of danger he had the ability to keep a cool head and a clear brain, as well as lead others in a dangerous enterprise.

Failure was a possibility in any such venture, but success would lay to rest any worries he had about taking on Ralph Barclay, and then there was the other consideration: Emily Barclay, a woman he was now sure he was in love with. If he had put that subject to the back of his mind this morning it was one that had pressed on him the night before and would come back to haunt him again. There was no way he could seek to live with her, and that he was set on doing, while she was taking money from her estranged husband.

That such a course would be rocky in the extreme would be eased by money, so many things were in life and not just for him. For his friends, they could earn enough to buy their way out of trouble – Rufus paying off his apprentice bond, Charlie doling out a heavy fine to cover his misdemeanours while retaining enough to set himself up, Michael able to go back to Ireland and put to rights his family's debt-wracked farm.

'If the risk is too great I would understand, John,' Winston said, his face anxious, for Pearce had been thinking for a long time – hardly surprising since this one stroke could solve so many dilemmas and, beyond that, open up many prospects for the future in terms of what he could and could not do to make a living.

'Where is the vessel berthed?'

It was Winston's turn to take time to respond. 'That I would keep to myself until I was sure a fellow was committed.'

'And what would it take to convince you that I could be?'

'You know, I am not sure.' Seeing Pearce react, and not well, he was quick to continue. 'I have thought on this so long I am almost made fearful by your willingness to so readily consider it. All the while that vessel sits in . . .' he paused, 'wherever it is, I am out of pocket to the tune of the cost of purchase, and a tied-up vessel earns nothing. While such a thing has not stopped me doing business it has constrained me, and I will not deny to you that a solution would allow me to speculate more in what is a booming market.'

'Have you put this proposal to anyone else?' Pearce asked, aware that it was a question he should have posed much earlier.

Winston emitted a hollow laugh. 'I have never got further than a mention that what I want might be illegal, most people being the type to shy away at the word and me of a mind to back away from eagerness for fear of being cheated.'

'Am I not to be feared for the very same reason?'

'You are singular in many ways, John: first, by that naval coat you so despise and the means by which you won it . . .'

'I have told you, it was as much accident as design.'

Winston beamed. 'Then there is your modesty.'

'There must be more.'

'There is – perhaps because having been a victim of the law, you respect it less. Yet you are a casualty of legal stupidity, not some repentant felon, and I go

273

back to the words I spoke to you in the Pelican about the shortage of suitable men to command ships in any sort of trade. There is no surfeit of people available to undertake such a task as that I have outlined, quite apart from anyone disposed to do so, and even fewer in whom I repose any measure of confidence.'

'Do I need to explain to you why I might be the right man, in the right place at the right time?'

'No, but I must have care even with that, eagerness being no substitute for clear thinking. But in your favour you are without employment if you do not wish to be a king's officer, you are badly in need of funds and, I think, John, you are not averse to risk.'

'Do you have the vessel's manifest?'

Winston's eyes narrowed, but he was too sharp to fall for a request, which, of necessity, would carry the ship's name. 'I have a list of the cargo.'

'Can I see it?'

'To ascertain the value, no doubt?' Pearce nodded. 'I have it in my office.'

'Then, if you are finished your breakfast, my friend, I suggest we repair to that place this instant.'

'You move with too much boldness.'

'Time and tide, Arthur, though that begs one question. How quickly could I be got to where this ship is?'

'If I told you that, I might as well just admit where she lays, and when you say "I", you mean "we".'

'You would be coming too?'

'How else will you know which ship is the one I own and how it is to be landed?'

'By giving me her name, perhaps, as well as the rest of the plan?'

Winston looked him straight in the eye. 'Which would repose in you a degree of trust bordering on foolishness.'

While Pearce was frustrated by the answer, he could see the reason for Winston's caution: given every bit of information about his vessel, a man he had only met once before might be tempted to act alone and cheat him out of everything, yet he wished to show him he could arrive at certain deductions.

'A Flemish trader, French goods, it cannot be as far off as the Baltic, more likely we are talking of the Flanders shore. It matters not: in time you will tell me that, just as you will show me the list, inform me of the minimum number of hands needed to sail her and you must, in all conscience tell me where the cargo can be safely landed, for I assume that in your deliberations that has already been decided upon.'

'I am beginning to wonder if your mind is not too sharp.' There was no joy in that, so Pearce stood up. 'I see you are eager.'

It was odd that Arthur Winston seemed put out, as if he was being pushed to do something against his will, which had Pearce reasoning that a notion in contemplation is a very comfortable place to be, while one in the act of execution can be quite the opposite. Winston had thought on this for a long time and very likely, quite often, had worked through various scenarios in his imagination, all of which would, naturally, end in success. Action brought on the possibility of failure, perhaps the permanent loss of both vessel and cargo, and that was less pleasant.

'More so than you know, my friend, so shall we go back to your place of business and see, first, if what you propose is possible?'

It took time for Winston to rise, but with a contemplative face he did so eventually. As they covered the short distance back to his chambers, Pearce talked as he walked, well aware that he was only telling Winston what he knew already, but his aim to convince him that his instincts were right.

'I am in need of funds to a level near impossible to achieve and that takes no account of time. There is no method I can think of, other than that which you have proposed, which will provide what I need either in the level or the speed.'

'Would it offend you if I said I feel it is being rushed and in such a way that makes me nervous?'

'I apologise, Arthur. Put it down to my nature, for I am a fellow who, having seen an objective, cannot abide anything other than an attempt to immediately achieve it.' Those words made Pearce smile, for the only thing that came to mind as he said them was his single-minded pursuit of the opposite sex. 'I am at your mercy in the article of time, but I am satisfied you know that I will not be dilatory once we have come to an agreement.'

Back in Winston's chambers, it was confirmed by his neighbour that he had indeed had another visitor, also that the fellow was eager for a meeting and would call back at the same time on the morrow. Then they went

276

into his room; the door being firmly closed, the list was produced and what he could see only served to increase Pearce's desire to be quick about the act. Given the amount of cargo, he guessed she would be light in displacement so it would need few hands to sail her if, as he suspected, it had to be a straight trip across the North Sea and one he would not undertake if the weather looked to be inclement. More important, what Winston had said about the value was true – the game was definitely worth the candle!

There were bound to be risks, but that was a state in which he had lived all his life; even just being with his father, boy and man, had occasioned such a thing many times, and his naval service, while it may have been reluctant, had been full of hazards, all of which he had overcome. Still, it had to be weighed and that he did, with the concomitant knowledge that there would be many unknowns – there always had to be and it was how they were dealt with that counted. The first of those was obvious, so finally it came to the crunch and he demanded to be told the port in which she lay at present, as well as the landfall he would be required to make on the English shore. It took half a minute of silent contemplation to get a reply: Winston was like a woman choosing a dress, or even worse, a hat, but finally he did answer.

'My ship is tied up in Gravelines, having been brought down by canal from St Omer. It will, of course, need a fair wind, but a north-easterly is fairly common in the North Sea and she can be brought in to St Margaret's Bay just north of Dover, where I have a cousin who farms nearby, hard by the village of Martin. He has assured me he can provide the bodies necessary to unload the cargo, which will, of course, occasion some payment. The notion was to agree some signal beacons on shore, certain lights at the masthead and have him watch for my arrival, he having been previously informed by coded letter that matters are in train.'

'And your vessel is of a type fit for the crossing?'

'It is one she has made many times before to the Port of London.'

'What happens to the cargo then, Arthur?' Again there was that seeming reluctance to answer, that hesitation, as though to divulge information was to weaken his hand. 'Since this would be in the nature of a partnership, I think knowing that would be necessary.'

A slow nod led to another delayed answer; it was like drawing teeth. 'I would sell it before it is landed, at an affordable discount, a method I have recently learnt that has supported the smuggling trade for centuries and one which removes the risk of interception by others.'

Now it was John Pearce's turn to hesitate: everything he was being told, payments for landing and discounts from pre-sale indicated a substantial drop in value. 'So, the final tally would be?'

'Speculative until the trades are complete,' Winston murmured, 'but surely enough to satisfy us both and, I would suggest, it is better to know what the profit would be prior to landing than take the risk of transporting the goods ourselves.'

Such a proposal made sense: it would mean hiring wagons and men to drive them, as well as carrying contraband through Kent, a county where the Excise was likely to be active. Yet having settled on a potential figure in his mind, and a high one, it was slightly galling the way it was being trimmed. Still, there was no point in pursuing that: the rewards would still be substantial and his task was to get it across the Channel.

'What of the Excise at the point of landing?'

'Thin on the ground and not zealous, I am informed,' Winston replied, before adding, 'If it is too risky for you, John . . .'

'Tell me about Gravelines.'

'Right on the Flanders coast, a dozen miles south of Dunkirk.'

Winston then produced a map of the Low Countries to explain that the estuary town was one through which he had traded for years. Once a Spanish possession, then French, it was at the sea end of a canal that joined the River Aa from St Omer, hence the ease with which goods could be shipped from the French interior and the type of ship which, without being precise, he said was equally at home on a canal as at sea.

'The townsfolk speak Flemish, but Gravelines has been a fortified French garrison town since the time of Louis the Fourteenth, though the walls are not manned by Jacobins at present. They are still locked up in Dunkirk, to where they fled when the Duke of York moved to besiege the place.'

'And failed to take it?'

279

'But he is still in the field leading the Allied forces, Dutch and Austrian as well as his own regiments, hence the reluctance of the French to sally forth and try to reoccupy places like Gravelines.'

'You know this?'

'I do, just as I know what was demanded of me as payment for the release of my property.'

'You went there?'

'As soon as I heard the Duke of York had invested Dunkirk and that the French had abandoned their other possessions in the Low Countries.'

'So who is guarding it now?'

'In the town, no one, but there are a pair of older forts guarding a narrow channel leading out to sea, which may now have some kind of occupying force to deter the French from raiding. But the type of vessel you will be taking out is much used in costal trade and so should arouse no suspicion.'

What Pearce was being told had to be filtered through what he already knew: the armies under the Duke of York were now reported to be nearer to Brussels and well away from the coast, so that meant Gravelines was in the possession of Britain or her Dutch allies. If it was so, then getting a ship out should be easy, so much so that he wondered at the need to use him, which would have become his next question if he had not stopped himself: profit lay in that employment. Yet he got an answer anyway – it was as if Winston had read his mind.

'I can guess what you are thinking, John, but I doubt my fellow will give up easily and in a zone of conflict the means to force the matter legally do not exist.'

'The duke may beat the French.'

That got a terse response. 'He has shown damn little ability to do so up till now, and if he loses to them what is an awkward task now will become ten times harder. In fact, I could lose everything.'

'Do you know if your fellow is fully manning the ship?'

'He will have an anchor watch, no more, I suspect.'

'You do not know?'

The reply showed a trace of temper. 'Not for certain, but why spend money on a crew when the scoundrel has no intention of letting her set sail unless I pay him a fortune?'

Tempted to ask how much that fortune was, Pearce decided against it: the man was upset enough. 'How do we get to Gravelines?'

'There is a packet still sailing regularly from Ramsgate to Flushing.'

Pearce looked at the map and declined that as a route. Flushing was too far away from Gravelines and on the wrong side of Dunkirk, which might make the journey risky and besides, being on a public boat with the Pelicans carried its own hazards.

'There must be another possibility.'

'There is. I confess I went into that before we had an army in Flanders and I found, through my aforementioned cousin, there are boatmen in Deal with oared galleys that can get you there in hours on the right tide and sea state.'

'These people would be smugglers, would they not?'

'I don't think that question requires an answer.'

'You know them, Arthur?'

In his reply, he seemed almost ashamed. 'I made their acquaintance thanks to my cousin, with some difficulty, for no one admits readily to such abilities or even the possession of such a boat. At one time I had it in mind to engage them to bring back my cargo.'

'But you decided against it?'

'John, if you were to meet these people you would understand. There are villains in this very city of London, but they pale by comparison to the men of the Kentish coast. Just to be in their presence is to fear for your very soul. If I engaged them I doubt I would see a brass farthing and I would not even be sure my life was safe.'

Pearce remained silent when he could have spoken: he had met such people before in his life, some quite recently from nearby Sandwich, and his opinion had been that they were no more villainous than any other breed. Certainly, when it came to robbery, they need not fear comparison with the rapacious speculators of the City of London.

'How do we go about engaging such fellows?' he asked, with a feeling that his rewards were about to sink some more. 'And paying them?'

It was a glum Arthur Winston who responded. 'That, I hate to say, is a task and an expense which of necessity must fall to me, to be set, of course, against the future revenues for the whole enterprise.'

It was Pearce's turn to frown: Arthur Winston was a

typical man of business, willing to speculate but not to bear any costs he could pass on. He was about to raise the method of getting back should they fail, but that was not a prospect to which he really wanted to allude. Problems might present themselves, and in the worst case he and his friends would have to risk taking the packet from Flushing to Ramsgate, and at some point Winston would have to provide the funds for such an eventuality.

'I will require charts and tide tables of the Flanders coast as well as the waters of the Channel, especially inshore ones of the landing place.' Imagining what could go wrong, the most obvious thing, apart from a failure to secure the ship, was to be intercepted while making the crossing. He had no notion of fancy manoeuvres – it would be 'set all sail and run' regardless, putting the vessel aground in an emergency if a Revenue cutter appeared.

'It goes without saying that these Deal boatmen cannot be told anything, secrecy is essential.'

That made Winston cross. 'Then why say it?'

'Only so I can be sure.'

Pearce was with Winston for another hour discussing every facet of the task, gleaning, by dint of subtle enquiry, scraps of information about the ship and the required crew, gaining his confidence so that more was being revealed than it had originally seemed likely that the city man intended to give away. And he hovered between excitement, caution, and sometimes, real fear, till in the end it was Pearce who was steeling him to the project with encouraging words and, finally, a statement of the position.

'It is simple in essence, Arthur. Right now you have neither your ship nor your profit and seemingly little chance of taking possession of either. With additional expenditure you might have both. So, do we proceed? A firm answer, for I cannot act if you are in doubt.'

Arthur Winston seemed to visibly shake before agreeing, but agree he did. 'I will set out for Deal first thing tomorrow. For the rest of today, I must see about getting decent prices committed for what we will fetch ashore.'

The latter statement, being made with a more positive tone, led Pearce to suspect that was where Arthur Winston was happiest, making trades.

CHAPTER SIXTEEN

Emily Barclay was startled when she came down to the parlour to find John Pearce. It was also an awkward moment when Mrs Fletcher, no doubt wondering at what seemed to her a stream of handsome gentlemen callers, lingered a fraction too long and observed the look the couple exchanged: not in any way a very clever woman, she had seen that sort of communion before and she had no doubt that, careful of her own reputation as an upright widow, she might have to keep a sharp eye on this Mrs Barclay. The two potential lovers made sure she was long gone before they joined hands and spoke in near-whispers.

'I will be gone for a very short period of time, but I also want to reassure you that, should the venture I am about to take come to a happy conclusion, then you may abandon the need for any support from your husband. You will, and I say this with joyful anticipation, become mine to take care of.'

'John, I—'

'Hush, Emily. I know you have doubts, just as I know what I am proposing flies in the face of everything you have been brought up to hold dear. It is in your eyes and your diffidence, but, and I say this with as much love as determination, you are dealing with me.'

There was such a temptation then to tell him how she had purloined the papers he thought lost, taking them from Heinrich Lutyens' instrument chest while he was, with the rest of the crew, fighting the blaze that would eventually destroy HMS *Grampus*. But would he be grateful, or could such an admission possibly turn him against her? Odd, there was temptation in the latter, a way of ending their intimacy in such a way that she could not blame herself.

'Is what you propose to do dangerous?'

He grinned, trying to deflect her curiosity. 'Whatever makes you think that?'

'Your nature.'

'Too bold, perhaps, but I fear if I were not, you and I would be in limbo for a very long time.'

'Such a notion is not without a trace of merit, John, for I seem to be rushing headlong into the unknown, which is not comfortable.'

'You are the mistress of your own destiny.' Pearce mentally cursed himself for one word in that statement, and he saw that it registered with Emily to underline her fear. The notion of being any man's mistress, a kept woman, was one to induce terror, not keen anticipation, so he added quickly, 'And you are a match for me in boldness.'

'No, John.'

'Courage then?'

'Foolishness, perhaps.'

The opening door had them moving rapidly apart, as Mrs Fletcher appeared with a tray. 'I thought you might like some tea, Mrs Barclay, you and your gentleman.'

The aplomb with which Emily replied was a marvel to the man who loved her, and yet another example of why he so admired her, for even he could see that the landlady was being overtly nosy.

'Lieutenant Pearce, Mrs Fletcher, who served with my husband, Captain Barclay, but I am sure you must know that, given the gentleman introduced himself.'

'Mr Pearce, he said.'

'Forgive me, madam, for failing to use my rank. I see it as my duty to call upon the wife of a fellow officer . . .'

'A fellow officer who is at sea,' Emily added in the minuscule pause, slightly shocked at her brazen lie. 'But thank you for your consideration, Mrs Fletcher, the tea will be most welcome.'

With a short curtsy the tray was put down and the landlady departed, Emily whispering, and not happily, once more, as soon as the door was closed, 'That is just a hint of what I might look forward to.'

It made the rest of their conversation awkward and stilted as they sat and took the tea, of necessity further apart, and it was also plain that Pearce could not linger, for to do so would only inflame what Mrs Fletcher had hinted at by her interruption.

'I could say you will become accustomed to it, but

that would be unkind. All I can avow is that you will be happier, even with such judgements, being with me.'

'And where will that be, John Pearce?'

'Wherever you choose to go, Emily, perhaps somewhere that we can live as man and wife without comment.'

'Man and wife?' Emily replied, with no great enthusiasm.

'Emily, I suspect you have yet to taste the joy of being a wife. I will make it my first duty to ensure that is remedied.'

Well aware of what he was driving at, her face went bright red.

That they parted with a stolen kiss did nothing to diminish her confusion. Emily, back in her own room, sat for quite a while in contemplation, aware that a decision could not be left to just hang; she must make up her mind which course she was going to follow and then set about doing so, and this in a situation where advice from a third party was worth less than a pinch of salt. The word that kept recurring was 'happiness', the word she wanted to concentrate on being 'regret'. What would she suffer in that regard when finally she set her course? That made her smile, it being so much like a nautical allusion.

The choice was not between Ralph Barclay and John Pearce, it was between living alone or with a man she suspected she was in love with, though being of a practical bent she was far from sure what love was supposed to feel like. Emily also knew she was incapable of dithering and that a conclusion was required. Alone, she would be miserable and always at the mercy of her husband; with Pearce she would at least have a chance of some joy in her life, and it was that that allowed her to contemplate undertaking two things. If, and this was another nautical allusion, she was going to nail her colours to the mast, then she would be best to do so wholeheartedly.

She would call at the offices of Mr Studdert and collect those court martial papers, which she could then turn over to John Pearce? If he loved her as he implied he did, then she would be forgiven for stealing them. If he could not accept her reasons for her actions then she would find his affection to be less than he seemed to mean when he spoke with her, which would save much in the way of future difficulty. The second undertaking would be to write a letter to Toby Burns, telling him that he must come clean about the things he had done for the sake of his own soul and provide, in writing, the means by which she could keep her husband at bay.

'I calculate we can manage,' Pearce said, 'though we might need you to swing those fists of yours to get clear.'

'What are we about, John-boy?'

'A possible end to scraping a living, Michael,' Pearce replied, his face very serious. 'Which I have had to do most of my life.'

'You're not alone there, Pearce,' Charlie said.

'I've told you what the cargo is and I have told you how much it is worth, and I have gleaned enough about the vessel to reckon she is of two masts and enough for us to handle without help. If the wind is fair and the sea is kind we can do the distance from Flanders in a single night's sailing, and I am happy to hover off the Flanders coast until conditions are right.'

'What are the shares to be?' asked Rufus, who then realised the way he had said that implied distrust of those present, when what he had meant was other parties. 'Ours, I mean.'

'Enough to set you up, but as to how much that will be, well, we need to see it sold for a figure. But know this, I cannot do it without you three and I will not do it if you turn it down.'

'What's to turn down?' Rufus replied, looking around the Pelican. 'A life in the Liberties.'

'There's sense in that, Rufus.' That got Charlie a nod; the youngster was not accustomed to such approval. 'And that goes more for you, Michael, than even we two.'

'It's God-given that such a thing should come along at such a time,' the Irishman responded with a smile and a slow headshake, evidence of how low he had been since getting back to this place, for he was a man of positive mien by nature.

'Miracles and saints bein' what you heathens believe in, Michael, so say a prayer and let's set on it.'

O'Hagan grinned. 'Happen you will say a prayer to the good Lord with me, Charlie?'

'My pleas go down, brother, not up.'

'Every one answered,' hooted Rufus.

'Are we on for this?' Pearce demanded.

It took time for Michael to nod, but he did so; the other two had never been in doubt. 'How do we get to this Deal?'

'By boat, Michael, through the good offices of a Thames waterman, a fellow I have engaged to take us downriver. He is sure he and his mate can get us clear.'

''Tis a long haul,' opined Charlie.

'We'll take turns rowing, not like the last time we went that way, trussed like chickens.'

'Then I,' Rufus cried, when he realised the route, 'beg to piss out his boat as we pass Sheerness.'

'That'll frighten the Nore fleet,' cawed Charlie. 'They'll be running out the guns when they see your weaponry.'

'Michael, you have those pistols still, and the means to fire them, so we will take them along, but only to threaten. The men recruited to aid us in crossing will be paid in advance for their service and must be told nothing. No word is to be said of what we are about or where we are headed.'

'Sure, they'll guess it's smuggling, John-boy.'

'Let them, for a guess is just that, but if they know anything for certain they are sure to let it slip. Tight lips at all times, for if those Deal scallies get a whiff, we could find them waiting to rob us at St Margaret's Bay, which, when I looked at a map, is not more than a long walk from where they reside.'

It took Arthur Winston two days to coach to Deal, make the arrangements, and get back, but he assured

Pearce on their subsequent meeting that everything was in place, including the prices promised for the cargo.

'Once I put out feelers I was inundated, John, and so was able to drive some very hard bargains, especially for the Lyon silk, the price of which has gone through the roof so desperate for it are the ladies of fashion. Once all costs are met I think you can look forward to clearing ten thousand pounds each, which I admit, is better than anticipated.'

Not by me, Pearce thought, who had started out hoping for substantially more, and he would be splitting that with his Pelicans. Still, he would be well found and it would be churlish to say he was disappointed.

'I see you are once more wearing your naval coat.'

'A garment that makes it less likely I will be examined by the tipstaffs when I come and go from the Liberties.'

'And getting your fellows out of there?'

There was an element of paying him back in Pearce's reply, for he was still holding to himself the name of the ship. 'Please do not be offended, Arthur, when I do not respond to that. You have no need to know, and while I trust you not to be loose of tongue, it is better for me that you cannot let slip anything at all.'

'Of course,' Winston said, with tightly pursed lips. 'But I need to know when you will be there, for I have already laid out part of the fee and I have no desire to languish in such a den of iniquity waiting for you to appear.'

'Our plan is to be there at some time on the morrow.'

That produced a weary sigh. 'Then I must take to a coach sooner than I wish, for I must tell you my posterior is sore from travel already.'

Reaching into his desk, Winston pulled out several sheets of paper, the required charts, as well as a hand-drawn map of the Gravelines quays and defences. Pearce recognised the layout of the Vauban fortress, a star-shaped interior redoubt with the main walls protected by outworks and canals, very like that he had seen at Toulon. What was different was the narrow access to the sea, which was one he was determined to closely examine.

Winston talking took his attention away from his perusal. 'This is the name of the man I contacted in Deal, a fellow called Barmes. We will find him in the Three Kings Inn, where he does all his business, which is right on the beach, and it is he who will secure our crossing. If you get there before I do, make his acquaintance, for I would wish you to cast your mind over the arrangements to ensure they meet our needs, for I readily admit I am in ignorance of too many things to do with the sea.'

'What does he know?'

Winston produced a sly smile. 'I borrowed from you in this, John. He thinks I am trying to get out of France a man with whom I did much trade, now in St Omer and under imminent threat of the guillotine, hence the need for speed. I am going to fetch him, get him to Flushing and thence to England and safety. Naturally, taking along enough men to protect us both.'

'A good story, which makes you sound noble.'

'Too much so, I feared, so I hinted, too, at a chest of valuable possessions, not honestly obtained. Let us hope my tale convinces him, for he is a devious cove, as they all are in that neck of the woods.'

That left Pearce to wonder if Arthur had been wise: in his mind an excuse elaborated upon was less likely to be believable, and the mention of valuables even less astute. Still, it was done now, so there was no point in saying anything. 'Tell me about Deal, for I do not know it.'

Except, Pearce thought, as a swimmer who failed to reach the shore having jumped overboard from HMS *Brilliant*. He knew the beach to be high shingle and the water off the town to be freezing cold.

Winston obliged and made it sound like the worst place in creation, full of vice and villainy, leading Pearce to reckon, being a London businessman, he knew nothing of the common seaport: if Deal was a place of rough folk, drinking dens, whores, pickpockets and violent robbery, so was every other anchorage John Pearce had ever visited, both in Britain and abroad.

Jack Tars lived for the day and were easily parted from their money, so it was obvious that those well practised in the art of extraction would gravitate to the place where they were gathered, and Deal was such a spot. Sailors were also rowdy and given to making trouble, so it was also the case that the means of keeping their most boisterous behaviour in check had to be present.

'When do you leave?' Winston asked finally, and that got him another look and John Pearce an apology for asking. The last thing handed over was a purse of money for contingencies. 'I have made a note of the sum enclosed for the final tally.'

Tempted once more to mention a failure and return through Flushing, Pearce knew by the weight of the purse that was covered, but he had to say something. 'To tell you the truth, I was going to ask you for some funds. I have spent everything Davidson advanced me.'

'Do this well and that is a worry you will never have again.'

'Amen to that.'

After a firm handshake, Pearce went on his way, aware that his extremities were tingling: there was a frisson of danger in the air and he was in his element.

The Pelicans ate heartily before they departed and they also bought some provisions to take as a precaution, then they dressed in thick, hooded cloaks bought by Pearce that both hid their features and provided protection against the elements. Their boatmen were waiting by the riverbank and as soon as they and their ditty bags were aboard they took them swiftly out into the stream, which, with the tide falling, would carry them a long way downriver without much effort. There were eyes upon them, from shore and from one floating bounty hunter, who sought to hail them to stop. He was ignored and bypassed with ease, unaware that, had he managed to impede them, he would likely have ended up swimming in the Thames for his life.

Before long they were swinging through the arches

of London Bridge, brightly lit and busy, with Pearce recalling the last time he had boated through that hazard, for the tidal rush around the massive stone piers could be deadly to a novice oarsman; it was different now – he was seeking his fortune not doubting his fate. Soon they were well past, easing through a mass of anchored shipping sat between Greenwich and the London docks, vessels either waiting to unload cargo, or take it on.

As the fall of the tide eased they took turns on the extra oars the watermen had fetched along, keeping up a steady pace, leaving behind the smoke and buildings of London. There was rarely open country and clean air on either beam all the way till they raised the Medway towns, this being such a working river. As promised, Rufus prepared to aim his piss at the lights of Sheerness, but they had stayed silent as they passed the anchored ships of the North Sea fleet, the great, hulking, black-painted leviathans of seventy to one hundred and ten guns, rocking gently and surrounded by their own filth.

Off Faversham, with dawn breaking, they were spotted by a guard boat intent on pressing seamen, but this was where Pearce's naval coat came into its own, for he was able to call out the name of one of the warships on the Downs station and hail the information that he was on his way to rejoin. Yet further on, the river estuary widened out and the tide turned, making the journey past the North Foreland a hard pull, and causing Pearce to wonder at how his watermen would fare on their return, though not for long, given it was none of his concern.

Then they were round the great white cliffs and into

the calm of the Stour estuary, with long mudflats to larboard, hauling along a low shoreline, through the first of what turned out to be hundreds of merchant ships, on past the first of the three rose-shaped Tudor castles, with the black muzzles of their numerous heavy cannon plugged to keep out the sea spray. These protected the most important anchorage on the east coast, the long bight of water where great convoys formed and made their landfall before proceeding upriver to London, protected from the run of the North Sea by the long bar of the Goodwin Sands.

Those vessels making a return paid off their excess deep-water crew here – many fewer were needed for the short journey up the Thames, those same sailors forming a well of employable men for those convoys heading out to the four corners of the globe. Thus, at any time, Deal was awash with sailors freshly in receipt of their wages after several months at sea and there was, according to Winston's gloomy description, a whole raft of folk who saw it as their bounden duty to relieve them of such coin, and whether it was by fair means or foul lay in the lap of the gods. As a concomitant to that, given the propensity of tars to spend everything they possessed as quickly as possible, Deal was also home to men impoverished and desperate for a ship.

The whole shoreline was lined with boats, hoys, clinker-built cutters and fishing smacks pulled up onto the shingle, and behind them the backs of a string of tall, grey houses, all with smoking chimneys. They passed the stink, as well as the floating blood and offal, of the local abattoir, where cattle and pigs were slaughtered, salted and barrelled for convoys which could be at sea for half a year. Boats plied to and fro taking men to and from their ships, hoys likewise with supplies, while hovellers cast lines to seek out lost anchors and anything else fallen or discarded in the shallows.

There was much legitimate trade in Deal, but Winston had opined the locals only truly prospered when the wind blew hard on a high tide from the north-east. That was the route from which danger came to this place, a screaming wind and high pounding waves, causing ships to drag said anchors and, if they did not collide with another vessel equally in trouble, fight to stay off the deadly Goodwins – that long, wide sandbar that would suck below any ship run aground, but not until the local boatmen, by legend ignoring the cries of the drowning, had stripped her bare of anything of value.

Like the whole of England's shoreline facing France, smuggling was a way of life here, a constant battle between the Excise and the men who resided there, with blood spilt and lives sometimes taken. There was a naval presence too, one ship of the line and a brace of anchored frigates, which made Charlie wonder at the number of sailors who must be present, until Pearce, who had recounted all the information he had received from Winston, moved to put his mind at rest.

'They have nothing to fear in this place. I am told the Press dare not enter Deal for fear of their own lives.'

'A rough town, then, as you tell us?'

'From what I am led to believe, Charlie, but it is no

worse than what you know.' Pointing ahead, he alerted the men rowing to a tall building with a flag aloft, bearing as a device a trio of crowns. 'That will be the Three Kings, set us down as close as you can.'

They landed on steep and crowded shingle, which had the watermen getting their bare feet wet, not that they seemed bothered, too eager as they were to get from John Pearce the second part of their agreed payment, a sum which they could not have earned in a month from their normal endeavour ferrying folk around the Thames. Their ditty bags were passed over and with a wave they departed.

'So, my friends,' Pearce said, as a gentle north-east wind plucked at his cloak, 'let us see what kind of food this place can provide.'

CHAPTER SEVENTEEN

'You're in luck, for the weather is good, light north-easterlies and a calm sea judged to stay that way for a day or two by those who read the sky.'

These reassurances came from Barmes, a grossly overweight, fat-jowled fellow who was busy filling his massive belly via a mouth rarely free of food. Pearce had finished his repast well before, only to be staggered that a man eating when he came in was still doing so now. Tempted to ask if an easterly was not an impediment to a Channel crossing Pearce stopped himself. Speed was no doubt more important on the return journey than that going out.

'The fellows you need to get you across the water will come upon my call if they judge conditions to be right.'

'We must await my principal, who is coming on the London coach.'

'Nothing will happen lest he does so,' Barmes insisted,

omitting to say that money would have to change hands before anything occurred. 'All being well, we will fetch him along to you as soon as matters are agreed.'

The dining room of the Three Kings was full, so this was a low-voiced conversation made easier by the loud buzz of everyone else present: naval officers from the Downs Squadron who, given his dress, looked at him with interest as soon as he removed his cloak; redcoats either making their way to, or taking leave from, the army of the Duke of York, seeking battle in the Low Countries; merchant ship captains and local traders; as well as men who were not engaged in any conversation at all, but seemed more intent on watching their fellow diners, making Pearce wonder what Charlie Taverner, who could spot a lawbreaker a mile off, would make of them. He, Michael and Rufus, having spotted a newly landed boat cooking fish over a charcoal brazier, had gone off to eat outdoors.

'Tell me of the arrangements.'

'You will have observed the salt marshlands north of Sandown Castle; that is where you will launch from before we lose the last of the light, this very evening, if, as I have already said, my fellows agree.'

If the fat fellow's eyes could convey avarice, John Pearce had a pair equally good at displaying caution and they reacted at the mention of the castle, which brought forth more reassurance.

'The Deal forts, Sandown included, have a military piquet but they are gunners and few in number. They have no interest in boats being launched and even less inclination to leave their warm fires unless subject to a general order to do so, and that is rare.'

'What about the Excise?'

'You are departing the English shore, sir, not landing, so they have no interest.'

In between filling his face Barmes instructed Pearce to make his way to the Ship Inn, which lay on the prosaically named Middle Street, and wait. 'If all is well, I will send a man to fetch you at the appropriate hour and Mr Winston will be taken to the rendezvous, should he arrive as promised to you.'

That had Pearce thinking once more that Arthur Winston was not a natural intriguer: he had been careful not to use his own name, in fact he had given this tub of lard no name at all. Winston should have done likewise.

'And if your man does not come?'

'Then you must find a bed for the night, sir, and wait for my messenger on the morrow, while praying that the weather holds, for a galley cannot go in any kind of sea or wind, and a decent tide at the right time of day is required to cross the Goodwins. It is common to wait a week or more for the conditions to be right, and not unknown to wait a month.'

That gave cause for a bout of misplaced impatience: Pearce had no notion to be stuck in Deal for any length of time but he was only too aware that, when it came to journeys over water, wind and tide were the factors in control.

'How will we know him?'

'He, sir, will know you, for he has clapped eyes on you this very hour, as soon as you identified yourself to me. And, sir, I would advise you to put your cloak on, for that coat you are wearing is one to induce caution in a place like Deal.'

Pearce reprised the arrangements to ensure there was no chance of an error before exiting the dining room, checked the arrival time of the London coach at the desk, which would not pull up till late in the day, then left, taking the advice to don his boat cloak. Once outside he signalled to his waiting companions, now seated on bollards. They rose and silently followed along a quite broad strand, which fell away on both sides – a street dissected by the kind of narrow alleyways with which every seaport abounded, so constrained no two people could pass, made dark by the high walls of the buildings either side, with the wind whistling through to tug at their clothing.

Middle Street, a lower thoroughfare than that fronting the beach, was crowded and full of hawkers, trundling carts and folk going about their business, including sailors in abundance, easy to identify from their dress and gait, a lot of them drunk, and the air of the place was generally one of merriment – hardly surprising given the number of places selling drink through open windows: it seemed every house was a dispensary of some beverage or other.

As a thoroughfare it conformed to what one could expect in a town that lived off the sea, with urchins either running around or gathered playing games. There were whores and hucksters, rough-looking fellows, local boatmen in tarpaulin hats and smocks, voices calling out inviting the foolish to find the lady, bait a bear or try the throwing of a fowl, the smell of food preparation mixed with unwashed humanity and the waste from man and beast, the whole overborne by the pervading odour of drying or cooking fish, for nothing could overcome the smell of a frying sprat. Charlie cuffed a near child who came close, with words that warned him not to try dipping, while Rufus opined on the street women, seemingly not put off by Michael's asserting that they were all likely to be poxed.

The brick-faced building they entered was an alehouse, the room they entered small, busy and with a blazing fire. Pearce, once he had the Pelicans seated, told them to take it easy on the ale and went off to do a bit of investigating, which entailed making his way back to the beach and hiring another boat, this to take him to St Margaret's Bay so that he could assess the suitability of the place for a landing, being in luck that the man rowing him was a talkative soul who seemed content that his passenger was just a fellow, with time to spare, out for an excursion.

They passed in their travels – Pearce had them pointed out to him – the naval dockyard, Deal Castle, behind which there seemed to be a rate of building work in progress, then on through the crowded shipping to the third of the fortresses, Walmer. All were similar in design, bristling with forty-two pound cannon that covered the whole field of fire to protect the anchorage and its approaches. They passed a run-down fishing village called Kingsdown and, not long after, the beach ended and the cliffs suddenly rose to form a bluff that cut off St Margaret's Bay. It was also the point at which the anchorage ended for merchant vessels, the seascape beyond now dotted with fishing boats.

'Good for crabs and lobsters 'tween inshore, Your Honour, but for fish you want to be out a bit, tho' you might find yourself contesting for a catch with them damned Frenchies from Calais.'

'That means rocks inshore does it not?' Pearce replied.

'Only a hazard t'at either end, for as you can see, I don't fear to row close to these here cliffs.' They now towered over the small wherry, grey mostly, rarely the white of myth, home to seabirds and stained at the base where the tide washed against them. 'You can walk the shore at low tide, though you'd be fish bait if you got caught, 'cause them cliffs is sheer, as you can see.'

It was not a long pull, something over a mile Pearce reckoned, and then they opened the bay where he was tasked to land the cargo, a strand of beach with a few pulled-up boats, the whole enclosed by steep hills with a winding path leading up to the heights. To the man examining it, and he stayed afloat to do so, the place certainly had the twin advantages of a decent shelving beach and of seclusion – by land there was only one way in and out. But that could also be a trap, and he then and there resolved that whatever happened when he got here – if he got here – then he must have a means to get clear by sea, which he could not do if his keel were stuck.

He would have liked to stay and see the effect of the falling tide, but ever mindful he was supposed to be a tourist, he indicated to his oarsman that he could take him back to Deal, which engendered a sly look.

'Take you round to Dover, if'n you has a mind to, Your Honour. T'aint far and the castle there is a sight.'

'Thank you, no, I have an engagement I must keep in Deal.'

The fellow was less chatty on the way back, given he had failed in his task of adding to his fee by an extension of his labours.

Once back in the Ship, there was no choice but to occupy the corner seat, which had a window by which the Pelicans could sit and watch the world go by, each with their own thoughts about what lay ahead, though the past, as was common amongst friends, was more often the subject of their conversation than an unknown future and Pearce, quite deliberately, barred any talk of future prosperity, that being to tempt providence.

They were fetched from the Ship Inn by a gruff-voiced messenger, to be told their principal was already on his way to the rendezvous and, after a short walk, crossed a narrow brook that fed the stinking abattoir, leaving behind the habitable stone buildings, passing instead, at the north end of the town, through the tarred canvas shacks of the local poor, eyed by glowering men and their downtrodden women and children, until finally they reached the marshlands.

They stayed well clear of the silent, low and brooding walls of Sandown Castle, its central dovecote catching the dying rays of a weak sun as the first of the lanterns were being lit inside, unsure if they were observed but certainly pleased they were not challenged, heading along a shore that had as protection nothing more than the bank of shingle thrown up by the normal tides – one, judging by the presence of sand underfoot, that was easily overcome by any kind of storm. Once atop that bank, they could see in the fading light that the tide was high, the sea state benign, while the wind was gentle on their faces.

Pearce did not like the look of the men who would launch and row the galley, quite a crowd given their numbers exceeded the number of oars, their grim expressions and bearded faces not softened by twilight, short-in-the-leg types with broad shoulders, none of them old, men who eyed Michael O'Hagan as if he was some kind of freak and mumbled insulting asides about long-legged Paddies who stole the grub of honest Englishmen – remarks that would have got them a clout had Pearce not restrained his friend.

Arthur Winston was there, well wrapped up, his hat clamped on his head and a thick woollen comforter round his neck and lower face. When he spoke, even muffled, it was as if he was in terror of what he might face and the brevity of the introduction Pearce made to his friends underlined that, for he shied away from any temptation to engage them in conversation after a general reference to their shared knowledge of the Pelican Tavern, quickly taking Pearce aside to whisper to him.

'I must tell you John, I am no great shakes on water, in fact being at sea upsets me and that, I must tell you, is on something more substantial than what we will sit in this night.'

307

'Then let us hope these fellows get us across in short order, and mind this, they would not risk their lives, so they will be unlikely to be risking yours.'

The boat itself, sat just out of the water on logs of round timber, was sound enough, light in weight by the look of its raked timbers, three times the length of a naval cutter though no wider in the beam, with seating for twelve oarsmen a side and room in the middle for enough cargo to make a trip worthwhile, this now covered with temporary seating for their passengers.

'The big 'un and that sack he's carrying just forrard of the middle of the boat,' growled the leader, he who had brought them here, the first time he had used more than one word, 'or he'll have us down head or stern; the rest of you take a place 'twixt the oarsmen as you see fit.'

'Where will you be?' asked Pearce.

That got him a look that implied he had no right to ask. 'Sat astern with an eye out for trouble.'

'Then I will be close to you,' Pearce replied, before moving to whisper to Michael. 'You face aft and I will face forward. Anything you don't like, let me know.'

'Holy Mary, John-boy, there is nothing going in to this boat I like at all.'

Pearce took out his watch and had a quick look. 'I think they will get us across safe and sound.'

'You're sure?'

'I am,' Pearce replied, before turning to a worried-looking Winston. 'Or I would not get aboard myself. Sit close to me, Arthur.'

That he did and when all the passengers were

aboard, the galley was run down on its logs on a falling tide, with the rowers leaping in just as their feet hit the tideline so that the momentum took the boat clear of the shore. The shipped oars, twenty-four in all, were in the water and quickly employed, the rhythm of rowing so quickly established it was obviously well practised, while those left ashore gathered the roller logs and took them to high safety.

There was a mass of shipping to navigate through and that too was impressive, for if Pearce, facing forward, looking at Arthur Winston's back, could not see the man in command, he could hear the one-word instructions that had oars on one side lifted, the opposite side left dead so that the galley turned easily in its own length, those same sticks rapidly deployed again so they were never still. If that was notable, so was the speed they achieved when they hit clear water, evidenced by the creamy water running down the side, as well as the quickly diminishing bulk of the ships Pearce could see over his shoulder.

'Goodwins,' the man said, with his nearest passenger wondering whom he was telling, only to realise it was he when the fellow continued, almost boastfully, 'No more'n a few feet of water under our keel now, a place where no sailing ship dare follow.'

There had been a bit of lift and drop from the run of the sea, but very little. That increased now as they went over the middle of the sandbar and hit a wave. There were, Pearce knew from his study of the charts, channels through the Goodwin Sands – not many, but the main ones, and those which concerned him, lay to the north and south, the latter being the route he would take to close St Margaret's Bay. These were waters constantly sounded, for the sands did shift, and the charts he had, the latest from the Admiralty, were very recent, yet he could not but worry and consider it would be a damn nuisance if he misread them and went aground.

Once they were in deep water half the oars were raised, which occasioned a degree of curiosity, but he reckoned they would only employ all twenty-four again either close to shore or if danger threatened for, even with a decent wind, he doubted there was a ship afloat that could run down a galley like this if it was going flat out. They were making good speed, with the fellow behind him, he assumed, counting off time by a method of his own, before he issued an order for the rowers to switch, those with their oars already working not lifting them until the others were in the water and working so there was no loss of momentum.

'How do you fare, Arthur?'

'Not well, John, not well, but I think my stomach might hold.'

It was dark now, with not much in the way of a moon and enough wispy cloud in the sky to make the stars indistinct. Wondering how they held their course with such assurance, Pearce craned to look and saw, at the feet of the man acting as coxswain, a half-shaded lantern, while in his hand, hanging from a thin leather strap, was a piece of fish-shaped metal which wavered very slightly. That being magnetic, it gave him true north, which was, as a method of navigation, primitive but effective.

* * *

There was no way of knowing how long the journey took: Pearce would not have been able to see the face of his watch, but its time passed quickly, and given there were two forts at the mouth of the River Aa, they had enough lights showing to guide them into the beach below the estuary, the galley grounding on soft sand. Their landing was carried out in silence, no greeting or well-wishing followed and, as soon as they were all ashore the boat was pushed back out to sea, to disappear into the gloom of the night.

'Thank God that is over,' came the heartfelt voice of Arthur Winston, as the clouds parted slightly to allow some starlight. 'What do we do now, John?'

'Wait for daylight, Arthur, there's no point in stumbling around in the dark. Let us go inshore and see if we can find some place to rest, and I would suggest, since we are unaware of what we face, that some sleep might be in order.'

'Now that we are back on dry land and my fears are at rest, perhaps I can get to know our companions properly.'

The introductions were reprised and as they began to walk over the soft sand it soon transpired that Charlie Taverner had managed to separate Arthur Winston a little, and he was softly beginning to tell his tale of past misfortunes and potential rewards.

'Can't help himself,' whispered Rufus, 'as soon as he smells a bulging purse he is off.'

'Happen *he'll* become a victim if this comes off,' Pearce replied. 'Charlie dunned.'

'Now that,' Michael added, 'I cannot wait to see.'

Dropping back, for Pearce had no notion to let Charlie just continue, his proximity brought the tale to a halt. What light there was, and it was slight, showed a dark mass ahead of them, which turned out to be a long wall running inland from the sea, perhaps part of the defences. It made no odds, for it was not manned and it gave them all, wrapped in cloaks, a place against which to lean and rest, with Pearce insisting that any temptation to keep talking should cease: sleep was more important.

'Do we need to set a guard?' asked Winston.

'We shall take turns, Arthur.' He had to peer hard to see the hands of his watch, 'but you may slumber in peace.'

CHAPTER EIGHTEEN

It was a group of cold, stiff souls, thick cloaks notwithstanding, who woke with the first hint of daylight, Pearce being the least so, having taken the last watch himself. Fearing he would nod off, he had taken to pacing up and down as all the things for and against what they were about fought a battle in his mind. Yet at the base of it was a chance of freedom from the kind of life he had always led, which had only ever occasionally been secure, and then never for long.

His father had shown an annoying indifference to money, pleased when he had some, able to act with equanimity when there was none, while his son had enjoyed the periods of comfort more than those of deprivation, especially the period immediately after the fall of the Bastille, when Adam Pearce's pamphlets had sold in their thousands; likewise in Paris, following on from their flight, at a time where there were still men of means eager to pay to hear a famous radical speaker.

A fear of dearth was not, he knew, an estate in which he was singular: even men of substantial means worried that, by some stroke of misfortune, they might lose what they had and fall into the hellish pit of poverty, and he knew, for he had even got his father to acknowledge the fact, that such insecurity often coloured their attitude to those less fortunate, the very visible poor who stood as a constant reminder of what they might face if their means of existence evaporated.

There is nothing like a dark night and no company to provide an excuse for introspection, and John Pearce was no different from the rest of humanity, having as he did, on his mind, not only the task before him but the possible benefits of a successful outcome as well as the potential for failure. He might be unable to get aboard Winston's boat and sail it out to sea, he might misread his course, for if he was wiser in the ways of the sea than he had been when pressed, he knew the gaps in his knowledge were too large for comfort, and no great imagination was required to conjure up a vision of a foul storm, for which the seas in which he would be sailing were notorious, one that could send him and his friends to perdition.

Time and again he conjured up an image of the voyage back to the English shore, sometimes an easy progress, at others storm-tossed, yet more with the vessel stuck on a Goodwins sandbank. The worst vision was of him and his companions in chains on the deck of a Revenue cutter, and when that recurred, which it did too often, he had to shake his head to clear it and replace such gloom with a more positive thought, often with the face of Emily Barclay, though that, initially a happy contemplation, soon led on to potential complications, for a liaison of the type he envisaged was not without problems. Thus, when the first light tinged the eastern sky it was more than welcome, for with the rising sun came things to do and an end to imaginings.

Emily Barclay was a victim of troubled dreams in which her husband had her in his power, and in this it was he as a slavering, ravenous beast of a man, worse than the kind who had so cruelly taken what he considered to be his marital due in the cabin of HMS *Brilliant*, the final act in a long strand of misbehaviour which had led to the conviction she could no longer live with him. The vision, which made her wake with a start, was of a grinning Ralph Barclay eating the papers she had left with Studdert, but she knew that was absurd. Having woken, sleep would not come back as her mind flitted between the faces of John Pearce, her hated husband and a mob of indistinct people pointing at her for her moral laxity.

Had she seen her husband then, she would have been more comforted, for Ralph Barclay did not sleep at all, pacing up and down his hotel room wondering if Gherson's suggestion was one he should pursue – that he knew of some villains residing in the eastern rookeries of the City of London, who might, for a fee, break into that attorney's office and steal what they both suspected lay there. What were the risks of success, what were the possibilities of failure, but more pertinent, what could be the consequences of discovery?

Naturally he would never know the names of the felons, just as they would never be given his name. But in doing what was suggested he was putting himself further into the hands of a man he was not sure he could forever trust. There might come a time when Gherson knew so much of his affairs that he would become a threat. Gnawing on that, Ralph Barclay treated it as a problem to be dealt with when the time came, his usual solution to such matters.

He deliberately turned his mind to the needs of his forthcoming command, not least his shortage of hands. He had written to those he wished to take on as lieutenants, admonishing them not to turn up without a decent band of followers, and if they could not provide enough of those, to get out in whatever locality they were presently based and press more. The pity was he would not have that bastard John Pearce on his muster roll: if Ralph Barclay took any pleasure from his ruminations, it was of the notion of having Pearce up at the grating, and that happy thought took him off to his slumbers as the first hint of dawn touched the sky.

There was, naturally, a curfew in Gravelines, with the town gates closed and secured at dusk, to be reopened at dawn, so there was no choice but to wait until full daylight to enter. Pearce left his companions eating bread and cheese, for he had other matters to see to – an examination of the long, straight canal that led from the walls and the watergate to the sea. In darkness, he had seen lantern-lit fishing boats heading out on the height of the tide. Now the first trading ship, with more following, was making its way slowly down the channel – not under sail, but poled so that it could not deviate from a sudden gust of wind and run aground in what had to be the shallows, these indicated by the boats resting on mud by the canal bank, one or two of which had begun to cant over as the tide dropped.

Also of interest was some of the detritus of the town, and the speed at which it floated by, which showed the flow of the current, indicating it was of a strength, combined with the tidal fall, to take a boat out to deep water without too much trouble. Pearce would need the same kind of conditions and he watched with deep interest as the crew of the first vessel went to work with purpose, setting just enough canvas, their fore course and outer jib, to get them out through the sandbanks on either beam under sail, an action repeated by those in its wake.

Daylight showed the formidable, reddish walls of Gravelines topped by the higher buildings, a number of church spires which testified to a deep devotion in a populace, while outside those walls stood angled bastions, water-bound outworks backed by deep earth; properly garrisoned even now, it would need to be invested and cut off from land and sea to be starved out. The misfortune of Gravelines was to be part of that cockpit of land in constant dispute, the scene of endless battles between their overlords fighting the ancient enemy, royalist France.

The town had a sleepy appearance as lazy trails of smoke rose in the morning sky, looking more of a place the world had forgotten than what it had once been, a point of strategic importance on the French border. The two shoreline forts were in a poor state of repair, parts of the land walls more gaps than defences, others needing to be supported by timber baulks, deep green where the waters lapped them at high tide. Beyond, lay shiny mudflats capped on the shoreline with gently banked sand, while behind that the Flemish landscape was flat and barren in appearance.

Most important was the lack of any discernible challenge from the forts as those trading ships eased by. Satisfied that exit seemed possible, he gathered up his party, making his way towards the first of the many bridges that crossed the canals and outworks which encompassed the main walls. All the vessels, barges and square-riggers were tied up on the outer quays below those bridges, nothing was berthed on the fortress side and Pearce was tempted to ask if Winston's was one of them, but he decided against it: if he had not been told already, he would not be told now.

There was no impediment to entry; the watch set by the town gate were more interested in personal comfort – the gatehouse had a roaring fire – than scrutinising those who came and went. Arthur Winston, on Pearce's instructions, had covered his lower face with his comforter – they dare not risk him being recognised – and they quickly found themselves in a wide street, with Winston leading them to a quiet tavern where he required them to stay until he had established how the land lay.

'Forgive me, John, but I must ensure we have not come on a fool's errand.'

Pearce took that for what it was, misleading if not a barefaced untruth: Winston wanted to make sure his ship was where he expected it to be and perhaps make a final judgement as to the wisdom of what he was about. He might even seek out the man attempting to cheat him and try to come to an arrangement, something that Pearce had kept at the back of his mind as a possibility; when it came to unknowns, that had always been one of them.

'Why in the name of all that's holy,' Charlie opined, as he sipped a wheat beer, 'did I not meet your Mr Winston when I was working the Strand? Ripe meat ain't in it.'

'You would have taken him, would you?' Pearce asked.

'As easy as kiss my hand, mate. I had him going last night an' that was without the aid of a drop of wine. Cat an' mouse it was.'

'Cat and rat,' said Rufus, which got him a friendly swipe, easily ducked.

'I am in need of a wander,' Pearce declared, standing up. 'I can't just sit here.'

'Suits me,' Charlie replied. 'Never be outdoors when you can be in.'

'Michael?'

'I'm with you John-boy, sure, my arse is itchy too.'

Pearce looked at Rufus. 'You stay here with Charlie. If Winston comes back tell him I am looking out for any threats to us getting clear.'

'He won't believe that, will he?' Charlie said.

Pearce smiled. 'No, he will think I followed him.'

'Which would not have been a bad notion.'

'Except he would have expected it,' Pearce replied.

He was aware of the number of questions in what Charlie was saying, as well as the way he was looking at him, and it was not just he who had them: they all did, and they were the same ones the trio had posed when he had first outlined the proposition. He was also aware that when it came to definitive answers he did not have any – it all came down to how he felt, and that was a combination of things made up of suppositions and needs.

'We are here on Winston's purse and he has provided the means to get us home again, should matters not work out, while the chance exists to make a real killing – not like your fantasy Charlie.' That got a frown – if he knew it was a fairy tale, he did not like it being referred to as such. 'Besides, having got this far, surely we must see the thing played out.'

'What do we really say if Mr Winston comes back afore you?' asked Rufus.

Pearce grinned. 'Tell him Charlie has a scheme to make him rich, but also tell him I have gone nowhere near the quays.'

He and Michael departed, Pearce suspecting his other friends did not understand: if Winston was annoyed to find him not where he should be there was nothing he could do about it – the man of business could not achieve what he came to do without the Pelicans. It was nothing to do with liking or respect now, for if Pearce had a degree of the former for Winston he was not much given to respecting anyone, if you left out those who had shared his misfortunes or proved, like Heinrich Lutyens, to be the kind of friends he could turn to when in need. The man he respected most was with him, drinking in everything he saw and storing it away in his mind.

The town had been laid out to make capture difficult even if the walls were breached, the only broad avenues running to north and south, the roads that crossed them east to west narrow enough to canalise any advance. Every group of buildings seemed to be laid out as a copy of the exterior bastions, designed to act as barriers to an invader's progress, and the high church spires were not just devotional but prime places from which to observe and aid the defence, all of that explained by Pearce before they got to the heart of the town and the walls of the citadel into which the defenders could retreat for a final stand.

Acting as the centre of Gravelines, before the fortress lay a large open esplanade where the town became bustling, with various markets purveying meat and vegetables, as well as all the trades that such a place needed to be self-sufficient. Groups of fellows, obviously in drink, were making merry around the edges, their raucous shouting getting them hard looks from the traders and their customers. Pearce ignored them; he was more interested in the walled citadel, for if there were any authority to pose danger to their enterprise it would be here. There was also a long set of buildings, obviously barracks, which lay along one side of a quadrangle within which troops could parade, as well as being a fire zone which would expose an attacker as he tried to cross to overcome the citadel walls.

Uniformed sentries, desultory in their manner, guarded the ramp to the citadel and their clothing was white, indicating they were either Austrian or Dutch; oddly, there was no flag showing anywhere to enlighten Pearce. Reassuringly there was also no sense of coming and going which would attend upon a well-manned fortress, more importantly from those exterior barracks, where any garrison not under threat would be housed. Pearce even took a quick gander inside one of the doorways before continuing on his way, not forgetting to keep Michael abreast of what he was observing.

'Empty barrack blocks, so there can only be a small number of troops here, and if they lack numbers they may well lack curiosity.'

'Listen, John-boy,' Michael said, cutting off the flow of information.

Exiting the esplanade into one of the narrow streets that fed it they had just passed another tavern, one set back from the road with an open courtyard to the front, and both had heard the sound of singing. It was Michael, stopping him talking, that allowed Pearce to hear what the Irishman had already picked up.

'English?'

O'Hagan nodded. 'Stay here, while I have a gander,' responding to a quizzical look with a slightly terse comment: 'Sure, one man looking will not cause a ripple, but two might.'

Pearce did not agree, because Michael was of a size to do that on his own, so he dogged his heels as the voices grew louder, enough now for the words to be

322

identifiable as a rude drinking song. The place they entered was packed, full of smoke and noise, with a fair number of men obviously drunk – there were women bearing jugs moving to and fro – but even more of their fellows engaged with females who were whores by their manner, some flirting, others occupying a knee, while there seemed to be a degree of traffic of both sexes to and from the upper floor.

'Full of the damned heathens,' Michael said, more in envy than anger, 'and all very oiled. Makes me harken for the Pelican.'

Pearce peered through the fug in vain for a place to sit – all the tables and chairs were occupied – while he was also aware they were being examined by quite a few of the drinkers – and not kindly, which had him whispering to Michael, 'Hard bargains by the look of them.'

'Sure, I would say they ain't much different from them lot that fetched us over last night.'

'They're certainly enjoying themselves.'

'And spending freely.'

Pearce shrugged. 'Nothing to do with us, Michael, and I am not minded to ask who they are.'

'John-boy, think on this, if they are like those boatmen from last night, they would not be here in such numbers if they could not come and go as they please.'

'Let us hope you have the right of it.'

'Shall we try for a place to sit?'

'No, time to be making our way back.'

A troubled Arthur Winston was awaiting them and

it was clear his annoyance was directed at John Pearce, an attitude that fell on stony ground. 'I think you are too sanguine about things, my friend, but I am not.'

'We heard fellows carousing in English,' Michael added. 'Lots of them.'

'You heard it too?'

'You did not say before this was a place much frequented by our countrymen.'

'It is a trading port and always has been.'

'Even with a war on?'

Winston threw his hands up in a gesture of hopelessness. 'Such a thing is of no concern to me, I am here upon my own affairs.'

'A fair point, Arthur. What about your ship?'

'She's berthed where I last saw her and still loaded.'

'Rigged for sea?'

'I would say so, yes, but I lack your knowledge.'

'Do I now qualify for a name?'

Winston had the decency to look abashed. 'She is called *Hemoine*. You must understand, John, that once a man has been cheated . . .' That became an unfinished sentence. 'After such a short acquaintance—'

This time he was interrupted, but gently so. 'It matters not, we are here now and I need to see her so I can decide what must be done to get her out to sea.'

Winston was up quickly. 'Then let us do that.' As Charlie and Rufus rose too, he added, 'I do not think it is wise that we go as a group. It will draw attention to us.'

'Suits me,' Charlie responded, sitting down again, 'though I am not much taken with this Flemish ale.'

'Good,' Pearce said, detecting a very slight slur in the voice. 'Then you won't have too much of it, given you will need a clear head. You stay here too, Michael, and keep an eye on him.'

As they exited, Pearce had Winston wrap his comforter around his lower face again. 'You dare not risk being seen, for it will not take much to deduce why you are here.'

They did not exit through the gates but instead went up on to the deep band of greensward, the grass-covered earth that backed up the fortress walls where the cold wind, light in its strength, seemed unusually biting. From this high elevation Winston pointed out a two-masted vessel, deep in the water, which testified to her being fully loaded, with the sails furled tight on their spars, a jolly boat hanging from her transom, berthed below the bridge they had crossed to enter the town, with Pearce asking what type she was.

'A Bilander and it is a common vessel in these waters.'

The broad beam pointed to the kind of shallow draught that she would need to sail canals, but it also indicated to him that this was not a vessel for any type of heavy sea, for with a limited depth of keel she would be much affected by the current, while at this high elevation he could feel the increase in the strength of wind that would play on her upper canvas. They watched for a while but no one came on deck or approached the vessel, while from their vantage point they could see the ocean waters, strangely grey under such a clear blue sky.

'Is there anyone here about whom we can get an opinion of the weather?'

'John, it is so calm I doubt I would be troubled by it and I am a poor sailor, as you already know.'

'I need to know if it is likely to hold.'

'Does your own experience not tell you?'

Pearce was disinclined to respond, mentally noting that Arthur Winston had become somewhat tetchy, behaviour he put down to the man's nerves. He was not a man of action, he was a fellow at home in an office or a coffee house doing business. Instead, Pearce looked at the sky, bright blue with a few lines of high, wispy clouds streaming to the south-east, with the shape of a half-moon just visible, like a daub of faint chalk. There was no indication that the weather had altered, and if it did not he would have it, on the course he was set to take, coming in right over his stern but at no great strength, which was far from perfect.

Yet it was good weather and that was not a lasting thing; to wait for it to be perfect could be weeks. In his mind he plotted a variation on his course: he would head for the Goodwins, the wind coming in on his beam to up his rate of sailing, sure that the lanterns of berthed ships in the Downs, as well as the lights of Deal and its castles, would alert him to the danger of sailing too close to the sandbank if he arrived there in darkness. Those same lights would aid him in navigating the deep water at the tip of the southern end, where he could set up his signal lamps and head into the shallows of St Margaret's Bay. Aware that Winston was looking at him and in a slightly worried fashion, he finally responded.

'My knowledge tells me that weather is a fickle mistress, Arthur, but with the tide making and high in the hours of darkness, if nothing changes in that sky above us we will attempt to take your *Hemoine* out at twilight. Now, I need to get close to her and see what numbers are aboard, and I would suggest that is something I should do alone, since even with that comforter over your face you might be recognised.'

Once out of the gates, Pearce wandered along the quays like a fellow out for an innocent stroll, hands behind his back, stopping occasionally to examine a barge or a ship long before he came to the *Hemoine*, noting, judging by how they lay in the water, that some of those he looked at were partially loaded, while others were showing copper and obviously empty, and on those the decks were all ahoo with coops and untidy ropes. Most striking was the lack of anyone present; they seemed a trusting lot in Gravelines.

Well short of *Hemoine*, her name was plain on the stern transom, he stopped to look, thinking she appeared to be in very good order, her black-painted sides shiny, and showing no signs of any of the kind of cracks caused by weather or sun. Moving closer, he could see the decks were clear, while the falls seemed to be of good rope and neatly arranged on their cleats in a way that would have pleased an inspecting king's officer, the only problem being a growling dog, a large creature with her paws on the bulwarks, which barked as he got to the edge of the gangplank.

As he was eying her, and no doubt alerted by the barking, an elderly, craggy-faced fellow, with bent shoulders, came up from below, his peg leg stomping first on the companionway steps and then the decking as he crossed to the gangway. Staring straight at him, Pearce was given to thinking he would have struggled to look benign, which he did not, even if he had smiled, while the way he cuffed the animal to silence was harsh. He had a hooked, many-times-broken nose, far from straight, beetle, near-white, overgrown eyebrows and untidy dewlaps of grey hair down his cheeks all topped by a greasy woollen cap. The gruff question he asked, more of a demand, was delivered in execrable French, which roughly translated enquired what he thought he was gawping at.

'Un bon bateau, n'est-ce pas?'

About to ask if he was the owner, which might start a conversation and provide some information, his flattering description was met with a jerked thumb and two words spat out with real venom. *'Privé'* and *'Marchez!'* There was no point in doing other in response than giving a shrug and moving on, which Pearce did with the same air of insouciance as he had used in approach. Aware he was being watched by the old misery, he stopped to look down into the next berthed vessel, a lugger, its deck being well below the level of the quay. He was hoping his adopted air of curiosity would send the irascible bugger back below, but it was not to be; the old fellow kept him under view, forcing him to walk on.

In truth, he had already gathered all the information he could reasonably hope to get and was, again, stuck with a series of unknowns. Were those furled sails of good canvas? Was there water in the well and how did it smell – of rot or just the usual odour of damp wood? What was the rigging like, though what he had seen looked to be sound and well maintained? More worrying was the fact that, if that old sod was keeping a sharp eye out, he could not get along this open quay without being seen. Against that he saw no evidence that he would have to deal with anything other than that one watch-keeper.

With a firmer step he retraced his walk, passing the *Hemoine* again, which was done under observation from those same beetle-browed eyes, though the fellow made a dumbshow of working on the binnacle brasswork. Pearce did not even look at him – he went by as though he had purpose, but the feeling of that basilisk look of deep suspicion boring into his back was palpable. Once back inside the walls, he made his way back up to the point at which Winston had first identified the ship. He lay down to avoid being spotted, then spent a whole hour watching the old fellow come and go from below, pleased there was no evidence of anyone else aboard, his back warmed by the sun, his front chilled by the damp grass. The whole quay remained relatively deserted, with only the odd person walking to and fro, which he put down to the low tide making it impossible to contemplate setting sail.

Back at the tavern, as he entered, he was met by a quartet of enquiring looks, most earnestly from Arthur

Winston, that met with a nod and the information that his supposition looked to be correct: there was only an anchor watch and not one that could not be dealt with. That was followed by a question.

'What are the signals you have arranged at the landing place?'

The look that crossed Winston's face had, once more, that air of caution, which irritated Pearce: what in the name of creation was wrong with the man? His eyes dropped, as did his head, and Pearce suspected he was wondering if that, too, was information best kept to himself, so he added, for it was the case, 'It matters not, but we must go to the market outside the citadel and buy some raw meat.'

CHAPTER NINETEEN

Given a clear sky and that gentle north-east wind, twilight was going to be a long drawn-out affair, and still that half of a moon was faintly visible in the clear blue sky, which suited the way Pearce wanted to approach matters. It would be best to avoid violence: that would attract attention from any people on the vessels berthed close by. Also, overlooked by the outer walls of the town, there was no way of knowing who might see what they were about. Possibly a concerned citizen could alert the estuary forts, which would induce unwelcome curiosity; *Hemoine* had to be taken over quietly and sailed out calmly.

The pistols, that same pair which Michael had wrested from the crimps, were quietly loaded in the tavern while those serving were out of view. The notion was advanced by Charlie Taverner that more shot might be an idea – there was only enough for a couple of reloads, but Pearce was of the opinion that unless they had in mind to put a ball in someone that would be unnecessary – as stated before by the Irishman, the advantage lay in the threat not the discharge. After a last look at his watch, Pearce announced it was time to go and, bill settled, they made their way out into the now deeply shaded street, heading for the city gate and bright, if low sunlight.

As they made their way towards the gangplank they could see smoke coming from the chimney; hopefully the miserable old sod was busy at his dinner. Pearce, as a precaution against being recognised, walked behind Michael O'Hagan, Winston, once more obeying the instruction to hide his face behind his comforter, bringing up the rear, while Rufus skipped along well in front tasked to play the fool.

How the dog would react was a factor, the hope being that the way the old fellow had cuffed it hard, argued against it being well cared for: folk who behaved in that manner tended not to overfeed their animals. Certainly it had its paws up on the bulwark again, but before it issued a growl, Rufus tossed the first piece of raw horse meat over the side, which, whizzing past its ear, took its eye before the smell – they had bought some high, well-hung produce – took its nostrils. The paws disappeared.

'Move,' Pearce hissed.

Michael broke into a run, Pearce following, both producing pistols at the bottom of the gangplank before gingerly making their way onto the deck. Rufus kept the dog busy with more meat, but two weighty bodies could not board a floating platform without the deck dipping and alerting the man left to watch. Charlie went to work on the line, tied around the aft bollard, preparatory to casting it off, Rufus making for the bows to do likewise, while Arthur Winston stood transfixed on the quay.

An indistinct voice called from below, to which Pearce did not respond as he and Michael, hearing the first stomp of that peg leg, took up a position on either side of the hatchway. There was an angry growling sound, obviously complaint, as he climbed the steps, but that ceased as he saw two pistols aimed at his head, while the light, coming from the east over the vessel's stern, shone on John Pearce's recognisable face.

'*Vous!*'

A finger went to Pearce's lips. '*Silence, mon vieux, au . . .*'

The pistol was waved and the message was clear. Michael reached down and grabbed at his clothing, hauling him up to deck level, which produced a whimper of terror, this as Pearce said softly in French that he had nothing to fear if he did exactly as he was told. Passing his pistol to Pearce, Michael dragged him, it had to be said without much protest, to the gangplank, indicating to Winston to come aboard, before Pearce instructed the old fellow to untie the dog, which was still chewing on the horse meat, and take him on to the quay.

'Cast off those lines,' Pearce called, now with two pistols aimed at the old fellow, not in the least surprised when his speaking in English got a shocked response. 'Everybody aboard and haul in the gangplank. Pole us out into the channel. Michael, the wheel.'

Charlie and Rufus grabbed the long poles, hooked at one end, which were sat on the bulwarks, these placed against the quay and their backs bent. As the gap widened between ship and shore they were transferred to either side to get it moving downstream. Pearce called to the old fellow, reverting to French, telling him to stay where he was and not to seek to raise the alarm, an admonition that only lasted until he thought himself out of range. At that point he began to stomp back up the quay towards the town gate, dragging a very cowed dog behind him, while Pearce jammed the now uncocked pistol into his waistband.

'Thank the Lord he cannot run,' Winston said, pulling the comforter off his mouth.

'We're not clear yet, Arthur, put it back on.'

'Would it anger you if I went to assess the state of my cargo? I need to see it has not perished.'

Pearce shook his head: there was nothing Winston could do on deck, and even if he had urged caution he knew the river current and poling was taking them downstream with relative ease. At some point he would have to get aloft and release some sail and it would be damned hard work with so few hands to employ at the task, but once they had dropped the canvas and sheeted it home it should be plain sailing, with little to do aloft until they were out in deep water. Then there would be ample time, safe from interference, to get set a proper suit of sails.

They edged into the long, straight canal now, the bowsprit pointing right out to sea and dissecting the two forts, both of which had the tide now lapping against their walls. That incoming sea would slow them down, which was the critical point. Pearce could only guess how long Peg Leg would take to alert his employer and also what that man would do to react. If there was a beacon within Gravelines that could be lit to alert the forts, it was something of which he was unaware and could do nothing about – yet another unknown.

Winston came back on deck and it was clear by his smile he was satisfied. 'I cannot fault him for his care, John, he has kept the 'tween decks dry and properly aired. No doubt the cook's fire has helped.'

'That we will have to extinguish for now.'

'The copper has a sack of peas coming to the boil.'

'Michael,' Pearce called, 'get below and douse that fire, but have a look to see what we have in the way of stores of food.'

'Will we need any?' Winston enquired.

'That fellow who has come to the edge of that jetty?' Pearce said, ignoring the question and pointing forward to a small wooden landing stage poking out from the southern fort. Winston turned to observe a white-uniformed fellow, a soldier and by the braid on his hat, an officer, standing overlooking the canal with a red flag in his hand. 'Do you think he is there for a purpose?'

The flag, which had been idle in his hands, was now lowered. To Pearce it was like a signal to heave-to, an indication to say he required to check their papers. Winston was on his way to the foredeck as he replied, obeying a shouted suggestion he pull his muffler up again while Pearce, as precaution, steered to get as close to the end of the jetty as was safe, calling for the poling to ease off so that they could pass by at a snail's pace.

He eased the pistol out of his waistband and held it hidden by his thigh. 'Be ready to get them going again, and hard.'

Winston was leaning over the bulwark, and what followed was a silent exchange, a wave as the flag dipped even more, and Winston calling something out that carried away on the breeze, this before he stretched out a hand to shake that of the man on the landing stage. As soon as contact was broken the red flag was dropped behind the parapet, to be immediately replaced by a blue equivalent, which was aimed and waved downstream, an indication to proceed, which had Charlie and Rufus poling again.

At the same time Michael came back on deck to report that there were a pair of food barrels, probably pork and beef, as well as a sack of peas, also the usual things carried by a sailing ship, but not much, given the holds were packed full of cargo, the conclusion of that exchange coinciding with the ship's wheel coming abreast of the flag waver, who lifted off his braid-edged hat in salute, Pearce replying with a touch to his forehead. In short order they were beyond the forts and into the tidal flow, so the poles were abandoned and the three Pelicans, now barefoot, were sent aloft to let go of the foremast mainsail. It took time, and the canvas flapped loose until they could get back on deck and loop the sheet lines on to the cleats.

'What was that all about?' Pearce shouted to Winston as the bows lifted on the incoming waves, forcing the man to grab a handhold and, grimacing, to put his other mitt to his stomach.

'He was demanding evidence we had paid our port dues, John. You will not have seen it, but in that handshake I slipped him a few guineas. At least the propensity to take a bribe has not changed since the French abandoned the place.'

That was praiseworthy, but there was no time to say it as his friends, having been ordered to lash off the single sail, were now busy on the bowsprit, freeing the rolled-up canvas preparatory to hauling that aloft also, and more would be necessary, since against an incoming tide the ship was making little headway. Pearce called to Winston again, made sure his belly was stable – that acknowledged with a wan smile – and got him aft to hold the wheel, admonishing him to hold the head steady, this while he kicked off his own shoes and went to the aid of his fellow Pelicans.

What followed was a period of hard toil on the yards, shrouds and the deck, it being doubtful that without the strength of Michael O'Hagan they would have got aloft all Pearce knew they needed – the whole interspersed with endless instructions to Winston so that he could make slight adjustments to their heading. There was shallow water to either side of their keel and if the vessel was taken aback and the head let fall they could end up running aground on unknown sandbanks.

In time, their combined efforts saw enough canvas aloft. There was now enough way on the *Hemoine* to show a wake, so Pearce retook the wheel and, now that he thought them out in deep water, he began to adjust the rudder and the sails to find the best point of sailing commensurate with the course he needed to follow, this as the last of the sunlight faded in the east, leaving a long orange-to-blue line along the horizon. Above, stars were beginning to show, as well as the crescent of a moon, which left the man on the wheel feeling very satisfied indeed – things had gone well.

'Astern, John-boy,' called Michael and in a tone that had Pearce spinning round.

Emerging from the mouth of the canal was a crowded, low-sided lugger, its great blood-red lanteen sail aloft, taut and lit by flaming torches in the hands of the men on deck. Grabbing the telescope in the rack by the binnacle, from the light they threw out Pearce could see the pointing arms all aimed in his direction.

'Pursuit?' demanded Winston, his voice strained on a face now devoid of blood: he was feeling badly the motion of the ship.

'It would be foolish to suspect otherwise, Arthur.'

'Can we outrun it?'

'As yet I do not know.'

His original intention had been to leave the sail plan as it was – they had way and time had not been of the essence, but, if that was a band of Flemish traders come to the aid of their confrère, that was no longer the case: it would be best to seek an increase in speed. He had two choices, but in such light airs, and given his course and the direction of the wind, he had to favour the spanker over dropping the course on the mainmast, for that larger sail would only take away wind from the forward canvas.

With sharp commands he had his friends on the lines to loosen the boom, so that it could be shifted to larboard. Raising such an amount of canvas was a doubly hard task with so few hands to work it, but eventually they got it up, lashed off and drawing, the increase in speed evidenced by the heel of the deck and the increase in white water running down the side.

'I think they have gained on us, John,' Winston said, his voice again unsteady, having kept an eye on what was, they were now in no doubt, a chase.

'Let us see what effect our spanker has.'

'Will we not need more?'

'If we do, it will have to wait till daylight. I cannot send my friends aloft in the dark, they are too few.'

Both looked astern, to what was now no more than a red distant glow of numerous lanterns: someone had seen the folly of flaring torches so close to wood, tarred rope and dry canvas and had them extinguished.

'If these fellows catch us, I doubt they will be gentle.'

'If they catch us,' Pearce snapped, 'they will find out what the opposite of gentle means. Now, search the ship and see what weapons you can find.' Pearce sighed then as a staggering Winston went below. 'What I would not give for a long nine, a barrel of powder and a garland of iron shot.'

That would have seen them off in no time, while in his heart Pearce knew his chances of outrunning a fore-and-aft-rigged vessel, given the minimal strength of the wind, were limited in a lumbering and fully loaded square-rigger. The Bilander had not been designed for speed; indeed, with its shallow draught it was not a creature for deep water either, and if the swell was slight, it, as well as the current, was playing on the lack of depth in the keel, this obvious by the way it kept seeking to fall off the course he needed to hold to.

Against that it was unlikely the lugger had any cannon either, so he was safe from that hazard, which would mean his masts and canvas would remain intact, and as long as that prevailed he could damn them to a continued pursuit of such length they might just desist, for if they were gaining, it was not swift. To board him from that much lower deck and get on the *Hemoine's* while she was under way would be damned difficult, so the only thing he had to fear was to be becalmed, an almost unheard of event in these waters.

At first light he would get more canvas set, topsails and maybe even an upper topsail on the foremast, though he did recall being told more than once that more sail did not always translate into more speed. For all he had got them out to sea, he was aware again of a lack of that deep knowledge which came from a lifetime of naval service. That would hamper him in making decisions, especially given he had no time for experimentation.

Winston came back up from below. 'There are a dozen cutlasses down in a rack but nothing else I could see.'

'No muskets?'

'No.'

Pearce, looking astern and calculating the distances, pointlessly cursed himself for not taking time to buy more powder and shot for his pistols, useless as such self-castigation was; but well-employed cutlasses, added to their greater deck height, could do great service. He ran through in his mind what would come should they get alongside, for they would have to – he would not heave-to. First they would try to take his wind, that then pressing their scantlings on to his, followed by those brave enough jumping up to grab on to his bulwark, at which point they would be at the mercy of him and his friends.

They were not likely to be fighters in the true sense, though he would not guess at the depth of their anger or commitment to the purpose. Unless they had the means to keep them away from their own side, the Pelicans would wreak havoc on those scrabbling fingers. Did they have those means? Only time would tell, as it would demonstrate the level of their determination – more unknowns. They could, of course, lower that jolly boat and abandon both ship and cargo, but Pearce saw that as a very last resort, given it would mean abandoning any chance of profit.

'Arthur, you best lay-down and get some sleep, for whatever happens we have a busy daytime at sunrise.'

That was an injunction he also gave to the others, as well as reassuring words that, from what he could observe, they should be safe overnight, and they went below, leaving him alone on the deck, with only the light for the binnacle for company, illuminating enough for him to see his watch and so call out upon the others in turn to hold the wheel for a spell. It was truly dark now, the half-moon reflecting off the black waters, the ship moving before the wind, so the whistle through the rigging was slight. Looking up at the star-filled sky, providing more glow than the moon, he calculated the odds once more.

If they pursued him all the way to the English shore it would be tricky, yet that depended on what they had in the way of weaponry, and it was doubtful if a boatload of suddenly gathered Flemish traders would run to much in that line. If they did, he would have no choice but to run the ship ashore and hope that, with aid being signalled for, there would be enough bodies to discourage a landing. Eventually he grew tired of speculation: that his mind wandered was hardly surprising, where it wandered to even less so.

It was Michael O'Hagan on the wheel when the first grey light tinged the eastern horizon, the unpleasant sight of that big red sail not a shock in itself, only in its proximity: they were no more than two cable lengths astern. As the sun rose on what was likely to be another clear day the lugger came into focus, as did the people on her deck and Michael, craning to look, was taken by what he saw. To get the telescope open and focused while keeping the wheel steady was difficult, but the excess time meant there was much more daylight available to show him the lugger's low maindeck, and even then it took him time to realise what he was looking at. He yelled out for John Pearce to wake up and as soon as he appeared, bleary-eyed and curious, with Charlie and

Rufus on his heels, he handed him the magnifier.

'Have a look at the men on that deck.' As soon as he did so, Michael said, 'Do you recall the tavern we entered?'

'Yes.'

'Well, I have to tell you, John-boy, if you have not already smoked it, those buggers back there look uncommonly like the folks we saw drinking and singing, and you know as well as I do they is not Flemish, but English.'

Arthur Winston's strained voice came from behind the quartet. 'I think I had better explain.'

CHAPTER TWENTY

'I found out that my agent had sold my cargo to another Englishman, but I had no idea to whom.'

'Well I have to tell you, Arthur, it looks like it was a gang of right hard bargains.' The question he posed then was obvious, even if Pearce thought he already knew the answer. 'Did you know he had sold it before you engaged me?'

Winston's nod was slow and full of meek regret – hardly surprising given the look he was getting was one that could kill – while he still appeared a bit green around the gills. 'I must confess that I did.'

'How?'

'He sent the letter with a British officer going on leave, though he, of course, had no idea what it contained.' The next words were delivered in a garbled fashion such was the speed of his speech. 'I thought it to be a set of projectors trying to make their way on my misfortune, businessmen like me, who would do what we are now trying to do.'

'Were about to do,' Charlie growled.

'What do you mean?'

'It be simple – we take to the jolly boat and give them behind us this barky and the cargo.'

'We could not get away from them in a jolly boat,' Pearce said, 'they would overhaul us in no time.'

'A nice notion, Charlie,' Michael added, 'if they be of a saintly nature. But having seen them closer than you, I take leave to doubt it. You recall those fellows who got us over in that galley? Well, those on our tail are of the same stripe.'

'I smelt smugglers on that Deal beach,' Charlie spat.

'And so did I,' Michael replied.

'If they are that,' Pearce added, grimly, 'they will be bloody-minded and might not just take repossession of the boat—'

'Repossession!' The word brought colour to Winston's cheeks as well as force to his voice. 'This boat is *mine*.'

'I was about to say, Arthur, that they could then just toss us into the sea, which is the common act of pirates.'

'You're mad.'

'No, it is they who are mad and by their lights they have every right to be. Let us say it's a possibility and not one I wish to test.'

'We got to get goin', then,' Rufus insisted, to both agreement and surprise. 'And outrun them.'

'Well said, young fellow,' Winston cried.

Pearce's reply was grim, as he looked around the cold

grey sea for any sight of another sail. 'We might not be able to, and there seems no one with sight of us to prevent them doing as they please.'

'So, John-boy, if we cannot do that, sure, we has to fight them off, for if I have no notion of where we are, I know that we are not close to shore and they are not far off our stern.'

His friends looked at him for enlightenment, but they looked in vain. There had been no casting of a log, no notation of the course and no writing both those pieces of very necessary information on the slate by the binnacle. If Pearce knew they were roughly somewhere in the North Sea, he had no idea precisely where and none of the skill required to make any more than an educated guess. Yet, not being about to admit his own failure to do what he should, he pulled out his watch and flicked it open.

'Then we need to find a log and cast it, so we can get some idea of our speed.'

'Damned slow,' Charlie replied, 'an' even I know that.'

'We cleared the Flanders shore about eight of the clock on my Hunter, so we have been at sea for just under nine hours. If our rate of sailing has varied it will not be by much.'

'Will that tell us what we need to know?' Rufus asked.

'Not exactly, but close is better than ignorance and it will allow us to decide how to act. There has to be a log and line somewhere, so go and find it.' He looked hard at Winston. 'Can I have a word?'

'Happen we might want to hear what he has to say.'

'Charlie,' Pearce replied wearily, indicating to Michael to take back the wheel, 'you will hear every word, for I will tell you verbatim.'

'Come on, Charlie,' Rufus insisted, 'let's get to it.'

Charlie was slow to move, but he did so eventually, the words he posed to Rufus just loud enough to be heard. 'What does "verbaithem" mean?'

'Search me, mate.'

'How do we stop them, John-boy?'

'Depends on what arms they have, Michael. I thought they were just a bunch of irate Flemish traders, but if they are not that . . .'

'How could I be so foolish?' Winston wailed. 'We might all suffer for my stupidity.'

'No we will not,' Pearce snapped. 'We are going to get to where we are supposed to be and the only question that matters is are we going to be alone when we do so?'

'I don't see how—'

Pearce cut right across Winston then. 'You don't have to see, Arthur . . . I do!'

'I'm sorry.'

'You have a great deal to be sorry about. Now, that explanation, if you please.'

Winston, who had shrunk visibly when barked at, no doubt also through his fearful imaginings and disturbed constitution, seemed to gather himself then. 'I do not want you to think that I approached you in anything other than a spirit of honesty, John. That day, when I first met you in the Pelican, was the happenstance it appeared to be.'

'That matters not, get to the point where it ceased to be honest.'

'The letter I spoke of came that same day, I got it upon my return to my bureau and damned unpleasant reading it made.' Seeing the impatient look on John Pearce's face, he continued hurriedly. 'I tried to engage some seamen to undertake the recovery, I told you that, but they all declined, not from the notion of regaining the ship, you understand, but more from the illegality of getting my property ashore and sold. I was driven to making increasingly generous offers, none of which were accepted. Then you came to see me.'

'Someone you took the trouble to enquire about?'

'Only because your name rang a bell and I asked. In truth, given you had taken the prizes you mentioned, I was surprised to see you at all.'

'Go on.'

'Well, when we were having breakfast and I discerned that you had come seeking employment, it occurred to me that you were a person who had possibly less fear of the law than most, an adventurous sort of fellow, and then you informed me that you needed money and perhaps a great deal of it.'

'So you thought, *How convenient.*'

'Please do not make me sound like a deceiver.'

'One moment, Arthur, if you're not that, you are damned untrusting. The required destination I had to drag it out of you, you held secret the name of the ship until we were across the Channel and, as of this moment, I have no idea of the signal those ashore are waiting for because you have yet to tell me.'

'Chase is no more'n a cable's length away now, John-boy,' said Michael, calmly.

'Three white lanterns at the foremast in a vertical line.'

'Thank you, and did I forget to mention that you lied from the very beginning of our second meeting?'

'For which, I hope, you will forgive me, but as I have said, I did not imagine this. Would it help if I offered you a larger share of the venture?'

'No!' Seeing the look of surprise on Winston's face, even if he tried to disguise it, Pearce added, 'You could have trusted me with everything, Arthur, and that is the one thing which you have not understood and which has irritated me no end.'

'Obviously,' he responded in a soft, regretful tone, 'I have misjudged you.'

'More than you know.'

'If you will not take an increased share, how can I make it up to you?'

'You cannot, and it makes no odds. We are in a bad situation and we have to get out of it. I have to find a way, without any of the weapons I need to effect it, how to encourage this lot pursuing us to desist. If you have any ideas, I would be grateful.'

'I'm sorry.'

'Is that for lying, or for a lack of imagination?'

The crack of what sounded like a musket was loud enough to carry, even if the range at which it was discharged was too far off to be a risk. It was a message being sent over the water telling Pearce to heave-to. He shot down below to where he had left the pistols – now wormed and unloaded – and came back on deck with one, horn in his other hand. Priming one quickly he cocked it, laid it on the bulwark so it could not be seen for what it was, and fired it off, only to turn back to face a curious Arthur Winston.

'Let's hope they think we have muskets too. The sound is not too dissimilar, even without a ball.'

'As long as they don't guess what little we've got in the way of powder and shot,' Michael replied.

'I think they will be a last resort, Michael, but load them anyway.'

The Irishman nodded; they were not much good unless you could see the whites of an opponent's eyes and would only be of any use if they were actually close to being boarded.

The cry came from the bows. 'By the mark, three.'

'They found a log,' Michael said. 'Bless them.'

Doing a quick calculation in his mind, Pearce grabbed the telescope and, tucking it into his breeches, ran for the mainmast shrouds, his still-bare feet gripping the tarred lines. He was over the cap in record time and well on his way to the crosstrees before Winston asked Michael what he was doing.

'Holy Mary, can you not guess? He'll be looking for our landfall and he will also look for any sails that might give those bastards pause.'

'Do you think he will succeed?'

Michael just shrugged, but looking aloft he could see Pearce throwing a leg across an upper yard, then securing

350

himself so he could use the spyglass, the point of that moving left and right before steadying, indicating he had spotted what he was looking for. That was held for a while before he searched the horizon in all directions, naturally including the pursuit, to observe that the man conning her had every available body standing on his bulwark to stiffen the lugger against the wind and improve her rate of sailing.

The faces were not yet distinct, but he could see the bodies of the more adventurous as, almost on the tips of their bare feet, they hung on to a shroud or a line as they leant out over the grey-green waters below, loose shirts billowing, but eyes fixed on the Bilander with a degree of concentration that testified to their determination. Pearce knew it was fanciful to think he could feel their hatred, yet he could not put aside the sensation, and since it was an uncomfortable one he returned the telescope to his breeches and, grabbing a backstay, slid back down to the deck.

'There are no vessels close by that can either aid us or prevent those fellows doing what they please, but I have seen the white cliffs below Ramsgate. We are close to home, and more to the point, close to requiring a change to a more southerly course. The pity is that will aid the pursuit.'

'How so?'

'They will shave the corner, Arthur. Still, it matters not, if we are going to put an end to this chase we have precious little time to think of a way to do it. Michael, hold this course for now while I see what I can find below.'

351

'I will join you,' Winston said, quick to dog his heels. Just as they reached the hatchway the pursuit discharged another musket, another demand to heave-to. 'You're sure it would not be wise to just surrender?'

'We do not know who these fellows are, only that we are in possession of what they see as their property, and they will be of a mind that it is us who have stolen it. Think of the likely nature of the men we might be dealing with, then ask yourself what you would do in their place.'

'I would certainly not commit foul murder. It is barbarous.'

'Well, I for one will not trust to their morality, on the grounds they might have none.'

'But if we dispute with them it will make matters worse.'

There was just enough light to see Pearce's grin. 'Not if we beat them.'

Michael's voice came down the hatchway. 'Well short of a cable now, John-boy, they'll not be long in trying musket range.'

The holds were full to capacity and Pearce was reminded of what he had noticed last night when coming below to sleep: literally there was no room to swing a cat below decks on a merchant vessel. Had there been a full crew they would have been squashed into a cubby hole in the forepeak, while the master used the poky cabin in which they had slept the night before. This caused something to occur to him he should have thought of before.

'Arthur, look in the lockers of that cabin and see if you can find any flags.'

'Why?'

'Please stop asking questions and do as I bid you.' The look that got, again barely visible, was still obvious: Winston was miffed to be spoken to in such a manner. 'Arthur, I have no time for hurt feelings and neither have you.'

Struggling to recall the exact cargo, Pearce called out to ask Winston, but there being no reply, he guessed he was inside the cabin and had not heard. It was packed so tight that nothing beyond the aft outer layer was available to him, and the space left to get round the whole was so cramped he had a genuine fear that, if it moved while he was between the scantlings at the bales, he might be crushed. Everything was wrapped in tarpaulins, making it difficult to see other than that which lay right before his eyes.

With some effort he pushed himself upwards, reaching forward a hand until it made contact with straw. Feeling further he felt cold glass and roundness: it was a flask and should mean quality brandy. It took even more effort to get higher, but stretched fingers told him the flagons lay close to the deck timbers and would be reached easier through the hatch covers.

An image of that low-decked lugger coming out in pursuit came to his mind at the same time as an idea. What he envisaged would not stop the pursuit but it might slow it down and that was better than nothing, so he struggled to get down till his bare toes touched the deck, then to squeeze himself out till he could breathe properly. There he found Winston holding a pair of flags, one the stripes of the Dutch Republic, another

353

the triple-turreted white castle on a red background of Hamburg.

'I have found the brandy.'

'I am all for an uplifting libation, John, but . . .' Winston was talking to himself: Pearce was running up to the deck, calling out to bring up the flags. By the time Winston reached fresh air he saw three of the Pelicans tearing at the covers of the hatches, pulling back the canvas to reveal the cargo, first some thin packets right up against the deck beams, then under those, row upon row of tightly packed brandy flasks in wooden boxes, each wide part of the glass wrapped in protective straw.

'Out with them.'

'What for?' asked Rufus.

'Can't you tell, lad?' Charlie joked, cutting off any explanation. 'We's goin' to get them drunk.'

'Get them out,' Pearce ordered, 'and line them along the larboard bulwark.'

'Might I ask you to take care, given they are quite valuable,' Winston said. 'French brandy fetches a very high price now.'

Pearce grinned. 'It always did, I seem to recall.'

'Now't amiss with apple brandy,' Charlie insisted.

'People of refinement don't agree, Charlie.'

Mock surprise was the response. 'You sayin' I ain't a nob, John Pearce?'

'No times for banter, friend,' Pearce jerked his head to indicate the lugger was close indeed. 'Rufus, get aloft with a line to the mainmast cap and drop it over. Quick now, before they are in range to take a potshot at you.'

Rufus had all the agility of his years and enough real fear to respond like a startled hare to what he was being told. He grabbed a spare line off a cleat and went up the shrouds like a squirrel, hand over hand, the rope over his shoulder. Once on the cap, he was told to throw his rope over and the first flagon was lashed on.

'Haul away, Rufus,' Pearce called and up it went on command, an act that was repeated half a dozen times.

The next report of the musket had Pearce looking at the lugger's forepeak, where a fellow, balanced on the bowsprit, was passing back the discharged musket, while one of his mates was handing him another loaded weapon. That had to be ignored: it would be a damned lucky shot to hit anyone at that range, muskets being inaccurate at anything over fifty paces, while the fellow was standing on a moving platform, rising and falling on the swell.

Pearce called up to Rufus to give him instructions, the first of which was to crouch down behind the mast and wait. 'Arthur, get below and fetch up the cutlasses.'

The man stood rooted to the spot, as if Pearce had not spoken, until the second musket was fired. This time the ball crossed over their heads, the crack of that making him move; Pearce ran for the binnacle, talking to the man steering.

'Michael, you're too much of a target and besides I need you with a sword in your hand. Let us change our course now and then lash off the wheel.'

'We'll need to trim the sails as well, that spanker most of all.'

Pearce grinned. 'The navy has made a sailor of you.'

He called to Charlie to lay the pistols behind the binnacle, then had him help trim the braces on the main canvas. Even if he knew it would cost them speed, he had Michael alter course and lash off the wheel before they could attack the set of the spanker, a sail they would not have been able to handle without the Irishman, with a struggling Charlie Taverner, using what breath he could muster, calling aloft to Rufus that he was an idle bugger, and getting as much abuse in reply.

For all he was hauling on a rope he was not sure he was totally in control of – not aided by the pitch and roll of the ship – Pearce experienced a strange feeling of pride then: they were in danger and it might be mortal, but they could still jest with each other, while nothing made him more satisfied than the way they obeyed every instruction he issued without complaint; in short, his Pelicans trusted him, and for a man who had had few long long-term friends in his life it brought a lump to his throat.

That emotion evaporated as another musket ball cracked by; the pursuit had closed to the point where the man on the lugger's wheel was edging his bowsprit close to the Bilander's taffrail, and, as expected, to windward. Those men stiffening the keel had abandoned the bulwarks and were now preparing themselves for boarding and it was obvious they had no shortage of weapons.

'Where's Winston with those cutlasses?'

He was not on deck so Pearce rushed below as another musket was discharged. Once down the hatchway he found Winston crouched down and visibly trembling, the cutlasses gathered in his arms.

'God help me, John, I fear I am about to soil myself and my stomach is in turmoil.'

The sound was so pitiful it halted Pearce's angry bark; clearly the fellow was terrified, and if he knew anything, he knew there was no time to do anything about it. 'Give me the weapons.' The hands that passed them over were shaking. 'For the love of creation stay here.'

'I must help.'

'The only help you can give is to pray to whatever gods you believe in.'

'I'm sorry, John.'

There was really no point in doing other than patting his shoulder and leaving. Back on deck he threw the swords into the bulwarks, calling on the others to get there and crouch down.

'We can't do a tot of rum, lads, but you might want to crack the neck off one of those bottles and have yourself a nip.'

'I'll drink when it's over,' Michael replied, which surprised Pearce: Michael was an imbiber of note.

'Bugger that,' Charlie whooped, as he lifted a flask and cracked it on the top of a cleat, severing a jagged edge. Then he lifted it and, keeping the glass clear of his mouth, had an untidy swallow, that before he growled. The brandy hitting the back of his throat caused that and was followed by a furious headshake. 'By Christ, that's a fine brew.'

They could hear loud shouting now and in amongst that clear indications of what they intended to do. There was no more musket fire now, they probably reckoned they did not need it, though Pearce harboured a hope, very faint he knew, that they had run out of powder or shot. The noise rose, the voices became clearer: their guts were going to be garters, their gizzards were going to be sliced open and most fearful of all were the threats to feed them to the fish.

Pearce, as the lugger took their wind, stood up and looked straight down into a vessel now close to coming alongside, into a sea of faces, more than two dozen in number, all screaming imprecations. A musket being levelled to take him, it was agony to hold still for several seconds before it was discharged, he ducking back down only just in time.

'Rufus, as soon as you think you can.'

'Not yet, John.'

Was it the wrong man in the wrong place, Pearce thought, before putting such a useless thought aside? What he did know was that he was required to cause another distraction, to stand again and let another musket fire at him – at all costs he had to keep their eyes on the deck. This time he stood and stepped out into plain view, only to see that the gap was close to gone and he was facing not one musket but three, all of them discharged as soon as he became visible.

He dived sideways and shouted as the balls cracked past him. 'Damn it, Rufus, now!'

Back to safety, he craned his neck to see if his instructions had been obeyed. The youngster had the first flagon, now stripped of straw, by the neck and he threw the dark green bottle, with Pearce watching it tumble through the air, its progress seeming to be dreamlike it was so slow. But there was no mistaking the sound of breaking glass, nor that the second was on the way.

'You too, Michael,' he called.

The Irishman, sitting with his back to the bulwark, lobbed another bottle into the forepeak and that too broke, Charlie at the same time standing just enough to throw another flagon at the head of the man on the wheel, every one braking on contact. Pearce grabbed the pistols and scurried across the planking, then got upright enough to discharge first one pistol then the second, which got heads ducking and stopped in its tracks the idea of reloading those muskets. Better still, it made those planning to board move and, as they did so, he heard the loud pained curses as they trod on the broken glass, his hope that such wounded feet would cut the numbers who could board and might even make them sheer off to clear their deck, granting him time to reopen the gap.

What followed, Pearce could not have foreseen: his idea had been merely to cause delay, coming to him from seeing those barefooted men stiffening the keel by standing on the bulwarks, reasoning that they would still be likewise when they came alongside. The notion of inflammable vapour had not occurred, while the flash he saw could only have come from a dropped musket, one that was already primed. There was a sudden burst of bluish flame and it rose high enough to shoot up that great red sail. More than that, short in duration as it was, it scared the men who lined up on the deck and had them running in all directions over all that broken glass.

There was one fellow with sense and a healthy fear of flames. He grabbed an axe and cut away the falls holding the sail, trying to get it clear before it set fire to anything else. The sail began to flap as the way came off the lugger, its head falling to starboard as the current pressed it over, and the gap between the vessels opened up.

An elated John Pearce stood to jeer and he moved towards the larboard bulwark without looking down. Unshod, he cut his own foot on the jagged top of the bottle from which Charlie Taverner had imbibed, and the sharp pain made him drop to his knees. Looking back he was able to see the blood oozing through his toes, as well as the gash on his sole.

CHAPTER TWENTY-ONE

It was impossible to know why the pursuit was not resumed, though Rufus, left aloft, was allotted the task of watching out for it – perhaps it was cut feet, maybe the mainsail was too damaged, it mattered not, certainly to John Pearce, who had spent an age while Michael sought to stem the flow of blood from his foot. Seeing it needed to be stitched, Rufus was fetched down to apply his superior skill and once that task was over, not without pain, a makeshift bandage was applied, though it was one which left Pearce hobbling, damned uncomfortable on a moving deck.

'Sure, you'll need a stick, John-boy,' Michael opined.

That was soon provided by cutting one of the hooked poles they had used to exit the Gravelines canal, with a bit of rope work, some padding and another section providing a rest for Pearce's arm. Even with that he had to walk on his heel, for to put any pressure on his toes might reopen the gash. He was on the wheel, the charts he needed on the deck before him, weighted down to keep them from flying away on the wind.

Now they were within sight of the Downs anchorage, perhaps another reason the chase had not resumed, making exceedingly slow progress into an up-channel current on the seaward side of the Goodwin Sands, the anchorage as full of shipping as it had been when they departed, the flag at their masthead that of neutral Hamburg, the hope being that such a standard would keep the curious at bay. Certainly the navy, if they were even at sea, would be cautious, but the worry was a Revenue cutter and Rufus, sewing done, was back on the mainmast cap as a lookout.

'Will that sun never go?'

Winston, who seemed to have found some passable sea legs, mouthed this complaint while looking east towards the seemingly endless, flat marshlands that lay between Deal and Sandwich, while simultaneously aching to close with the high bluffs to the south of Walmer Castle. Pearce wasn't listening: he was too busy trying to make sense of the charts, seeking out landmarks, while the light held, to give him some clue as to his precise position in relation to the ten-mile-long sandbank, aware that if he got it wrong they would, like so many ships before them, end up stuck, praying for a tide to wash them clear before a storm and heavy seas came along to send them to perdition. Charlie was employing a weighted line to test the depth, one he had spent hours knotting at fathom intervals, for a search of the ship had found no such item.

362

'It would be a blessing if it clouded over.'

Pearce made that remark knowing it required no further explanation: there was barely a cloud anywhere, so even with a much less than full moon, a clear sky full of stars meant a luminous sea, so anyone on those cliff tops would be able to see what he was up to when he changed course.

'You fret too much, John.'

'Do I, Arthur? It strikes me you might be too sanguine.'

'In this I trust to what I have been told. The Revenue men are not numerous, while the coastline they have to protect is endless, and what does it matter if there is one fellow? The chances of a strong party being in one place is slight, and in the right place even slimmer, I fancy.'

Pearce was tempted to remark that, for a man who had so recently turned to jelly, Winston had quite surprisingly recovered his self-confidence. Perhaps it was the advantage of the fearful to be able to shed their terror as quickly as it occurred.

'Let's get those lanterns rigged before the light goes. I am going to change into my naval coat.'

'To gain respect?' Winston asked, almost amused.

'No, Arthur, to keep myself warm.'

In some nine hours of darkness there appeared to be no trouble about timing the tide so that Pearce could safely beach, the notion being that he do so well before it was at its lowest and haul off slowly, which would allow for the unloading, while once that was completed, it still falling would allow him to float out on a much lightened vessel, the task then to get Winston's ship back to the Thames and to anchor: he and the Pelicans could then boat back upriver to the Liberties. Up in the bows Charlie was casting his weighted line, calling out the depth under the keel as well as reassuring Pearce that under him he had sand, not rock, for the approach into St Margaret's Bay was not generous in that regard.

What had been white cliffs faded first to grey, then to black, and it was only then that Pearce got Rufus aloft with a working lantern and some of that straw from the brandy bottles, used as tapers to light the signal lamps. As soon as the last one was fired, two red lamps appeared onshore, the reply signal, to tell the men sailing the *Hemoine* that not only were the men who would unload it present, but that no one who could interfere was around. Pearce, as he saw them, was only aware he had been holding his breath by the quantity of air that escaped from his lungs.

'By the mark, one,' Charlie called, 'and shelving fast.'

'Anchor, Michael.'

The splash of the stern anchor sounded as though it could be heard in France; was it imagination that had Pearce thinking it echoed around the bay? The time it had taken to rig that anchor cable to the capstan had underlined the lack of his ability to help. Much discussed, the notion was to use the tide, the stern anchor and the unloading in combination to keep just enough water under the keel to stay afloat: Pearce never mentioned that it would also allow for a rapid departure if necessary.

The ship was hardly moving, with Pearce listening for the first scrunch as the shallow keel on the bow touched the layer of sand that lay just beyond the shingle of the beach, that was now a strand awash with lights. By faint outline he could see that a number of men were carrying a ramp and he edged the wheel to bring the Bilander in so that the bowsprit was pointing slightly off, that allowing the ramp, which he suspected had grappling hooks, to be attached.

'Michael,' he called, as he felt the slight shudder under his one good foot. That had the Irishman and Charlie Taverner leaning on the capstan to halt the inward drift, while Rufus let fly the scrap of topsail, which they had used to get inshore, the north-east wind having held steady.

'We have made it, John.'

'We have, Arthur.' There was a loud clunk as the ramp dropped onto the forward bulwark and within seconds the first head appeared, lantern held high enough aloft to show a very fat face, a visage, added to a body shape, made more obvious when he came closer, which had John Pearce say in surprise, 'Barmes?'

'The very same,' replied Winston, as a party of men swarmed up behind him.

'Why is he carrying a pistol?' Pearce demanded. 'And why is it aimed at me?'

The laugh from Arthur Winston made him examine the man's face, lit from below by the binnacle, which made him look like the very devil. More worrying was that he, too, had a pistol in his hand, one of the pair belonging to Michael, and it was no more than two feet away, pointed right at his gut, so he was only vaguely aware of those rushing past him.

'Let me say, Pearce, you have done quite brilliantly, though I confess to being worried at one time that I would forfeit my life on this venture.'

'You're a peach,' Barmes said, with Pearce aware that he was not the referred-to fruit.

'Thank you,' Winston replied, 'but I cannot tell you how simple it was.'

'John-boy?'

The cry came from Michael and there was just enough light, as he flicked his gaze past Winston, to see both he and Charlie with hands held out from their bodies, while others had taken over control of the anchor cable. He was looking into Winston's eyes again by the time he replied, and that was to tell his friends to do nothing, his next call being to get Rufus back down on deck.

'Do I warrant an explanation?'

There was a sneer in the response. 'Are you not so clever that you can work it out for yourself?'

'I suspect the Pelican was not "happenstance", as you called it.'

'It was, but in the end a most fortuitous one. I was pursuing a number of schemes, as one must, for not all will come to fruition. You, unwittingly, provided the pattern by which I could see this one in the round.'

'The Pelican is not much frequented by sea officers.'

'True, but it is a prime place to seek out the needy.

366

A man badly in debt, offered a decent sum, is a fellow easily tempted. My first impression was that you were such a fellow and so open about your dilemmas, as well as the problems of your friends, that I wondered at my good fortune to the point of near-pinching myself. Then you mentioned your prizes, which I have to admit came as a disappointment, since you seemed perfect.'

'Did you know my name and background before we spoke?'

'No, but you would not credit what information you can extract from an Admiralty doorman for the price of a tankard of ale, especially when the fellow in question is one he purports to despise as a low creature undeserving of his rank. My enquiries regarding you were general, but interesting, and helped to fill out a conversation that led to what I was really after. You are, after all, not the only king's officer without employment.'

The hatch covers were off again and the first of the cargo was being rushed down the ramp to disappear into the dark and Pearce paused to watch that, really to give himself time to think through what he was being told.

'The day I came to see you, you were expecting a visitor.'

'You have a quick mind, certainly speedy enough to make that association, which I believe I acknowledged previously.'

'Another naval officer in need of money?'

Winston nodded. 'But not one who, it turned out,

had your quite exceptional advantages, or, I have to say, your needs, not to mention your writ-bound friends from the Liberties, who even had protections, forsooth. It is a pity this is not an enterprise I can repeat, for the fellow was very much in need of funds.'

Pearce was back at that breakfast, reprising the conversation. This man had sucked him in, providing such a complete answer to his needs, and that had blinded him. It had been clever the way he'd been drawn in by the drip of information: there had been no ship name because the target vessel was unknown and there was a very good chance the men unloading the *Hemoine* were the very same folk who had rowed that galley across the Channel. If there was nothing he could say, he felt he had to do something, had to find some line by which he could puncture this bastard's certainties.

Pearce leant to take up his makeshift stick, an act that got him a slight dig in the stomach with Winston's pistol, so his notion of clouting him needed to be immediately abandoned. But the act had turned him so he was now partly facing the beach, and the first thing he noticed was that the line of lanterns, those carrying the contraband goods, were not ascending the steep hill that enclosed the bay.

He had stood off in daylight in that Deal wherry and had a picture in his mind of the shape of the bay and the arc of near-vertical hills from the beach to the heights, cut by a winding track, with no way out to north or south when the tide was in, because of the sea. Yet the line of lanterns was heading for the cliffs and, just at that moment, one he had half an eye on was extinguished, the next in line the same, in a way that seemed altogether too sudden.

'So this ship is stolen, after all?' he said, prevaricating so that he could make certain what he had seen was not some illusion.

'Profit without much in the way of expenditure, which is a very sweet trade.'

'Except those who you took it from will not just let such a theft pass.'

Winston laughed out loud. 'You were right to think them smugglers. Can you see them going to the forces of the law, to say that their contraband has been stolen? I think not. And should they search for the miscreant, it will not be me, will it? – given my identity and my face is unknown to them – which is not the case with yours. You even had me hide mine, so convinced were you of my tale.'

'So you were not in terror, or really ill, but in hiding when you stayed below?'

'Correct, and banking on your seeing off the pursuit.'

'And if we had not?'

'I daresay that would have taxed me somewhat, but I did have the threat of retribution, or perhaps the means to convince them I could buy them off with the purchase of their cargo, while I have to add there is no hope of yield without risk – a point you put so eloquently to me, I recall. Was it not you who persuaded me to proceed with this venture?'

'Is your name, I wonder, really Arthur Winston?'

'Enough,' Barmes insisted.

That was barked in a way that indicated to Pearce it was not his real name, and he suspected the fat fellow's name to be false as well. Yet he was curious as to their association: was it of long-standing, or had one sought out the other merely as a way of doing business? Speculate he might, but more vital was what was about to happen now.

'Do you intend to kill us?'

'No, no, that, as I said, is a barbarous notion. Once the cargo is unloaded and we are gone, I have it on good authority a certain party of gentlemen will come down from the heights and effect an arrest.'

'There will be no contraband.'

'We shall make a small sacrifice,' the fat man sneered.

'Enough,' his companion added, 'to satisfy those who oversee the Excise, and what are you doing, in the name of creation, beaching a ship so secretly in such a secluded bay with not another soul in sight?'

'Have you bribed them?'

'He's not short on questions, is he?' spat the fat one, given Pearce had addressed that to him.

'He was long on greed and that is all that matters.'

Pearce turned his head to see the goods being fetched out of the hold, a task being carried out at speed, then he looked back again to see lanterns appear and suddenly it all made sense. The cliffs were chalk, perfect for tunnelling, which meant these villains had to be local, so there would be a route inside that would take them up to the heights and habitation unseen. That he had bribed the local Excise men was likely, not that it made any odds, except that there would be little point in pleading he and his friends had been duped.

'Last bales coming out,' called a voice, just as the ship began to heel over, which told Pearce that she was now well and truly beached and any notion of sailing her away before the tide came in again was gone; they had thought of everything.

'Time to go, I think,' said the man who had made a fool of him, the sudden thought coming to him, entirely inappropriate, that Charlie Taverner was an amateur by comparison.

'Right, everybody off,' called the fat man.

The tip of Winston's pistol – Pearce could not think of what else to call him – was lifted to his hat in mock salute. 'Let me say this, John Pearce, you were very nearly a worthy adversary. There were times when you had me jumping, and to think, when I offered you more of a share, you turned me down! Such a sense of nobility, *mon ami*.'

That had him laughing again, a sound that faded as he departed the ship and walked up the beach, leaving the fat fellow to deliver the last message. 'Stay on board the ship and make no attempt to follow, for if I say I am more of a barbarian, you will understand.'

Then he too was gone, waddling down a ramp that disappeared from the top of the bulwark as soon as he was off it. He watched as the lanterns disappeared, all except the last one, which was held in one of the fat fellow's hands. In the other he had his pistol, which he raised and discharged, sending out a flash, as well as a sound that did echo round the narrow bay; then the light went out. By the time the fat man had carried out his last task, a gunshot to alert the Excise, the others had joined him by the binnacle. Pearce was no longer looking at the cliffs, he was looking at the rim of the heights and, sure enough, before that echo died away, pinpoints of light appeared.

'That was a sign.' Pearce said, having given his friends the briefest of explanations.

'We're trapped,' said Rufus, 'so we'll have to fight them.'

'We still has the cutlasses,' Charlie added.

'Belay,' Pearce barked. 'That is to risk a hanging if any of them are killed.'

He pulled what money he had left from his pocket and, emptying out the purse, handed half of it to O'Hagan. 'Michael, lower yourself over the side and help the others down. There's a path right in the middle of the bay and it's the only way in and out, but with a low tide you can go north. You might get wet feet but I know it is possible to walk to Deal from here and the tide is still falling.'

'How do you know?'

'There's no time to explain,' he replied.

In truth, he did not want to say he had taken his boating trip without telling them anything about it: vital was the fact that 'Winston' had no knowledge of it. In the gloom he thought he saw Charlie Taverner unwilling to accept that statement, but Michael cut him off, for he at least must appreciate the need for speed.

'What about you, John-boy?'

'With this foot, I can't go anywhere and if I tried I would slow you down, so I will stay by the binnacle, so they can see me. In coming for me it will give you a chance to get clear. If you can get away, best you try to get in touch with Mr Lutyens, I'm sure he will help you. There is money owing to you and I from a fellow called Davidson, which he knows about.'

'Pearce?' said Charlie, not in complaint, but worry. 'How in hell's name can we just leave you?'

'Charlie, there's no time to waste, every one of you is in double jeopardy. Get off from this damned boat and find at the very least somewhere to hide till the tide is right out. Now go!'

'A hand, John Pearce,' asked Rufus, holding out his own.

He took each hand in turn and, with a lump in his throat said, 'Take care, all of you.'

It was agony watching those lights weaving down the steep slope, trending left and right as they followed the steep, winding path. His foot was throbbing, but the real pain was seated in his damaged pride. Once they got low enough he walked away from the binnacle light to look onto the beach, and there, as he had been told there would be, was a line of contraband, several barrels and bales, hardly a problem for a gang that must have cleared thousands in money from those packed holds.

Finally the lanterns were on the beach, with no indication of a hue and cry, so perhaps the others had got clear. The crunch as the Excise men came down the beach was like the knell of doom, for Pearce knew he could look forward to a life of misery from now on. Then he put his hand in the pocket of his blue broadcloth coat again, to touch that tin of earth from Paris, which had travelled with him. What would old Adam Pearce say about his son now, and would he ever get those bones out of their Parisian resting place?

'You there, don't move,' called a voice, and John Pearce burst out laughing, wondering as he did so if they would go below and fetch for him his ditty bag, and most of all, his shoes.

EPILOGUE

A week in the Sandwich gaol was not unpleasant, given
he had enough money left to pay the warder for food
and comfort as well as a medical man to tend to his
now-healing foot, though it would not yet take a shoe.
More troubling were his own thoughts, for, hardly
surprisingly, he could not get out of his mind what had
just happened, and every reprise of recent events made
him feel more of an idiot than the last. With hindsight
he could see so many flaws in the way he had been
deceived that it beggared belief he had fallen for them
in the first place.

Still, he would soon have more to worry about: a letter
to Davidson, pen and paper provided by the warder for
a fee, had established his affairs were still up in the air,
nothing was resolved, so the fine he was expecting of
one hundred pounds, standard for smuggling as he had
been informed, he could not pay. So it was either hard
labour or transportation he was facing, and he was up

before the Justice of the Peace in an hour.

He had written to Emily Barclay too, but that letter, to his mind unfinished, was yet to be sent. Time to put the last touches to a missive that would tell her that, while he loved her deeply, the notion of their being together was one she would have to put aside, if indeed she had ever truly harboured it.

I have instructed Davidson to provide for you as best he can, and said that any prize money should go to you unless it can be used to secure my release, not that I think that a likely event once sentence has been passed. Please be assured once more of my deep love for you and my wish that if you can find happiness you should do so. It would probably be best to forget you ever knew a man called John Pearce.

With that he signed it.

'Lieutenant John Pearce?' asked the clerk of the court.

All he could do to that was nod and reply yes; he had used his naval rank in the hope it might ameliorate what was coming. The court was crowded with the usual set of ghouls, many hoping for a hanging, no doubt, but there was a commotion at the back as three men elbowed their way to the front, and that made Pearce curse. What the hell were his Pelicans doing here? The charges were read out and he entered a plea of guilty, all the while glaring at the body of the court, where his friends now sat, a look that was returned with bland indifference.

'The fine for evading the excise duty is set by statute at one hundred pounds. Do you have that sum to pay to the court?'

'No.'

The Justice was about to speak when Charlie Taverner stood up and cried out, 'May it please, Your Honour.' That got him a jaundiced look over the magistrate's half-glasses. 'Is it not the case, that if a fellow convicted of smuggling can provide two men for His Majesty's Navy, who have the skills of the sea, the fine is waived?'

'That is so.'

'Then can I say that my mate here and I,' Rufus stood up, looking far from confident, 'were approached by this here Lieutenant Pearce to join up for the bounty, which we will happily put aside in his favour.' Charlie held up his piece of parchment. 'Even having this.'

A sharp instruction was given and the clerk of the court took from the pair their protections, which were handed up to, and closely examined by, the Justice of the Peace, before he looked back out to the well of the court.

'You are volunteering for the navy?'

'That's right, Your Honour.'

That set the court a-buzzing: if it was not expected for men to condemn themselves out of their own mouths as smugglers, that was what this pair were doing, for only a fool would believe their connection to the man in the dock was other than that. The navy was not much given to taking criminals – in truth they were dead against it – but smugglers were the exception, given they were bound to be at home on a ship and thus highly valued.

'You are competent seamen?'

'We are,' Charlie replied.

'Both of you?'

'Yes.'

The magistrate paused for a moment to consider his response, but when he did speak it was with firm purpose. 'Sergeant of the Court, take these men into custody to be handed over to the receiving officer of the Impress Service at Dover. You, Lieutenant Pearce, have satisfied the needs of justice and you are thus free to go.'

'I protest.'

The words he was about to utter, that he would not accept the verdict, died in his throat: Michael O'Hagan was shaking his head, and in truth, any intervention he could make was too late. Charlie and Rufus were already on their way. Minutes later, a free man, he hobbled out of the courthouse to join the Irishman.

'That was madness!'

'Was it, John-boy? We talked long, this last week, while we hid out in Deal to see what became of you.'

'Where I must go to look for those who near did for us all.'

'You'd be wasting your time, they would be unlikely to show and if they did, what can we two do against so many? Charlie and Rufus had no mind to go back to the Liberties, as I have not myself, but I will wait to find what risk I am under, since you say my name is not known. It was plain we all owed our freedom to you . . .'

'They did not have to go back,' Pearce protested.

He knew, even as he said the words, they were false. Charlie and Rufus with writs against their name could not just wander the land in safety: if it was not the

Liberties, it was more likely to be the same kind of risk Pearce felt he had faced before going into the court.

'Take it for what it is, John-boy, two men who consider you a friend, doing what they thought best and that included for themselves. They have no love of sea service, but even that is better than what they had afore. At sea they are safe from the law.'

'And what of us, Michael?'

The Irishman just smiled; if he was aware of the turmoil in the mind of John Pearce he said nothing. Just abandoning Charlie and Rufus he could not do and live with himself, while he was at a stand to know what to do with his life, Emily Barclay notwithstanding. It was the same dilemma he had laboured under ever since coming back from Paris, the lack of a clear path to a decent future, for he was not fitted for much. Those prizes might pay out, and then again they might not, and even then the sums were not great enough to provide security, which, if it engendered a painful reminder of how foolish he had been in going to Gravelines, also harked him back to the reason. The solution was obvious, if not entirely pleasant: he needed security for both himself and the woman he loved, he needed to help his friends and there was only one place that could be achieved.

'You must see I have to find a way to repay them, or at the very least ease their lives.' Michael nodded and gave a look that told Pearce he understood what that meant. 'How do you feel about being servant to a naval lieutenant?'

'Sure, I would be a cack-handed one.'

'Not as cack-handed, or -headed for that matter, as the man you will be obliged to see to.'

'So, John-boy, where to now?'

'First back to the town jail to retrieve a letter I wrote, then we must go to Dover and see what we can do for Charlie and Rufus.'

'And then?'

'Then, Michael, I am going to beard the First Lord of the Treasury, whom you might know as William Pitt, as well as a companion of his called Henry Dundas. They made me certain promises and I intend they should keep them.'